Picking Daisies

Hope you enjoy the book.

Charles P. Sharkey

Ringwood Publishing
Glasgow

First published in Great Britain in 2025 by
Ringwood Publishing, Glasgow.
www.ringwoodpublishing.com
mail@ringwoodpublishing.com

ISBN 978-1-917011-09-9

British Library Cataloguing-in-Publication Data
A catalogue record for this book is available from the
British Library

Prologue

It was a balmy late summer's night. A full moon slowly appeared through scattered clouds above a farmhouse left to decay for years. The two-storey house, isolated and forgotten, was surrounded by a few acres of uncultivated land and was hidden from the nearest road by a pine woodland. In an outhouse once used as an abattoir, blood dripped from a deep gash in a large oak table. The grain of the wood was slashed with recent cuts and scores that were fresh against the ancient, dark marks of animal butchery. The killing table had survived the elements and ravages of time that had destroyed everything else in the barn.

A colony of rats had been using the barn as a nest for years and had seen the butcher at work. Now that he was gone, a large brown rat leapt onto the table, its black eyes catching the moonlight that flooded through the gaps in the roof. It sniffed around, twitching its whiskers, its long, naked tail hanging over the edge of the table. While gnawing at the cuts in the wooden surface with its sharp teeth, it squealed, frantically forcing its claws into a deep gash and pulling out a long sliver of human flesh. The other rats emerged from the darkness to fight for the food, their frenzied shrieks carrying into the night.

The dilapidated wooden barn nestled on the leeside of the house, sheltered from the worst of the weather during the harsh winter months that ravaged the glen. The sandstone walls of the house had seen better days, but it had been built to last and stood strong and silent under the pale moon that cast a narrow sheen on the pitched slated roof.

The only sign of life was coming from a downstairs

window, where a yellow glow seeped from the closed wooden shutters. The front room had become his domain. He was sitting at the dining table, sewing on his mother's sewing machine, fussing over a cotton dress pinned to a mannequin torso, unaware of the dried blood under his long, dirty fingernails. The table was covered with spools of thread and rolls of chiffon, cotton, and silk. He smiled, a twisted grin that released a convulsion of tiny spasms around his mouth, causing dress pins to fall from his lips onto the floor. His mother's voice made him stop sewing for a moment.

Don't get too excited. Take your time, Son. Do it right.

He had almost finished. Just the sleeves and the hemline to do.

Once he had completed the dress, he hung it on the back of the door to admire his work. He grinned again. Mother would be proud of how he'd mastered her precious sewing machine.

Darling, you're such a clever boy.

Startled by the sound of a constant thudding over hypnotic clicks and an endless whir, she emerged from her stupor. She began to panic, her bloodshot eyes and gaunt face streaked by the shards of light from long cracks in the boarded window. She sat up, recoiling in terror at every creak the floorboards made on the other side of the heavily bolted metal door. He was back.

Hot tears stung her eyes as she frantically pulled at the long chain attached to her left ankle. The stubborn bolt anchoring it to the wall defeated her efforts to free herself. Her long, dark hair was moist with sweat. Her erratic breathing stopped as the door slowly opened. Silhouetted by the light from behind, he stood in the doorway. Exhausted and weak from the little food she forced herself to eat, she let out a scream that sounded hollow and utterly helpless. She grasped and kissed the gold crucifix that hung around her neck, mumbling a desperate prayer in Polish.

He smiled, enjoying the fear his mere presence induced in her, before approaching slowly and sitting on the edge of the bed with the new dress on his lap. He stared into her terrified face before pulling aside the thin duvet that had been covering her pale, naked body. She was getting too thin … like the others.

'Why are you doing this to me?' she pleaded.

'Be quiet. Don't make Mother angry again,' he snapped, pushing the fringe of his dark hair from his intense eyes.

He removed a folded leather sheaf from under his apron and systematically placed its contents on the bedside cabinet. She drew away from him as he lifted a syringe and put the needle into a small glass bottle. He extracted enough of the contents to make her docile before grabbing her forearm and carefully injecting benzodiazepine into her upper arm. When he released his hold, she began to struggle again, the hard leather restraint rubbing into the skin around her ankle. Unmoved by her distress, he sat impassively until she slowly weakened.

Her eyelids grew heavy, blinking rapidly. A strange sensation moved through her body, sapping the little strength she had left. Her pleas echoed around her head like the voice of a lost child searching for a way out of a maze. His face became blurred as though it was melting into the darkness. She tried to fight the overwhelming need to sleep. Her body began to spasm.

She became still.

He rose, walking into an adjacent room and switching on the light. It flickered and buzzed into a dim blue glow, barely revealing the grubby, white-tiled bathroom. Rolling up his shirt sleeves, he turned on both taps in the tub before going back into the room.

He unlocked the padlock that secured the leather strap to her ankle before casting it and the attached chain aside. He put his arms under her, easily lifting her limp body and carrying it into the bathroom, where he lowered her into the water. The cold shock revived her a little. She opened her eyes. Drowsy and weak, the drug made her compliant. She sat shivering in the tub as he began to wash her, the dried blood from the sores around her ankle slowly diffusing into the water.

Now washed and dried, he began to cut her hair with a large pair of dress scissors, putting the clippings in a plastic bag to dispose of later. Her expressionless eyes looked into the distance as he dressed her in the new blue cotton dress, fussing over the sleeves that consumed her cold, lifeless arms. Once she was sitting back on the bed, he fixed her crudely cut hair with kirby grips. Breathing heavily now with excitement, he carefully began to put makeup on her that showed this skill was learned over several years. Finally, he fitted a blonde wig with more kirby grips in a way that pleased him, brushing it back to how he remembered Daisy had looked. Satisfied he had her back again, he fetched her music box from the other room.

After winding up the shank mechanism, he placed the music box on the bedside table and became lost in the moment. The tiny ballerina on top of the box, pirouetting to Brahms' *Lullaby*, bewitched him. A dazed smile was fixed on his face until it finally stopped playing.

Play it for me again, Son. Daisy loved her music box.

Chapter 1

Friday: 1st of September 2023. Four years later.

Duncan Webster wore a dark blue rugby top with the collar up. The top, a size too small, clearly defined the muscles around his shoulders and upper arms. His dark hair was short at the back and sides, combed into a side parting so straight it looked like it had been done with a razor blade. Though he shaved every morning, a shadow of stubble remained on his dimpled chin. His blue eyes were the only tokens of colour in his otherwise monochrome face.

Duncan went down the gears to get the camper over a steep brae as Buachaille Etive Mòr appeared in the distance. He loved driving the 1970s reconditioned Volkswagen, and had been chuffed when his uncle agreed to let him have it for the long weekend.

Changing up the gears again, he glanced at Erin, who was resting her head against the passenger-side window, using her jacket as a pillow. Beside her, Skye, her friend Hannah's cockapoo, was snuggled up fast asleep. Unlike Duncan, Erin was quiet and shy, and looked much younger than her twenty-one years.

They had met in a bar on Byres Road during their first year at university. He remembered how beautiful she had looked as she stood alone at the bar, sipping a glass of white wine and anxiously looking at the clock above the gantry. Duncan couldn't take his eyes off her. 'I think I'm in love,' he mouthed, before finally finding the courage to go over and speak to her, leaving his best mate, Jack Hardy, sitting on his own playing solitaire on his phone.

After about ten minutes of small talk, her friend, Hannah Bain, arrived. Her long, straight hair was dyed so black it had a blue sheen. She wore a long leather coat, short black skirt, fishnet tights, and Doc Marten boots. The only thing she wore that wasn't completely black was a T-shirt printed with The Cure's third album, *Faith*. Her dark eye makeup made her pale, thin face look ghostly white – clearly the effect she was looking for. Hannah quickly made it clear to Duncan that his presence was not welcome. He retreated with his half-finished pint and his tail firmly between his legs.

'Another knock-back,' Jack smirked, with more than a hint of pleasure at his friend's discomfort.

'I was doing alright until her stupid pal turned up. She looks like Morticia Addams,' Duncan moaned, resentfully staring over at Hannah.

'I don't think you're in her league, mate.'

'What do you mean?'

'She's drop-dead gorgeous!'

'They're probably lesbians anyway,' Duncan scoffed, still reeling from the rejection.

That would've been another uneventful evening for the pair, until later that night Duncan returned from the toilet to find both of them sitting with Jack, laughing at one of his corny jokes.

'Hi, again,' Duncan said, staring straight into Erin's eyes as she moved over to let him sit down. 'Would you like a drink?'

'Okay, a glass of white wine,' replied Erin, moving her hair away from her eyes and smiling at him.

'And I'll have a pint of cider,' said Hannah with a mocking grin, handing him her empty glass.

Duncan headed to the bar, leaving Jack in the middle of another one of his dreadful jokes.

Despite the unpromising start, Duncan and Erin exchanged phone numbers that night and within a few months were sharing a flat not far from the place they met.

Jack took a bit longer to persuade Hannah. In a desperate attempt to win her over, he dyed his hair black and bought a second-hand leather jacket with *AC/DC* embossed across the back. With his leather bomber, skinny-fit black jeans and white T-shirt, he looked more like a teddy boy than a goth.

'Jack, what were you thinking?' laughed Hannah, when she bumped into him at the university bar. 'Are you into heavy metal these days?'

'No, but the jacket was only thirty quid out of Oxfam … I've got tickets to see Ocean Colour Scene next Saturday. My mate can't make it now, and he gave me his ticket. Do you fancy going?'

'Okay, but only if you promise not to wear that jacket.'

Jack spent the next two days trying to get tickets for the concert, eventually paying over the odds on a dodgy website. He only told her about it when they had been going out regularly for a few weeks. He never wore the jacket again.

'Are we nearly there?' asked Erin, patting the dog's head and stifling a yawn.

'Maybe another thirty minutes,' said Jack from the back of the camper, while checking Google Maps to see how far they still had to go.

'Jack, have you got your lighter?' asked Hannah, expertly rolling a joint on her lap.

'Hannah, you can't smoke weed back there. Wait until we stop,' insisted Duncan, pulling the sun visor down and putting on his sunglasses as the road straightened out before him.

'Okay, don't get your knickers in a twist,' muttered Hannah, putting the rolled joint in her tobacco tin for later.

Glen Etive was impressive in any weather, but the bright sunshine made it staggeringly beautiful. Buachaille Etive Mòr stood out from the rest of the mountains that flanked the long road through the glen. The only sign of human settlement for the last few miles was a solitary white house that did not seem to have any reason to be there, surrounded by a sea of heather and bracken.

'This place is stunning,' said Jack, taking pictures on his mobile phone through the side window.

The camper had to slow down when it found itself behind a line of traffic, mainly motorhomes and caravans, all heading north towards Glencoe and beyond. Duncan took off his sunglasses and turned on the radio as the first clouds began to appear over the mountains, casting their shadows on the peat bogs and blocking out the sun for the first time that day.

'Turn that up!' shouted Jack excitedly as he and Hannah began singing along to 'Vampire' by Olivia Rodrigo.

'I used to think I was smart
But you made me look so naive
The way you sold me for parts
As you sunk your teeth into me, oh
Bloodsucker, vain fucker
Bleed me dry, like a goddamn vampire ...'

They were soon in the shadow of the Buachaille and Duncan needed a break from driving. He turned off the main road towards the Kingshouse Hotel. 'Let's go in here for a pint. I need the toilet anyway.'

It was lunchtime and they were lucky to get a table outside the old building that had been spared from demolition a few years earlier when the hotel underwent a major rebuild. People were wandering around wearing backpacks and carrying hiking poles. The hotel was a popular stop for those walking the West Highland Way, which partly explained why it was so busy, even at this time of year. Jack left the dog with Hannah and went into the bar to order the drinks, while Duncan went to the toilet.

Hannah took pictures of the deer that had wandered up to

the front of the hotel after one of the kitchen staff scattered food out for them. 'This is beautiful,' she declared, lighting a cigarette. The first few draws gave her the hit she had been craving since they last stopped for a break at the Drover's Inn. 'Erin, are you okay?'

'No. I told you we shouldn't have come. I don't know how to tell him.'

'Can't you just leave it until we get back, like we agreed? Cheer up, otherwise he will know there's something wrong.'

'There *is* something wrong. I don't want to be with him anymore. I need to find my own flat.'

'Erin, please tell me you never told him about ...'

'No, don't be daft!'

'That's him coming back.'

'Hasn't he got the beers in yet?' complained Duncan, putting his mobile phone on the table and taking a seat beside Erin. 'What's up with you?'

'Nothing, I'm just tired.'

'You're always bloody tired. I'm the one that's been driving for nearly three hours, and you're the one that's fucking tired!'

'Fuck you,' mouthed Erin, moving along the bench away from Duncan.

Jack came back with the drinks, shocked at the price he had to pay for them. 'What's up?' he asked, putting the drinks down on the table and looking at their glum faces.

'Nothing,' said Hannah, patting Skye, who was feeling ignored and looking for attention.

'C'mon, let's have a drink,' insisted Jack. 'That round cost me a fortune. I was going to get everyone something to eat, but it's seventeen pounds for a venison burger and some chips. There's no way I was paying that. It's a good job we brought our own food and booze. This place is a fucking tourist trap.'

'This weather is amazing,' said Hannah, putting on her

sunglasses and lifting her glass of cider.

'Hooray, global warming has finally come to Scotland,' proclaimed Jack.

'It's weird,' said Hannah, checking the temperature on her mobile. 'It's twenty-four degrees, which must be a record for September.'

'But once that sun goes down, the temperature will plummet,' said Duncan. 'It's also going to be raining tomorrow.'

'Oh, for God's sake, don't ruin the moment, Mister Doom-and-gloom,' said Jack, lifting a cigarette from the packet Hannah had left on the table. 'Let's try to have a bit of fun before we have to go back to uni.'

'Excuse me,' said Hannah, addressing the barman who was clearing empty glasses from the next table. 'Could I have a bowl of water for my dog … and would you mind taking a picture of the four of us on my phone?'

After posing for a few pictures with the Buachaille and the red deer in the background, they finished their drinks and decided it was too expensive to buy another round. Jack climbed into the passenger seat while Erin went in the back with Hannah and Skye. Duncan switched on the radio and they got back on the A82, continuing along the twisting road through the stunning Glencoe scenery. The mood lifted.

After about fifteen minutes, they turned onto the B863 and drove along the south side of Loch Leven towards the village of Kinlochleven. The brilliant sunshine on the still waters of the loch reflected the forest of pine trees on the far shore, where the massive Mamores ridge dominated the landscape. They drove through the village, continuing for a few more miles along the north side of the loch before turning onto a steep gravel road that led them into a forested area that was more remote than the website had suggested.

'Are you sure this is the right way, Jack?' asked Duncan.

'Yes, it's not far now.'

Following Jack's directions, they reached a rough, stony track that pushed the VW's suspension to its limit.

'I'd better not get stuck in here. This road's a fucking nightmare,' ranted Duncan, as things began to clatter and fall in the back of the camper.

'You'd think they'd fix the road if they're renting out their cottage,' complained Hannah, trying to stop the grills on the small gas cooker from rattling and frightening Skye. Like Jack, Erin was on her mobile, looking at Google Maps to see how far they still had to go, but the road did not seem to exist, even on the app. The app suddenly froze.

'I've lost my phone signal,' she groaned.

'There's the cottage up ahead,' shouted Jack, relieved that his directions had finally got them there.

'Thank God,' Duncan sighed, his hands still clamped tightly on the steering wheel. The road became a little more even as he drove onto an open gravel area and parked at the side of the cottage.

Everyone got out, eager to see just what they had rented for the weekend. Skye ran around in crazy circles, happy to be out of the camper and surrounded by so many new smells. While Hannah and Erin unpacked the bags, Duncan and Jack went out with Skye to see what the back of the house had to offer. They suddenly realised how far up they had travelled from the main road. The back garden overlooked a dense forest that ran down to the distant lochside. Jack became a little overexcited when he discovered there was a large metal firepit and a purpose-built stone barbecue in the back garden. Duncan found a large bag of charcoal stashed in a woodshed, which had enough logs in it to last a month.

That evening they had a barbecue, and afterwards the friends sat around the firepit and drank beer. As the sun was slowly slipping behind the mountains, it cast a yellowish-red glow that burnished the craggy slopes and gullies.

Jack was suffering from the midges and was frantically

scratching the red welts that covered his arms as he tried to roll a joint. 'Nasty little bastards,' he moaned. 'I didn't think they'd be out at this time of year.'

'It's probably because we're sitting near pine trees,' suggested Duncan, sipping his beer and worrying about how much damage he might have done to the underside of his uncle's camper.

'This is much better than a hotel,' said Hannah, holding tightly onto Skye, keeping him away from the sparks jumping from the fire. 'Jack, tell that scary story you wrote about the haunted mirror.'

'Okay, give me a minute to find it on my phone. Here, take this,' he said, passing the joint to Erin.

'Here we go again, another one of his daft stories,' sneered Duncan, staring over at Erin, who looked away. She no longer cared if he hated her smoking cannabis or not.

Scrolling down his mobile to where he had saved the story, Jack looked up to see if he had everyone's attention. He began to read in his best scary story voice.

'*Alice Pride loved to collect antiques, and one day, she found a beautiful oval mirror at a flea market. It had a silver frame with intricate carvings of roses and vines. She bought the mirror for a few pounds and took it home, hanging it in her bedroom above her dresser.*

Over time, she felt a strange connection with the mirror. It made her feel beautiful, even when she wasn't looking or feeling her best. Alice could spend hours in front of it brushing her hair, doing her makeup, changing into different clothes or just admiring her reflection.

One night she felt compelled to undress and admire her body in the mirror. After a few minutes, Alice became uncomfortable, as though someone was looking at her. A gust of wind rattled the bedroom window and she suddenly emerged from a strange trance. She got dressed and sat on the edge of her bed. There was an odd scent in the room that

12

reminded her of church.

That night, she had a vivid dream and saw herself in the mirror wearing a white dress and a pearl necklace. She looked happy and radiant. In her dream, she heard a sinister voice say, "You are mine, Alice. You belong to me. Now take off your dress …"

Alice woke up with a start, cold sweat on her forehead. She realised that she was naked under the bed sheets, with her nightdress draped over the mirror. Alice got up to get the nightdress but could not stop her urge to admire herself in the mirror. She looked at her reflection, but something was wrong. Her eyes turned dark and her skin became pale and wrinkled, her mouth now a twisted scowl. Alice tried to back away from the mirror, but her body wouldn't move. She heard a cruel and mocking laugh as her reflection changed again, this time morphing into an old man with long white hair, dark piercing eyes and a wicked smile. He wore a black evening suit with a pink carnation in the buttonhole of the lapel. "Hello, Alice," he said in a slow, rasping voice that caused a shiver to run down her back, as though he had somehow touched her with his ice-cold hands. "I've been waiting for you for such a long time. You see, this mirror was a gift from me to you over a century ago. But you died two days before our wedding in the arms of another lover, my brother, Christoph, and on that day, I swore to find you again. And I have. I found you, Alice. And now, you are mine and only mine once again."

He reached out from the mirror, grabbing her by the neck. Alice felt his cold fingers grip her throat tightly. She felt her life slipping away as he pulled her closer to the mirror. He said, "Don't be afraid. We will be together, forever. Come with me into the immortality of the mirror." He kissed her on the neck until the blood began to drain from her face and the mirror cracked open into a black void that trapped Alice forever.'

13

'Is that it?' mocked Duncan.

'I don't think I'll ever get undressed in front of a mirror again,' said Hannah, taking a long draw from the joint Erin had passed her.

'That was brilliant. Did you make that up, Jack?' asked Erin, who had barely listened to the story, the cannabis making her lightheaded.

'He just writes daft ghost stories so he can do his shit Dracula impersonation,' scoffed Duncan.

'That's a bit harsh. At least I'm trying to have a bit of fun. You've been in a shit mood all day.'

'Jack,' pleaded Hannah. 'Let's not start arguing.'

'I still can't get a signal on my phone,' complained Erin. 'I told my sister I'd give her a call when we got here.'

'I don't have a signal either,' said Hannah.

'We're too far off the beaten track,' explained Jack.

'You can phone her tomorrow when we go to Kinlochleven. You'll get a signal there,' suggested Duncan.

'It didn't look like there was much to do there,' said Jack. 'What about heading up to Fort William?'

'I thought we were going to do a bit of hillwalking,' said Hannah.

'Fuck that, if it's going to be raining tomorrow, I'd rather be in a pub,' declared Jack.

'I didn't come all the way up here to sit in a pub all day. We could've just stayed in Glasgow.'

'I'm with Hannah,' said Duncan.

'Well, fuck it. I'm here to enjoy myself,' Jack proclaimed, taking a rolled-up piece of paper from his pocket.

'What the fuck, Jack?' moaned Duncan. 'I thought you stopped taking *them*.'

'No, that was you, when you started all that body-building shit. So, don't be so boring. Who wants one?' asked Jack, swallowing one of the pills with a swig of beer. 'We're here to have a bit of fun.'

Hannah took one and passed the rest to Erin.

'No fucking way,' shouted Duncan, stretching over and grabbing Erin's wrist.

She let the paper wrap drop from her hand, turning to Duncan with her mouth open and the pill on her tongue. She closed her mouth defiantly.

'She's just swallowed a fucking eccie,' shouted Duncan at Jack. 'You're a fucking idiot.'

'Lighten up. It will only last a few hours. It's not like we're shooting heroin.'

The mood became sombre for a while as Duncan sat and sulked.

Still scratching, Jack threw another few logs on the fire, causing the red-hot embers to flare up wildly into the air. The flames were now so large that the fire could be seen from the other side of the loch. 'Hopefully that keeps the midges away; they're driving me fucking nuts.'

'You all think I'm boring, don't you!' shouted Duncan, turning to Jack. 'Do you have any left?'

'Here. If you're sure you want it.'

'Give me it. What the hell.'

Jack began to tell one of his jokes, with a punchline that only he seemed to find funny. 'This is a tough gig,' he complained, before throwing another log on the fire.

'Do you think there's a God?' asked Erin, out of the blue.

'There's no such thing as a God. It's all made-up rubbish,' declared Jack.

Erin took another draw from the joint. She was feeling quite philosophical. 'But how do you know? What about the Bible, don't you think that's true?'

'That's what I mean. It's all made-up. Do you really think we all came from Adam and Eve? According to the Bible, they only had two sons, Cain and Abel. I can't remember who killed who …'

'Cain killed Abel,' interrupted Duncan. 'At least check

your facts before you start pontificating your pagan beliefs.'

'I think he means bullshitting, Jack,' said Hannah.

'I know what he means. My point is, where did the next generation come from?'

'What do you think, Hannah?' asked Erin, passing her the joint.

'I don't really care. If there is a God then he's pretty useless. Look at the state of the world.'

'And you lot think *I'm* boring,' said Duncan. 'Jack, I think whoever sold you those pills ripped you off. I've had more of a buzz out of a sherbet Dip Dab.'

'They don't kick in for about half an hour, dude. Lighten up for once and find your inner self,' said Jack sarcastically, while making the peace sign with both hands.

'Dude,' laughed Erin, who suddenly had a fit of the giggles.

'Very funny,' muttered Duncan.

'Right, I've had enough,' asserted Hannah. 'I'm going to take Skye for a walk. He's bored sitting here.'

'I'll come with you,' said Jack, getting to his feet and stretching his arms. 'We can stick on my playlist when we get back. The eccies will have kicked in by then. Let's have a Highland rave.'

'You're nuts, and your playlist is piss,' moaned Duncan.

'It's starting to get a bit chilly,' said Hannah. 'I'm going in to get my jacket. Jack, do you want yours?'

'Aye, bring my Harrington, it's on the bed. Can you also get the torch?'

Jack and Hannah followed Skye along a narrow path that ran alongside a dense woodland on one side and a fast-flowing burn on the other. They walked for about ten minutes until they came across an opening in the trees that someone had cleared. There were a couple of crude wooden benches and a lopsided table, which had been there so long it was covered in moss. Hannah sat down and rolled a couple of joints. She handed one to Jack as Skye lay down at her feet.

It wasn't long before the last of the daylight began to fade. Jack switched on the torch, which clearly needed a new set of batteries. He knocked the top of the torch on the table and the light brightened for a few seconds, then faded back to a weak pale-yellow beam that dissipated into the darkness after only a few yards. 'We'd be better off using the torch on our phones than this stupid thing,' said Jack, taking a long draw from his joint and switching the torch off. He looked back towards the house before turning back to Hannah. 'I think something's going on between the two of them.'

'What?' asked Hannah, sure that Jack knew nothing.

'I don't know, but she doesn't seem happy. He treats her like shit. He's been a shit to her for weeks. Something's up.'

'It's nothing to do with us. Let them sort it out themselves.'

The cloudless sky quickly became so dark that the stars were radiant. Jack tried to make out the different constellations. He soon gave up as the endless expanse became overwhelming to look at for any length of time, especially after taking the ecstasy pill and smoking another joint.

Now that the sun had disappeared, a chilly wind started to blow up from the lochside as the trees around them began to sway and creak eerily, unsettling Hannah. 'We better go back,' she said. 'This is getting too creepy.'

'What was that?'

'What? Please don't, Jack. You're scaring me.'

'There's someone standing over there,' said Jack, turning the torch back on and shining it towards the noise. He couldn't see anything other than the trees moving in the wind. 'Who's there?' he shouted, the fear obvious in his voice.

'My God, I can see something,' said Hannah, holding Skye's lead tightly as he began to bark at a figure that moved slowly towards them.

'Duncan! Is that you? Stop fucking about!' shouted Jack,

picking up a stick and brandishing it.

'It's okay, it's me,' replied Duncan as he came into the light of the torch, clutching his left hand to his chest and looking distressed.

'Oh my God, you scared the life out of us,' shouted Hannah, now more angry than frightened.

'What's wrong?' asked Jack, walking towards him. 'What happened?'

'Nothing.'

'Then why are you crying, and what happened to your hand?'

'We had an argument. She went off her head,' explained Duncan, wiping the tears from his face and shaking his head. 'You shouldn't have given her that pill.'

'Don't blame me.'

'Where's Erin?' asked Hannah.

'I don't know. I thought she ran off to find you two.'

'Did you hit her?' demanded Hannah. 'You better not have laid a hand on her! Where is she?'

'I didn't touch her. I promise. My head is spinning like hell. I don't know where she is.'

'What happened, mate? What the hell happened?' pleaded Jack.

'I feel sick,' groaned Duncan, before throwing up on the picnic table.

'Let's head back,' said Jack. 'She's probably in the cottage.'

'C'mon Skye, let's go and find Erin.'

Chapter 2

Wednesday: 6th of September 2023

Disturbed by the sound of a door slamming in the flat above, Frank Dorsey woke up a few minutes before his seven o'clock alarm was due to go off. He reached over for his phone and cancelled the alarm. He turned to look at Liz, who was still sleeping, and eased himself out of the bed without disturbing her. Since they had started dating, she rarely stayed over, always worrying about her two cats being left alone for too long. She must have had too much wine the night before and forgotten about the cats.

After a shower and shave, he got dressed and went into the kitchen, making himself a coffee to go with his habitual morning nicotine fix.

The morning light began to fill the small kitchen, and he could see his reflection in the window. Now on the wrong side of forty, the grey hairs in his sideburns were finally taking over. Liz didn't seem to mind the grey hairs, or even the twelve-year age gap. If she did, she never mentioned it. He finished his coffee and put out the cigarette just as the kitchen door opened.

'Why didn't you wake me?' she asked, coming in wearing his dressing gown.

'I thought you said you were off today.'

'I said I was working from home. There's a difference. Do you want another coffee?'

'Why not?'

While she was making the coffee, Dorsey went into the bedroom to get his phone. For the first time in months, he had little to do when he got to the office. Another long investigation involving organised crime was over, and the statements and productions had already been passed to the Crown.

'That was a good night. I really like Claire,' said Liz, sipping her coffee and taking a cigarette from Dorsey's packet. 'We should invite them over to mine some night.'

'What's wrong with inviting them here?'

'I'm not cooking in this kitchen. You only have two small pots and a frying pan in that cupboard. There are no utensils other than a wooden spoon that's still got baked beans burned on it. Unless you're planning to make them beans on toast.'

'Okay, maybe your flat is a better idea. Anyway, I'd better get a move on. I can drop you off.'

'Or you could just phone in sick, and we could go back to bed,' suggested Liz.

'Are you serious?'

'No. I just wanted to see if you'd be up for it.'

'You're just a tease.'

'I wish we could, but I've got too much paperwork to do for that fraud trial I was telling you about. I'm going to have a shower before I head home. I'll get a taxi.'

'Okay,' he said, kissing her and lifting his packet of cigarettes from the table. 'I'll phone you later.'

'Leave me a couple. I need another coffee to wake me up.'

'It's time you started buying your own,' he joked, leaving her the packet of cigarettes. 'I'll get a packet on my way to the station.'

'Before you go, I was thinking Montenegro might be a good idea. The reviews online are great. It's got beautiful towns and villages, and it's not full of tourists. The weather is still pretty good at this time of year.'

'I don't know much about Montenegro, but if it's got decent weather and you think it's okay, just go ahead and book it. Let me know how much it is, and I'll transfer what I owe you.'

'I'll have another look at it later.'

It was a dull grey day and the streets were still wet from the rain that had drenched them during the night. He bought a packet of cigarettes from the corner shop before getting into his car and taking the twenty-minute drive to London Road Police Station.

'You're looking tired, Frank,' said Detective Sergeant George Mitchell, handing him a coffee. 'The gaffer was down looking for you about ten minutes ago. He wants to speak to you urgently.'

'What about?'

'Something about a missing student in the Highlands.'

'What's that got to do with us?'

Dorsey finished his coffee before going up to Chief Superintendent Knox's office on the first floor. He took a seat and waited for his boss to finish the phone call he was on. Eventually, Knox put the phone down. 'Frank, I've had a call this morning from the Deputy Chief Constable.'

'Is it about a missing student in the Highlands?'

'Yes, but she's no longer missing. That was a call from Glencoe. They've found a body. Cullen had already asked if you'd take over the case as senior investigating officer. Now he'll be ordering you to. Her father is the MSP Desmond Keenan – no doubt one of his cheese and wine friends.'

'What does it matter who her father is?'

'It matters to Cullen. He's the one who has to deal with the politicians on a daily basis.'

'Which division is overseeing the investigation?'

'Inverness CID are running the case, and it's their resources you'll be relying on, along with uniformed officers from Fort William. You can set up a local incident room at Glencoe Police Station.'

'Why do they need me? Surely they've got one of their

21

own senior officers to act as SIO?'

'Inverness CID are in the middle of two major surveillance operations involving organised crime, leaving them without any senior officer above the rank of inspector to deal with this case. Cullen insists on having a chief inspector as SIO and believes you are the best person to run the investigation.'

'Do they know if it's the missing student they found?'

'The body is in a peat bog just three miles from where she was last seen. Who else is it going to be? It was found by a mountain rescue dog this morning. The body is still submerged in over two feet of water in a ditch. The local uniformed officers have secured the area and are waiting for the scenes of crime team to arrive from Inverness.'

'Is there any sign of foul play? Could she have just gotten lost, fallen into the ditch, and drowned?'

'They're not sure.'

'Before we go any further, Andrew, I can't do it. I've got to give evidence in the High Court next week for that murder in the Gallowgate. I was the SIO in that case and could be giving evidence for days. I've also promised Liz I'd take the following week off so we can have a break together before she starts prosecuting a fraud trial at the end of the month.'

'Frank, you can come back and give your evidence when needed. I'll make sure that they have you on standby with at least a day's notice. Mitchell can stay up north until you return, then he can come back and give his evidence. You know how these High Court cases are, deals at the last minute.'

'What about Liz? What do I tell her?' asked Dorsey, showing no sign of succumbing to the pressure Knox was used to putting on his detectives when he wanted his own way. 'She probably already booked flights to Montenegro. You'll need to find someone else.'

'Frank, I don't know,' said Knox. 'I don't ask you to do much for me. I'm under a lot of pressure here from Cullen.'

'So you've already told him I'd do it!'

'He's not a man to take no for an answer. What can I say? I'm sorry, I should've spoken to you first.'

'Okay. I'll speak to Liz.'

'Great. I owe you one. As I've said, you'll be SIO and oversee the investigation in Glencoe. Detective Chief Superintendent Fiona Mackie will be your immediate superior officer. She'll remain in Inverness, dealing with the media and providing you with the resources you need. Cullen will have strategic command over the different regional divisions that may need to be deployed. The only suspect, if there was any foul play, is the boyfriend, Duncan Webster. He was the last person to see her before she went missing. He had bruising to his left hand and was interviewed under caution at Glencoe, but he wasn't charged. He said he punched a tree after she told him she was seeing someone else. That injury now looks pretty damning. If he punched a tree, you'd expect more than a few bruises on his knuckles.'

'Depends how hard he punched it. Anyway, we still need to find out how she died before we even think about arresting him.'

'I'll arrange for our family liaison officers to visit the family. Here's the file emailed to me this morning before they found the body. I'll leave it to you to tell DS Mitchell.'

'Where are we staying?'

'Don't worry, we'll get you booked in somewhere decent before you leave. If she did fall in the ditch and drown, you'll be back tomorrow.'

'But if it was murder, I could be there for weeks.'

Back in his office, Dorsey took out the paperwork from the file that Knox had handed him. Along with three statements and various productions, there was a report of the case by PC Susan Dixon, the local police constable who initially investigated the disappearance. He slowly perused her summary, underlining key points of interest.

The disappearance of Erin Keenan was reported to Glencoe Police Station on Saturday, the 2nd of September 2023 at 7.30 a.m., by her boyfriend, Duncan Webster, and two other friends, Hannah Bain and Jack Hardy. All four, including Keenan, are second-year students at Glasgow University and were on a long weekend break. They had rented Craggy Wood, a cottage, which is roughly a mile inland from the B863 on the north side of Loch Leven. It can only be reached by a poorly maintained track that runs up as far as the cottage and the woodland from which it gets its name. The booking was made online through the Airbnb website and paid for in advance for three nights, from Friday, the 1st, to Monday, the 4th of September. Erin Keenan is a twenty-one-year-old white female, five foot six, with green eyes, and curly shoulder-length auburn hair. She was wearing light blue jeans, a blue puffer jacket, and brown hiking boots.

According to the statement obtained from the boyfriend, Duncan Webster, after Hannah Bain and Jack Hardy went for a walk with their dog, he remained in the back garden of the cottage with Erin Keenan. They began to argue when she explained her intention to get the bus back to Glasgow in the morning. During that argument, she told him she was seeing someone else and wanted to break up. In his rage, he kicked over a firepit, and she ran off into the woods. He then went after her but couldn't see where she went. At that time, he punched a tree in his frustration, injuring his left hand. He eventually found Hannah Bain and Jack Hardy at a small picnic area about a quarter mile from the cottage, but there was no sign of Miss Keenan. According to Bain and Hardy's statements, the time between when they left for their walk and when Duncan Webster found them at the picnic area was around thirty minutes. All three stated they were unaware that Erin Keenan had been seeing someone else.

The three friends then spent the next few hours searching for her. They searched the area around the cottage and the woods. *Hannah Bain found Erin Keenan's mobile phone on the grass near to where she had been sitting at the firepit. They eventually gave up looking for her and returned to the cottage, hoping she would be there when they got back.*

At some point while they were searching the Craggy Woods, their dog, a black and white cockapoo, ran off and did not return. After a sleepless night waiting for Miss Keenan and the dog to turn up at the cottage, they drove to Glencoe Police Station in the morning to report them missing. They did not report her missing sooner because Duncan Webster had too much to drink and was unfit to drive. There was also no phone signal, so they could not phone for help. They all thought that Miss Keenan would return at some point. It was only as the hours passed that they became concerned that something might have happened to her.

That day, I made enquiries in Kinlochleven, Ballachulish, and Glencoe village. I noted that there was no evidence of Miss Keenan checking into any other accommodation, nor did she take a bus or a taxi out of the area. At the time, I believed she managed to reach the B863 and got a lift, or she went further inland and got lost, succumbing to the cold. I, along with another two constables, checked all the CCTV in the immediate area and found nothing of interest. By the end of our shift on the Saturday, I informed the CID in Inverness that I was concerned for the safety of the missing student.

On Sunday, the 3rd of September, Inspector Bill Crawford arrived from Inverness and took over the case, initiating a police search of the woodlands near the cottage. This was extended further inland on the Monday morning with the help of the local search and rescue team from Glencoe and many local volunteers.

Since her disappearance, her debit cards haven't been used, and she has made no attempt to contact her family. Duncan Webster was interviewed under caution by DI Crawford but was later released without charge. I attach the relevant productions, including photographs and a copy X-ray of Duncan Webster's left hand, and a photograph of the four students with Hannah Bain's dog taken in Glen Etive the day she went missing.

Dorsey looked at the photograph of the four students. They were all smiling, except the young woman on the extreme left of the picture, whom he assumed was Erin Keenan from the description in PC Dixon's report. He then studied the copy X-ray of the hand for a moment. There were no broken bones, but the photographs showed an area of bruising around the knuckles. He gave the summary to Mitchell while he read the statements of the three students. The statements didn't add much beyond what was in the summary, other than the fact that Hannah Bain confirmed that Erin Keenan was wearing a gold Claddagh ring her mother had given her for her twenty-first birthday. It was the only piece of jewellery she wore.

'What do you think?' asked Dorsey, as Mitchell continued to slowly read the summary of evidence, writing down everything of interest in his notebook. 'Knox thinks it was Webster.'

'He might be right. It does look like the boyfriend did it,' said Mitchell, looking at the pictures of Webster's hand and the copy of the X-ray again. 'If he did punch a tree, you'd expect the injury to his hand to be more serious than just some superficial bruising.'

'That's what Knox said. But according to all three statements, he was only alone with her for about thirty minutes. That wouldn't have given him time to dispose of the body. It was found three miles away from the cottage in the middle of a peat bog.'

'True. So where does that leave us?'

'I'm not sure.'

'If he punched her and that made her run off, get lost, fall in a ditch, and drown, then that might be enough to charge him with culpable homicide.'

'I don't think we'd get that to stick in court, but that's for the lawyers to argue over.'

'Do we know anything more about the body?' asked Mitchell, handing the file back to Dorsey.

'No, they're waiting for the scenes of crime officers to arrive from Inverness. I think we'd better get going. It's a bit of a drive. We'll go to your place first. Pack enough for a week and we'll see how it goes.'

Chapter 3

There was something ominous about the dark clouds gathering over the imposing mountains that made the road towards Glen Etive feel more like the entrance to Mordor than the gateway to the Highlands. Dorsey slowed down and pulled over to let a large lorry pass as the rain started to come down. It had been fine when they left Glasgow and had only started to cloud over when they reached Tyndrum, but now it was like a different day entirely.

The rain was torrential, and the mountains had all but disappeared into a wall of greyness on either side of the glen. They passed Buachaille Etive Mòr, unaware it was even there, leaving Glen Etive and descending into the twisting road that took them through the immense wilderness of Glencoe.

Dorsey was loving the new car he had only picked up from the showroom the week before. He had never had a BMW 5 Series before, and it was a joy to drive. This was the first time he'd had a chance to feel the power of the engine as he took the challenging road with ease. Even Mitchell was waxing lyrical about the array of gadgets on the large dashboard and the heated leather seats.

'I wonder what this hotel is going to be like,' said Mitchell, who liked his home comforts.

'The usual basic three-star rubbish. Knowing that tight git, Knox, we're probably sharing a double bed.'

'Like Morecambe and Wise?'

'Well, I was thinking more like Laurel and Hardy. Was that lightning?'

'Think it was,' said Mitchell, just as a deep roar of thunder reverberated through the glen.

The rain increased its intensity, and Dorsey slowed down when the drop in visibility made the bends in the road treacherous. 'Shit. I meant to phone Liz before I left. Give me a minute.' He pressed the speed dial on the dashboard, but her number rang out. 'I hope she's not booked that bloody holiday yet.'

'Where were you going?'

'Montenegro. It's in the Balkans, before you ask.'

'I know where it is. It used to be part of Yugoslavia. The capital is Podgorica.'

'Well, you know more than me.'

'I think Liz and Claire got on well last night,' said Mitchell, changing the subject.

'Yeah, it was a good night. Liz thinks we should maybe have a night at her flat sometime. She obviously thinks my flat's a midden.'

'Is it serious between you two?'

'Who knows, early days. I'm not planning to get married again, if that's what you mean,' responded Dorsey, not keen on where the conversation was going. He switched Bluetooth on, which immediately began to play *Wish You Were Here* from his album playlist. Mitchell went back to looking at the map on his phone.

Splashing through the deep torrents of water running off the mountainside and slightly distracted by Pink Floyd, Dorsey almost missed the turnoff to Kinlochleven. Mitchell kept him right just in time. The windscreen wipers were struggling to deal with the deluge, and visibility was now only a matter of yards. The greyness was beginning to overwhelm them.

'George, can you phone Inverness again and get them to give us the GPS for the location of the body? After we get to Kinlochleven, I've no idea where to go.'

The GPS directions were finally sent with a text giving

more information. 'Got it,' said Mitchell, scrolling down the text. 'The locus is around five hundred yards from some ruins on the Old Military Road that's part of the West Highland Way ... We've come the wrong way. We should've stayed on the A82 and headed towards the Ballachulish Bridge. The Lairigmor ruins are on the Lochaber side of the loch, so the body's not actually in Glencoe.'

'Will I turn back?'

'No, we've come too far. Just stay on this road to Kinlochleven, then follow it through the village and around the other side of the loch. There should be a sign for a place called Callert, about two miles before we reach North Ballachulish. According to the text, there's a footpath from the car park that takes us to the ruins, where scenes of crime have set up a base. It's the only shelter for miles. I can't see the path on Google Maps; we may have a bit of a hike to get there ... Shit, I haven't got any waterproofs with me!'

'Why can't we just get on the Military Road if the ruins are right beside it? Why are we going this way?'

'The Old Military Road was built by Redcoats three hundred years ago to march on after they defeated Bonnie Prince Charlie and his Jacobite army at Culloden in 1746. It's not built for cars and is now just another part of the West Highland Way.'

'George, how do you know all this?'

'I don't, I just googled it. Here's another interesting fact: there's a flower called Sweet William, named after the English general, the Duke of Cumberland, who defeated the clans at Culloden. But in Scotland it's called Stinking Billy.'

'Any other useless information?'

'Not if you're going to be like that. Don't you think we should just head straight to the police station in Glencoe? We'll get everything we need at the post-mortem,' suggested Mitchell. 'We don't have the right gear for trekking across country in this weather. We could end up lost trying to find the locus. It's just one massive bogland according to this map.'

'Okay, I've got my parka and a pair of wellies in the boot, so I'll drop you off at The Stag's Head. You can book us in and take my suitcase up to my room. Then get someone from the police station in Glencoe to pick you up and take you there. You can set up the incident room the way we do it. I'll head back once I've spoken to the pathologist.'

'Are you serious? You can't go on your own.'

'George, this is not up for debate. I'll drop you off at the hotel.'

They drove slowly into Kinlochleven, which was all but deserted apart from a drenched young couple carrying sodden backpacks and sheltering in a shop doorway. The hotel was on the lochside on the north of the village. Dorsey pulled into the car park and dropped off Mitchell, who was still complaining about Dorsey's decision to go to Lairigmor on his own.

Chapter 4

The rain stopped as quickly as it came on, but the sky remained a homogeneous hue of grey that smothered the mountains in the distance and seemed to come right down and touch the dark waters of Loch Leven. The drive along the B863 was straightforward enough and gave Dorsey a chance to phone Liz again. She picked up this time.

'Did I wake you up?' he said sarcastically, putting the call on loudspeaker now that Mitchell was no longer in the car.

'Don't be funny. I've been working hard all morning. This case is a nightmare to prepare.'

'I phoned you twenty minutes ago. I thought you would've phoned back by now.'

'Well, you didn't phone me. I've had no missed calls from you.'

'I must have pressed the wrong number. Anyway, the reason I'm phoning is that I'm on my way to Glencoe. A missing student from Glasgow has been found dead in a bog. She either got lost and fell into a ditch and drowned or was murdered. I won't know until I get there and speak to the pathologist.'

'Why are you doing it? Is that not something Inverness should be dealing with?'

'They are, but Cullen insisted that I take over as SIO. She has been missing since Friday and the body was only found this morning.'

'Okay, what about Montenegro? Do I book it or not?'

'I'd leave it for now. I'll know what's involved in a few hours. If she drowned in a bog by accident, then I'll be back in Glasgow tomorrow. I'll phone you when I know what's happening.'

'Okay. I know it's selfish, but I hope she fell into the ditch and drowned. If it's a murder, you could be up there for weeks ... even months.'

'I know. I'll phone you later, bye.'

'Bye. Take care.'

His phone rang as soon as he hung up. He looked at the number on the monitor and realised why Liz never got his earlier call. He had called his ex-wife by mistake.

'Helen?'

'Yes, you called earlier. Sorry I missed it.'

'That's alright,' he said, quickly deciding not to let her know he called her by mistake. 'I was phoning to let you know that I'm on my way to start an investigation in Glencoe. I may be away for weeks. It's likely that I won't be able to come on Saturday. If I'm not back before then, tell Daniel I'll make it up to him.'

'Frank, you can't keep letting him down like this. He was looking forward to going.'

'I'm not saying that I'm not taking him. I'm just warning you that I might not be able to, depending on what I find out in the next couple of hours.'

'Why are you dealing with a case in Glencoe anyway?'

'It's a long story. I'll phone him later.'

'Okay, maybe Richard can take him.'

'I need to go.' *Why did she have to even mention him?* Glad both calls were out of the way, he put Pink Floyd back on to clear his head.

The wind had not let up, and the trees along the road were being battered in all directions. He had not passed a single car by the time he reached Callert, which he discovered to be a small lochside settlement of holiday-lets on the shores of the loch.

He drove into the car park, where there were already half a dozen police and mountain rescue vehicles parked beside a large white mobile forensic unit and the ubiquitous blue police portacabin that uniformed officers used at major crimes, as a shelter as much as anything else. There was no one there. He assumed everyone was at the locus. Battered hard by the freezing wind, he put on his heavy parka over his suit jacket, zipping it up as far as the fastener would go. He struggled to stay on his feet while trying to put on his wellingtons. He was beginning to think what he had brought might not cope with the wild conditions. He checked the portacabin to see if he could get some waterproof trousers, but it was locked.

Once on the path, the wind blew straight into his face and he could feel his skin going numb. Visibility was only about twenty feet, and the mountains that surrounded the glen were completely shrouded in a thick grey mist. The wind howled like the wailing of banshees through the thickets of gorse bushes that were one of the few shrubs tough enough to survive in such a hostile environment. He had to force his way forward along the slippery, undulating footpath towards what looked like an endless mass of sodden bogland. He was now wishing he had listened to Mitchell. The path was so steep in places that he began to feel a burn in the back of his legs. Even though it was no longer raining, his clothes were saturated with the water blowing off the heather by a fiendish wind that constantly changed direction. He was sure that one night in this would give anyone hypothermia.

An hour into the exhausting hike, he was tempted to turn back, but persevered. He tried to think of the sheer misery the clans must have faced while fleeing from the Redcoats after their defeat at Culloden. As it started to get dark, he switched on the torch on his mobile to keep on the path. He noticed there was no signal on his phone and the battery had only twenty percent of life left. He was now sure the student must have simply got lost, fallen into the ditch in the dark, and drowned. He was starting to think he might meet a similar fate if he didn't find the ruins before his phone battery died on him.

After another twenty minutes, he was relieved to see lights up ahead and the outline of a building that he assumed was the ruins Mitchell mentioned and where the local police had set up a temporary base. He walked on, no longer able to feel his hands and wishing he had been sensible enough to bring gloves with him. He shuddered to imagine how cold the place must be in the depths of winter.

A ghostly figure appeared from the side of the ruins, battered by the wind, standing staring in his direction. It then began walking along the path towards him. From what he could initially make out, it was a female, wearing the kind of gear that was needed in this part of the world. Freezing and wet, he was already suffering from outdoor clothes envy.

'Chief Inspector Dorsey? We were told you were on your way … PC Susan Dixon, glad to meet you, sir.'

'I read your report, Constable. It was extremely helpful. I hope you've got a fire in there and some way of making coffee,' he said, now desperate for a cigarette and to commandeer a dry jacket and pair of gloves from someone.

'No fire, sir, but there's coffee and we've got spare waterproofs you can borrow. I'm surprised you decided to walk here, sir.'

'What do you mean? How did everyone else get here?'

'Those involved in the search obviously walked from the Craggy Woods. The rest of us were brought in by helicopter when the body was found.'

'Where was the body found?' he asked, wondering why the possibility of a helicopter was never made known to him.

'Over there, sir,' she replied, pointing towards a forensic tent which was glowing from the constantly moving torchlight inside.

'Who's in charge of forensics?'

'Dr Jamali. She's still out there. We tried to relay cables

from the generator we have inside, but we were thirty feet short. An extension is on its way,' she explained, leading Dorsey into the ruins where she introduced him to Detective Inspector Bill Crawford, who had been in charge for the last four days. He was surrounded by an exhausted team of uniformed officers and detectives, who all got to their feet when they realised the new boss had arrived.

Dorsey had seen a hundred Bill Crawfords in his time in the CID – middle-aged, prematurely balding, overweight, and counting the days to retirement. His beer belly was resting on his belt with such panache as though it had paid to be there. Wearing a grey suit with buttons no longer able to reach the other side of his jacket, he looked like someone who didn't give a shit anymore. Despite this, his handshake was still full of the man's need to be taken seriously, squeezing Dorsey's hand harder than was necessary.

'What do we know about the body?'

'Not a lot. Dr Jamali wanted the surrounding area searched before she started work; she's been out there for a couple of hours,' explained Crawford. 'We're just taking a rest. We've been at this since seven and everyone is knackered.'

Dorsey took the cup of coffee from Dixon and lit up a cigarette.

'You can't smoke in here, sir,' said Crawford, who looked like he had just made that rule up on the spot.

Looking around the ruins and at the tarpaulin that covered the roof flapping wildly in the wind, Dorsey ignored him and continued to smoke. 'Was the dog, a black and white cockapoo, found?'

'The only thing found apart from the body was a rucksack, which was recovered about five hundred yards away, tangled up in a thicket of gorse bushes. There was nothing inside it and it's been bagged and sent up the road to be examined,' explained Crawford.

'Erin Keenan didn't have a rucksack when she went

missing. Is there any indication that she just got lost and fell into the ditch and drowned?'

'What? Did nobody tell you?' smirked Crawford, turning to look at DS John Grant, who was standing just behind him, before addressing Dorsey. 'According to Dr Jamali, the body is dismembered and has probably been there for years.'

Dorsey dropped his cigarette and put it out with his heel, turning to face the DI. 'Take that smirk off your face. When I asked you what was known about the body, you said not a lot. You should've told me then that the body was dismembered and had been in the ground for years, because that obviously means it's not Erin Keenan. So, when I ask a question in future, make sure you tell me what I need to know.' He gave the rest of those present the same stare that had just immobilised Crawford, before turning to Dixon. 'Constable, can you take me out and introduce me to Dr Jamali?'

'Of course, sir. Here, you'll need these,' she said, handing him a jacket and a pair of gloves.

Dorsey cast his sodden parka aside and put on the waterproof jacket. Dixon gave him one of her hiking poles, before leading him towards a path that was already well-trodden by those coming and going between the ruins and the body. Traversing the spongy peat bog was difficult even with the hiking pole, and Dorsey struggled to keep up with Dixon as the wind tried its best to knock him off his feet, only staying upright because the sodden bog anchored his boots. When they reached the forensic tent, he was glad to see that the forensic team had made a standing area out of plastic duckboards. Satisfied he would be able to make his own way back, he instructed Dixon to head back to the ruins.

Dorsey found Dr Jamali sitting on a camping chair in white hooded forensic overalls, writing in a leather-bound notebook. Two of her team were working in and around the tent, which was flapping violently and would have taken off down the glen if not for the thick ropes that criss-crossed over it, tied to two-foot metal stakes sunk into the ground. The tent covered the immediate area where the body was found that morning and was glowing from inside like a giant firefly.

'Hello, Dr Jamali,' said Dorsey, causing her to look up from her notebook and remove her reading glasses. 'I'm Chief Inspector Frank Dorsey, and now in charge of this investigation. Can you give me a verbal update on the victim?'

'Well, Chief Inspector, it's not who we thought it was. It's not the student that went missing six days ago.'

'I know, DI Crawford has just told me.'

'Also, this body has been dismembered, and each part has been individually wrapped with pieces of blue cotton, which may have been a dress at one time. The main torso and head are intact, but there are two knife wounds to the neck. The arms and legs have been severed. It's also been here for some time. How long exactly, it's impossible to say, as all the normal post-mortem indicators have been usurped by the fact it's been submerged in this bog.'

'Is it female?'

'Yes, the body is female, naked apart from what it was crudely wrapped in. From what I can make out, she's in her late teens to early twenties, short dark hair, five foot six, and ethnically white northern European. The body is submerged in two feet of water in a trench. It may never have been discovered but for the unusually dry weather, which must've caused the level of stagnant water in the ditch to drop due to evaporation, exposing the right hand and lower arm to the elements. There are two holes on the back of the torso in the upper trapezius muscle and on the wrists and ankles. The body parts were hung up with what I can only deduce were butcher's hooks. The knife wounds to the neck would have been inflicted to sever the main blood vessels. This would all have been done after death to drain the blood.

'The left ankle also has skin damage that indicates that it was tethered with some type of strapping which rubbed and blistered the skin, causing an infection. She's clearly been the victim of an abduction and was probably repeatedly raped over a period of time before she was killed. So, Chief Inspector, you don't just have a missing persons case on your hands … You have a murder. I've still to determine the cause of death, but once dead, the killer butchered the body to make it easier to dispose of.'

'Can you say how long it's been here?'

'It's impossible to say much more than I've already said until we get the body back to the lab and I conduct a full autopsy,' explained the doctor. 'If you'll come with me, I think the scenes of crime officers have finished photographing and measuring everything. There were four different boot prints found, but I'm quite sure they'll be mine and those who found the body before the area was cordoned off. I can't see boot prints lasting too long in this wet mush, although I could be wrong.'

He followed the doctor over to the ditch where one of her colleagues was looking for evidence of insect activity and had just finished taking soil and plant samples from around the submerged corpse. The entomologist got up from his knees and handed Dr Jamali a high-tech LED lamp and stood aside. She took the lamp and held it over the waterlogged ditch. At first, Dorsey couldn't see anything other than ferns and thick tufts of heather around the dark peaty water, until the doctor increased the intensity of the LED light. He then noticed the faint outline of the body parts just under the surface of the water, as though it had been put into a light brown bath of formaldehyde. She pointed to the left hand and forearm, which were clearly in the initial stages of decomposition.

'Why is it still underwater?' asked Dorsey.

'After removing the cotton material and making a cursory

examination, I was satisfied it was not the young woman we expected to find, so I decided to leave it underwater. I didn't want to disturb things too much until we were ready to remove it. I've ordered a refrigerated cadaver van, which is on its way. You see, Chief Inspector, if we simply remove it now, the body will immediately start to deteriorate – look at the hand and forearm. While it's in this stagnant water, the flesh is being preserved, making my job of figuring out its identity and probable cause of death much easier.'

'Is it going to Inverness for the post-mortem?'

'Yes, I'll have it done by midday tomorrow. I'll be able to give you a provisional report sometime in the afternoon, assuming DI Crawford gets the extension cables that I asked for. We need proper lighting here to do our work.'

'Thanks, Doctor. I'll let you get on with it and make sure you get your cables,' said Dorsey, before heading back to the ruins. On top of finding the missing student, he now had to uncover whoever murdered the body being recovered from the bog. This was not what he signed up for. He was now likely to be away for months.

The wind had died down, making things more tolerable for everyone. Dorsey borrowed a camp chair from inside the ruins and set it up on the only flat area of *terra firma* he could find nearby. The cable extensions had finally arrived, and the technical crew soon had the forensic high-intensity LED lights set up and connected. The area around the white forensic tent was now lit up like a fairground attraction, powered by the large generator in the ruins.

'Do you mind if I join you, sir?' asked PC Dixon, carrying a camp chair. 'The refrigerated lorry has arrived at the car park. They'll be moving the body shortly.'

'Sit down. You might help me understand a few things about this place and how a body would end up here in this wilderness.'

'I'll do what I can, but I've never been in this part of the glen before.'

'But you must know Kinlochleven and the area around it fairly well.'

'Yes, but Glencoe Police Station covers a massive area, and we rarely come to out-of-the-way places like this. You don't walk in these bogs unless you have to. Whoever dumped the body must know this area. Not many non-locals would know about the path from Callert.'

'According to Dr Jamali, the victim has been in that bog for years. Her ankle was bound and she was probably raped for some time before being killed, dismembered, and dumped here. She could've been murdered anywhere.'

'I've never dealt with a murder case before.'

'Until I did my first murder, I'd never dealt with one either. If you had to bring a dismembered body out here, how would you do it?'

'Obviously, it's not something I've thought about.'

'I'm asking you to think about it now. How would you do it?'

'I don't think I'd come this far if I had to carry it, even if it was dismembered and I made a couple of trips. The Callert path is the best way to get here on foot, but it's a bit of a hike.'

'What about this road? You could drive a car on it if you had to.'

'Yes, on this stretch, but you can't get here from the main road, even with an off-road jeep. For what it's worth, sir, I spoke to the dog handler who found the body. He has a specially trained ex-army rescue dog that has also been trained to find cadavers.'

'I thought it was part of the mountain rescue team?'

'No, not officially anyway. I asked him to help. Alex Munro is an ex-soldier. He was in Afghanistan and moved back here a few years ago with the dog. He sometimes helps the mountain rescue team to find missing hillwalkers.'

'Can you get me his details? I may want to speak to him.'

'He's from Brig. I'll ask him to come down to the station to speak to you. He can be a bit strange until you get to know him. He was severely injured in Afghanistan and keeps to himself.'

'That's them,' said Dorsey, getting to his feet as he heard the unmistakable sound of a helicopter in the distance. 'Once they remove the body, there's not much more to be done here.'

'I'm going to head to the station now, if that's alright, sir?'

'How are you getting back?'

'I'll walk back the way you came. At least I've got the right gear for it.'

'You hang back with me. I want to wait until the body is on its way to Inverness,' he said, as the whirring blades of two police helicopters got closer.

Dorsey returned to where the scenes of crime officers were preparing to raise the body from the waterlogged trench. The senior forensic officer, DS Jock Kilbride, was supervising the lift. Kilbride was a huge man in his late fifties, well over six feet tall, with short grey hair and a matching beard. His forensic bodysuit stretched to cover his broad shoulders and barely reached his rubber boots. Dr Jamali insisted on more support around the head of the body to minimise the risk of it separating from the trunk. Once more lifting straps were secured beneath and around the remains, DS Kilbride gave the order to begin.

With the help of the bright LED lamps, Dorsey and Dr Jamali watched the forensic team raise the head and torso from its waterlogged grave using a small, motorised pulley system. The bog made a loud sucking noise, as though it was reluctant to give up its gruesome secret. It was disturbing to watch. For the first time, he could see that it was still recognisable as a young woman. The limbs were then retrieved. He could make out the grim black holes where the hooks had been inserted when the body was butchered. The doctor pointed to the discoloured circular injury to the left ankle, an obvious indication that the victim must have been tethered for some time before being murdered.

When the body was finally clear of the bog, it was photographed by one of the scenes of crime officers. Dr Jamali then conducted a further preliminary examination before it was placed in a specially insulated coffin.

Once the body was safely in the coffin, Kilbride offered his hand to Dorsey. 'Jock Kilbride. I'm in charge of forensics. I take it you're the new SIO?'

'DCI Frank Dorsey. It can't be easy working in these conditions.'

'No. We searched the wider area when we got here, but we'll have to come back in the morning to do a fingertip search of the ditch now the remains are out. Dr Jamali's got her work cut out identifying this body.'

They stood aside to watch the coffin being carefully carried back across the duckboards that were now laid all the way to the ruins. Seen from a distance, it looked like the solemn cortege of a Highland village carrying their clan chief to his final resting place, only this coffin was placed in the bay of a waiting helicopter. Dr Jamali, DS Kilbride, and the four-man forensic team took up the remaining passenger space.

When the first helicopter took off, the downdraught from the rotor blades blew the gorse bushes and heather in all directions. The clipped whirring of the two helicopters and their bright searchlights made Lairigmor look more like an army field camp in a war zone than a remote bog in the middle of nowhere.

Satisfied that there was nothing more that could be done until morning, Dorsey ordered the rest of the detectives and uniformed officers back to the police station via the Callert path. He then signalled to Dixon to follow him and the crew of electrical engineers to the second helicopter. It was not often he felt the need to pull rank, but there was no way he was walking back to the car park.

While the helicopter hurtled towards the Callert car park, the first one had already landed and the coffin was being transferred to the refrigerated van.

When they landed on a grass verge a few hundred yards from the car park, Dorsey remembered that he had left his sodden parka at the ruins. He was relieved to find he hadn't also left his car keys. He sent a text to Mitchell to bring him up to speed.

Now driving in a slow-moving police convoy across the bridge to South Ballachulish, Dorsey took his phone out of his pocket and phoned Mitchell. 'George, I'll be there shortly. Did you get my text?'

'Yeah, Jesus, Frank, we might be on this case for months. This is a much bigger deal than I was expecting. Whoever killed her must be a psychopath.'

'Yeah, and we still don't have a clue what happened to Erin Keenan?'

'I was just about to call Glasgow to get someone out to visit the Keenans and inform them that the body found wasn't their missing daughter.'

'Keep all the details of the murder under wraps as much as possible. There's nothing to show any connection between the two cases. According to the pathologist, the body could've been there for years.'

His mobile went silent; the battery was dead. He wasn't sure if Mitchell caught the last part of the conversation.

The forensic team were well on their way to Inverness when the returning police cars filled the remaining spaces in the station car park. The detectives were desperate to get into the warmth and take their wet gear off.

Once the detectives had changed, Dorsey made his way

to the front of the muster. The din of voices quickly subsided, and all eyes turned towards the chief inspector.

'We all know now that the body found this morning was not the young student we were looking for. At this time, she is still a missing person. The body that was recovered is on its way to Inverness, and tomorrow we should find out more about her after the post-mortem. In the meantime, we concentrate on finding Erin Keenan. She is our priority. As it stands, we have nothing to show she was abducted or murdered, and she may very well be alive. As you all know, thousands of missing persons cases are reported every year, and most are found alive and well. People disappear for all sorts of reasons, so we must keep an open mind.'

'What about the fact she has not used her bank card or attempted to contact her family or friends?' interrupted DI Crawford.

'I was coming to that. This young woman has no history of running off. She's highly intelligent and was due to continue a degree course in a few weeks. The fact that her bank card has not been used and she has not attempted to contact family or friends are the reasons this was assessed as a high-risk missing persons case. Although there is nothing yet to link the missing student to the body recovered today, the fear is obvious. However, as far as the public is concerned, we are not linking the two cases.'

'Good luck with that, sir,' said one of the Inverness detectives.

'Who are you?' asked Dorsey abruptly, annoyed at being interrupted for a second time.

'Detective Sergeant John Grant. Sorry to interrupt you, sir, but won't the media just treat both cases as if they're linked anyway?'

'They'll do what they want to sell papers. We don't know how long that body has been lying in that bog. Until that's established and we find a connection, we treat them as separate cases. For that reason, I'm splitting you into two teams. DS Mitchell will head the team investigating the body found today. DI Crawford will continue to lead the search for Erin Keenan. That means continuing to search for her as if she is still alive. From tomorrow, all annual leave is cancelled.'

There were audible groans from some in the room that irked Dorsey even more than the earlier interruptions. He held up a picture of Erin Keenan. 'If this were your daughter or sister, you'd still be out there looking for her now! Anyone who has leave booked, cancel it or go back to Inverness and stay there. I don't want you here. And so I'm perfectly clear, no one in here is to speak to the media about this investigation or risk facing a disciplinary hearing for gross misconduct. The two teams will also be split into twelve-hour shifts, 8 a.m. to 8 p.m. dayshift. I'm sure you can work out what the night shift will be for yourselves.'

There were a few muted laughs and murmurs of discontent from some, but most were beginning to understand the kind of boss under whom they were now working.

He continued. 'The team leaders will decide on the rota for their squads, including detectives, uniformed officers, and admin staff. So, get your excuses ready now, because once your shift is agreed, you're stuck with it. The first two shifts will start at 8 a.m. tomorrow. DI Crawford will now run through the state of the investigation as it stands, as much for my benefit as yours.'

The inspector took over, going through the date, time, and area where Erin Keenan was last seen. He confirmed that door-to-door enquiries, including checking hotels, holiday-lets, shops, pubs, and all available CCTV in the area, had come to nothing. There had been no sightings of her.

Crawford continued. 'The last person to see her was her boyfriend, Duncan Webster, who was interviewed under caution but not charged. He remains the prime suspect for her disappearance. However, until we find Erin Keenan, there is nothing to charge him with, as she could have simply gone missing for any number of reasons. The two other friends who travelled with her that day have been eliminated from our enquiries but remain as potential witnesses for when we discover what actually happened to her.'

'Sir, is it possible that the three of them were involved in killing her?' interrupted one of the detectives from the back of the room. 'If she went missing around eight in the evening, they had all night to dump her body and agree on their stories.'

'We'll look at all the options, but we need evidence or everything is just speculation,' said Crawford, looking flustered.

'It's the only thing that makes sense,' continued the same detective.

'Well, find me a fucking motive for why three students would murder one of their friends …'

'Right,' interrupted Dorsey. 'Let's keep this civil. We look at every possibility until it's eliminated as a possibility. Continue, Inspector.'

Crawford cleared his throat. 'There's no evidence of her taking a bus or taxi out of the area, although the possibility that she hitched a lift is more difficult to rule out. Hundreds of vehicles on the B863 and the A82 have been stopped, and statements have been obtained from those travelling on those roads after 6 p.m. on the 1st of September. Nobody saw anything suspicious, and those questioned were cleared for various reasons, including alibis and other exculpatory evidence. Lochs and rivers have been scanned from the air with drones and helicopters and a full team of divers are on standby, but so far nothing suspicious has been spotted. Forensics found nothing at the holiday-let that would indicate that anything untoward had occurred within the cottage. Despite the massive deployment of resources and manpower, we have found no clues, and her disappearance remains a complete mystery.'

Once Crawford had stopped, he handed the floor back to Dorsey.

'Thank you, Inspector. At least we all know how much has already been done and the effort everyone has made to find her. Tomorrow, we'll have a preliminary PM report for the body found today, so we will be able to see what that gives us to help identify her. Now you can sort out your rotas. PC Dixon, you'll work with me as I need your expertise and local knowledge.'

'Sir,' shouted the desk sergeant from the back of the room. 'The chief superintendent is insisting she speaks to you. She intends to make a statement to the media this evening.'

It was after nine when the two Glasgow detectives arrived at their hotel. Dorsey's first impressions of The Stag's Head were not great; it looked like a hotel designed by Sir Walter Scott, with its tartan carpets and thick velvet wallpaper. He almost knocked over a grotesque-looking stuffed fox that greeted them in the foyer. He hated taxidermy and couldn't understand why a hotel would think it acceptable to have dead animals scattered around as decor.

There was no one at the reception desk, and he pinged the bell on the counter a little harder than he intended. While they waited, he picked out one of the brochures from a display tray. It was offering a trip along the loch to the visitor centre in the village of Glencoe and to a local distillery to learn about the making of malt whisky, neither of which interested him much.

'Hello, sorry there was no one here. We're a bit understaffed today,' said a young woman in a smart blue uniform, her smile warm and welcoming. 'We were all shattered when we heard they found a body this morning. Do you think she was murdered?'

'I'm sorry, we can't discuss the case. Is the restaurant still open?'

'Oh, I'm so sorry, the restaurant closes early during the week at this time of year. The last orders were at nine.'

'Are you telling us we can't get anything to eat?' moaned Mitchell, his stomach rumbling in protest.

'It's too late for dinner in the restaurant, but I can ask the chef to make you both a plate of sandwiches, which you can have in the bar.'

'Well, it's better than nothing,' said Dorsey. 'Where's the bar? I need a pint.'

They drank their pints and ate their sandwiches while waiting for the news update to come on. Mackie had agreed with the decision not to link the two cases or to reveal any details of the condition of the body found in the bog, other than to provide the victim's description and confirm that it was being treated as murder.

Dorsey paid for the sandwiches and the barman took away the empty plates, returning a few minutes later with two pints of lager. 'They're on the house; the manager paid for them,' he said with a distinct Eastern European accent. 'Have you found the missing girl yet?'

'How did you know we were police officers?' Dorsey asked.

'Someone from the police station phoned this afternoon asking for Chief Inspector Frank Dorsey. The name on your debit card,' he grinned, handing the card back. 'You don't have to be a detective.'

Mitchell laughed, spitting out some of his beer as the barman went back behind the bar to continue cleaning the dust off an array of malt whisky bottles lined up on the top shelf of the gantry. Before Dorsey could think of something to say, Chief Superintendent Mackie appeared on the TV screen, looking nervous and holding what Dorsey assumed was the press release they had agreed to earlier. She introduced Erin Keenan's father, Desmond Keenan MSP. He was dressed in a casual check shirt open at the neck, beads of sweat gathering on his forehead from the heat of the studio lights bearing down on him. He stared into the camera, grim-faced, holding the hand of his distraught wife, whose eyes were tearful behind her glasses. He then made an impassioned plea to anyone who may have seen their daughter to contact the police. His voice broke as he spoke directly to Erin. 'Darling, if you're able to, please contact us. We all love you. Your mum and sister are sick with worry, we all are.' He could no longer speak and put his arms around his sobbing wife. The press photographers seized the chance to capture their distress, taking the pictures they needed for the morning papers.

CS Mackie then delivered the short press statement that clearly left the gathered journalists with more questions than answers. She stuck to her brief and ignored suggestions of a link between the two cases. Holding a picture of Erin up to the cameras, she made a direct appeal for members of the public to come forward if they had any information about either of the victims. She then abruptly called an end to the press conference as the journalists fired questions after her.

'Rather her than me,' said Dorsey, finishing the pint the hotel manager had sent over. 'You fancy another?'

'No, not for me. It's been a long day. I think I'll head up and have an early night. I want to speak to the kids before Claire puts them to bed.'

'Sure, give them my love,' said Dorsey, the word 'love' sounding awkward. It was a term of endearment he rarely used.

After a double whisky on his own, Dorsey went up to his room. He placed his suitcase on the bottom of the bed and took out his toiletries, putting them in the en suite. The room had the usual blandness of a three-star hotel, with nothing much to do other than watch TV. He flicked through a few channels before turning it off abruptly; the image of the dismembered body being sucked out of the bog was still too fresh in his mind. He called Liz, but her phone just rang out.

He went out to the balcony with a miniature bottle of Glenfiddich malt whisky from the mini bar. The loch had all but disappeared in the darkness, but he could still hear it lapping up onto the pebbles on the foreshore below. He wasn't keen on malt whiskies, preferring blended instead, but he was sure drinking blended whisky in this part of Scotland was sacrilege. It would have to do.

Chapter 5

Thursday: 7th of September 2023

Mitchell was already sitting down to his full Scottish breakfast when Dorsey joined him. They were both up early, and apart from a group of German-speaking tourists who were clearly dressed for serious hillwalking, they were the only ones in the breakfast room. The glen was basking in the early morning sunshine.

Mitchell nodded towards the window that dramatically framed the loch and surrounding mountains. 'Stunning. It's like a different place.'

'You know what they say about the Scottish weather … Is it self-service in here?' asked Dorsey, looking around for a member of staff.

'It's a buffet. You need to help yourself.'

The weather was in sharp contrast to the day before, making Dorsey feel energised. While having his scrambled eggs and toast, he made a call to CS Mackie, who agreed to have the case upgraded to a major investigation and arrange for more resources to be deployed.

It was now obvious to Dorsey that the empty rucksack was an item of interest and of potential evidential value. He thought of nothing else from the moment he woke up. 'George, if it *was* her rucksack, then there's every chance the killer's DNA will be on it. If it is and he's on the police database, then this case might be more straightforward than we thought.'

'Frank, if it was, and he's careless enough just to stick it in some gorse bushes, then we're dealing with someone who is not very bright or doesn't care if he gets caught. Do you think we're dealing with a local?'

'Strangers to this area wouldn't be aware of the path from Callert, and that's the only conceivable way that anyone could've brought the body to that place. I've walked it; there is no way anyone would carry a body that distance.'

'But it wasn't a body; it was body parts. He could have made a couple of trips.'

'Even so, it's a bit of a hike for anyone. George, can you concentrate on the locals with records of violence or sex offences? I'm going to head up to Inverness to speak to the pathologist. I can't sit around and wait for the provisional autopsy report.'

'What about the suggestion that the three students were in some way involved in their friend's disappearance?'

'Seems highly unlikely. I'd rather you concentrate on the body in the bog. I want to keep these investigations separate. Until there is something that links them, they are what they are: a murder and a missing persons investigation. When you've finished your breakfast, I'll drop you off at the station,' said Dorsey, who had eaten enough, getting up to finish his coffee with a cigarette in the beer garden.

Inverness was a two-hour drive from Kinlochleven, giving Dorsey time to think about the case. The drive through the countryside was pleasant enough until he found himself behind a slow-moving caravan that wouldn't pull over for at least five miles. Eventually, the caravan pulled into a lay-by to let him and a dozen other frustrated drivers pass. He put his foot down.

A couple of miles from Inverness, his phone buzzed. He didn't recognise the number that came up on the dashboard. He took the call.

'Sir, it's Crawford. We've had two sightings of Keenan since the TV appeal last night. She was seen in Fort William the day after she went missing, but even better than that, she was also seen in Glasgow yesterday.'

'That's fantastic news,' said Dorsey, unable to remember if he was ever told Crawford's first name.

'I'm heading to Glasgow with DS Grant to see if there's any CCTV to confirm she's no longer our problem.'

'Let me know how you get on.' He smiled at the irony of the case. He and Mitchell had travelled all this way to look for a missing person who was likely already back in Glasgow when they left, only to be landed with a bizarre murder case. Then the doubts started to rise in his mind. *Why hasn't she used her bank cards or tried to contact anyone all this time? If it's her, then she clearly doesn't want to be found, but why?*

He checked his satnav. The morgue was only around the corner.

The post-mortem of the unknown female had already been carried out by the time Dorsey got to the morgue and the pathologist was now working in her office. The lab assistant knocked on her door and nodded for Dorsey to enter. She was sitting at a small desk, typing on her laptop. She looked quite different from the person he recalled from the previous day. No longer in the unflattering white bodysuit, she was wearing a loose-fitting Aran knit sweater and jeans. She had short, lustrous black hair, smooth olive skin, and wore black eyeliner around her large, dark eyes. She looked like someone who was visiting from a very far-off exotic place, not someone who lived and worked in the grey, windswept Highlands of Scotland.

'I wasn't expecting you to come all this way to pick up the report,' she said. 'I could've simply emailed it.'

'Preliminary reports throw up more questions than answers. I prefer to ask questions and hope that I'll get the answers I'm looking for.'

She looked at him intently for a moment before responding. 'So, what questions do you want answers to?'

she asked, gesturing for Dorsey to take a seat. 'I can only give you answers to what I know.'

'First of all, the obvious one: do you know the cause of death?'

'That may seem obvious and often is the easiest one to answer, but not in this case. The dismembered limbs, as you probably expected, were done after she was killed and almost certainly to make it easier for the killer to dispose of the body. There's no obvious physical injury, internal or external, that's serious enough to explain how she died.'

'You mean how she was murdered?'

'No, how she died or was killed.'

'Surely the injury to the left ankle shows that she was a prisoner of some psychopath who abducted, raped, and murdered her before dismembering the body and disposing of it in the bog? Am I missing something?'

'Right now, the cause of death is unclear. My position on this may quickly change once I've had a chance to carry out further tests on the internal organs and when I get the toxicology report back from the lab. Remember, Chief Inspector, I only promised a provisional report today. It will take a few days before I'm able to provide the full PM report.'

'Okay, I understand.'

'I've taken hair, blood and other fluid samples and will be sending them for a toxicology examination. The surprising thing is that although she was clearly restrained for a lengthy period by whoever abducted her, there is no evidence that she was raped.'

'What?'

'Yes, it surprised me as well. The hymen is fully intact, with no sign of attempted penetration injuries. Very strange. There are distinct thumb and finger bruising marks on her left arm and needle-like puncture marks on the upper arm. This suggests she was being injected with some kind of drug, most likely a sedative of some kind. If administered over time, a person would gradually become more tolerant of the effects of a sedative, and the dosage would have to increase. That may have resulted in an overdose; whether intentional or accidental, it may be impossible to say unless there is a substantial amount of the drug still in her body from the time of her death. I also took scrapings from under her nails, but there was next to nothing there to show she may have put up a fight. I believe that could be explained by the fact she was likely kept in a state of docility. Her fingernails have a distinct blue tinge to them that would indicate there was some respiratory issue prior to death. This might have been caused by whatever drugs were injected into her arm. At the moment, that's the most likely cause of death, but I must have all the tests done before I give a final opinion. I cannot simply speculate.'

'Okay, Doctor, you can understand why I felt the need to speak to you directly rather than trying to understand all this in a report. How easy would it be to get those types of drugs?'

'There are a number of possible sources. It could be a doctor, nurse, or chemist, all of whom have access to these drugs, or it could be someone with a medical condition who was prescribed them. They could even be obtained from an illegal website. I think you should wait until we get the toxicology report to see if we can name the type of drugs that were used, otherwise you'll have an impossible job trying to trace them.'

'So, when do you think we'll have the toxicology report?'

'Within a few days. I'll email you as soon as we receive it. I assume your next question is going to be what was the time, or, more likely in this case, the date of death?'

'You assumed right.'

'We may be lucky, because if the body was found in the open or simply buried in normal earth, then it would be almost impossible to get a time of death that had any degree of accuracy. But, as I told you yesterday, because the body was submerged in a peat bog, the normal textbook signs of death are absent. This is due to a lack of bacteria in the stagnant water that prevents the usual decomposition of the flesh, hence the reason the body looked as though it had only been in the bog for a few days. This is clearly not the case, as the skin and hair have absorbed the tannin that comes from the peat, causing a red colourisation and leather-like texture to the skin that takes months, if not years, to materialize.'

'This is all new to me.'

'Let me show you.' She turned the laptop towards Dorsey and clicked onto a picture of the corpse taken that morning during the autopsy. 'You see how red this side of the lower back and buttocks looks? The skin here has also started to show the beginnings of the mummification process that could preserve the body for centuries. Don't worry, it's not been there that long. The only part where decomposition has started to take place is in the right hand and forearm, which at some stage became exposed to the air. That may have happened when we had a mini-drought up here recently.'

'Okay, I understand that, but is there nothing else to give us an idea of how long she was in the bog?'

'What I can say is that the condition of the body indicates that she was placed in the bog within twenty-four hours after she died. How long she was there is a trickier question. I've sent hair, skin tissue, and two bones from her hand to a colleague at Edinburgh University's forensic department, who may be able to calculate the deterioration of the calcium in the bones to give a reasonable approximation of the time of death to within a couple of months, or even weeks.'

'How long will that take?'

'I'd hope to have the results in maybe three or four days.'

Dorsey just nodded.

'Don't look so despondent, Chief Inspector. There's quite

a bit about her that I can tell you now. Further to what I mentioned to you yesterday, she's somewhere in the region of eighteen to twenty-one, with dark brown hair, five feet six in height, and thin-boned. So, she's likely to have been quite a slim person in life.'

'Anything else?'

'I can also tell you that the limbs were severed after the body was bled to make the dismembering a less messy operation. To do this, a sharp knife was used to puncture the skin and enter the thoracic cavity.' The doctor moved her hand to her upper chest to show the area she was meaning. 'This severed the carotid artery and the jugular vein. He may have hung the whole body from the Achilles tendons at this stage to let the exsanguination take place over something he would've used to catch the blood.'

'So, how long would it be hanging upside down for?'

'Could've been a few hours, who knows. He could have even left it like that overnight. It is likely the same knife was used to cut the skin and ligaments, then a saw of some kind was used to cut through the bone before it was finally severed with a cleaver or even an axe. The teeth marks indicate that it was a fine saw, maybe a hacksaw.'

'This is gruesome.'

'Death usually is. The dismembered parts were probably hung for another while to drain the rest of the blood away.'

'So, he knew what he was doing – a butcher or doctor.'

'I'm surprised you didn't suggest a pathologist. This type of crude butchery is not something that he was trained to do. He could've gotten the idea to bleed the body from the internet with a couple of clicks. What is needed is the mind to carry out such a gruesome task, and that would point to the killer almost certainly being a homicidal psychopath. He would have no empathy or emotion for the victim. The dismembering of the body and bloodletting would've been seen by him as a necessary task to make it easier to dispose of the body.'

'It must have made some mess, all that blood?'

'This whole ghastly business would have obviously produced a massive amount of blood. Even if cleaned up, the use of luminol spray and ultraviolet light would still show the indelible stains that the blood will have certainly left behind.'

'All this happened when she was already dead?'

'Yes. Apart from the injury to the left ankle, bruising to the forearm, and the needle marks on the upper left arm, there are no other obvious ante-mortem injuries. The rest are all post-mortem. I'll have to carry out further tests on the liver and kidneys to see if there is any toxic damage to them which may have caused them to fail. The contents of the stomach are also being investigated; it may give us an idea of what exactly she digested prior to her death.'

'What about the blue cloth the body was wrapped in?'

'I was coming to that. Remember, I'm a pathologist; the body always comes first. When the fabric was laid out, it was clearly material that once made up two identical blue cotton dresses, which were cut up to wrap each section of the body in. The material is with forensics and is being examined for blood, semen, or fibres that may have DNA that can be checked against the police database for a match with the killer.

'What I can tell you at this stage is there is no label on the material to help find where the dresses were bought, which is unusual. Nothing from what I can see shows they were removed. They may have been made to order, but I'd still expect labels. However, I'm no expert in dressmaking. The only other thing I almost forgot to mention is that her hair seems to have been cut crudely. It's uneven in places as though she or someone else cut it with no concern as to how it looked. Everything I've told you so far will be in the provisional report, which I'd have finished by now if you were the patient type and just waited for me to send it.'

There was a light knock at the door and the lab assistant entered. 'This has just been handed in,' he said, passing an A4 brown envelope to the doctor.

'Ah, good. This might be of help to you, Chief Inspector. I sent one of our friends in the anthropology department a copy of the post-mortem photographs from the neck up. This is what he was able to do with it,' she said, looking pleased with the results before handing the photographs to Dorsey. 'That's what we think she would've looked like in life. AI is pretty amazing.'

They took his breath away. It was a picture of a young woman, who looked like she was alive when it was taken. He looked back at the doctor and queried, 'If it wasn't for some sexual gratification, then why keep her captive?'

'I didn't say he wasn't getting sexual gratification from abducting her and keeping her as his prisoner. It simply wasn't sexual intercourse that interested him.'

'What about sodomy?'

'Chief Inspector, we no longer use that old biblical term. It's all now classed as rape. And no, there is no indication that took place either.'

'What, then?'

'Your guess is as good as mine.'

'Do you think he's killed before?'

'Whoever did this to this poor soul obviously has a psychopathic personality and a deviant sexual disorder. I'd be surprised if this is the only young woman abducted for his perverse satisfaction. I'm afraid there may be other victims lying undiscovered in the bogs around Glencoe.'

'I was aware of that possibility. I've ordered a second search of the area today within two miles of where this victim was found.'

'You may have to widen your search. There are thousands of places around Glencoe and beyond where a body could be dumped and lie undetected for years. Remember, we wouldn't have found this victim if Erin Keenan hadn't been reported missing.'

'No, because no one was looking for her. Which is sad.'

'Any word about Miss Keenan's whereabouts?'

'There have been two reported sightings of her after last night's press statement. One sighting was six days ago in Fort William, and the other one, more importantly, was yesterday morning in Glasgow.'

'Good, let's hope it's her. I was beginning to think she might've been abducted by this monster. I'll email you my provisional report and the morgue pictures later today. You can take these enhanced "in life" pictures that may be useful in finding out who she is.'

'Thanks, you have been extremely helpful, Dr Jamali. Please phone me if anything else of interest comes up.'

'Of course.'

On the way down from Inverness, Dorsey went through the list of things that had to be done in his head. He concentrated on the body from the bog in the hope that Erin Keenan was safely back in Glasgow. He would have to arrange a further press conference and release the digitally enhanced photograph of the victim. Her identity was crucial to finding her murderer.

His phone buzzed. It was Liz.

'I'm sorry I missed your call last night. The TV was rubbish, so I went to bed early. How are things going? I saw the news report about the body found in Glencoe.'

'Yeah, things are a bit hectic at the minute. It was actually found on the other side of Loch Leven. I was at the morgue this morning. We've had to commandeer the church hall in Glencoe to set up an operations room. I'm heading back to make sure it's up and running. How're you getting on?'

'I'm still trying to get my head around this fraud case. There is just so much paperwork. I guess we can forget about Montenegro. You're going to be up there for a while.'

'Yeah, I'm afraid so. I never should've let Knox talk me into accepting this case. I'm stuck with it now. Even if the missing student turns up, I've got this murder to solve.'

'I think you protest too much, Frank. I know how much you lot love a good murder. Why else would you be in the murder squad all these years?'

'Very funny.'

'What day are you at the High Court next week?'

'Not sure. They'll let me know when I've got to go down.'

'I'd better let you get on with finding your killer. I'll phone you later.'

As soon as Dorsey walked into the office, Mitchell handed him the list of convicted sex offenders. He looked briefly at the names and addresses of over a hundred men convicted of sexual offences in the central Highland Region in the last ten years.

'George, try to get that reduced. We don't have the manpower or time to interview this lot.'

'Frank, it is reduced. I've removed all the minor stuff.'

'Reduce it again. Take out all domestics and rapes.'

'Rapes?'

'Yes, she was not raped. It's not sex he's after. Well, not normal sex, if there is such a thing. So, take out all the domestics and rapes and concentrate on the weirder offenders, like stalkers, flashers, and the voyeuristic types. According to Dr Jamali, the person we're looking for has some perverse character defect. We can start by looking at the first thirty who stand out on the list, the perverts and the weirdos. Get them in, and if necessary, pay them a visit.'

'It's still going to take some time to get through,' said Mitchell.

'George, we have no other leads, so the sooner we start, the sooner we get results … Now, can everyone be quiet for a minute?' shouted Dorsey, addressing the room of detectives.

'Is the church hall set up yet?'

The room went quiet as the detectives stopped what they were doing and looked at each other.

'Not yet, sir. The engineers are still installing the phone and computer cables. It should be finished this afternoon,' explained one of the detectives.

'Where is everybody else?'

'DI Crawford and DS Grant are in Glasgow viewing CCTV footage and two other detectives from their team are doing the same thing in Fort William while the rest are involved in the search,' the same detective explained.

'Okay, everyone get back to what you were doing … Can someone get me a cup of coffee?'

Even though he was not speaking directly to Dixon, she got up and walked towards the kitchen area. 'What do you take in it, sir?'

'Just milk.'

Dorsey went into the office allocated to him beside the incident room. He took out the AI-generated photograph that Dr Jamali had given him. It was quite disturbing to look at, considering it was taken after she had been lying in a peat bog for what might have been years.

'Your coffee, sir. I brought you some biscuits,' said PC Dixon, placing them on his desk.

'Thank you.'

'And here's the list of missing persons you asked for, sir.'

Dorsey took the pages of names and looked at them for a few minutes. 'There's hundreds here. They can't all still be missing.'

'We checked the Police Scotland database and with the Scottish National Missing Persons Unit. That's how we've managed to get it down to a couple of hundred for the last five years. If you could give me more information about her, then we'll be able to remove a lot more from that list.'

'Here, take these and copy them,' he said, handing Dixon

the envelope with the digitally enhanced pictures. 'That's how they think she would've looked in life.'

'Oh my God. She was beautiful.'

'Ask DS Mitchell to arrange for a press release to as many newspapers and TV stations that are willing to put it out there.'

'Sorry to interrupt, sir,' said one of the new admin staff who was manning the phones. 'Bad news. I've just had a call from Fort William. The female sighted there has turned out to be a local primary school teacher.'

'Okay, let's hope DI Crawford has better luck in Glasgow. Dixon, any update from the search at Callert?'

'They've found nothing so far, sir.'

'Do you have the address of the dog handler? I've forgotten his name.'

'It's Alex Munro. I tried calling him, but he's not great at answering his phone. I'll get his address for you now, sir.'

It was only a short drive along the A82 and over the Ballachulish Bridge. The satnav took Dorsey right to the door. The house was a small bungalow, sitting five hundred yards off the main road and facing the loch. He parked on the driveway behind a red hatchback. He rang the doorbell and instinctively took a step back, as he always did. Years of knocking on the doors of violent criminals made it an unconscious habit.

The door was opened by a woman, likely in her late forties, wearing a district nurse's uniform. She looked hard at Dorsey for a few seconds before saying in a defensive tone, 'What's wrong?'

'Nothing's wrong. I'm Chief Inspector …'

'I know who you are.'

'I was looking to get some advice from Alex about his dog.'

'Oh, right,' she said. 'He's not in but will be home shortly. Would you like to come in and wait? You look like you could do with a cup of tea.'

Dorsey nodded and followed her into the kitchen at the back of the house, thinking that he must stick out like a sore thumb to the locals. He took a seat at the kitchen table while she put the kettle on.

'As a matter of interest, how did you know?' Dorsey asked her.

'Alex googled you last night to check out who is in charge of the investigation. The picture doesn't do you justice.'

Before he could say anything else, the front door opened and Munro came in. 'Whose bloody car is that parked halfway up the driveway?' he shouted from the hall, while taking off his waterproofs and boots. 'I've had to park on the grass.'

'There's someone here to speak to you, so stop shouting, for God's sake.'

Dorsey got to his feet when Munro came into the kitchen with a perplexed look on his face, his dog by his side. The ex-soldier was wearing a grey flat cap and had long hair down to his shoulders. His weather-beaten face was sharp, almost gaunt, which made his vivid blue eyes look like they were trapped in the wrong body.

'Chief Inspector, is there a problem?'

'No, I just wanted to thank you for finding the body yesterday.'

'That wasn't me. It was Major,' he replied, as the dog at his feet stared at him, panting. 'Go to your bed,' ordered Munro. The dog got up and disappeared into the other room.

'That's some dog,' said Dorsey, surprised by Munro's lack of affection towards it.

'He's an old dog now. How can I help you? We didn't find anything today, but I suppose you know that. We're covering a vast area, and I was told that it may be extended all the way up to Fort William. That's a lot of ground to cover. You need more people and more dogs to do that kind of search.'

'That's another reason why I wanted to speak to you. I'll be getting more officers from other divisions across Scotland, and we are planning to extend the area up to ten miles from where the body was found. We're going to make an appeal for members of the public to help with the search. Can you tell me how your dog is able to find bodies?'

'What do you want to know? You must have used these dogs before.'

'No, we don't have a lot of use for them in Glasgow. Most murder victims we deal with are found lying in the street or in a rundown tenement.'

'Okay, Inspector. If it helps you understand how we work, Major is a specially trained ex-army dog that worked with me in Afghanistan. We were both injured when an IED blew up our Snatch Land Rover. The driver and another dog were killed. We were both invalided out in 2016. Major was given to me after we both recovered. Most rescue dogs search for people who are still alive; Major is trained to pick up the scent of human remains. A lot of our guys over there would end up butchered by those crazy Talibans, and their remains dumped somewhere in the desert or mountains for the wolves to get them. Major was trained to find them. It was gruesome work. We also helped find mass graves of whole villages that were massacred by the Taliban for supporting us and the Afghan government.'

'Thanks, Mrs Munro,' said Dorsey, as she handed him a cup of tea and put a plate of chocolate biscuits on the table beside him.

'I'm not his wife. I'm his sister.'

'Sorry.'

'Just call me Eileen.'

Munro took off his heavy pullover and hung it up behind the kitchen door. It was only when he turned back to speak that Dorsey noticed the damage to the left side of his face, where he had clearly undergone extensive plastic surgery.

Munro's eyes met his stare. 'Yeah, the whole side of my body looks like that. Anyway, that's in the past.'

'It must have been bad out there.'

'Helmand Province. Should just have been named Hell. That's what we called it, anyway.'

'I still don't know why the army sent you there, and for what?' interrupted his sister as she sat at the table, shaking her head and sighing heavily.

'Eileen, just drink yer tea for God's sake. It wasn't the army. It was George Bush and the British government that got us into that fiasco.'

But his sister hadn't given up on venting her anger. 'When Scotland gets its independence, there will be no more young Scots going off to fight and die in wars.'

'Aye, okay, Eileen, give it a rest. The chief inspector is here to talk about Major, not the bloody Afghan war.'

'I'll be quiet. You don't listen to me anyway.'

'Sorry, like I was saying, Major can find bodies that are buried up to ten feet deep and pick up scents on the ground or in the air and follow them to where they're buried. He can also find the place where a body was, even if it's been moved to somewhere else.'

'He's a German Shepherd?'

'Aye, they make the best cadaver dogs, although there are a few other breeds that can be trained up.'

'He's a special dog; I've been told he's the only one around here. I'm surprised that the mountain rescue team doesn't have any.'

'Their dogs are trained to find people alive; the clue is in their name. If they think there may be a fatality, then they might ask me to help, which I'm happy to do when I can. But usually, they know where to find the people they're looking for, and they've got their helicopters and drones now, so they don't normally need us.'

'It must take a while and cost a lot to train a dog like

Major.'

'Aye, it can take years to get them trained to this standard. I know that K9 Search and Recovery Scotland use a Springer Spaniel that can detect bodies under deep water. You may have noticed we've a lot of water around here. I can phone them to see if they can help. I may be able to get a few other dogs to join the search with Major. I know that some were sent to Ukraine to help there, but I'm sure they're now all back in Scotland.'

'I appreciate this,' said Dorsey, offering his hand to Munro. 'I'm glad I came to see you. Let me know how you get on.'

'Before you go, I heard you found the student we were looking for in the first place.'

'No, there was one that was a false sighting in Fort William, and I'm still waiting to hear from my team in Glasgow. If it was her, they would've phoned by now. As it stands, she is still missing and she is our main priority. At least she may still be alive … I'd better be going. I appreciate any help you can give us. Thanks for the tea, Eileen.'

'You didn't eat your biscuits, Chief Inspector,' she said with a smile.

'I'm watching my weight.'

He had only turned the engine on and lit a cigarette when DI Crawford called.

He sounded down. 'Boss, we've spent all day in Glasgow going through the CCTV footage. We saw no one who fits her description.'

'That's not good. Maybe it was some crank who phoned that in. You can never trust anonymous phone calls. Some people get a kick out of this sort of thing. Don't let it get you down. I'll see you tomorrow,' said Dorsey calmly, but as soon as the call was over he thumped the steering wheel with his fist. 'Fuck it!' he shouted. The pressure was back on.

That night, Dorsey struggled to get to sleep. He couldn't

get the case out of his mind. Even though he had only been on the case for two days, Erin Keenan had now been missing for seven, and there was still no evidence as to what might have happened to her.

Chapter 6

Early the following morning, Dorsey drove to the local petrol station. While walking to the shop to pay for the petrol, he was stopped in his tracks when he saw the display of newspapers outside with the enhanced picture of the unknown victim on most of their front pages. He lifted the rubber rain shield and took out one of the national tabloids, which had the heartless heading, 'The Lady in the Bog'. The others were a little less lurid, but the body now had a nickname that would stick. He lifted one of the newspapers. He was now certain that the phones would be ringing all day. He handed a copy of the *Daily Express* to Mitchell when he got back into the car.

'What do you think?'

'That's got to get a result.'

'It's on the front page of most of them. We'll need to take half a dozen uniformed officers from the search to man the phone lines. It's going to be like a BT customer service helpline in there today.'

Dorsey drove the rest of the way deep in thought, hopeful that they might be on the verge of getting somewhere. Someone must know her. She didn't look like the type of person who'd be going through life unnoticed or unloved.

With twice as many police officers now involved in the investigation, Glencoe was looking more like a police academy than a sleepy Highland village. Dorsey threw his cigarette butt out the window as they pulled into the police station car park.

The early shift was already manning the phones. PC Dixon had one receiver at her ear, watching another phone ringing persistently on the desk. She nodded to Mitchell to take that call while she frantically noted down information on her notepad.

'We've got two positive identifications of the victim already,' she said, holding the notepad up for Dorsey to see as she continued speaking to the person on the line.

Dorsey tore the page out of the notebook as other phones began to ring around the office.

'Can someone get those phones!' he shouted at the other detectives coming on duty. He read the details in Dixon's staccato handwriting. *Lena Kaminski, Polish. Worked as a waitress at The Royal Hotel in Oban between April 2018 and March 2019.*

Within an hour, they had over a dozen confirmed identifications, the last sighting being when she left her job at the Loch View Hotel in Fort William on the 17th of August 2019, planning to hitchhike to London. This was confirmed by four work colleagues who never heard from her again and didn't expect to. They confirmed that they had all been interviewed by the local police after she had gone missing but had heard nothing since. Although they confirmed that she was from Poland, none of them knew which part of that country she came from.

'Sir, I've just spoken to the duty officer from the Missing Persons Unit at Fort William,' said Dixon, after finishing another call. 'He dealt with the case at the time and confirmed that the parents had contacted the station when they couldn't get hold of their daughter after she stopped phoning home,' she explained, trying not to speak too fast in her excitement. 'She always phoned her mother every other day and that suddenly stopped the day she left her job at the Loch View Hotel. He checked the local bus company, but they had no record of who travelled on their buses. Fares were often

71

paid on the bus, and at the time, it was only cash payments they took from those who had not booked in advance. He then contacted Buchanan Bus Station in Glasgow, who checked their CCTV. There was no sighting of her, but they explained that she could've gotten off the bus anywhere en route. However, a few days later they called him to say that a mobile phone was recovered from the bus on the 19th of August 2019. Two days after she left the job in Fort William … Sorry, Chief Inspector, am I going too fast?'

'No, continue.'

'He recovered the phone which was unlocked by one of their IT experts and confirmed that it was her mobile. Because her work colleagues believed she was heading to London for work, he contacted the Met and gave them her details as a possible missing person. The last thing in his log was a call he made to the family in Poland, telling them that they recovered her phone in Glasgow and that she was believed to have travelled to London and would likely contact them when she was able to get a new mobile. He heard nothing from them or the Met since and assumed she had been found in London.'

'Did you get the contact details of the family?'

'Yes, they live in Krakow. The mother speaks good English, the father not so good. I have their phone number,' she said, suddenly dreading that her boss was going to ask her to contact the parents to tell them their daughter was found dead and had been lying in a peat bog for all these years. She handed the notepaper with the details on it to the chief inspector who went into his office to make the call that he knew was his duty to make himsclf.

A Police Scotland press conference was set up at the Royal Highland Hotel in Inverness and was due to air on BBC Scotland's six o'clock news. Deputy Chief Constable Cullen sat alongside Chief Superintendent Mackie, both dressed in their formal uniforms and looking stern as the programme producer called out the countdown.

Dorsey watched the live broadcast on his laptop with Mitchell.

'Good evening,' said Cullen. 'We've called this press conference to update the public on what is now a major investigation in the Highland region. Chief Superintendent Mackie will provide you with the details of what we have discovered at this early stage of the investigation.'

Mackie stared directly into the camera and began to speak slowly. 'On Saturday the 2nd of September 2023, it was reported to the local Glencoe police station that a young woman who was staying at a cottage near Kinlochleven with three of her friends had gone missing the previous evening. Her name is Erin Keenan, a twenty-one-year-old Glasgow University student. This is her photograph … I appeared on TV last night to ask the public to help with our investigation, and the public response resulted in two sightings. Unfortunately, I've been advised by the officer in charge of the investigation, Detective Chief Inspector Frank Dorsey, that both these leads have now been investigated and turned out to be false, which was extremely disappointing to us, but, more importantly, devastating for her family.

'At this stage she is still believed to be a missing person, and the search for her will continue with further resources being added to what is now the largest police operation for a missing person in the history of the Highland region. No stone will be left unturned.

'As was previously released to the press, a body was discovered in the Lairigmor area near to a section of the West Highland Way. It was quickly confirmed that this was not the missing student but has since been identified as Lena Kaminski, a Polish national who is believed to have gone missing in August 2019. This is now a murder investigation. Her family have been informed.

'We're holding this press conference to appeal to anyone

who may have seen Lena Kaminski after the 17ᵗʰ of August 2019 or can give us any information about her. We're also again appealing to anyone who may believe they have seen Erin Keenan at any time from the 1ˢᵗ of September, this year.'

The deputy chief constable tapped the microphone in front of him. 'We will not be taking any questions but will provide further updates as the investigation proceeds.' With that declaration, Cullen lifted his hat and gloves from the table. The two senior officers got up from their seats and ignored the questions being hurled at them from the scrum of reporters. The press conference was over.

Dorsey turned off his computer and turned to Mitchell. 'What do you think?'

'They gave out the victim's name, and we still haven't had a formal identification.'

'Do you want to phone and tell them they fucked up?'

'That's above my pay grade.'

'What time are the parents due to arrive?'

'They're due in at Glasgow Airport at 8.30 p.m.'

'That's just over two hours. I know it's going to take you well over your shift, but could you get one of the uniformed officers to drive you to the airport and pick them up? We need to find them a decent local hotel.'

'No problem. I'd better go now. It'll take over two hours to get to Glasgow.'

'George, tell them that the hotel bill will be paid by Police Scotland. It's the least we can do for them.'

Chapter 7

Dorsey had finished breakfast and was reading a copy of a local newspaper that someone had left on a nearby table when Mitchell joined him, looking tired. It was raining outside, and according to the weather forecast it would be like that all day.

'Did you pick up the parents?'

'Yeah,' replied Mitchell. 'They asked all sorts of questions; most I avoided answering. The mother was utterly distressed and crying for most of the drive back. It was hard to watch. We dropped them off at the Kingshouse. It was the only one with a double room I could get. I told them we'd take them to Inverness to identify their daughter today. Do you want me to do it?'

'No, I'll go up. I want to speak to the pathologist anyway. How're you getting on with the interviews?'

'We've interviewed twelve out of the first thirty we agreed on. We've found nothing of interest so far. There's another eight coming in this afternoon. We'll have to pay a visit to the others on the list if we can't get a hold of them or they refuse to be interviewed.'

'Okay … I phoned Crawford before you came down and called off the search today.'

'Why?'

'It's just for today, we can restart it again tomorrow when we should have the cadaver dogs. There's no point sending out uniformed officers in this weather; some of them have been searching non-stop for over a week. They need time

75

off, or we'll have officers unable to do their job because they're exhausted. If Erin Keenan's been in the open all this time, she'd be dead from exposure by now. If she's still alive, she must be somewhere against her will. According to Dr Jamali, whoever held Lena Kaminski captive is likely to have kept her for weeks, even months, before she was disposed of.'

'So, are we linking the two cases?'

'No, not officially. But if he's got Erin Keenan, there is every chance she is still alive.'

'Whatever happened to the dog that everyone seems to have forgotten about? It wasn't even mentioned in the press conference last night.'

'You're right, George. We'll put out a public appeal on social media and get something in the local newspapers for tomorrow. I'll make sure it's mentioned at the next press conference.'

'If you ask me, the only explanation is that she was picked up after she reached the B863 and offered a lift, probably to Kinlochleven or Ballachulish. If the dog was with her, whoever picked her up would've had to take the dog, otherwise I don't think she would've accepted a lift. What other possible scenario is there? If she got lost around Lairigmor, we'd have found her body by now.'

'I think you're right. Can you deal with that today?'

After Mitchell finished his breakfast and Dorsey had smoked a couple of cigarettes out under a canopy at the back of the hotel, they drove to the police station. After dropping Mitchell off, Dorsey drove on to the Kingshouse Hotel.

Tomasz and Anna Kaminski were already sitting in the foyer when he arrived. He introduced himself and escorted them to his car. Like Mitchell, he found it hard to answer their questions. Using his years of experience dealing with murder victims' loved ones, he deflected the questions where the answers could only cause more distress.

The rain was torrential, not unlike the day he had driven up from Glasgow to start the investigation. When he had run out of things to say, both Tomasz and Anna withdrew into themselves. He absent-mindedly turned on the radio, immediately turning it off again when he realised what he was doing. It was going to be a long journey.

He was relieved to reach the morgue, but knew the suffering of his two passengers was only going to get worse when they had to go through the ordeal of identifying their daughter. He asked them to sit in the waiting room and went through to speak to Dr Jamali.

Dr Jamali was in her full autopsy PPE. 'Oh, sorry, usually only the dead see me in this. They found a young man's body in the River Ness last night. It looks like a straightforward suicide … Give me ten minutes to get changed. I take it the parents are here?'

'Yes, they're in the waiting room.'

Before leading the grief-stricken Kaminskis to the mortuary viewing room, Dr Jamali explained to the parents that their daughter's body had been preserved by the peat bog she was found in, making her still recognisable, which wouldn't normally be the case. Seeing how distressed they were, she then gave them the choice of simply providing a blood sample so that a DNA match and their previous identification of the digitally enhanced photograph would save them from having to make a formal identification of the body. However, they both insisted on seeing their daughter. The doctor smiled sympathetically and put her hand on Mr and Mrs Kaminski's clasped hands before leading them along the corridor to where the body had already been prepared for viewing. Dorsey followed solemnly behind.

When the white sheet was removed from the face, they simply held each other and sobbed. Dorsey waited for a moment before speaking in a respectful tone, 'I'm sorry, but I have to formally ask you if this is your daughter, Lena

Kaminski?'

'Yes, yes, that's our Lena. Our darling little girl,' sobbed Mrs Kaminski as her husband simply nodded and blessed himself. They both shuffled forward towards the trolley, the dread of what they were looking at etched on their faces. Mrs Kaminski bent over and kissed Lena's forehead, speaking softly in Polish as tears fell onto her daughter's face. She turned to Dr Jamali. 'She's so cold, my poor child is so cold.'

The doctor nodded but said nothing. She continued to watch the heartbroken parents trying to make sense of what had become of their beautiful daughter.

'She had a gold crucifix and chain that we gave her for her confirmation,' said Mrs Kaminski, her voice trembling as she looked up from the body. 'She always wore it.'

Dorsey and Dr Jamali looked at each other before the doctor spoke. 'She wasn't wearing a crucifix when she was found.'

'If it's recovered in the future, we will return it to you,' said Dorsey.

After a few more minutes, Mr Kaminski, whispering in Polish, led his wife by the hand back out to the waiting room.

Dr Jamali put the sheet back over the face and nodded to her assistant to move the trolley back to the cold storage unit. 'That was tough,' she said. 'It never gets any easier, especially when it's someone so young.'

'It's hard to imagine what they're going through.'

'It's a terrible way we make our living, Chief Inspector. I often wonder why I didn't find something more pleasant to do with my life.'

'The reason you do it is because you can, and you care about people.'

'Is that why you do what you do?'

'I guess so,' said Dorsey.

'I'll have the results from the toxicology department this afternoon. If I get it early enough, I'll email you my final report later today.'

'That would be helpful. I'm dreading this journey back. What do you talk to them about?'

'You talk about their daughter. They now only have memories of her. So let them tell you what she was like. What music she loved or even hated. Anything that helps them cope with their grief. That's what you talk to them about.'

After dropping the parents off at their hotel, Dorsey arrived at the police station to find the place in what could only be described as a state of euphoria. 'What's going on?'

'Sir, we've got a confession. DI Crawford and DS Grant are in the interview room with him,' said Dixon. 'The statement is being typed to have him sign it now. He's confessed to the murder and rape of Lena Kaminski, but denies being involved in the disappearance of Erin Keenan.'

'Why did no one phone me?' asked Dorsey, knowing what he had just heard didn't add up.

'I did, Frank, twice,' said Mitchell. 'You didn't pick up. I was concerned that the interview was being done without a lawyer or an appropriate adult present. The guy clearly has mental health issues. Crawford outranks me, that's why I tried to get hold of you.'

'Sorry, George, I was with the parents at the morgue and switched my mobile off. I forgot to turn it back on. Why's there no lawyer?'

'Crawford said he didn't want one.'

'What the fuck are those two playing at?'

'Sir, this is the statement based on DI Crawford's handwritten notes of the interview,' said Dixon.

'Why do they need this when it should all be on tape?' asked Dorsey, taking the typed document and slowly reading it.

'Apparently, he refused to say anything if he was put on

tape,' said Mitchell.

'This is getting worse. Who is he?'

'Roddy Thomson. He's on our list of sexual offenders. He lives with his sister in Glen Nevis near Fort William,' explained Dixon, looking surprised at how strangely her boss was reacting. 'We've asked the station at Fort William to seek a search warrant. We're still waiting for it to come through. Even though he denies having anything to do with Erin Keenan, I wouldn't be surprised if that's where we're going to find her.'

'She's not there and he didn't kill anyone, least of all Lena Kaminski … Dixon, can you get me the number for his sister? George, ask DI Crawford to come and see me, and cancel that request for a warrant.'

Dorsey went into his office and perused the alleged confession again, making sure he was right before speaking to Crawford. He could deal with this in one of two ways, and one of those ways would only make matters worse. Dixon texted Dorsey the sister's phone number. He made the call.

He had just put the phone down when Crawford barged into his office, his face flushed and breathing heavily. 'Sir, I was told you want to speak to me?'

'Take a seat, Inspector.'

'Before you start, sir, this is my arrest. You can't pull rank and finish the interview. That's not on!'

Crawford had the look of a man who had just won the lottery and wasn't sharing it with anyone. It was his revenge for being humiliated by having an outsider put in charge of a case that he had only four days to solve, as though he wasn't up to it in the eyes of his superiors.

'Before you go any further, I have no intention of even speaking to Thomson, never mind trying to steal your thunder,' said Dorsey. 'You're second in command here. Virtually all the detectives here see you as the man who should be running the investigation, and maybe you should be. I never asked to take this case on.'

'Where's this going?'

'The man you've got in there is a fantasist; he never killed anyone.'

'How can you know that? You haven't even spoken to him! This is just sour grapes, instead of being grateful that I've solved this fucking murder for you! I don't know what your problem is!'

'I'm trying to save you from embarrassing yourself. This confession states that he killed her and dumped her in the bog. There's no mention of dismembering the body or wrapping it in the blue cotton material. Everything he said here has been in the papers and on television.'

'That doesn't mean he didn't do it!'

'He also said he raped her. Lena Kaminski was a virgin when she was murdered. Did you not read the provisional PM report?'

Crawford began to shift uncomfortably in his seat, as though he couldn't remember where he put his lottery ticket.

'I've also spoken to his sister. She has just told me her brother was sectioned over six months ago after setting fire to a barn for no apparent reason. He was only released from hospital two days ago. At the time of Lena Kaminski's disappearance on the 17th of August 2019, he was again in hospital for a total of eight months – three months before she went missing and a further five months after we know she was last seen. He also has a history of admitting to crimes he didn't commit.'

There were now beads of sweat on Crawford's forehead and Dorsey noticed an obvious change in his demeanour. He waited for a response.

'Okay, Frank, what do you intend to do now?'

'I don't intend to do anything. There's no damage done. But what I suggest *you* do is phone the hospital and get them to confirm the dates he was sectioned. If they agree with what the sister has told me, then you tell DS Grant you've spoken to the hospital and you believe the confession is false. Once you do that, take this confession and shred it. Take a DNA swab from him, and we'll check it if we get the DNA of the murderer. If I'm wrong, and it is him, I'm giving up being a detective.'

'You must be thinking I'm fucking incompetent.'

'No, I don't, but I think you're just like the rest of us, desperate to solve this case. That's how we all feel. In future, if a person is questioned and stops simply being someone of interest and becomes a suspect, the informal interview stops and his lawyer or the duty lawyer must be contacted. If there is to be a confession, it must be done on tape with the lawyer present and, if necessary, with an appropriate adult if there is any hint that the suspect has mental health issues. Even if he was the killer, this evidence would be inadmissible in court. That way, we don't have situations like this occurring again. We do it by the book, or we risk jeopardising the investigation.'

'Okay. I'll make this up to you, Frank. You could've made a big deal out of this and made me look like an idiot in front of everyone.'

'That's the last thing I want. You're second in charge here, and we need to work together. Remember, I put you in charge of finding Erin Keenan. DS Mitchell is in charge of the murder investigation, and even though you outrank him, you should've let him carry out the interview. Now, put this behind you and let's move on.'

'Thanks, Frank,' said Crawford, who took a deep breath before facing his damage limitation strategy.

Dorsey sat quietly for a few minutes before going into the main office and asking Dixon to give him an update in relation to the list of sex offenders.

'Admin have transcribed the interviews that were done yesterday,' she told him. 'We've since checked them all out, and they either have alibis or were ruled out for other reasons.'

'So, who do you have left on that list to be seen?'

'Well, the rest haven't responded to the telephone requests for them to come in. There's one who was convicted of exposing himself twice at the Highland Games in Kinlochleven. Drunk, of course. He's married with three kids.'

'Never mind him, who else?'

'There's Ross Wallace. According to his record and social work report, he was convicted three years ago of secretly taking pictures on his mobile phone of young women in the sauna dressing rooms at a hotel where he worked. He got two hundred hours of community service and was placed on the sexual offenders register for two years. There's been nothing since.'

'Where does he live?'

'He lives in Appin.'

'Ask George to come in and see me. We'll pay this character a visit.'

'DS Mitchell has gone out. He left when you were speaking to DI Crawford to pick up another suspect who refused to come in on a voluntary basis.'

'Okay. Can you put all the transcribed interviews on my desk and I'll go through them all later. Who did he go with?'

'He went on his own to pick up Hamish Murray. He's a forestry worker who was convicted of sexually assaulting a teenage girl at a swimming pool when he lived and worked in Dundee around four years ago. He got six months for it.'

'Okay, I'll leave Wallace for later. I need to go and get something to eat. Phone me if anything happens.'

He hadn't eaten since breakfast and had a sudden urge to buy a fish supper. He drove through the deserted village to the chip shop on the main street, but when he got there it was closed. He just sat there, the stresses of the day going through his head. His phone bleeped. It was an email from Dr Jamali with an attached report from Edinburgh University. He scanned through the technical jargon and graphs to the last page with the conclusions.

The Forensic Conclusions Re: Deceased Lena Kaminski.

This opinion is based on the case papers provided to us along with a detailed statement by Dr Jamali.

We understand that the body of Lena Kaminski was submerged in approximately two feet of stagnant water in a peat bog. If the water was stagnant then oxygen would be unable to enter it, creating an oxygen-free environment technically known as anaerobic, which prevents the growth of bacteria that would otherwise cause the decomposition of flesh. The ecology of bogs is unique and contributes to the preservation of human and animal tissue, similar to the tanning process used in the making of leather. The tannins and sphagnum in the water released from the peat moss cause a natural mummification of flesh. The first stages of this process can be identified by the discolouring of the skin and hair, which takes on a reddish hue, growing darker in time. The condition of the body of Lena Kaminski shows it has undergone this process for four to five years.

Further tests of the bone fragment from the right hand have shown the calcium in the bones has dissolved, causing bone deterioration that has allowed a further, more accurate finding. This indicates that the length of time the body has been submerged in the stagnant water is just under four years. We have concluded, with a reasonable degree of certainty, that the body was placed in the bog in mid to late October 2019, approximately two months after she was last seen alive on the 17th of August 2019.

He didn't have to read the rest of the report; whoever had Lena Kaminski kept her alive for around two months. The report proved the killer did not kill his victims until he was finished doing whatever the hell it was he did to them.

The noise of a car backfiring brought him out of his thoughts. It was a black pickup heading south at what was clearly excessive speed, but it had been a long time since he gave out a speeding ticket. He still fancied getting his hands on a fish supper and decided to drive to Kinlochleven to try his luck there. His phone buzzed. It was PC Dixon.

'Chief Inspector, there's been some trouble with Hamish Murray. DS Mitchell's sent a code twenty-one. I managed to get him on his radio. When Murray refused to come in on a voluntary basis, he threatened to pay him a visit at his work in the morning. Instead of making him relent and come in, he flattened DS Mitchell with a punch that may have broken his nose.'

'Where is he now?'

'He backed off when Murray threatened to decapitate him with a pickaxe. He is now heading to the hospital in Fort William.'

'Right, I want every available officer to be ready to leave in five minutes.' He hung up and began to make a U-turn, almost hitting a parked car.

When Dorsey pulled up outside the station, there were half a dozen PCs and four detectives standing at their vehicles. He got out of the car and shouted to PC Dixon. 'You come with me and keep me right. The rest of you follow behind. Let's get this bastard!'

They drove in a convoy as if heading to a major incident. Dixon phoned the procurator fiscal's office in Inverness to request a warrant. She supplied the details required while Dorsey drove at speed towards South Ballachulish.

He pulled up when Dixon pointed to an end-terraced house on the opposite side of the road. 'He lives there with his elderly mother, sir. I don't see his car outside. He normally drives a black Hyundai.'

Dorsey now realised that the pickup that drove past him

at speed outside the chip shop was Murray making off. 'Can you put out an alert to stop that car? It was last seen heading south at speed on the A82.'

'Yes, sir,' said Dixon. 'But how do you know where it's heading?'

'I'm a detective … Wait here,' said Dorsey, getting out of the car and gesturing to the rest of the squad to stay in their vehicles as he crossed the road to Murray's house. There was a flickering light coming from the front room. He peered through the window. An elderly woman was sitting in front of the TV with knitting lying on her lap. She looked like she was asleep. He pressed the doorbell a couple of times and waited before looking back through the window. She hadn't moved. He rattled the letterbox.

While he waited for the door to open, two detectives crossed the road towards him. 'Murray's not here,' he shouted. 'Can everyone just go back to the station! I'll be back shortly.'

When he turned to look through the window again, the old woman was gone. He rattled the letterbox again.

'Sir,' shouted Dixon, standing at the open passenger-side door. 'They stopped him on the A82, near Tyndrum!'

'Okay, I'll be back in a minute. Stay in the car.' He then heard the lock on the door being opened with some difficulty. The shawled woman who appeared was how he'd imagined a Highland granny would look a hundred years ago.

'Why are you banging the door? I'm not deaf. What do you want? Who are you anyway?'

'I'm Chief Inspector Frank Dorsey. Is it alright if I come in and ask you a few questions?'

'If it's about that big eejit again, he's not in. Come in anyway, I've just put the kettle on.'

After a chat and a cup of milky tea, Dorsey reemerged from the house and crossed back over to his car. 'Did you manage to get that warrant?'

'No, sir, no one's got back to me.'

'Well, don't bother. According to his mother, Murray was arrested for drink-driving last Friday afternoon and was in police custody until he got bail from Fort William Sheriff Court on Monday morning.'

'It looks like he has a stonewall alibi for Erin Keenan at least.'

'When we get back to the station, I want you to check with the custody officer at Fort William and get the exact time he was arrested and released. If it's as his mother said, then score him off the list of potential suspects. It sounds like he's just a violent drunk.'

'He put up a fight before they got him in cuffs. They searched his pickup and found a half-empty bottle of whisky. He refused to give a roadside breath test.'

'He has obviously been driving drunk again.'

When they got back to the station, the noise from the cells made Dorsey decide that interviewing Murray when he was clearly still drunk was not a great idea.

It was over an hour before the duty lawyer arrived and asked to see his client. Dorsey told him he'd be better coming back in the morning when his client was sober, as they did not intend to interview him. The young solicitor insisted he had to see his client.

Within ten minutes, the lawyer had to be rescued from the cell, his nose dripping blood and his briefcase and papers scattered on the cell floor. He had become another victim of Murray's violent temper.

After another struggle, Murray was put back in handcuffs and left to howl and wail in his cell. The custody sergeant cleaned the blood from the lawyer's swollen nose. He looked like he had not been out of university long and was on the verge of tears.

'You're lucky. I don't think it's broken,' said the sergeant.

'Thank God,' sighed the lawyer, dabbing the blood on his

upper lip with a tissue.

'He'll need to get another lawyer,' said Dorsey. 'You're now a potential crown witness against him. I'll get an officer to take a statement from you before you leave.'

'Do I have to? I'd rather just forget about it and get back home. I've had a terrible day.'

'It's up to you, but I did warn you.'

'I should've listened.'

By the time Dorsey got back to The Stag's Head, Mitchell was back from the hospital and had gone straight to his room.

The receptionist said that Mitchell's face was badly swollen and he looked terrible. 'He didn't want anything to eat and just wanted to go to his bed.'

Dorsey decided not to disturb him and let him get a good night's sleep. He went into the restaurant and ordered the steak pie and chips, which he followed with a pint of lager and a whisky chaser. He went out to the front of the hotel and had a cigarette. With nothing else to do, he went to his room and lay on the bed fully clothed, quickly falling into a deep sleep.

Chapter 8

Sunday: 10th of September 2023

The next morning, Dorsey waited for Mitchell to join him for breakfast. He was shocked when he saw him. Mitchell's nose was badly swollen, and the skin under his eyes was turning black and blue. He looked sore and a little embarrassed.

'George, that looks bad. How're you feeling?'

'Not great. He punched me before I knew what was happening. The hospital couldn't do much. They need to wait for the swelling to go down. All they gave me was painkillers.'

'We've got the bastard who did it in custody. George, take next week off and go back to Glasgow. I'll drive you to the station at Tyndrum. You can be home with Claire and the kids in a few hours.'

There was no argument from Mitchell, who was just desperate to get home and be with his family. He buttered a piece of toast, but one bite was enough. His face was too painful to chew anything. He stared out at the loch, looking miserable.

It was cold and overcast but dry. Loch Leven looked benign, but Dorsey knew better as he changed up a gear and drove at speed along the B863. This place was as dangerous as it was beautiful. He reckoned that the average human wouldn't last more than five minutes in the icy water. He glanced over at Mitchell, who was staring straight ahead, probably worrying about Claire and his kids' reaction to his swollen and bruised face. He felt sorry for him.

Once he had dropped Mitchell off at the station, he

headed back up the A82 just as the sky turned dark and it began to rain. He could feel the steering wheel vibrate in his hands as a long deep rumble echoed through the glen. The sky cracked open. The jagged streaks of lightning made Buachaille Etive Mòr look like something from a Gothic novel.

When he reached Glencoe, the village had that empty Sunday morning feeling about it. As quickly as it came on, the rain stopped.

It was agreed that most of the Inverness detectives would take alternative Sundays off unless there was a breakthrough in the case. He was surprised to see Dixon at her desk, typing away as if she had been there all night.

'Why are you in today? I told you to take the day off.'

'I'd rather be working. There's not much to do around here on a Sunday. How's George?'

'He's okay, he's on his way home. Has Murray been making any more trouble?'

'Not a peep. He's out cold.'

The custody sergeant let Dorsey through to the cells area. He pulled over the spyhole cover to see Murray lying in a crumpled heap in the corner of the cell, moaning. He wondered if Murray had any idea just how much trouble he was in. Once he was fit enough, he'd have him formally charged and kept in custody until his court appearance at the Sheriff Court on Monday morning. He was no longer of any interest to Dorsey, who had no time to waste on a violent drunk, despite what he did to Mitchell. He had a psychopath to catch.

After going back over the statements of the sexual offenders, Dorsey sat back in his chair, put his hands through his hair and sighed. He phoned through to Dixon. 'I think we should pay the guy in Appin a visit.'

'If you mean Ross Wallace, there's no need to. He has since phoned and agreed to come in tomorrow and provide a statement. We already have his DNA.'

'Okay, do you know where the next two on the list live?'

'I've got their addresses here. One lives in Fort William and the other a few miles further on in Inverlochy. We can stick the addresses in the satnav. They won't be hard to find.'

'Do you know anything about them?'

'Only what's on their record. Sean Muir is thirty-six, married with two kids. He was convicted six years ago of grooming a fifteen-year-old schoolgirl and getting her to send him inappropriate pictures of herself. He was also charged two years later with doing the same thing to another teenage girl, but he was acquitted of that charge. There is no record of him providing a DNA sample.'

'What about the other one?'

'The other guy is James Carling; he's forty-three, unmarried. He was an IT worker before he was convicted of exposing himself to a nineteen-year-old German tourist. He was convicted a second time two years later for possession of heroin and fentanyl. He got community service for the first conviction and six months for the second. Both Muir and Carling were put on the sexual offenders register at the time. We have Carling's DNA on the police database.'

'Let's pay these two characters a visit and ruin their Sunday. We'll take your car.'

The fifteen-mile drive took about twenty-five minutes along the A82 and gave Dorsey a chance to get to know Dixon a bit better. He discovered she had moved to Glencoe after finishing her police training in Inverness. She was now in her late twenties, and after five years in Glencoe, she was considering going back to Inverness to take her detective exams.

'I'm sure you'd make a good detective. Don't leave it too long or you'll never do it.'

'What age were you?'

'I was in my early twenties. Maybe a bit too young and

naïve at the time, but you soon learn.'

'It's funny, I can't imagine you ever wearing a police uniform.'

'Neither can I.'

They drove into Fort William, the road taking them around the town centre before turning up one street and down another until the satnav told them they had reached their destination.

The house looked like any of the other houses in the short, narrow road, a small semi-detached with white pebble dash and dormer windows. The curtains were drawn and there was no car in the drive. 'It doesn't look like there's anybody in,' said Dixon, turning off the engine and turning to look at Dorsey. 'Do you want me to stay in the car?'

'No, I might need some backup,' he said with a smile. 'I don't want to end up with a broken nose like George.'

Before they got out of the car, a man appeared, looking anxiously at them and then looking around at his neighbours' houses for any signs of twitching curtains.

'Are you Sean Muir?' asked Dorsey, standing at the open passenger door. 'Can we have five minutes of your time?'

'Okay, what is it?'

'Can we come in?'

Muir nodded and turned back towards the house. 'Please, can we do this quickly? My wife and the kids will be back soon. I know why you're here. Come into the living room.'

The house looked like a normal family home on a dull Sunday morning: children's toys scattered around, a morning newspaper lying open on the coffee table, and the radio on in the next room. 'Mr Muir, you'll no doubt be aware of the investigation that is ongoing at present in relation to a missing student and the murder of a young Polish woman. We've no reason for suspecting you of being involved in any of these matters, but because of your record …'

'What, one conviction over six years ago?'

'You were also charged with the same offence four years ago.'

'You can't bring that up. I was acquitted. She was a lying bitch and put me through hell. I'd like you to both go now! I'm not answering any questions without a lawyer. I know how you lot twist things. I'm not going through that again. I'd like you both to leave now.'

'We're not accusing you of anything, but you can see that your past makes you a person who we must speak to, if only to eliminate you from our enquiries. We require you to provide a DNA sample.'

'No fucking way … Get out of my house.'

'You have a choice, my friend. You can provide a sample, or we can come back with a warrant when your wife and kids are here.'

'A warrant, for what?'

'To search your house and require you to provide a DNA sample.'

Muir's facial expression of anger turned to submission as he threw up his arms. 'Right, let's get this fucking over with.'

Dixon got the DNA swab kit from her jacket pocket and took a mouth sample from Muir before Dorsey began to ask some questions. The interview was hurried on account of Muir's sudden willingness to cooperate, answering most of the questions before Dorsey had finished asking them. He even let them have a cursory look around the house.

'What do you think?' asked Dixon, once they were back in the car.

'No, it's definitely not him. He's too afraid of his own shadow. At least we've got his DNA sample. I could always be wrong.'

'Would we have gotten a warrant granted if he refused to provide the sample?'

'No, it was a bluff.'

'Well, it worked. We've still got Carling to visit,' she said, making a three-point turn. 'At least we've already got his DNA.'

Dorsey had never heard of Inverlochy, which was on the outskirts of Fort William. They were there in five minutes. The grey concrete five-storey tower block seemed out of place and would have looked more at home in the east end of Glasgow. They took the lift to the top floor where their final suspect and last hope of a breakthrough lived, or so they thought.

It didn't take many knocks at the door before an elderly woman, still in her dressing gown, opened the door opposite. 'If you're looking for the guy who lived in that flat, you'll have to bang a lot harder than that. He's been dead for a year. Good riddance to him. He was a drug dealer and a thief.'

Chapter 9

Dorsey was up early and decided to drive to Callert as he was keen to speak to Munro before they resumed the search. It was a dry day, and the car park was so full he had to park further up the road and walk back. Apart from the police cars, there were mountain rescue vehicles that had come from all over Scotland. Munro had not let him down. He introduced himself to a four-man team from the Cairngorms who were getting changed outside their vehicle, their dogs pacing around the large cage in the back, barking excitedly. He thanked them for their help and for coming all the way from Braemar to join in the search.

The path to Lairigmor was nothing like the first time when he had to battle against the fierce winds on wet sodden ground. That day now seemed like a long time ago. The mountains on both sides were free from the mist that smothered them when he was last in the glen, and he could see just how vast an area they had to cover.

The Lairigmor ruins were still being used by the scenes of crime unit as their base, and he spoke to DS Kilbride. 'Morning, Jock. Have you finished the forensic report?'

'I sent the report to Mackie on Friday.'

'I haven't seen it. In future, can you make sure that you send any reports to me first?'

'Sorry, Frank, I assumed she would've sent you a copy. I emailed it to arrange for the DNA database to be checked. She was probably waiting for that to be done before she sent it to you.'

'Okay, can you tell me what was in the report?'

'We found Lena Kaminski's DNA on the rucksack and a second unidentified DNA profile.'

'That could belong to anyone.'

'It could, but I've no doubt it belongs to the killer.'

'I'm listening.'

'We found a hair on the blue material used to wrap the body parts. It matched the unidentified DNA on the rucksack. This unidentified profile is of a white male, but when it was checked on the police database, there was no match.'

'Shit. He's not on the database.'

'No. Either he doesn't have a serious criminal record or has minor convictions that didn't require him to provide a DNA sample. It could also be that he committed offences before the requirement to provide DNA came into force. Then, there's also the chance that his DNA has been removed from the database.'

'Why would it be removed?'

'There are time limits on some charges that mean we have to delete them when they expire, although that wouldn't apply to serious charges like rape, abduction, or murder.'

'What if he's a foreigner?'

'I thought of that. We've sent the unknown DNA profile to Interpol. We are waiting for them to get back to us.'

'Okay, at least we have his DNA. What about the footprints?'

'There were four distinct types of prints, and we checked them with the boots of the dog handler who found the body and the two police officers who originally cordoned off the area before we arrived. Dr Jamali's were easy to eliminate as she was wearing sole covers. The treads and boot sizes of the rest all match the ones we expected to find. I'm afraid, Frank, there's no other unaccounted prints. With the length of time that body was there, I wasn't surprised.'

'If Interpol comes back with a match, let me know first.

I'm the SIO in this case, not Mackie.'

'No problem, Frank.'

Dorsey looked back along the glen. 'I was hoping to have a word with Alex Munro.'

'Good luck with that. You'll need to run to catch up with him,' said Jock, pointing down the glen. 'They won't be back unless they find something or they finish for the day. These guys are tough and just keep going. They're going to concentrate on this side until they reach the forest at the other end where uniformed and local volunteers are already searching. They'll then come back down the other side all the way back to Kinlochleven.'

Dorsey decided to leave them to it. He went over to where the body was recovered and stared down at the ditch for a few minutes, the image of the body being sucked out coming back to him vividly. He glanced around in a vain hope of finding Lena Kaminski's gold crucifix lying undetected somewhere in the thick clumps of heather and moss. He quickly gave up and went back to the ruins, knowing that the crime scene would soon disappear back into the unforgiving landscape and be forgotten. 'Jock, did you find anything else of interest in the ditch?'

'No, nothing. Is there something you think might be there?'

'It was just that her mother said she always wore a gold crucifix.'

'If it was there, we would've found it. We used metal detectors in and around the ditch this morning. Not a bleep.'

'Okay, thanks. I think I'll head back.'

'Enjoy the walk.'

When he got back to the station, Dorsey was still troubled that CS Mackie had held back the DNA profile of a prime suspect and hadn't told him. He checked his emails. There was one email from Inverness sent that morning at 11 a.m. with a copy of the forensic report and the results of the checks done on the DNA database. The email simply confirmed what Kilbride had just told him. He also checked Friday, but there were no emails from Mackie or anyone from Inverness CID. *What was she up to? Probably looking to take the credit if there was a match found.* Now, he wouldn't put it past Mackie if she planned only to tell him of the match after the suspect was arrested by *her* Inverness team of detectives. Even Knox wasn't that devious.

Still angry, he studied the large Ordnance Survey map of the Highlands in the incident room. An area between Kinlochleven and Fort William was marked out with a black marker, as though the killer was only allowed to commit his crimes and dispose of the bodies within it. But they had to have a limit, otherwise they'd be overwhelmed by the sheer size of the task they faced. He looked at one of the incident boards and the picture of the four students with the dog at Glen Etive, showing what Erin was wearing when she went missing. He stared long and hard at the pictures of Webster's hand. There was nothing else.

He then turned to the second board with the enhanced morgue picture of Lena Kaminski. Beside it were pictures of the bog where she had been discovered, and the morgue stills showing the injuries to her left ankle and close-ups of the bruising and needle marks on her arm. Below these were forensic stills showing the blue dress material, the rucksack, and the various boot prints. The first list of sex offenders they thought might be of interest was still pinned to the board, but now all the names had been scored out. Like the other board, there were no pictures of suspects, or even people of interest, on which they could focus. Both cases had the same problem. They had nothing to go on. There was no line of enquiry for either case other than chasing up sex offenders who might not have been required to provide a DNA sample when they were arrested or had it removed due to the time limits. Unless Interpol were able to match the DNA profile on their database, that crucial piece of evidence would only be of use once they had a suspect to match it with.

Dorsey knew he had to do something to increase the odds of finding the killer. He phoned Deputy Chief Constable Cullen.

'Yes, sir. I know it will be costly but it could solve this case. We have his DNA, but it's not on the database. It might be the only way to catch him and save Erin Keenan from the same fate as Lena Kaminski. He could also go on to kill more young women.'

There was a long pause. Dorsey was sure Cullen was weighing up the cost to the police budget against the possible fallout if he refused and the killer was only beginning his reign of terror. The question for the press in the future would be why it wasn't done. Now he'd received a formal request from the SIO on the case, the buck would stop with Cullen.

'Okay, Frank. I'll instruct Inverness CID to start a voluntary DNA screening programme in Glencoe. This better work. It's going to put a large dent in our budget.'

His elation at getting Cullen to sanction the screening programme was short-lived; he received a call immediately afterwards he could have done without. It was Knox.

'Frank, they're bringing in the Gallowgate trial, and the advocate depute wants you to give evidence tomorrow. She has one expert to call before you, but she has agreed most of his evidence in a joint minute with the defence and thinks he'll only be in the witness box for a couple of hours.'

'Shit, Andrew, could you not have phoned me earlier?'

'If you check your phone, you'll see that I've called you twice already. I'm not your bloody secretary!'

Chapter 10

The train took nearly two and a half hours to get into Queen Street Station, arriving on time just after 9 a.m. He was eager to get into the High Court and get his evidence over with as quickly as possible, but knew from experience that there was a good chance he'd have to stay overnight at his flat and continue his evidence for a second day. He quickened his stride along Argyle Street as the sky darkened over.

The rain held off, and he was soon at the Saltmarket. He was early and stood outside to have a cigarette as the hordes queued up to go through the security checks. He smiled when he saw Professor Jenkins coming up past the old morgue building, where he had dissected more bodies than Jack Klugman did as Quincy, M.E.

'Morning, Professor. Looking as debonair as ever.'

'Ah, Chief Inspector. Morning, I didn't know you spoke French. One must keep up appearances. I hear they're taking me first. I won't be long. They've agreed most of my evidence. This case should've been a plea.' With that, the professor made his way to the North Court, waved through by security who didn't bother to even look at his security pass. He had been attending the High Court before they were even born.

Dorsey went into the building and checked into the witness muster at the North Court in the old building. There were already four officers from his squad sitting in the waiting room, anxiously going over their evidence in their notebooks. They got to their feet, but he gestured with his hand for them to sit down. He decided to seek out the advocate depute dealing with the case, and went into the courtroom by the side door reserved for court officials and the lawyers. The defence advocates were already in their wigs and gowns, laughing and joking among themselves. He asked the clerk of court if she could contact the advocate depute.

'No need to, there she is now.'

Dorsey turned to see the senior counsel for the Crown wheeling in a trolley of arch lever files, followed by the procurator fiscal who was assisting her in the case. She had so much of her own grey hair underneath her court wig that she looked like an eccentric character out of a Dickens novel.

'Can I have a word?' he asked, as he showed his warrant card.

'I've already spoken to Chief Superintendent Knox this morning. We'll try to get through your testimony this afternoon. The defence counsel has agreed most of your evidence by way of a joint minute.'

'That's good to know. I've got something urgent to do in relation to another case. Is it okay if I go now and come back before midday?'

'I don't think that would be a problem. I expect once we get the preliminary matters out of the way, Professor Jenkins's evidence will likely take us up to lunchtime, but you never can tell,' she added, with a wry smile while nodding in the direction of the defence counsel.

Dorsey went back out to the front of the building and phoned London Road Police Station, requesting the address of Erin Keenan's parents. It was now raining heavily, and people were scurrying for shelter from the downpour. Glasgow always looked dreich in the rain. He flagged down a taxi.

Within minutes, he received a text from the family liaison officer with the address and some helpful information about the Keenans.

It took twenty minutes before the taxi pulled up outside a large detached Victorian house in the Pollokshaws area on the southside of Glasgow. The house was enclosed by a high stone wall and there was a wrought iron gate entrance to the driveway, where three cars were parked outside the house. He unlatched the side gate and walked up the gravel path. He rang the doorbell, almost expecting a butler to answer.

The door opened, and a teenage girl greeted him. 'Come in, the station phoned to let us know you were on your way. I'm scared to ask, but have you found Erin?'

'No. I'm sorry. I take it you're her sister?' replied Dorsey.

'Yes, Orla. Pleased to meet you. Here, let me take your coat.'

'It's okay, I won't be long. I just have a few questions to ask your parents.'

The house was enormous; the hall was as big as his whole flat. Orla led him into the living room where her parents were waiting anxiously.

Erin's father, Desmond Keenan, got up and approached him. 'Take a seat, Chief Inspector. They wouldn't tell us why you were coming. Have you found Erin?'

'No, I'm sorry, that's not why I'm here. We don't know where she is. That's what we're still trying to find out,' said Dorsey, taking a seat opposite the parents.

'Do you think she is still alive?'

'There's no reason to believe she's not.'

'We're sick with worry,' said Mrs Keenan, the sleepless nights etched on her face. 'People are posting on social media that she's been abducted or even murdered by the same man who killed that young woman from Poland.'

'That's not true. We don't know what happened to Erin. We're still treating her as a missing persons case. There is nothing to link both cases.'

'But whoever murdered that young woman might have

Erin?' pressed the father. 'Is that right, Chief Inspector?'

'Like I've said, we have no evidence to link Erin's disappearance with the murder. The reason I'm here is that I would like to know a little about Erin's relationship with Duncan Webster.'

'Webster? Why?' asked Mr Keenan, looking towards his wife. 'Do you think he's got something to do with her going missing?'

'We have no evidence he did anything. His hand was badly bruised. His position is that he punched a tree after she told him she was seeing someone else and wanted to split up.'

'I never liked him. He's an arrogant bastard … If he laid a hand on my daughter, I'll …'

'Has he ever hit her in the past?'

Mr Keenan turned and looked at Orla. 'Did she tell you anything?'

'No, but he was a bully, criticising her all the time.'

'Why haven't you told me this before?' snapped her father, looking sternly at Orla.

'She told me not to.'

'Okay,' said Dorsey. 'Did you know she was seeing someone else and planning to split up with him?'

'No, it's not something she would've told us,' Mrs Keenan explained, turning to look at her daughter.

Orla shook her head. She looked uncomfortable and turned away when Dorsey stared in her direction.

'You will be aware that her computer was examined and we found nothing on it to indicate she was in another relationship or that Webster was violent towards her. Okay, the family liaison officer will keep you updated if there are any developments,' said Dorsey, getting to his feet. 'I'm sorry, but I must phone a taxi and get back to the High Court. I'm giving evidence in another case this afternoon.'

Mr Keenan sat in his chair, shaking his head. 'Is that all

you have to tell us after twelve days? You must have found something to explain how our daughter disappeared. She didn't just vanish into thin air. I'm unsatisfied with the lack of progress. If you think she's been abducted and murdered then I'd rather you told us, instead of all this rubbish about Duncan Webster.'

'I believe Webster has not told us the whole truth about what happened the night Erin went missing. I need something to undermine his first statement. He may have been lying about how he injured his hand.'

There were more questions from the father that Dorsey could not answer without compromising the case. He moved towards the door. 'I need to go. I can't be late for court.'

'I can drive you,' offered Orla. 'Just give me a minute to get my coat.'

'It's alright, I can get a cab.'

'It's no problem.'

Dorsey waited in the hall until Orla came back down from upstairs. She took a set of car keys from a tray on a table near the front door and led Dorsey to the cars parked outside. The locks on a black Mercedes pinged and the doors opened with a loud click. He went to the front of the driveway and opened the gates as she manoeuvred past the other vehicles before stopping to pick him up. He got into the passenger seat, amazed that someone so young could be driving a car like that.

'Is this your dad's car?'

'No, it's Erin's. Dad bought it when she passed her exams to go to university … Duncan was using it after Erin went missing. My dad just got it back a few days ago when his lawyer threatened to take Webster to court.'

'You must miss her.'

'Every minute of every day.'

'I suspect there might be some things you didn't want to say in front of your parents. You seemcd uncomfortable when I asked if your sister was seeing someone else. Do you know if she was?'

'No, but she said something to me a few weeks before she went missing that seemed a bit strange. She said she thought she might be gay. I thought she was just joking, but a few days later she said it again and made me promise not to tell anyone.'

'Did she say why she thought that?'

'No. I'm still not sure if she was serious about it.'

'You said Duncan was a bully. What did he do that made you think that?'

'He's a control freak. He stopped her going out with her friends and belittled her. Erin was happy before she met him. I hate him.'

'Do you think he would have harmed her?'

'I wouldn't put it past him. He's all nice and polite when he's in company, especially in front of my parents, but they've not seen how scared she is of him when he's been drinking and treating her like shit.'

'Have you seen it?'

'Yes, he was shouting and bawling at her when I went up to her flat a few weeks ago. When he opened the door and saw me standing there, he acted as if nothing had happened. When Erin came out of the bathroom, I could tell she had been crying. I should have told my dad then, but she made me promise not to.'

'Just let me off here,' said Dorsey.

She pulled up at the Saltmarket opposite the High Court. 'Is she still alive?'

'We don't know, but we'll do everything possible to find her.'

'Please don't mention the lesbian thing to my parents. They're a bit weird about that sort of thing. Now I wish I never told you.'

'Don't worry, I can't remember what we were talking

about. Old age is a terrible thing.'

'Thanks. You're not *that* old.'

'I'll take that as a compliment, and thanks for the lift.'

By the time Dorsey returned to the witness waiting room, the Crown and defence had reached a deal. One of the accused had pleaded guilty to culpable homicide on the grounds of diminished responsibility, while the charges against his co-accused were dropped. Relieved that was now out the way, Dorsey drove to his flat.

It felt strange to be back, as though he had been away for months. He decided to make a coffee before phoning his ex-wife. The kitchen was cold. He chain-smoked a couple of cigarettes. The meeting with the Keenans had unsettled him; it made him see their anguish firsthand and just how little he had to offer them that might ease their pain.

He phoned Helen to see if it was convenient to go over and spend a couple of hours with Daniel, maybe take him for something to eat.

'Frank, I'm sorry. Daniel's got his rugby sevens at six. Richard has already agreed to take him.'

'When did he start playing bloody rugby?'

'It's just training sessions he's going to. He wants to get into the school team.'

'Okay, I'm only in Glasgow until tomorrow, then I have to go back up to Glencoe. I'll phone him and try to arrange something for next week.'

'Please don't arrange anything if you're not going to be able to make it. I know what you're like.'

'Helen, just tell him I'll give him a call. I have to go.'

He then phoned Liz, who was preparing her files for another day in the custody court in the morning. They agreed to meet after she finished work.

'Yeah, half six is fine. It will give me a chance to get something to eat.'

'Why don't you wait and have something when we're

out? I'll meet you in The Granary. They have a decent pub menu.'

'Okay, don't be late as usual.'

He sat in the bar on his own for about fifteen minutes before Liz arrived, apologising for being late. He gave her a kiss on the cheek and ordered another pint of Guinness and her usual gin and tonic. Liz took off her coat and hung it over a nearby chair.

'How did the High Court go today?' she asked, as he placed the drinks on the table and sat opposite her.

'Last-minute deal. The main guy pleaded guilty to culpable homicide and his mate got off … How was your day?'

'Hectic. I had the custody court to deal with, and a sheriff who was just being difficult for the sake of it. Anyway, I'll have a different sheriff tomorrow. How's the investigation in Glencoe going?'

'We've got little to go on. The student's disappearance is a complete mystery. We have DNA for the suspect in the murder case that's not on the police database. We don't have any tangible leads in either case. Let's talk about something else.'

Liz ordered a glass of white wine to go with the spaghetti carbonara she picked from the pre-theatre menu, while Dorsey stuck to what he knew, another pint and a burger and chips.

'It's a bit bizarre they have a pre-theatre menu on a Tuesday,' said Liz.

'I think it's even more bizarre they have one any night of the week. There's not a theatre within a five-mile radius of this place.'

'There's the Citizens Theatre. That's only a couple of miles away.'

'Which has been closed for the last few years, and God knows when it will reopen.'

'Yeah, I know that, but they still put on their plays in the Tramway, which is nearer still. So I don't think it's bizarre that they have a pre-theatre menu. It's just that I don't think there's many people that go to the theatre on a Tuesday night.'

He unintentionally yawned.

'Am I boring you?' she asked sternly.

'Of course not. I'm sorry. I've been up since five this morning. I'm just tired. I didn't mean to yawn.'

'I'll let you off this time, but you've made me feel self-conscious.'

'I'm sorry,' he repeated, just as the waitress arrived with the two plates of food.

Chapter 11

Wednesday: 13ᵗʰ of September 2023

Dorsey woke the next morning in Liz's flat. Not wanting to disturb her, he eased himself out of bed and lifted his clothes from the floor to get dressed in the living room. Her two strange looking Sphynx cats were sitting together on the settee and staring at him. He was sure they were jealous. They made him feel uneasy, as though they were planning to pounce on him for stealing Liz's affection. He ordered a taxi from the app on his phone and quietly made his way out of the flat and downstairs to have a cigarette before the taxi arrived.

He took the cab back to his flat. After a quick shower and changing into the only clean shirt left in the wardrobe, he took a fresh tie and put it on with the suit he had worn the previous day at court. According to the train timetable on his phone, he still had an hour to kill before he had to get to the station. Enough time for a coffee. He thought about the night before and Liz's suggestion that he should sell his flat and move in with her. Although her economic arguments were sound, there was no way he was ready for that. He was used to the freedom that living on his own gave him and he hated those furless psycho cats. He packed some clean socks, underwear, and toiletries into a holdall. Satisfied he had what he came for, he booked a taxi to take him to Queen Street Station in time for the 9.30 a.m. train to Tyndrum.

Once he got on the train, he noticed two text messages from Dixon asking him to phone urgently. He had only one thought – they must have found her.

He phoned Dixon. 'What's happened?'

'Sir, I've been trying to get hold of you. I didn't want to phone in case you were in court … They found another body.'

'Is it her?'

'We don't know yet. Scenes of crime have cordoned off the area. I'm waiting at the old ruins.'

'Where was it found?'

'In the bog on the other side of the road, just about half a mile from where the other body was found. One of the cadaver dogs found it.'

'Okay, it's a pity they didn't do that side first. Let me know if you find out anything else. I'm on my way back.'

The train journey back felt much longer than the same journey he made in the opposite direction only the day before. The theory of relative time that he had read about once came to mind, but he brushed it aside. He had other things to think about, none of them good. His phone buzzed. It was Knox. He decided to ignore it. He wasn't in the mood to speak to him. He phoned Mitchell instead.

'How're you doing, George?'

'I'm okay. I've been trying to get a hold of the PF at the High Court to see if they need me in today.'

'Don't worry, I was at the High Court yesterday; they agreed a plea. Someone from the Crown should have phoned you to cancel your citation.'

'Thank God, I was dreading having to go to court looking like this. My nose is still swollen and I've still got those hideous black and blue bags under my eyes.'

'When do you think you'll be able to go back to the hospital to get it fixed?'

'I've got to wait until this swelling goes down before they can try to straighten it. I'm not looking forward to that. What's been happening in Glencoe?'

'That's why I phoned you. They've found another body.

They don't know if it's the student. I'll phone you later when I find out. Just look after yourself and have a rest.'

'Okay, Frank. It doesn't look good,' sighed Mitchell, with his usual mastery of the understatement.

After speaking to Mitchell, his mobile immediately buzzed again.

'Frank, you're beginning to piss me off. Why don't you answer your bloody phone?' complained Knox.

'Sorry, Andrew, but I had the phone on silent,' he lied.

'Right, okay. Have you heard that they found another body?'

'Yes, I'm on my way there now.'

'Do you know if it's Keenan?'

'No, but I'll find out soon enough.'

'Well, keep me up to speed. I'll need to send someone out to speak to the family before they hear about it on the evening news. I don't want their lawyer on the phone again.'

'I'll let you know when I know.'

It was almost midday by the time the train arrived at Tyndrum Station. He had a minor panic when he couldn't find his car keys in his jacket pockets, before remembering that he had put them in his holdall. Panic over, he clicked the fob and opened the driver's door. He was relieved to be behind the wheel again as the skies opened up and the rain battered the car bonnet.

The road was quiet but it still seemed to take forever to get through Glen Etive and onto the last stretch towards Glencoe. He had already made up his mind to go straight to Lairigmor. He pulled into a lay-by and phoned the station. 'Have we got any information about the second body yet?'

'No, sir,' replied the duty sergeant. 'Dr Jamali has just phoned. She is on her way and will be at Callert shortly. The police helicopter is waiting there to take her to Lairigmor. Scenes of crime are at the locus, but they don't want to touch the body until the doctor gets there.'

'Is it Erin Keenan?'

'They don't know, sir, but the body is dismembered and wrapped in blue material. It's the same as the last one.'

'Okay, phone me if you hear anything else. Can you arrange for the police helicopter to wait at Callert until I get there? I'm not walking across that bog in this weather.'

'Of course, sir. I'll get on to them straight away.'

When he arrived at the car park, the rotor blades on the police helicopter were turning slowly. He noticed Dr Jamali's car alongside the police vehicles and the forensic unit. He parked on a grass verge and got changed into his wet gear before joining the pathologist and her two assistants in the bay of the helicopter. Apart from a nod and smile, the noise of the helicopter taking off drowned out the possibility of any meaningful conversation. The anticipation of what lay ahead made everyone sombre.

The scenes of crime officers had already set up a forensic tent on the other side of the road where the second body was obviously found. He made his way across the boggy ground to where DS Kilbride was standing outside the tent in his white overalls. 'Looks like we have a serial killer on our hands. It's the same MO as the first one,' said Jock, the rain running down his face into his beard.

After changing into their PPE, the doctor and her assistants unwrapped the sections of blue material from the body parts and carefully placed them into production bags. Dorsey could now make out that the body was that of a young woman. Dr Jamali carried out a cursory examination of the dismembered body while it was still in the waterlogged ditch, dictating her observations into her digital recorder. Once finished, she explained her initial findings to Dorsey. 'She's white, European, and has been here for some time.'

'So, it's not Erin Keenan?'

'No, but I'll need to wait until we're ready to lift her before we can have a proper look at her facial features. I

112

can tell she is quite young, late teens or early twenties. She has been dismembered and has the same hook marks as the other body. There's also a similar injury to her left ankle. As you saw, the body parts were wrapped in a similar, if not identical, blue cotton material … Are you okay, Frank?'

Dorsey was suddenly lightheaded and had to stop himself from falling headfirst into the ditch. The moment quickly passed. 'I'm okay. I don't think there's any doubt now that we're dealing with a serial killer who seems to have a dress fetish.'

'That's about the size of it. Maybe you should get a forensic profiler involved. This is weird stuff.'

'I'll speak to Professor Jenkins. He's a pathologist and also lectures on forensic profiling.'

'I know him. He was my professor at university.'

'I'm not much use here and I need to get back to the station,' said Dorsey, suddenly feeling lightheaded again.

'Frank, are you alright? You should go back to your hotel and rest. You look exhausted. Everything here will be taken care of. I've got your mobile number and I'll let you know if there's anything else of interest.'

'I need to go back to the station first. We'll speak soon.'

Dorsey walked back to the ruins to find somewhere to sit out of the rain and gather his thoughts. He was not someone prone to dizzy spells and blamed it on skipping breakfast that morning. After a few minutes he made his way to the bay of the helicopter, which took him back to the car park. The wind and rain made the short journey nerve-racking and only added to his feeling of nausea.

Relieved to be back on the ground, he walked back towards his car. Before reaching it, he threw up violently on the grass verge. He took a paper hankie from his pocket and wiped his mouth. He noticed specks of blood on the tissue. After inhaling the brisk air coming off the loch to clear his head, he got in his car and drove back to the station.

The incident room was packed. Those handling phones and operating computers had chairs to sit at, while the rest of the muster had to find somewhere to stand. As Dorsey walked across the room, DI Crawford ordered all phones to be put on hold, and the constant clicking of keyboards stopped. All heads turned towards the chief inspector, who was standing in front of the incident boards.

Now that he had complete silence in the room, he spoke to them with a passion he had not felt in years. 'Most, if not all of you will know that a second body was discovered this morning in Lairigmor, only a short distance from where Lena Kaminski was found. The MO is identical. What I'm going to tell you this evening is not to be discussed with anyone not involved in the investigation.' Dorsey looked around at the stern faces. 'We now have two murder victims. It's clear they have been killed by the same person, who disposed of them in the same manner, only half a mile apart. We're dealing with a serial killer who seems to have been getting away with this for years, so God knows how many he's killed.'

'Sir,' interrupted one of the detectives, 'are we now linking the missing persons case with these two murders?'

'Yes. If this killer has Erin Keenan, then if she is not already dead, she will be if we do not find her in time. We now must widen our hunt for this man, as it is likely he may not even live in this area. Time is running out. Let's get this bastard before he murders anyone else!'

Chapter 12

The second body was quickly identified by DNA tests as Evinka Janik, a 19-year-old Slovakian who was last seen at the end of July 2020. She had never been reported missing, but she was wanted by the police for questioning when she disappeared after being accused of stealing from guest rooms in a hotel where she worked. She wasn't one to stick around for the police to arrive. Despite the COVID restrictions at the time, Evinka was last seen hitching on the A82 near Tyndrum, where her ex-boyfriend had dropped her off.

Two previous investigations into her criminal activities resulted in her having to give a DNA swab, which she obviously didn't know at the time would be used to identify her murdered body. Dr Jamali obtained skin tissue from under her nails, which confirmed that her killer's DNA matched that of the same man who murdered Lena Kaminski. She must have fought for her life when she realised her fate.

Evinka's parents were both dead, and Dorsey had the sad task of meeting her younger sister at Aberdeen Airport and taking her to identify the body. It was only when he spoke to her about Evinka and witnessed her distress that the dismembered body parts became more than just a murder victim; she was a person who had been brutally robbed of her young life by an evil stranger she had met by a simple twist of fate.

The MO of the murder of both victims was almost identical, with the only notable difference being the two kirby grips discovered in Evinka Janik's hair, which seemed odd to Dr Jamali. The toxicology reports for both victims confirmed that they died after being injected with the antipsychotic drug benzodiazepine and the opioid fentanyl until they eventually died of a lethal overdose administered intentionally or by an accidental, misjudged dosage. The police were treating both deaths as premeditated murder. The recovery of the second body added little to the investigation in terms of new evidence. They already had the suspect's DNA from the first victim, and if Evinka had a phone, it was never recovered. All that her corpse added was more pressure to find the killer.

With both bodies found wrapped in a cotton fabric, a clothes specialist re-examined the material and confirmed that it was cut from at least three identical dresses that were not commercially made and was the work of a very competent dressmaker. The material and the thread were impossible to trace, with most local suppliers suggesting that they had been bought online. The subsequent questioning of Royal Mail and other delivery drivers in the area also came to nothing. The CID now had their own code name for the investigation, *Operation Dressmaker,* and the killer was now simply referred to by many of the detectives working on the case as *The Dressmaker*.

After the toxicology report confirmed that the benzodiazepine and fentanyl were found in the systems of both bodies, there was an appeal to the public to come forward if they were taking, or knew someone who was taking, this medication. This resulted in hundreds of lines of enquiry, but no suspects. It was obvious that the killer was unlikely to volunteer himself to scrutiny, but they hoped a family member or friend would be sufficiently suspicious of him that his name would be put forward. Those persons who volunteered of their own volition or were named by others were interviewed and DNA swabs were taken, eliminating them from the investigation.

Now that the police were openly accepting that they were dealing with a serial killer, the fate of the missing Glasgow student had become a matter of national interest. There were heated debates on radio and television about the police handling of the case and their failure to find her. The new tagline for most newspapers was *The Bodies in the Bog Case.* It was a headline, unlike the previous one, that they wouldn't have to change if more bodies were found in similar circumstances.

With Interpol unable to find a match for the killer's DNA profile previously supplied to them, the identity of the prime suspect for both murders and the whereabouts of Erin Keenan remained a mystery. The investigation dragged on, but with no new leads to follow up on, it was practically moribund.

The list of sex offenders in the Highland region remained the only hope of a breakthrough and resulted in hundreds more hours of police work with still no suspect being identified. Those who had not previously provided a DNA sample or had them deleted from the database were given the option of agreeing to do so or having a visit from two uniformed officers to their homes or workplaces. The samples from the willing and coerced were then checked with the unidentified prime suspect's profile. One by one they were duly eliminated from the enquiry when no match was found.

When Dorsey was finally told by Crawford that they had no sex offenders left to visit who were not already on the database and that everyone on the list had been eliminated as a possible suspect, he ran his hands through his hair and sighed. *What the hell are we missing?*

The case was becoming as stagnant as the water that both bodies were found in.

After being away for more than three weeks, Dorsey was glad to see his old partner back at work. Dorsey brought him up to speed with the investigation, which didn't take him long to do.

'So, we've still got nothing to go on?' Mitchell asked.

'Nothing,' said Dorsey. 'I bet you're sorry you came back.'

'I didn't know I had an option. So, what do we do now?'

'I'm planning to arrange a meeting with Professor Jenkins and Dr Jamali. I think we need to get a profile on this killer. The scale of the investigation is so wide that we need to look at this from a different angle.'

'I still think we should look at Duncan Webster again. I'm still not convinced he injured his hand punching a tree. There is still nothing to link Erin Keenan with these murders.'

'I may have him re-interviewed and see if he is sticking to his story. But first things first, I want this profiling done to give us something tangible to work with … Anyway, how's the nose doing?'

'It's fine. It's probably straighter now than it was before that nutcase broke it.'

'Maybe you should write to him in prison and thank him,' Dorsey said with a smile.

Chapter 13

Dorsey hadn't seen Daniel for weeks and decided to head back to Glasgow for a break now that Mitchell was back in Glencoe and could keep an eye on Crawford and his team. He always felt strange when he went back to his old house. Now that it had been signed over to Helen in the divorce settlement, he was getting used to using the doorbell and wiping his boots before he went in.

'Frank, you don't look so good,' Helen said. 'What's the matter? Is everything okay?'

'I'm fine. How are you?'

'Great. He's in his room playing on that bloody gaming console you got him last Christmas. You're soaking. Let me take your coat.'

Apart from when the three of them had lunch together, he spent most of the day watching Daniel kill aliens for fun on his Xbox. Daniel still had a way of answering every question with one-syllable words that were sometimes incoherent. So much for all that money spent putting him through private school.

He put his coat on at 5 p.m. It was the agreed time for him to leave before Richard Hamilton got back from visiting his own two kids from a previous marriage. He said his goodbyes and took a taxi to Shawlands to meet up with Liz at The Granary for a couple of drinks before he headed back to Glencoe. He ordered a pint and took a seat at the window. It was now raining outside and Liz was late as usual, even though she only stayed around the corner. He looked at his watch. It was ten past six. He sent her a text just as she walked into the bar.

'My God, this weather is miserable. Sorry I'm late. I had to deal with a problem I had with a trial tomorrow. We forgot to cite the witnesses … I'll get them in,' she insisted, shaking the rain from her umbrella onto the floor. 'Guinness?'

'No, can you get me a lager? This has a weird taste to it.'

He watched her being served at the bar. She was confident, beautiful, and elegant. He often wondered what she saw in him. She smiled at him as she returned with the two drinks.

'How did it go with Daniel?' she asked, putting the drinks down and taking off her coat.

'I find it hard sometimes. He's obsessed with his computer games and it's hard to have a conversation with him about anything.'

'He's a teenage boy. That's what they're all like. I wouldn't worry about it.'

'I'm not. I just wish he wasn't such hard work. He still hasn't forgiven me …'

'For divorcing his mother?'

'I didn't divorce Helen. She divorced me.'

'But did Daniel know why?'

'Yeah, his mother told him. I thought he'd be over it by now. Especially now she's in a relationship. Anyway, that's in the past. I'm sorry. I shouldn't even be boring you with this.'

'That's okay. What time's your train?'

'Half past nine.'

'Any progress with the investigation?'

'No, everything we investigate comes to nothing. I've never dealt with a case like this. Since you brought it up, I was wondering if you'd be able to come up to Glencoe on Wednesday afternoon. I might need some legal advice about the case.'

There was a painful silence before she said anything. 'Is

that why you phoned me to meet you? Not to see how I've been doing or to tell me you've missed me?'

'Liz, you know I've missed you. Why do you think I'm asking you to come to Glencoe?'

'You've just told me it was for legal advice. You're not the most romantic man, are you, Frank?'

'I've never pretended to be romantic. But you do know how I feel about you.'

There was another long silence while his hopeless attempt to express his feelings was being analysed by a lawyer's mind. She smiled. 'I guess you wouldn't be you, if you were any other way. Maybe that's why Daniel is the way he is. The apple doesn't fall far from the tree.'

'I don't know if that was meant to insult me or my son.'

'It wasn't meant to insult anyone. Let's stop this. What legal advice do you need? Surely, I can just tell you what you need to know now?'

'Not really. I've arranged a meeting with Professor Jenkins, Dr Jamali, and CS Fiona Mackie to see if we can get a profile on this guy.'

'I'm surprised you haven't done that already.'

'The problem is their other commitments. This is the first chance I've had to get them to agree to go to Glencoe at the same time. I think it would be helpful if we had a legal mind at the meeting. Would you be interested in coming up? You can submit your fee and expenses to Police Scotland.'

'No, Frank, I can't just drop everything and go to Glencoe. Anyway, it's not my jurisdiction. You should get the PF from Inverness to join the meeting. I don't think my boss would agree to it. And apart from that, I'm an employee of the Crown. I can't charge a fee or expenses privately for legal advice, especially if it's given as part of a criminal investigation.'

'Okay, I obviously didn't think this through.'

'Have there been no new leads in the last few weeks?'

'No, everything we try comes to nothing. We've got the guy's DNA, but we don't know who he is.'

'DNA means nothing until you have something to compare it to. Let me speak to my boss and see what she says. At least that fraud trial I'd been working on turned into a plea. She might let me take the day off to go up now that's out of the way. But I can't promise anything.'

'You can only ask. Do you want another drink here or do you want to go somewhere else?'

'Let's go to Heraghty's. At least there's a bit of atmosphere in there.'

Chapter 14

Monday: 2nd of October 2023

The detectives faced another tedious day of putting the new statements on the Home Office Large Major Enquiry System and cross-referencing them with everything that was previously uploaded. The system only added to the detectives' frustration as all the suspects highlighted by HOLMES had been previously eliminated. By midday they were left with little else to focus on.

With all the disappointments, Dorsey knew he had to keep the squad's spirits up, afraid apathy would quickly creep into the investigation. He was also aware from experience that too often in the past, the police had the evidence they needed in the mountains of statements, reports, and interviews they already had in their possession. With the constant leads that went nowhere, some detectives were already becoming overwhelmed and despondent with the sheer magnitude of the task they faced. The negative reporting from the press became a source of pressure they could all have done without. It was his job to keep the force under him focused on doing their jobs until the end, as bad as that might turn out to be.

After a long day at his computer, Dorsey had had enough. He suggested to Mitchell that they have an early finish. As usual, Dorsey took a pile of statements with him to go over later. His hotel room had become a second place of work when he could no longer cope with the constant interruptions in the office.

The two detectives had become bored with the food at The

Stag's Head and its lack of any discernible atmosphere. They decided to start having their evening meals in the restaurants and pubs around Kinlochleven to break the monotony.

They had become accustomed to the silence from the locals when they walked into the bar at the Tailrace Inn on Riverside Road. However, it was busy and the novelty of them being there soon dissipated. They began to relax a little. After a couple of pints to take the edge off, they both ordered the steak and ale pie from the standard pub grub menu.

'Today was another waste of time. We have no new leads whatsoever to go on,' said Dorsey, the stress etched on his face. 'I think if he was a local, we would have found him by now. My gut is telling me he may have some connection with this place, but doesn't actually live here.'

'He could be someone who comes here from time to time with his work, just passing through. Maybe a delivery driver?'

'Maybe, George, but the problem is that he probably looks as normal as the next person. Even psychos don't tend to broadcast that they are mad. The only thing we know about him is he uses the A82 as his main route to pick up his victims, although there's a possibility that he picked up Erin Keenan on the B863. If only there was CCTV on these bloody roads.'

'Frank, that's why he uses them. He knows how little CCTV there is around here.'

'With that much traffic on the A82 every day, it's hard to see how we pick him out if we've no idea what he looks like. We don't know what type of vehicle he drives or what he does for a living. The DNA screening is too slow.'

'I was speaking to one of the forensic team,' said Mitchell. 'They are using the electoral roll to invite people in to give their DNA swabs, but it's full of problems. Not everyone votes and some they've written to have been dead for years. They've taken dozens of angry phone calls from furious relatives.'

'That's why we need to focus on suspects fitting a forensic profile and bring them in first,' explained Dorsey. 'I've finally managed to arrange for Jenkins, Jamali, and Mackie to come to Glencoe this Wednesday and put their heads together to see if they can work out what type of killer we're dealing with.'

'Do you still think Erin Keenan is alive?'

'I have to think that until we find out otherwise.'

'He could have family connections here and that's how he knows the place so well?'

'Maybe … Anyway, I'd like you to be there on Wednesday along with Crawford. I'll have to run through the main points of the case for the benefit of the experts. I use that word loosely as far as Fiona Mackie is concerned, but I thought having her there would at least give the top brass some idea of the enormity of what we are dealing with here before they start complaining about their police budget again.'

'Is there anything you want me to do?'

'You can help me gather all the relevant evidence we have so they have everything they need before the meeting. I think I'll also ask DS Kilbride to be there.'

'No problem … I'll get the pints in. You're such a slow eater,' said Mitchell, getting up and heading to the bar.

Chapter 15

The following morning, Dorsey spent his time preparing for the meeting. With the help of Mitchell, he compiled a dossier of the evidence in the case to send to each expert to help them prepare in advance. The less time they had to spend going over the history of each case, the more time they'd have to concentrate on the suspect's profile. Even though there were thousands of statements, hours of video, and interview transcripts, virtually all of it failed to provide any evidence of value.

The DNA screening programme had so far been unable to identify a suspect. The profile from the dress material and the rucksack needed someone to match it with. The experts would have to make what they could from the other forensic evidence they had in relation to the dismembering of the two bodies, the use of dress material to wrap them in, and the type of victims the killer preferred: young females on their own in an area of Scotland where hitchhiking was not unusual … until now.

He double-checked everything before sending the emails. He was surprised to receive a response back from Dr Jamali within minutes, confirming she had received the attachments and would be travelling down that night. She suggested meeting up for dinner.

He left the office at lunchtime and headed back to the hotel to read the paperwork in his room. It was a cold but bright sunny day. The scenery was stunning. If he hadn't been dealing with the stress of the investigation, he might have taken more notice of the beauty of the place. He passed a young man with a backpack walking towards Kinlochleven with his thumb out for a lift. He was tempted to stop, only changing his mind on recalling the warning posters uniformed officers had spent weeks plastering all over the area about the dangers of accepting lifts from strangers. He accelerated around him, glancing in his rearview mirror. He smiled as the disgruntled hitchhiker put his thumb away and stuck up his middle finger.

After going through the summary he had written for the meeting, he had a shower to clear his head. He was thinking about what to wear; all he had in the wardrobe was a couple of work suits and half a dozen shirts that were looking washed out. Even his ties had been knotted and unknotted so many times they looked permanently twisted in places. He went into his holdall and lifted out a pair of jeans and a casual dark blue shirt.

While he was having a cigarette out on the balcony, his phone buzzed. It was a text from Dr Jamali. *I'm in the bar if you want to join me before dinner.* He sent a text back telling her he would be there in five minutes.

The bar was quite busy for a Monday night. He couldn't see the doctor until she waved and smiled at him from the other end of the bar. She was wearing a black evening dress and pearl necklace and looked like she was having dinner at the Ritz. He now wished he wore his suit; he felt a little awkward in his casual shirt and jeans.

'I know I'm a bit overdressed,' she said as he joined her at the bar, 'but I don't get out much these days. What are you having to drink?'

'I'll get it,' he replied, ordering a pint of lager. 'I'm feeling a bit underdressed.'

'No, you suit casual, it makes you look younger. This is a bit of a weird place,' she added, looking around at the various stuffed animals that Dorsey had become used to over the weeks and now hardly noticed.

'Yeah, I asked the manager about the over-the-top taxidermy. Apparently it was the previous owner's collection of things he'd killed over the years. Some of the Americans that come every year think they're wonderful. That's why the present owner decided to keep them.'

'I'm surrounded by dead things all day, but it's not what you want to be looking at when you're having dinner. Is this where you usually eat?'

'There's not a great deal of choice to be honest. At this time of year, some of the restaurants don't even open during the week.'

The doctor was easy company and liked talking. Dorsey was happy to listen when she began to tell him about her family's move to Scotland in 1979, when she was only two years old. The Iranian Revolution was something that Dorsey knew little about. For him, Iran was a country of Ayatollahs and religious fanatics that he had little interest in.

Dr Jamali explained how her family was forced to flee the country after the Shah went into exile. Her father was a Sunni Muslim and an important member of the Shah's inner circle. They had to get out. They left the country as the Ayatollah Khomeini returned from exile in Paris just weeks before the country became an Islamic republic. If they had not left when they did, there was little doubt her father would have been arrested and executed like so many of his family members and friends who left it too late to escape to the West. Apart from what she watched on TV, she had no memory of the country and would never return while it remained under the control of the Ayatollahs and their fanatical Shia supporters.

'Why did your family decide to come to Scotland of all places?'

'We lived in London for a few years before my father was eventually offered a professorship in planetology at

Edinburgh University.'

'I assume that's to do with the study of planets,' he asked, now drinking a whisky with his second pint.

'Yes. This probably sounds weird, but my father once told me that the Shah would ask him to read the stars and tell him what the future held for him. My father had to pretend to read them even though it was only planets he studied and he could hardly tell one star from another. This is even more weird – he warned the Shah about the revolution almost six months before it happened.'

'What, by reading the stars?'

'Of course not, I told you he couldn't read the stars. Well, no one can read the bloody things unless you believe in all that astrology nonsense. My father read an article in an American magazine about Jimmy Carter withdrawing his support from autocratic tyrants around the world, and the overthrow of the Shah was not a concern of the Americans. This was giving a green light to those already protesting for an Islamic republic. Obviously, my father couldn't show the Shah the article and had to pretend that he saw a revolution coming in the stars … There's a very good-looking woman just come in, looking a bit lost.'

Dorsey turned to see Liz; she was dressed as if she had just come straight from court. 'So, you made it,' he said, getting up to greet her with a kiss on the cheek. 'This is Dr Jamali, the pathologist on the case.'

'Just call me Sana. Dr Jamali sounds like I'm about to prescribe you something.'

'Pleased to meet you,' said Liz, taking her coat off. 'Frank has told me how helpful you've been with the case … I love your dress.'

The three of them had dinner together. The limited menu didn't impress Dorsey's two guests. After a couple of glasses of wine, Liz and Dr Jamali chatted incessantly as if they had known each other for years. With the after-dinner talk being all about things that Dorsey had no interest in, he paid the bill and made his excuses. He went upstairs for an early night, leaving the new best friends to get drunk together. They hardly noticed him getting up to leave.

Chapter 16

Wednesday: 4th of October 2023

After lunch, Dorsey had the incident room set up for the meeting that he hoped would give a direction for his team of detectives to pursue. He had asked Mitchell and Crawford to attend as heads of both sub-teams while PC Dixon would take minutes of the meeting.

CS Mackie arrived wearing her dress uniform as though she was appearing at a press conference. The epaulettes on her tunic displayed her status as Chief Superintendent of Police Scotland's Highland Division. Confident in her seniority, she took the seat at the top of the table, which she assumed her rank granted her. She was a woman in her late forties, with greying hair caught in a bun at the back of her head, keeping it clear of her stern, narrow face. She had travelled down from Inverness with Jock Kilbride, who was now having a cigarette in the car park after having to endure the chief superintendent for the two-hour drive from Inverness, which had tested his limited small talk skills to the maximum. Never had the draw of a cigarette felt so good.

After pleasantries were exchanged with the other detectives, CS Mackie asked if someone could fetch her a cup of tea. The other detectives turned to Dixon, who reluctantly got up to fetch it from the tea trolley. 'Just one sugar and a little milk,' she shouted after her.

Not long after the quorum of detectives was complete, Dr Jamali arrived with a briefcase full of documents which she emptied onto the table. She chatted with Mackie, whom she had known for years but hadn't seen since her promotion to chief superintendent.

Liz arrived shortly after, casually dressed in jeans and a sweater. Dorsey introduced her to the others and they waited another fifteen minutes before Professor Jenkins appeared, blaming ScotRail for being late. He took off his heavy coat and hat, placing them over a nearby chair. More out of habit than anything else, he then took out his gold pocket watch from his waistcoat, looking at it briefly as though he had somewhere else to be. He clicked it closed and took a seat opposite Dorsey.

'Chief Inspector, since you asked us all to be here, maybe you should give us a run-through of the case and evidence as it stands today,' suggested Mackie, in a tone of voice that was obviously acquired moving up the ranks to where she was now.

What would she sound like if she ever became chief constable? Dorsey wondered, as he began to go through the salient points of all three cases, referring to the contents of the dossier and using the incident boards as a prompt when necessary. 'I have decided to concentrate this meeting on the two murders as we have virtually no evidence in respect to Erin Keenan to consider. As it's now beyond doubt that the same individual abducted all three, any profile based on the forensics obtained from the two murder victims will be invaluable in our efforts to trace Erin Keenan. What I need to find out is the type of person you think is most likely to have committed these brutal crimes yet has no past criminal record.'

They all looked at each other, unsure about the pecking order or who was best qualified to answer first. All except Professor Jenkins, who had no doubt about whom Dorsey was looking to get the answer from, but the cagey old professor deferred his observations and invited Dr Jamali to provide a summary of her post-mortem findings.

Dr Jamali smiled at the professor, before speaking in a

132

very slow and precise manner. 'You'll see from my reports on both murder victims that the toxicology tests confirm the level of benzodiazepine and fentanyl found in the livers of both victims was the ultimate cause of death. The damage to the liver is the only perimortem injury found in both bodies, but there were also signs of respiratory issues, likely caused by the fentanyl. The large doses administered over the period of time they were captive resulted in increased liver enzyme levels and liver damage. Their high levels of sodium indicated that both likely suffered from dehydration and malnourishment, which would have been a contributing factor in their inability to absorb the drugs. The level of sedation was probably increased as the drug became less potent due to the victims' increasing tolerance. The stomach contents were negligible in both cases as it was likely neither had anything substantial to eat in the twenty-four hours prior to their deaths. Most likely because they were under the influence of the drug and incapable of eating, or the killer decided not to provide food as he no longer felt the need to.'

'Why would he do that?' asked Mackie.

'Because by that time his intention was to kill them and dispose of their bodies.'

'Could they not simply have been too scared to eat?' asked Liz, who was attentively taking notes.

'At first, their fear would certainly suppress any hunger, but as time went by their hunger would be powerful enough to demand satisfaction, despite the obvious terror they were enduring. They would not have survived so long if they'd not eaten.'

Liz nodded.

Dr Jamali passed around photographs of the victims from the pile of papers that she had in front of her before continuing. 'The likely date of death is detailed in my report and in the report from Edinburgh University, which tested the bones for calcium deterioration. It is estimated that the killer kept his victims alive for around two months after they were abducted before killing them and disposing of their remains.'

'So, he keeps them for sex and when he's bored with them, he murders them?' queried Mackie.

'As I've stated in my PM report, there's no evidence of sexual intercourse or any other sexual activity, although that doesn't mean there was none. He almost certainly has some other sexual perversion that drives him to commit these crimes. What that is remains to be determined. The ante-mortem and post-mortem injuries are also detailed in the report and there is no need for me to go into them, other than to say they are the same for both victims.'

'How did he dismember them?' asked Mackie, a question which showed everyone else at the table that she probably only gave the detailed dossier a cursory perusal.

'As I *stated* in my report, a sharp knife was used to cut the skin and ligaments from the bone. Some kind of saw, with relatively fine teeth, probably a hacksaw, was used, with the final break likely achieved with a cleaver.'

'Could he be a butcher or even work in a slaughterhouse?' asked Mackie.

'The cuts are not done with any real skill and I'd be surprised if he was someone who learned to do this professionally. The knowledge could've been gleaned from the dark web. It's his callous execution of the butchery that sets him apart from most killers. It's not easy to dismember a body; it takes a certain type of individual.'

'It's pretty gruesome,' said Mackie, her facial expression showing her revulsion.

'You'll see from the pictures that the body parts were wrapped in a blue cotton material which, when put together, made up two identical dresses and what was left was random sections of a third dress. The dress material was forensically examined and is the same cotton fabric used for both bodies which, along with the DNA recovered, confirms the same individual committed both crimes.'

Dr Jamali took a deep breath and looked for someone else to take over. Professor Jenkins had been unusually quiet while he listened to his former student without interrupting. He turned to her and smiled. 'Thank you, Sana, for that very concise and helpful summary. The years you spent listening to my ramblings at university weren't wasted.'

Dorsey noticed a slight blush on the doctor's cheeks, which he thought unusual for someone who was normally so comfortable in her own skin. He supposed everyone was the same; praise from our elders and superiors was always a difficult thing to take nonchalantly. He decided to spare her blushes and turned to the head of forensics to make his contribution. 'Since the issue of DNA has now been mentioned, maybe Jock could explain the problem of having an unidentified DNA profile and why the screening programme is necessary.'

Jock Kilbride began shifting through his papers to get the information he needed. He made a nervous cough, as the lab technician was not accustomed to speaking in such a forum. He passed around documents from the National Database website, containing lists and graphs that required explanation. He coughed again to clear his throat. 'Under the present law, police officers are legally entitled to obtain mouth and hair samples from arrested persons. From these samples, DNA profiles are extracted. DNA is the same for every person except for slight variations in the code which are responsible for different physical characteristics such as height, eye colour, skin tone, and hair colour. These differences are critical for the use of DNA in forensic science. When profiling, we don't examine all variations between individuals. Instead, we target areas of DNA that are known to differ widely between individuals. Other than gender, the areas of DNA we use don't contain information that could be attributed to physical characteristics such as eye or hair colour.'

'I think we are all aware of DNA, what does that mean in this case?' interrupted Mackie.

Her interruption put Jock off for a moment, and he coughed again before continuing. 'The hair found on the blue material on the torso of Lena Kaminski confirmed to us very quickly that we were dealing with a white male suspect. The nail scrapings from Evinka Janik confirmed we were dealing with the same individual for both murders. Unfortunately, even though we have two crime scene profiles of the suspect, he is *not* on the database. Therefore, a comparison cannot take place.'

'Jock, can you give us an update on the screening programme? I assume we are all here because no match has been found yet?' asked Mackie.

'The screening programme has already eliminated hundreds of males living in the ten-mile catchment area around Glencoe, but it's a slow and time-consuming procedure. My forensic team have also encountered several problems. Firstly, they're covering a vast, mainly remote, geographical area. They rely on the electoral register for the names and addresses to send the appointment letters. The obvious issue with this is that not everyone has registered themselves on the electoral roll. Others have moved away or died. But the biggest problem is that many have simply ignored the letters sent to them.'

'That's not what I was hoping to hear; this programme is costing the taxpayer a great deal of money. If it's not working, then maybe …'

'With all due respect, ma'am,' interrupted Dorsey, 'he didn't say it wasn't working. It has problems that'll take time to resolve, but we're eliminating hundreds from the enquiry every day, saving police time dealing with spurious allegations that are being made on a regular basis. It will eventually leave us with a manageable number of males in the area to concentrate our resources on.'

'Chief Inspector, it seems like it'll take forever. It's not like the killer is going to come in and give a swab.'

'That's not the point of the screening. Its primary function is to eliminate up to ninety percent of the adult male population in the area we are concentrating on.'

'Even so, it still seems like a bit of a sledgehammer to crack a nut.'

Dorsey decided he was not getting into a pointless argument with someone who was too lazy to even read the case papers. Even if she was his senior officer, he was still the SIO. 'I never asked everyone here to discuss the merits of the screening programme. It is what it is, ma'am.' His voice rose. 'If you have an issue with the cost of the programme, I suggest you take that up with the deputy chief constable. He authorised it!'

There was an awkward silence. The only sound was the nervous shuffling of papers and the torrential rain that was pouring down outside. Some in the room lowered their heads to look at their hands. Dorsey waited for a response, but Mackie didn't know how to reply. She wasn't used to being put in her place by a lower-ranking officer, even a chief inspector. She clasped her hands before responding weakly, 'Maybe I will.'

Crawford had to hide a grin with his hand.

'Before we go any further,' declared Professor Jenkins, the tone of his voice giving immediate gravitas to his words. 'We're here for one reason and one reason only, and that is to try to provide a profile of the killer. Everything else is police business and should be dealt with at the appropriate time. Let's all take ten minutes to calm down. I need a cup of strong tea. Then we can get back to doing the work Police Scotland is paying us to do.'

Chapter 17

Dorsey got up and immediately left the room before he said something he would regret. Mackie remained in her chair, her face fixed in an angry scowl. Everyone else congregated around the tea trolley.

Outside, Dorsey lit a cigarette, venting his anger at the miserable weather while the rain battered off the car park tarmac. He was sick of the place.

Liz came outside to check on him. 'You shouldn't speak to her like that. She's your boss.'

'She's an idiot.'

'She's only thinking of the budget and having to justify it to her bosses.'

'Liz, she doesn't need you to stand up for her.'

'I know, let's go back in. It's cold and miserable out here.'

'You go in. I'll be in when I finish this,' he said. 'I'll be alright, I'll just be relieved when she heads back up to Inverness.'

When he returned, everyone was seated. Professor Jenkins had his folder open and looked ready to start his contribution. Avoiding eye contact with the chief superintendent, Dorsey took his seat opposite the professor.

The professor tapped his fingers on the table, clearly waiting for everyone to settle down before beginning his observation. 'Good, let's get this over with. I've a dinner date back in Glasgow this evening and she doesn't like to be kept waiting. I've looked at all the papers and have come up with a profile of sorts, which I am happy to hear your views on.'

'Go ahead, Professor,' said Mackie, retaining her superior

tone.

'Firstly, I think it's not in dispute we are dealing with a white male. The DNA profile has confirmed that fact. Secondly, I believe we're dealing with one individual, a lone wolf, so to speak.' He raised his eyes over the rim of his narrow glasses to see if anyone had an issue with that observation. No one did. They were all too busy taking notes as though they were at one of his university forensic lectures. 'Thirdly, he is likely to be somewhere between his mid-twenties and mid-to-late forties.'

Liz put a question mark next to what sounded like an unsubstantiated fact and asked, 'Professor, how do you know he's in that age group?'

'I didn't say I knew, Miss Baxter, I said he's likely to be in that age group. The reason is simple: that's generally the age group of males that commit serial murders and violent sex crimes of this type. This is based on data collected over the last fifty years by the FBI and our own National Crime Agency. Serial killers outside that age range are rare.'

'Okay, but he could be older or even younger?'

'Miss Baxter, this is how profiling works. If I knew his exact age, I'd tell you his exact age. Any other questions before I go on?'

'No. Sorry, Professor, please continue,' said Liz, looking a little embarrassed.

'The fact that he used identical blue dress material to wrap the dismembered remains of both victims indicates a bizarre sexual fetish of some kind. It is almost certain from the sizes of the dresses when reassembled in the lab that they were specially made for them to wear while they were alive. As it has been confirmed, they were not commercially made and there's a strong likelihood he made them himself as part of his sexual fantasy. Although the dresses are not perfect, they're apparently made to the standard of a very good amateur dressmaker.'

'It reminds me of that freak in the *Silence of the Lambs* film who had a sewing machine,' said Liz. 'What was his name?'

'Hannibal Lecter,' said Crawford.

'No, it wasn't, he was the evil psychiatrist. The serial killer was Buffalo Bill; he used his victim's skin to make a dress for himself, something to do with metamorphosis,' explained Jock Kilbride. 'Our guy's mad, but not *that* mad.'

'Wouldn't that make a story?' said Jenkins sarcastically, beginning to look annoyed with the nonsense he had to listen to. He continued with his opinion. 'I understand from the reports that it has not been possible to find out where this material came from, which is a pity. However, this behaviour gives us some information about this man. He has obviously learned from someone how to use a sewing machine. According to the lady who examined the material, although not impossible, it's unlikely he simply taught himself from scratch to sew to this degree of competence.'

'Maybe he's been on *The Great British Sewing Bee*,' suggested Crawford, which even brought a smile to Mackie's face.

The professor ignored Crawford's comment. 'Furthermore, I note from the post-mortem report that both victims had traces of makeup on their skin and when these were forensically examined, they were found to have identical chemical compounds. Which, according to the expert who examined them, came from the same products. Since the two young women were held captive for around two months, this makeup must have been put on them. The likelihood is that their abductor instructed them to use the makeup or he put it on them himself, probably while they were heavily sedated.

'The two kirby grips found in the hair of the second victim are interesting. I understand it's rather old-fashioned and because both victims had their hair crudely cut short, a rather disturbing picture has developed in my mind. I believe they were dressed in the blue dresses, had makeup applied and had a wig of some sort attached to their own hair with kirby grips. Why would he do this?' He stopped speaking to look around the table.

'To make them look like someone he has had an obsession with,' said his former student, Dr Jamali.

The professor continued after taking a sip of cold tea. 'This obviously throws up an important question.' He stopped speaking again, raising his head as though waiting for a member of his class to put up their hand and provide the question so *he* could provide the answer. It was typical Jenkins; everything, even murder, was pure theatre to him.

'*Why*?' said Dr Jamali, obligingly.

'Exactly ... *Why*?'

'He has an Oedipus Complex,' suggested Dr Jamali, who was now back at university in her mind, and giving the critical answers the professor was looking for while the rest of the class sat in silence.

'Exactly,' he said.

'Professor, before you lose the rest of us, can you explain what this is? We didn't all do the classics at Oxford,' said Crawford, who was starting to think the whole profile exercise was just a waste of time.

'I think Dr Jamali can explain it as well as I can,' said Jenkins in his usual condescending manner, even when offering what might have been intended as a compliment.

Dr Jamali was in her element. She began to explain what the professor taught her, back when she was his brightest student. 'The syndrome is based on the Greek myth of Oedipus, who developed an infatuation for his mother and conversely a hatred for his father, whom he saw as a rival for his mother's affection. Freud developed this type of thinking and how it explains the psychosis that can lead certain individuals to suffer from mental illness and often

141

extreme criminal behaviour based on a memory of someone they were obsessed with. The condition is often explained as a narcissistic personality disorder. Not everyone who has this condition goes on to be a criminal and may simply grow out of it by the time they reach adulthood.'

Dr Jamali looked up from her notes briefly to see how well the Oedipus theory was going down, then continued. 'This individual has had something happen to him in childhood or even later in life that has caused a critical malfunction in his mind. He may have been a child that was abused by a parent or someone else who had authority over him.'

'Like a priest?' suggested Crawford.

'Maybe,' said Jenkins, wiping his glasses with a tissue. 'I believe we may be dealing with someone who has a mother obsession, which might explain the dressmaking skill and the fact he is likely to have put his victims in a style of dress that he remembers his mother wearing on some occasion that has become fixated in his mind. His mother may have either been his abuser, or saved him from being abused; perhaps by a violent, sexual deviant father or even a stepfather. That is the most common reason for the condition to develop into a violent or sexual aberration in later years, although not exclusive.'

'Professor, the fact that he makes dresses and has likely done so for quite some time … would that suggest a feminine trait? Something his abuser found distasteful?' asked Liz, hoping he wasn't going to deride her question like he did the last time.

'That's a possibility. He may have a gender issue on top of the abuse that's added to his isolation and deviant way of thinking. It is almost certain that he has been isolated for most of his life, probably an only child who had no real friends. Even if not convicted for any crime, he may also have been institutionalised in a psychiatric hospital for lengthy periods of his life or put in the care of the social work department

142

and maybe even placed in foster care for some time. This person looks like he's never been in prison, otherwise you'd not only have his DNA on the database, but his fingerprints. He would have been caught within hours of those checks being done if he had a criminal record.'

'Could it be someone other than the mother?' asked Mitchell, breaking his silence for the first time. 'What if someone had rejected him, like a wife or girlfriend?'

'That's also very possible. The main point I am trying to make is that we've someone who may have sought medical treatment in the past or been sectioned under the Mental Health Act. I think, Chief Inspector, that is a line of enquiry you should consider looking at.'

'Professor, what about motive?' asked Mackie.

'I would've thought that was obvious. He does it to vent the anger trapped inside his mind since childhood and, unfortunately, he gets pleasure from it. He's now the one in control, probably for the first time in his life.'

'What if he *was* charged with a crime in the past and his mental illness was used as a defence? How would that have been dealt with?' asked Mitchell, looking up from his notebook again and turning in Liz's direction.

'If that was the case and a special defence under S51A was accepted, which is essentially the same as the common law plea of insanity, then it would result in an acquittal.'

'So, he'd just walk free?' continued Mitchell, a man who Dorsey knew only spoke when he had something meaningful to say.

'It depends on his mental condition at the time of the acquittal. If the person is no longer deemed to be suffering from a mental illness, then they are free to leave the court and an acquittal is recorded, as if he or she was never charged or prosecuted.'

Mitchell continued to press Liz. 'So, he'd have no criminal record.'

'Yes. If the crime was minor then the Crown would probably just drop the case after consideration of the psychiatric reports. Even if the matter did proceed, the most the court would be able to do is order the accused, if still suffering from the mental illness, to continue or obtain medical treatment for whatever illness they suffered from,' explained Liz, with the confidence of a lawyer, who had prepared her brief.

'What if the crime was serious and the person was still regarded as insane?' asked Mitchell, who looked like he was enjoying having control of the agenda for a while.

'If the alleged crime was serious and the defence of insanity was upheld but the person was still assessed as mentally ill, a hospital order would be made and the accused would be sectioned to the care of the appropriate hospital. In many cases where the crime is regarded as heinous or the accused is seen as a danger to the public that would likely be the State Hospital at Carstairs.'

'Thank you, Miss Baxter,' said Mitchell, avoiding using her first name and keeping proceedings formal as if he was in a courtroom. 'Just one other thing. If he gave a DNA swab and was acquitted, what would happen to that profile?'

'What *should* happen is a better question. According to section 18 of the Criminal Procedure Act, it should have been destroyed, as is the case for all accused who are acquitted in a criminal court. Maybe Jock is better qualified to explain what happens to these samples.'

Jock looked blindsided, clearly unprepared to answer the question Liz Baxter had batted so deftly in his direction. He shuffled his papers again, making his customary nervous cough before speaking. He read directly from the document that was now in front of him. 'The retention of DNA is dependent on the outcome of the case.' He coughed again before finding his stride. 'It can be retained indefinitely after a conviction but must be destroyed if the accused is found not guilty. However, there are exceptions allowing DNA to be retained in specific sexual or violent offences even where those proceedings end without a conviction. In such cases their DNA data can be retained for three years, but the court can extend this in special circumstances. With all other offences it can be retained for two years after which it *must* be destroyed. That period cannot be extended.'

'If a person is sectioned after they are acquitted due to an insanity plea, how long are they kept in hospital?' asked Dorsey, who had been unusually quiet.

'How long they're sectioned for would be for the doctors treating them and the Mental Health Tribunal to decide. Most of those with high-risk levels of mental health issues may never get out, whether they committed a crime or not,' explained Liz.

'But there must be plenty that do,' queried Mackie.

'I wouldn't know, but I'd expect so,' replied Liz.

'What about the fact he dismembered the bodies and hung them on hooks to bleed them?' asked Crawford. 'Would that not make him some kind of psycho?'

'Well, exactly, although I prefer to use the proper word *psychopath*,' said the professor, stealing another look at his watch. 'He obviously cut up the body to dispose of it, but most people who have been convicted of murder would not be able to carry out such a gruesome task. That behaviour would point to a psychopathic personality, someone who lacks fear or has no empathy for what he has done. This makes this killer a very dangerous and ruthless individual.'

The meeting continued for a further hour, but the main idea that came out of the discussion for Dorsey was the fact they may be dealing with a killer with a history of mental illness that could be traced. It would fit the profile Jenkins had so clearly explained. If the killer had been charged in the past, he could've simply been acquitted without leaving a trace on police files, and any DNA or fingerprints would have been destroyed. On the other hand, Dorsey knew that this was all hypothetical and that there was every chance the killer had never been arrested before and that was the simple reason he was not on any police systems.

Crawford was given the task of conveying the salient points of the meeting to the rest of the team at the shift change so everyone could focus on the enormous task of going over those previously interviewed who might fit the profile. Using the professor's profile of the killer, with the help of Dixon's copious notes, the detectives were instructed to immediately eliminate all males under twenty-one or over fifty years old and those with siblings. They were looking for a loner, someone who lived in isolation and had some history of mental illness. They began to check online for any historical crimes going back twenty years. With nearly fifteen thousand sex-related crimes recorded in Scotland every year, the task was daunting. The geographical area had now expanded to cover the whole of Scotland.

Before he left, Dorsey asked Crawford to give the same instructions to the backshift squad, who often had little or nothing to do during the night shift other than laboriously go through statements of witnesses who had little to add, if anything, to the enquiry.

He then drove back to the hotel to get changed. He was taking Liz to The Lobster Pot for dinner to thank her for coming to the meeting.

Chapter 18

Monday: 9th of October 2023

With hundreds of old, weird, and hopeless cases being collated online, the incident room had become awash with possible suspects, with detectives flagging up a new one every couple of hours. After nearly a week of this frenzied activity, Dorsey had had enough and decided it was time to rein in their enthusiasm and prevent his head from bursting. He held an impromptu briefing to try to get the genie back into the bottle.

'This is not a criticism,' he began. Everyone in the incident room braced themselves to be criticised. 'We've got to get a handle on the type of cases you're bringing to DI Crawford and myself to look at. Firstly, check if the potential suspect is dead!'

There was laughter, but not from the few who had failed to check this crucial fact.

'Secondly, check if he was in prison during the dates we know these women went missing. If he was, then he's obviously not our guy. The same goes for those that ended up in the State Hospital, or any other hospital for that matter.'

Crawford pitched in with his own grievances. 'Someone kindly brought me a case from 1996, the guy was in his late fifties at the time. For God's sake, do the maths. Use the profile that you've been given; that's why we gave it to you. I know we're all desperate to find this bastard, but give me and the chief inspector a break. Make sure you cover all the basics before you decide to bang on about a crime you found on some dodgy website.'

147

'Okay, briefing over, back to work,' ordered Dorsey, sure that it would make them all think twice before bringing another pile of suspects for him to work through. He went back to his office.

Crawford followed him in and closed the door. 'Can we have a chat, Frank?'

'Take a seat, Bill. You've obviously got something on your mind.'

'Frank, I'm not sure how you're going to take this.'

'Try me.'

'I was in one of the local pubs the other night having a few beers with some of the lads, when I noticed Alex Munro sitting on his own. He's a strange-looking character and he didn't speak to anyone the whole time he was there, except the barmaid when he went up to the bar and ordered his beer. Even then he hardly said two words to her.'

'Okay, he's a man who keeps himself to himself.'

'For some reason, he made me think about the profile we've been working with.'

'Is this going where I think it's going?'

'Hear me out, Frank. You know his sister is a district nurse?'

'Yeah. I met her when I went to see him.'

'I spoke to Dixon yesterday to find out what she knew about him. Munro apparently moved to Glencoe to live with his sister in 2018. That was a year before Lena Kaminski disappeared, two years before Evinka Janik. Dixon said he was medically discharged from the army after being blown up by a roadside bomb in Afghanistan. That's all she could tell me about him.'

'I've got a feeling you've done some more digging.'

'I found out the regiment he was in from a couple of locals in the pub – it cost me fifty quid. It happens to be the same regiment Jock Kilbride served in as a medical reservist. Jock didn't know him personally, but said he had a few friends still in the regiment that he could speak to. He phoned me an hour ago.'

'Go on.'

'Jock told me that Munro was invalided out of the army after his Land Rover was blown up by a roadside bomb in Afghanistan.'

'Bill, you could have asked me all this. He told me what happened to him. Munro and his dog were badly injured.'

'No, not according to Jock. Munro's dog was killed.'

'You mean Major?'

'If that's what it's called.'

'Maybe it was another army dog he was given when he was discharged, and that's the one he now calls Major.'

'Not according to Jock's army friend. There is no chance he'd be given another cadaver dog. Do you know how much time and effort it takes to train these dogs? Anyway, he wasn't in any position to look after one. Munro was hospitalised for a long time after he was injured. There was some gossip in the regiment that he ended up in a psychiatric hospital, but he wasn't sure about that.'

'Is that it?' asked Dorsey, not convinced that what he heard amounted to enough to think Munro was now their prime suspect.

'You've been banging on about using the profile the professor came up with. That's what I've been doing. Think about it. He's a loner. His sister is a nurse, so he's got access to drugs. He has no previous convictions, so he's not on the DNA database. He has likely been in a psychiatric ward and he only came back here to live shortly before Lena Kaminski was murdered. He fits the profile.'

'Okay, what else have you managed to dig up about him?'

'That's it. I contacted the regiment's discharge unit and advised them of the nature of our investigation, but they refused to give me any information about him without a warrant. You could get that warrant.'

'Bill, I am not sure where all this takes us. Do you really think he's our serial killer? It was Munro and his dog that found the body in the first place. Why would he do that?'

'I don't know, maybe to make us think it couldn't be him. I'd like to at least put him under surveillance and get a warrant to get his army records released.'

'Bill, can you give me a bit of time to think this over? I'll let you know what I think before the end of the shift.'

'There's one other thing. He was one of the first to get a letter asking him to provide a voluntary DNA sample. He didn't respond to that or a follow-up request.'

'Fuck, okay. I don't think it's him, but you've convinced me he must be looked at as a possible suspect. Put him under twenty-four-hour surveillance. I'll try to get the warrant for his army records, including the medical records. This is good detective work, Bill. If it's him, I'll make sure you get the credit you deserve.'

'Frank, I don't want the credit. It's teamwork. We all get the credit.'

'In the meantime, make sure only the officers you put on the surveillance are told Munro is a suspect. I don't want this spreading around the station. That's how things leak from an investigation. If it is him, we want him to lead us to where he's keeping Erin Keenan. If it's not already too late.'

Dorsey sat in silence for a long time after Crawford left. He had a new respect for the man he had been so dismissive of when they first met at Lairigmor. Even if it turned out not to be Munro, it was good detective work to even find out what he had discovered with a little bit of lateral thinking. It was their first serious suspect, and the fact Munro had not provided the voluntary DNA sample was at least suspicious. He looked at the list of main points he had noted during the profile meeting and ticked them off. He then wrote down a corresponding profile of Munro: male, comfortably within the age range, access to drugs, seen as a bit of a loner, not on the police DNA database, no criminal record, drives and has his own vehicle, lives in the area with a good knowledge of the terrain, and he lied about the dog. The only question mark he put was against Munro's mental health.

Chapter 19

It was just after 8 a.m. the next morning. Crawford and Grant drove to the north side of the loch to relieve the two detectives who had spent the night waiting for Munro to leave his sister's house. They had nothing to report to the inspector other than that Munro had arrived at the house in his Jeep and never left.

'He's still in there. I take it he doesn't have any work to go to?' asked one of the detectives, handing Crawford his binoculars and high-spec zoom camera. 'I took a few pictures when he arrived, and that was it.'

'I hope he didn't see you sitting here. I don't want the bastard to know we're on to him,' said Crawford, who was now convinced that Munro was the serial killer.

'No chance. He turned onto his driveway and went straight into the house with the dog. He didn't stop and look around or anything, and he can't see the car from the house. I had to cross over to get a look at him through those bushes.' The DC pointed to a gap in a yew hedge on the other side of the road.

'Okay, you two head back to the hotel and get some breakfast. Same time tonight, unless you hear from me. Remember, no one is to know we're doing this. Report everything back to me.'

As the other car made a U-turn and headed back towards the A82, DS Grant bumped their car onto the grass verge. Crawford got out to have a closer look at the house through the gap in the hedge. The place was still. Munro's Jeep and his sister's hatchback were in the driveway, and there were no lights on in the house. He used the binoculars to zoom up to the large front window that he took to be the living room, but all he could see was the reflection from the glass.

He went back to the car to speak to Grant. 'Wonder when the sister starts doing her rounds?'

'If she's a district nurse, probably when it suits her. We're not following her, are we?'

'No, but maybe we should've brought another car. What if they're in it together and the sister knows where he keeps them? I should've asked Dorsey.'

'Why do you need to ask him? This is your idea, not his. Do you want me to phone and get someone to come out here and tail her if she appears? We don't need to tell Dorsey anything.'

'No, leave it. We'll concentrate on Munro. I'll speak to Dorsey tonight when we get back.'

Grant shook his head and went back to scrolling through his WhatsApp messages. He was unhappy that Crawford seemed to have changed his attitude towards the chief inspector, and it was beginning to get to him.

'I think we should find somewhere else to park. We're too obvious sitting here,' said Crawford, turning on the ignition.

'Where else is there? The loch is on one side and there's nowhere to park on the other side and still be able to see the path to their house. If they do come out, they can drive either way around the loch.'

'Look!' said Crawford. 'We're too late now to do anything.'

The Kia hatchback drove onto the main road and was now heading straight towards them. They both sank down in their seats as the sister's car approached slowly. Eileen Munro stared at them for a few seconds as she passed by, before changing up gear and heading off in the direction of the Ballachulish Bridge.

'Shit, I think she's on to us,' said Crawford. 'She's probably on the phone to the brother right now.'

'Fuck. Then we can't stay here. Let's find somewhere else to park before he clocks us next.'

Dorsey was about to leave when Crawford returned to the station, looking glum. He had spent the entire day waiting for Munro to leave his house. Apart from taking his dog for a walk along the shore of the loch, the suspect had remained in his house and out of sight of the two frustrated detectives.

'This might cheer you up,' said Dorsey, handing him a copy of the warrant to obtain Munro's army history and medical records. 'We've already instructed to have it served on the MOD, and we should get a response tomorrow.'

'Why don't we just get a warrant to search his house and get him to provide a DNA sample?'

'If he's got her then she's not in that house. His sister lives there, for God's sake. I checked Google Earth and, apart from the house, the only outbuilding is a small garden shed. We managed to get the floor plan from the builders. The house is just over twenty years old. It has an alley kitchen, a living room downstairs, and two bedrooms and a bathroom upstairs. There's no basement area under the house.'

'What about a loft?'

'There is a loft, but you've seen the pictures of the bodies. He didn't do all that in a loft.'

'Okay, I agree, but there must be somewhere else he keeps them.'

'If you're right about him, we must bide our time. We need him to lead us to where Erin Keenan is. If we bring him in, we need grounds to charge him to get a swab, otherwise he can just refuse to give one. He's not going to tell us where she is if we arrest him and his lawyer advises him to make no comment, swab or no swab.'

'Frank, I know all that, but if he knows we're on to him,

he might never lead us to her. What if she dies of hunger while he sits in his fucking house watching telly all day?'

'Why would he think we're on to him?' asked Dorsey, fearing the answer.

'His sister came out this morning when we had just arrived to relieve the night shift. She drove by slowly and stared at us. I think she knew who we were. Then again, maybe she didn't and I'm getting a bit paranoid.'

'Okay, we need to get his military and medical records tomorrow. I'll chase it up first thing. Hopefully the night shift gets a result before then.'

'You head back up the road and if anything comes in, I'll phone you.'

'Up the road? Frank, I've been staying at the Ballachulish Hotel for the last three weeks. The drive up and down from Inverness was killing me. Half my team is staying in it. Mackie agreed to it.'

'That makes sense.'

Crawford's mobile phone buzzed. He looked at the text message and his sullen face broke into a grin. 'That's the other surveillance team. Munro's on the move. They're tailing him towards the Ballachulish Bridge.'

'Okay, make sure their GPS is on. We'll get it up on my computer.'

They went into Dorsey's office and closed the door. Even though the other detectives, including Mitchell, had been kept in the dark, they knew something was going on. Dorsey switched on the GPS tracking app that immediately showed the Glencoe area in 3D format. There was a flashing red light that pinpointed the unmarked police vehicle on the B863, heading west. Crawford let out a deep breath and ran his hands through what was left of his hair.

The flashing stopped at the bridge for a few seconds before moving off again and onto the A82, now heading southeast on the south side of the loch. 'He's heading this way. Maybe we should get another car to take over in case he spots them following,' suggested Dorsey.

'I'll do it. The other car can fall back and follow me on their GPS,' said Crawford, just as his phone bleeped. 'Munro's stopped at a petrol station just outside Ballachulish.'

Time seemed to stand still as they watched the stationary dot flashing in the same spot for nearly ten minutes. Then it began to move. Crawford wiped the sweat from his brow, the tension getting to him as he watched the dot move slowly through Ballachulish, making its way to Glencoe village.

'I think you should at least let them tail Munro for a couple more miles. You can take over when he reaches the village; he's got the option then to either carry on the A82 south or take the B863 back along the south of Loch Leven,' said Dorsey without taking his eyes off the tracker as it entered the village and stopped again.

'If he thinks he's being followed, maybe he's just taking the piss!' sighed Crawford, pulling up his belt which immediately fell back to its preferred fold in his midriff. His mobile buzzed again. 'Shit, what's he up to? He's just stopped outside the station.'

Alex Munro paced up and down the small reception area after pressing the bell on the counter longer than was necessary, causing everyone in the station to look up from their desks. The duty sergeant made his way to the front counter to find out who was being so impatient.

'We're not all deaf in here, Alex. What's the problem?'

'I want to speak to the chief inspector!'

'He's just about to go off duty. Can I help?'

'No, Malcolm, you can't. Tell him I want to speak to him right now or I'm lodging a complaint!'

'Take a seat, Alex, and calm down. I'll have a word with him.'

Dorsey could hear Munro shouting from his office and

156

turned to Crawford. 'I think he wants to speak to you?'

'Well, it sounds like he's asking for you, boss,' replied Crawford, his face flushed and looking like he was on the verge of a heart attack as the duty sergeant knocked and put his head round the door.

'Sir, Alex Munro.'

'It's okay, Malcolm, take him through to the interview room. I'll speak to him in a minute. Bill, you head off. The operation is over for now. Get some sleep. I'll let you know what our next move will be in the morning.'

'This case is doing my head in. I need a drink,' responded Crawford, before leaving without another word.

Dorsey let Munro sit for a while to cool down. Even though they had their suspicions about him, there was absolutely no evidence that Munro was the killer. This was going to be awkward. He looked through the list of circumstantial evidence again that fit the professor's profile. Male, within the age range, lived in the area at the times of the disappearances, has knowledge of the terrain, has his own transport, and possible access to drugs through his sister. It all amounted to nothing; half the male population in the ten-mile catchment area fit the first five traits. Half again would have some access to medication that could be used to sedate a victim. Failing to provide the voluntary DNA sample was also not evidence, as there were still hundreds who hadn't come forward.

'Sir, Munro is banging on the interview room door and demanding you see him now,' said the duty sergeant.

Dorsey entered the interview room, bracing himself for a tirade of abuse, but Munro just sat there with his arms folded and stared at him.

'What's the problem, Alex?' he ventured.

'I'm not speaking in here with all this shit.' He nodded to the CD recorder and then the CCTV camera on the wall above Dorsey's head.

'They're not on. This is not an interview, just a chat. What are you afraid of?'

'I'm afraid of nothing, but how do I know they're not on?'

Dorsey pressed the power button, the recorder flashed and bleeped, and the empty CD compartment opened. 'There's nothing in it to record on, and if the CCTV was recording you'd see a red light come on underneath the camera. We can't record anyway without your knowledge and without a lawyer present. It would be inadmissible in court. So, do you want to tell me why you're here?'

'You've put me under surveillance. Why?'

Dorsey knew he couldn't deny the surveillance which had been a bit of a fiasco and probably a mistake in the first place. 'We have a duty to eliminate everyone we can from this enquiry. Those who failed to provide a voluntary DNA sample when asked put themselves under suspicion. That is the whole point of the screening process. You haven't provided a sample after you were sent two separate requests to come forward. Why?'

'I don't have to, it's voluntary.'

'By not coming forward, that puts you on a list of people we couldn't eliminate and who we've a duty to look at closer,' said Dorsey, maintaining a moral high ground that he didn't feel he deserved to be on.

'I'm not the only one who didn't give a sample. Half the guys in the pub said they were not providing one. Have you put all of *them* under surveillance?'

'No, not yet. Why wouldn't you help with the investigation by giving a sample?'

'The same reason the rest are not giving one. We know that once we give it, you lot just keep it on the police database forever. I've checked it online. You're supposed to remove it if someone is eliminated, but you don't. I don't want the police having my DNA on your database forever.'

'I know what's been in the paper and I know what's on the internet, but we've a legal duty to remove any voluntary DNA profiles that don't match our suspects.'

'Nobody trusts the police to do that. I trusted you, but instead of coming and saying all this to me, you've had me followed. It was me that found the first body and it was me that got more men and dogs involved that found the second one, and you put me under fucking surveillance as a suspect!'

'Trust works both ways. I can say the same thing about trust to you.'

'What do you mean?'

'You told me your cadaver dog was injured and the army gave it to you when you were discharged after your Land Rover was blown up by a roadside bomb.'

'And?'

'Well, that's not completely true, is it?'

'How do you think I ended up like this!?' shouted Munro, turning the scarred side of his face towards Dorsey.

'I know you suffered that injury from an IED, but your dog was also killed along with the driver, and the army never gave you Major. He's not an army dog and probably not a cadaver dog either. So you lied to me.'

Munro bowed his head and was silent for a moment. When he looked back up at the chief inspector there were tears in his eyes. 'How'd you find that out?'

'That doesn't matter. Is it true?' Dorsey waited for a response.

The ex-soldier seemed to be reliving the trauma of the explosion. His hands started shaking and his eyes became blank, spit bubbling from his mouth.

'Are you okay?'

He was far from okay, but before Dorsey could get to him, he fell off the chair, hitting his head hard on the floor. The convulsions now took over the whole body as if he had just received an electric shock. Dorsey took off his jacket and put it under Munro's head before turning him on his side. He put his fingers in Munro's mouth to make sure he wasn't choking on his tongue before calling for help.

Within ten minutes, a paramedic who lived in the village and worked with the mountain rescue team arrived. He explained to Dorsey that Munro was prone to seizures and he had dealt with him in the past. After an anticonvulsant injection was administered, the spasms stopped and the colour slowly came back to Munro's ashen face, but he was still in a daze and unable to get to his feet. The medic carried out various tests that confirmed his blood pressure levels had become dangerously low. 'He'll be okay. He'll need to rest to let the medication stabilise the condition.'

'He hit his head when he fell on the floor.'

The paramedic gently felt the lump that was on the side of Munro's skull and made an immediate decision. 'He'll have to go to A&E in Fort William. He's likely to be suffering from concussion and maybe even a fractured skull.'

'Will I call an ambulance?'

'No, I'll take him. By the time an ambulance gets here I'll be halfway to Fort William.'

'I'll send a marked police car to escort you to the hospital. Thanks for all your help and for coming out at this time of night.'

'It's not a problem, Chief Inspector. The guy's a war hero!'

Munro was assisted out to the paramedic's car and helped into the passenger's seat by two uniformed officers. Within minutes it was on the A82 heading north at speed. Dorsey phoned Munro's sister and explained what had happened to her brother and offered to send a car to take her to the hospital. She declined the offer.

The drama was over.

The shattered chief inspector drove back to his hotel, desperate to get his suit off and have a shower. The words

The guy's a war hero repeated in his tired mind like a mantra.

He was too late for the restaurant and ordered room service. He fell asleep on top of the bed before it arrived. After a few knocks failed to get a response, the night porter left the tray at the door.

Chapter 20

Driving to Fort William, Eileen Munro was not too concerned. She had picked up Alex in the past from the same hospital after he had one of his seizures. She often had to deal with his attacks by giving him his injection. He was usually fine within twenty minutes. She was surprised the paramedic had felt it necessary to take him to the hospital, but she wasn't aware that he had suffered a fall and injury to his head.

It was only when she got to the Accident and Emergency department at the Belford Hospital that the seriousness of her brother's condition became a concern.

After losing consciousness in the paramedic's car on the way to Fort William, Alex was immediately admitted to intensive care. She felt her knees going weak when the doctor explained that her brother was in theatre undergoing an emergency operation for a suspected brain haemorrhage.

She spent the rest of the night in the waiting room until the ICU doctor approached her and confirmed that Alex was now out of theatre but in an induced coma on a life support machine.

She asked to see him. The doctor nodded, and she followed him along one corridor and down another to the ICU ward, where she was able to look through the glass panel to where he was lying.

He was unconscious. The only thing moving was his chest with the help of a ventilator. An intravenous drip was attached to his arm while a heart monitor bleeped monotonously at the side of the bed.

Her breathing was heavy as she noticed the post-operation skull cap that covered the scars of the surgery.

His long hair had been shaved off. The old plastic surgery scars, which were normally hidden by his shoulder-length hair, made the side of his face look like melted plastic. She usually avoided looking at the damage to his face, but now she couldn't stop staring at it. The pain he had suffered must have been horrendous, but he never complained – not to her anyway. His face sallow and gaunt, he now looked like an old man and not the young handsome boy she remembered from the first time he arrived home in his uniform, his face beaming with pride. For some reason, the words of a Wilfred Owen poem she had learned at school came to mind: *To children ardent for some desperate glory, the old lie: Dulce et decorum est pro patria mori.* The tears ran down her face as the doctor took her arm and led her away.

She was advised to go home and get some rest. They now had to wait and see how his body responded to the operation. 'We have your number and we'll contact you if there's any change in him,' said the young doctor, who walked with her to her car.

Chapter 21

By the next morning, everyone in the station was aware of the botched surveillance of Alex Munro and his seizure in the interview room. Most were shocked that the man who found Lena Kaminski was even a suspect.

It was midday before Munro's medical records were emailed to the station. Dorsey scrolled down the pages to the period leading up to his discharge from the army in 2015. According to the surgeons treating him, he had been lucky to survive the explosion that had left parts of his body broken and stripped of flesh. The report confirmed he had undergone extensive plastic surgery to the whole side of his face and body, which took most of the blast that killed the driver. There was no mention of the dog, but Dorsey reckoned that wouldn't be of interest to those treating him.

He took a deep breath when he reached the psychiatric reports, which were extensive. He wasn't sure how he felt at that moment, part of him hoping that Munro wasn't their man, which seemed counterintuitive to his overwhelming desire to find the killer. It was no surprise to him that Munro suffered from PTSD after what had happened to him. The doctors confirmed that while recovering from the horrendous physical injuries, their patient's mental state deteriorated rapidly. Instead of a lengthy period of convalescence, he was transferred to a psychiatric hospital.

For the next six months, Munro's mind had descended into depression and intermittent episodes of delirium, with unpredictable violent outbursts. He was heavily sedated for lengthy periods until his gradual recovery and subsequent discharge in 2016. The covering letter from his GP confirmed a lengthy list of medications that he was still taking daily, which included benzodiazepine and fentanyl to deal with seizures.

Dorsey felt the sickness rise in his stomach. Maybe Crawford was right. Even though what he read in the medical reports gave him a degree of sympathy for Munro, if he was the killer then that sympathy was misplaced. He had to do his job and get a DNA sample one way or another. Then he remembered that Munro's Jeep was parked outside. He looked at the covering letter from the GP and phoned the surgery.

'Can you put me through to Alex Munro's doctor, please?'

'Can you give me your name and date of birth, please?'

'I'm not a patient. I'm Chief Inspector Frank Dorsey.'

'Can I ask you what it's about?'

'No, just tell the doctor I need to speak to him urgently!'

'Hold the line and I'll see if he's free.'

Dorsey tapped his pen on his desk, listening to a piece of annoying music for a few minutes before the doctor took his call.

'How can I help you, Chief Inspector?'

'Thank you, Doctor, for sending the medical reports of Alex Munro so promptly.'

'I didn't have much of a choice.'

'I see that Munro has a history of seizures, and he's on long-term medication for them.'

'That's correct.'

'I take it he's not fit to drive with this condition?'

'Yes, that's also correct. I reported this to DVLA shortly after he moved to our practice and first complained of seizures. He was sent for a brain scan, which confirmed a neurological post-traumatic condition that was caused by the injuries he suffered in Afghanistan. His licence was revoked on medical grounds.'

'Thank you, Doctor. That's what I thought.'

He stopped tapping his pen and called the forensic lab in Inverness.

He then went out to the front of the police station where Munro's mud-splattered Jeep was parked on the pavement and put on a pair of latex gloves to try the door handle on the driver's side. It opened. Munro must have been in such a rage that he didn't even bother to lock it. He looked around the dashboard, avoiding touching anything. There were scores of cigarette ends in a polyester cup, a half-empty bottle of Irn Bru, and a pair of muddy boots in the footwell on the passenger's side. In the back was the dog's cage with an old tartan blanket covered in dog hairs and mud. There was nothing obviously suspicious in the Jeep, but he knew he now had Munro's DNA once Jock and his team got their hands on the vehicle.

He lit a cigarette and waited for the tow truck that was on its way from a garage in Kinlochleven. He knew by the end of the day they would find out if Munro was in any way involved in the two murders and abduction of Erin Keenan.

Mitchell, who had been watching him from the station, went out to speak to him. 'You really don't think it's him, do you?'

'He fits the profile.'

'Frank, that profile could fit half the detectives in here. It's too vague.'

'Okay, but then we'll eliminate him. If it isn't him and he'd given a DNA sample when he was asked, then he'd have saved us all this bother.'

'I phoned the hospital, but they wouldn't tell me much. They confirmed he's still there and will be for a while.'

'That will give forensics enough time to get his DNA from his Jeep and any other evidence they might find. He shouldn't be driving this thing anyway. I spoke to his GP;

his licence was revoked on medical grounds. It's going to be impounded after Jock's finished with it. Even if he's not the killer, he's facing a charge of driving while disqualified and the court will likely forfeit it.'

'I think this is all wrong – we'd never have found those bodies if it wasn't for him. Crawford was wrong before and he's wrong again,' said Mitchell, turning to go back into the station.

Dorsey sighed and threw his half-smoked cigarette into the drain at his feet.

It was after 5 p.m. when confirmation came in from the lab that the Jeep had safely arrived in Inverness and their forensic team was working on it. Fingerprint lifts were taken from various parts of the car and crucial DNA samples were obtained from the Irn Bru bottle and the cigarette ends. A full forensic examination of the Jeep was ongoing and everything else recovered from it. Jock Kilbride advised Dorsey that he was confident that if Erin Keenan had ever been in the Jeep, he'd find some trace evidence of her.

While he waited for the results from Inverness, an email arrived from Munro's regiment. He read through the various conduct reports of his time in the army, virtually all positive and often glowing. There were even two bravery commendations and one recommendation for the military cross for actions under enemy fire during a mission behind Taliban lines. The pages and pages of redacted material made the rest of the report impossible to read. The redacted sections mainly related to a six-month period prior to the accident that brought an end to his time in Afghanistan. The document was signed by the Regimental Colonel, Julian Chambers OBE.

He phoned the number under the colonel's name and was surprised to be immediately put through.

'This is Chief Inspector Frank Dorsey of Police Scotland. Is that Colonel Chambers?'

'Yes, how can I help you, Chief Inspector?'

'I received the army records of Alex Munro.'

'Yes, I ordered that they be sent to you.'

'You'll have seen from the warrant that was sent to the regiment the other day that we are dealing with a murder investigation.'

'Is Munro a suspect in your murder investigation?'

'He is one of many suspects we are looking at, but that's about as much as I can tell you at the moment. The report you sent contains large sections of redacted material. The warrant we sent requires full and complete disclosure of his army records.'

'Well, we have the right to redact material that is operational in nature or a matter of national security.'

'This relates to his time in Helmand Province some six years ago. The army is no longer in Afghanistan, so how can it be either operational or a matter of national security?'

'That was not my decision; the army lawyers made the redactions. What I can tell you is that we withdrew from Camp Bastion in 2014 and Munro was part of the regiment left to train the Afghan army who took over the camp at that time. He unfortunately suffered severe injury when the Land Rover he was in was blown up by an IED. He was later discharged from the army on medical grounds.'

'I know all that. I've seen his medical records. I need to know what is in the redacted part of the file you sent me.'

'Well, Chief Inspector, I can't help you.'

Frustrated, Dorsey decided to call the colonel's bluff. 'Okay, I'll have no option but to cite you to give evidence under oath in relation to what is in these documents.'

'Hold on a minute. I'm not a witness to anything.'

'I'm afraid you are. You provided these documents and it's your name that's at the bottom of them. So you'll be required to explain in court why parts of these documents have been redacted.'

There was a long pause, and some finger tapping on the colonel's desk. 'I cannot see how this information would be of any interest to you. If I tell you what's been redacted, you must promise me as a gentleman not to let it go any further.'

'I promise,' said Dorsey, feeling for a moment that he had accidentally phoned Lord Kitchener in Khartoum.

'Okay, I will tell you what I can, but I can't see how it can possibly be relevant. Two months before he was seriously injured, Corporal Munro had made a complaint against two fellow soldiers who he accused of raping a 14-year-old Afghan girl in a village that was suspected of helping the Taliban. The military police investigated the claim and although the girl initially supported the rape accusation, she quickly withdrew her statement under her father's insistence. The matter was put to rest.'

'Why was it put to rest when you had the evidence of Munro?'

'That was not my decision. I'm not sure what all this has to do with your present investigation, but that's everything there is to know about Corporal Munro. I can't for the life of me think how this man turned from being an exemplary soldier into a murderer, but stranger things could have happened. War can make a good man turn bad.'

'I never said he is a murderer. We're trying to eliminate him from our enquiries.'

'Well, I hope you do that. It's never good for the regiment's image if one of our men goes rogue. Good day, Chief Inspector.'

Dorsey was still not sure what to think one way or the other. He decided he'd had enough for one day and went to get Mitchell to go for a pint, only to find Mitchell had already left.

Dorsey got back to the hotel to find Mitchell sitting on his own in the bar. He ordered two pints and joined him. He put one of the pints down beside Mitchell's half-empty glass. 'You left early.'

'I think early is the wrong word; not as late as usual would be more accurate. Anyway, other than Munro, there's no other leads to follow, and as I'm not in the loop for that, then I'm as well here as anywhere else.'

'Is that what's bugging you, the fact that I didn't tell you about the surveillance on Munro?'

'You should've told me. We've been partners for years, and you kept me in the dark about a possible suspect. Why?'

Dorsey took a sip of his beer. Part of him wanted to explode; it was worse than speaking to his son when he was in a sulk. 'George, it was an operational decision to keep the surveillance between me and the detectives that were involved in it. That way it wouldn't spread all over the station and leak out to the locals. You know how easy that can happen, especially in a place like this.'

'So, you think I would've gone off and told everyone what you were up to … Frank, that's just another one of your insults that I've had to put up with over the years.'

'That's not the reason I didn't tell you. I knew you'd be totally against it and I was afraid you might talk me out of going ahead with the surveillance. I had to give Crawford the chance to check out Munro. What if I didn't and it turned out to be him? This isn't about who's right or wrong. It's about chasing every lead, even if they go nowhere.'

'I still think you should've told me.'

'Okay, now I wish I had. I was wrong and I apologise. Now can we stop fucking about and enjoy our beers?'

The mood lifted. Mitchell had made his point. Dorsey told him about his telephone conversation with the late Lord Kitchener. It brought a smile. The detail of the army record and what the colonel went on to disclose only reinforced Mitchell's scepticism about Munro being involved in the murders, but he held his tongue. They would find out soon enough. Dorsey went to the toilet, while Mitchell went to the

170

bar and ordered two more pints.

Dorsey waited for an elderly man who was washing his hands to leave before he called the labs in Inverness. The line was engaged. He sent a text message to Jock's mobile: *Have you been able to check the DNA yet?* He washed his face and then stared at himself in the mirror. He looked like he hadn't slept for days. He couldn't remember an investigation that he had wanted to be over more than this. It was starting to take its toll.

When Dorsey returned, Mitchell was back at the table with the pints, absentmindedly tapping the palm of his hand on the table to the fiddle music that was now being piped through the bar.

'I didn't think you were into traditional music,' said Dorsey, taking his seat. Before Mitchell could respond, Dorsey's phone buzzed. It was Jock Kilbride. Mitchell stopped tapping the table as Dorsey listened to the call without saying anything.

'Okay, Jock. Thanks for phoning. I know, it is what it is,' said Dorsey, before placing his phone on the table and letting out a deep sigh.

'Well?' asked Mitchell.

'You were right. It's not Munro. The DNA didn't match and all they found in the Jeep were dog hairs. We're back to square one.'

Chapter 22

Monday: 23rd of October 2023

Over the next couple of weeks, the detectives continued to check the internet for old crimes that might reveal a suspect. Case after case was reviewed, but virtually all were in the police DNA database, and no match was found with the unknown suspect. Now that Alex Munro was eliminated as a potential suspect, the investigation had gone cold once again.

The gloom that settled on the police station only got worse when Mitchell took a call from the CID in Fort William, who informed him that Alex Munro had passed away during the night. He had spent almost two weeks in a coma before his life support was switched off.

Dorsey took a few minutes to process what Mitchell had just told him. 'I'd better phone Crawford.'

Apart from occasional expletives, Crawford just listened. When Dorsey finally finished, there was silence on the other end of the phone. 'Bill, are you still there?'

'Frank, I won't be in today,' answered Crawford, immediately hanging up.

That night, Dorsey was fast asleep when he received a phone call from DS Grant.

It took him a minute to pull himself together. 'Say that again.'

He listened as Grant told him that Bill Crawford had lost the plot. 'Boss, the manager wants him out of the hotel. He's been drinking all day. I managed to get him up to his room.'

'I'll be there in twenty minutes.'

It was after midnight when he reached the Ballachulish Hotel. The hotel was in darkness, and he had to wait for the night porter to let him in.

'The manager wants him out in the morning. He was abusive to the other guests in the bar,' said the night porter as he led Dorsey through to the reception area.

'Okay, son, we'll sort it.'

Grant was sitting in the foyer on his own, looking grey in the dull light coming from the reception.

Dorsey took the seat beside him. 'What's been going on?'

'He's sleeping, but he's been drinking ever since he heard Munro died.'

'It wasn't his fault. Munro is just another victim of the Afghan war. He could've taken that seizure at any time.'

'Bill thinks he's messed up again.'

'Everybody makes mistakes. I've made plenty.'

'You've no idea how much he respects you, and he thinks he's let you down. Bill's a good detective; maybe he's just been doing it too long and he's burnt himself out on this case.'

'Okay, if he's asleep we should just leave him, but I want you to get him up early and have him ready to leave before he can get his hands on any drink. I'll be back here first thing tomorrow to talk to him. I want you to take him home. Is he married?'

'Divorced, he lives on his own. He's got a daughter who lives in Aberdeen.'

'He can't be on his own. He'll just go back on the drink.'

'He could always stay with me. My wife and kids love the guy.'

'Okay, both you and Bill take a week off, longer if necessary. Now, get some sleep. I'll be back first thing in the morning.'

A chilly wind greeted Dorsey as the porter let him out. He sat in his car for a minute before turning on the ignition. He sighed before backing out onto the road and making his way along the B863 to the hotel.

When he got back to his room, he was wide awake and knew he'd never get back to sleep. He took a miniature whisky from the minibar and sat on the balcony, listening to the silence, taking a long draw from a cigarette that had nothing left to give. He went to bed.

Chapter 23

It was the morning of Munro's funeral. Dorsey woke in a cold sweat. His mind seemed hell-bent on trying to recall the surreal dreams that plagued his sleep, but he could only remember bits and pieces, none of which made any sense. The room was pitch dark. He checked his phone for the time. It was just after 6 a.m. He put the bedside lamp on and sat for a minute, trying to clear his mind.

He decided there was no point in trying to get back to sleep. He got up, showered, and shaved. There was nearly an hour to kill before they started serving breakfast. He got dressed and made a cup of coffee. He opened the balcony door to be met with a blustery wind that tempted him to have a smoke in the bedroom. Fearing he might set off the fire alarm, he put on his overcoat and a woolly hat that Liz bought him the last time she was up.

By the time he lit his cigarette, the coffee was already lukewarm. There were a couple of lights shining down on the lochside, but he could not make out where they were coming from. Then the first sign of life emerged from the gloom as a fishing boat left the quayside, its diesel engine puffing and spluttering. He watched it move along the loch, its navigation lights bobbing in the swell. He wondered how far out the small boat would venture to catch fish; the Atlantic was at the other end of Loch Linnhe and its likely destination.

Dorsey let out a sigh and lit another cigarette. He was becoming accustomed to the cold balcony. He was thankful that at least they never arrested Munro, as that would have legally placed him in custody and put a duty of care on the police. The paramedic was there within minutes; what else could have been done? As it stood, he was sure he had nothing to worry about, but it still troubled him. The last thing he needed was a complaint alleging he had in some way contributed to the death. He had enough to deal with. He took a sip of his coffee, which was now cold.

He got ready and went down to the breakfast room. There was no one else there, apart from two female members of staff who were busy setting up the buffet. The one thing about being down early was that the cooked food was fresh, and he helped himself to a couple of slices of crisp bacon and scrambled egg before sitting at the window that looked out over the loch. He was now regretting not ordering a wreath for the funeral. Mitchell had talked him out of it after Munro's sister turned down the offer of a police escort and made her feelings clear about exactly who she blamed for her brother's death. Maybe George was right. He was no longer sure what to think.

Mitchell eventually joined him, wearing a black suit, white shirt, and black tie. Dorsey couldn't understand how Mitchell always managed to look like his clothes had been pressed and prepared for him by a butler every morning. Even his shoes were always bullied to a shine that Dorsey had never even managed as a police cadet. His own tie had the same knot in it for days, and he buttoned his jacket to hide the wrinkled shirt that hadn't been ironed since he bought it.

'Morning, Frank, you're up early,' said Mitchell, taking a seat and tucking a napkin under his chin. He had his usual full Scottish breakfast.

Dorsey acknowledged him with a nod.

'Frank, are you not eating that?'

'No, I thought I was hungry … Are you planning to go to this funeral?'

'No, but I thought it would at least show the locals that we are being respectful.'

'Well, I don't have a black tie,' said Dorsey, slightly annoyed that Mitchell was taking some kind of moral high ground. 'I'm surprised you didn't bring your Bible down with you.'

Mitchell, who had just used his knife to slice a piece of black pudding to dip into his egg yolk, put his knife and fork down and stared at Dorsey. 'What's that supposed to mean?'

'Well, Munro was a mason like yourself. I know how you lot stick together.'

'Frank, what the hell is up with you? And I'm not a fucking mason, anyway!'

'Nothing … Sorry … Just eat your breakfast. I didn't sleep well last night.'

'Frank, the fact that Munro died was nothing to do with us. He came in of his own volition to make a complaint. He was never arrested or even formally interviewed as a suspect. If he had given a voluntary DNA sample when he was asked, we wouldn't have wasted time even considering him as a potential suspect.'

'But you never did.'

'Never did what?'

'Ever suspect him.'

'No, I didn't, but Crawford made a strong case. You had to check Munro out. It's as simple as that. How was anyone to think he'd take a seizure and end up dead? All that shit that's been posted online is just rubbish.'

'I know, but it doesn't stop me feeling bad that he's dead.'

'We all feel bad about it, but what can we do?'

'You're right.'

'Any word about Crawford?'

'Grant called me last night. Crawford went in to see the police doctor and got something to deal with the stress he's been under. He's got high blood pressure. Crawford just needs a rest. He'll be back next week.'

'Frank, you can have this black tie if you want. You're the boss after all.'

'No, George, you keep it. It suits you. I'm going down for a smoke to let you finish your breakfast in peace.'

Under an overcast sky, Dorsey and his team of detectives watched the funeral procession in silence from the south side of the Ballachulish Bridge. Two pipers from Munro's regiment led the solemn cortege across the bridge with more than a hundred mourners walking slowly behind the hearse. Eileen Munro was dressed in black, her brother's dog walking by her side with a regimental rosette on its collar. The whole glen had come out to pay its respects.

The sound of the pipes brought a lump to Dorsey's throat. They were playing 'Flowers of the Forest', a lament for a fallen soldier that drifted over the dark waters of Loch Leven and along the mountainside. There was a deep rumble of thunder that was soon followed by a ragged streak of lightning that ripped open the dark skies. The rain began to fall like tiny bullets that riddled the surface of the loch. The rain ran down Dorsey's face as he turned to go back to his car. He was now utterly sick with dealing with death.

Chapter 24

Monday: 1st of November 2023

It was a miserable wet day in Glasgow's West End, but Duncan Webster could only feel the anxiety rushing through his body as he weaved his way through the pedestrians coming the other way along Byres Road. The phone call the previous evening had made him feel sick. He hadn't slept all night and the constant worry was taking its toll. He crossed the road to Curlers.

The pub was quiet, and Duncan was relieved to see Jack sitting in the far corner. He gave him a wave before going to the bar. He then took a seat beside Jack with his half pint of lager shandy. 'Where's Hannah?'

'She's at a lecture. She'll be here shortly. So, what's up? You look terrible.'

'The police phoned last night. They want to interview me again.'

'Why?'

'I don't know,' said Duncan, nervously tapping his beer mat on the table.

'Maybe they've found Erin.'

'Maybe.'

'Why didn't you fucking ask them?' snapped Jack.

'I don't know. I just didn't think.'

'When do they want to speak to you?'

'I've to go to London Road Police Station tomorrow morning.'

'Do you think she would've told them about the drugs?'

'If they found her and she told them about the drugs, it's

not me they'd be wanting to speak to. It's fucking you, Jack! You gave them to her.'

'Maybe she told them you fucking punched her in the face!'

'I never fucking punched her or gave her any drugs,' Duncan insisted, throwing the beer mat at Jack. He then turned to see if anyone heard Jack's accusation. Apart from the barman, who was busy washing glasses and nodding along to whatever music he was playing through his earphones, the only other person in the bar was a middle-aged man who was sitting at a table next to the front door, drinking a pint of Guinness and looking intently at his mobile phone. Duncan placed his pint down on the table and leaned towards Jack and repeated, 'I never fucking punched her.'

'Well, I'm only saying what the police suggested to me happened.'

'Keep your voice down. I think that guy might have heard what you said.'

'I don't think so. He's probably looking at porn on his phone,' sniggered Jack.

'Don't stare at him,' whispered Duncan, after another cursory look over his shoulder.

'All I'm saying is you need to find out why they want to speak to you. You need to get a lawyer … There's Hannah now.'

Hannah came straight over to the table, her hair wet and face flushed. She put her bag on the floor and sat down. 'So, what's this all about?'

'Do you want a drink?'

'No, Jack. I don't have much time. I have to prepare for a seminar this afternoon. So, what's up, Duncan?'

'The police want to speak to me again. They want me to give another statement.'

'Maybe they found Erin,' suggested Hannah, clasping her hands together at her lips as though she was about to offer up a prayer to a God she didn't believe in. Instead, she just mumbled something incoherent.

'If they've found her, she's probably told them about the drugs,' said Jack.

Duncan slapped the table with the palm of his hand and stared at Jack. 'If I get a lawyer, they'll think I'm guilty of something.'

'Just stick to what you told them the first time,' advised Jack, taking another sip of his pint.

'Instead of worrying about yourselves, are neither of you two concerned about Erin? What if she's dead?'

'Of course we're worried about Erin, but if the police find out about the drugs we could all end up in prison,' explained Jack. 'Especially if they find her dead in a bog somewhere from hypothermia.'

Duncan grabbed Jack by the scruff of the neck. 'They were your fucking drugs!'

Jack pushed Duncan's hands away. 'Lighten up for fuck's sake. It doesn't matter who brought them, we all took them. We all agreed not to tell the police about them, and not to tell them about you driving down to the main road, out of your fucking head!'

'I was looking for her.'

'It was you that made her run away in the first place.'

'I wish you two would stop arguing. If they found Erin alive, she would never tell the police about the drugs. I've known her for years.'

'But what if she's found dead?' said Jack. 'They'll do a toxicology test and find the ecstasy in her system.'

'I've had enough of this. I need to go. My seminar is at two and I haven't had any lunch yet.'

'This is more important than a fucking seminar,' barked Jack. 'Remember it was you who actually gave her the ecstasy.'

'You shit, Jack! You fucking shit,' shouted Hannah,

lifting her bag from the floor and getting up from her seat. 'Duncan, I think you should get a lawyer before you go anywhere near that police station. And Jack, I think you should find yourself another girlfriend. I'll be moving my things out of the flat when I get back.'

'Hannah, for God's sake.'

Hannah was tempted to pour what was left in Jack's pint over his head until she noticed the man near the door looking over.

Jack looked at Duncan for some support, but he just shrugged his shoulders as she made her way out of the bar.

'You shouldn't have said that to her,' said Duncan.

'I know, I'll speak to her when she gets back from uni.'

'It might be too late.'

'She'll be alright when she calms down … Did you find out who Erin was supposed to have been seeing?'

'I don't think you want to know,' said Duncan.

'Try me,' insisted Jack.

'I wasn't going to tell you, but what the hell … It was Hannah.'

'Hannah! Are you having a laugh?'

'I knew she was seeing someone behind my back. That's why we weren't getting on. She started to lie all the time about where she was going and who she was meeting. But I had no idea who she was seeing.'

'Maybe you were just being paranoid, mate.'

'You think? I found this in the flat the other day,' said Duncan, putting a pink iPhone on the table. It's her old phone. It's got nude pictures of Erin and Hannah on it.'

'For fuck's sake. You're making this shit up to mess with my head.'

'Jack, I'm telling you the truth. Why would I lie? They had been sending them to each other. There's the mobile phone if you want to see them.'

'Fuck, no. Why haven't you fucking deleted them?'

182

'Because I didn't think you'd believe me.'

'When she told me that night she wanted to finish with me, I just lost the plot.'

'So, you did punch her!'

'No, I didn't. I told her that I was going to tell her parents and show them the photos. That's when she freaked out.'

'Shit, don't tell the police about that phone for God's sake. Wait a minute, wouldn't the police have gotten the photos from her new phone?'

'I don't think so. They would've found them long before now. That's probably why she kept her old phone.'

'Fuck it. Do you want another pint?'

'No. If the police do have them, then they'll try to use them to prove I had something to do with her going missing. I need to go and find a lawyer.'

Chapter 25

Since the discovery of the second body, the Central Highlands region had become gripped by an existential fear that made even the youngest in the area vigilant. Most children were dropped off and picked up from school by their parents or other family members. Teenage girls attending colleges were now too scared to walk home on their own and their tutors insisted they go home as far as they could in groups of two or more. Most boys just carried on as before, but even they were afraid to venture too far now that the days were getting shorter.

The police put up posters in every school and college in the area warning pupils of the dangers of accepting lifts from strangers and to report anything suspicious to them or their teachers. The bodies in the bog and the missing Glasgow student were now seared in everyone's minds, and no one felt safe while the killer remained at large.

The remains of both victims were eventually released by the Crown for burial and repatriated to their own countries. Chief Superintendent Fiona Mackie attended both funerals as a representative of Police Scotland and offered her condolences on behalf of the people of Scotland. She reassured both families of the victims that the police would not rest until their loved ones' killer was brought to justice.

With Duncan Webster providing a no comment interview, that line of enquiry was put on the back burner. The fact that he followed his lawyer's advice not to answer any questions didn't surprise Dorsey, but supported his suspicions that he was hiding something. What that might be, he still wasn't sure.

With weeks passing without any results, the pressure on Dorsey was now palpable. Since he had taken over the case, the officers under him had been working twelve-hour shifts six days a week. They were becoming exhausted and frustrated with their failure to find any new leads to catch the killer, and, if she was still alive, to save Erin Keenan. Dorsey was putting in as many as fourteen hours a day, seven days a week.

Dorsey was at least grateful to see DI Crawford back at work and looking well. He was wearing a new suit that he had bought after losing some weight while he was off the drink.

Under pressure from all sides, Dorsey held a public meeting at a local primary school assembly hall to persuade more of the locals to provide voluntary DNA samples as the initial take-up had dropped off dramatically as a result of conspiracy theories spreading on the internet about the true purpose of the screening programme.

Despite his reassurances, some of those attending protested that they were being treated like criminals and didn't trust the police to destroy their DNA samples after they were eliminated from the enquiry. He explained that the police had already wasted precious time and resources investigating spurious and often malicious incriminations of individuals, which came to nothing. He further explained that the swab programme would put an end to anonymous phone calls naming people without any reasonable cause and allow the police to concentrate on those who refused to provide a sample.

Despite his efforts, the numbers coming forward for the programme continued to fall and the chief constable ordered the testing to stop. The DNA screening programme was a complete failure.

To put further strain on the police, they also had to deal with social media platforms used by hundreds of amateur detectives from all over the country and their followers. They were coming up with all kinds of theories and culprits and were simply muddying the waters further. This distraction was wasting officers' time as they had to monitor these platforms for any clues that might appear, perhaps even from the killer. The police hoped that he got some thrill out of the morbid curiosity around the case and would be unable to stop himself from making some revealing comment. Any comments deemed suspicious were followed up by a visit from the police, but so far there was nothing to show for their efforts.

The number of statements taken was now in the thousands. The fact that the A82 and the B863 were poorly served with speed and public space cameras didn't help the investigation identify any suspect vehicles. Previous checks of CCTV cameras, mainly from petrol station forecourts, in respect to Erin Keenan's disappearance, resulted in hundreds of vehicles being traced and drivers and passengers interviewed. There was nothing of interest found.

The cost of the investigation was enormous, and the decision was taken by Deputy Chief Constable Cullen to scale back the search for Erin Keenan. The scores of police officers, mountain rescue teams, and local volunteers went back to their normal lives. Dorsey's squad of detectives was reduced to a team of ten, and now only the local newspapers continued to feature stories of sightings of Erin Keenan, none of which came to anything.

With winter approaching, life in the glens gradually returned to normal, and people went about their lives as if it had all been a bad dream. The papers had nothing new to report and turned their attention elsewhere. Even the cranks on social media had found other things to obsess over.

Chapter 26

Saturday: 11th of November 2023

Another day with no new leads to follow up, Dorsey
was laboriously going over the new statements obtained
during further routine vehicle stops and uploading them to
HOLMES. He was beginning to feel worn out; the lack of
progress in the case was getting to him. The case felt like a
jigsaw puzzle bought from a charity shop with crucial pieces
missing.

He got up and put on his jacket, and went into the incident
room. He stared at the large Ordnance Survey map, now
peppered with coloured pins that meant very little. He just
couldn't see the clues anymore. What was he missing?

Then Dixon took a call from the operations hub at the
church hall. 'Sir, I think you should take this. Someone
thinks they've seen Hannah Bain's dog.' She handed the
phone to Dorsey.

The civilian operator repeated what she had been told.
'Yes, sir, he was at an Esso station near Spean Bridge and was
sure he saw the missing dog in the back of a Volvo Estate.
He took pictures of the dog and the number plate of the car
when the driver was in paying for petrol. He was too scared
to photograph the man in case he saw him and knew what
he was up to. The car has left the station and is driving south
towards Fort William. The lad has just sent a WhatsApp with
the pictures. I'm sending them to your computer now.'

Dorsey handed the phone back to Dixon. 'Get as much
detail as possible.' He then went back into his office and
switched on his computer, which seemed to take forever

to boot up. Clicking the link, the pictures slowly appeared, showing the dog and the registration plate. He was in no doubt that this was Hannah Bain's missing cockapoo, but he still checked it against the picture of Skye on his laptop. He looked at the markings around the dog's face. They matched. The adrenaline was now pumping through his body as though someone had just replaced his old, dud batteries. He took a deep breath before going back into the muster room.

'Right, we're back in business. DI Crawford, DS Grant, and DS Mitchell, unless you're desperate to go home, we've got a sighting of a suspect with the missing dog. PC Dixon, check the registration number on the picture I've sent to you of a Volvo Estate and get the owner's name and address from DVLA.'

The incident room went from a gloomy office at the end of a long, tedious shift to a surge of activity with detectives and uniformed officers desperate to be on the task force; no one wanted to be left back in the office as they had invested too much to miss out on the arrest. Just the idea of seeing what he looked like set some of their pulses racing.

'Sir, I've got it. It's an Angus Sloan. He has a place out in the sticks a couple of miles from Spean Bridge. I've sent everyone the GPS directions to their mobiles,' shouted Dixon.

'Good! How far is Spean Bridge?' asked Dorsey, putting on his raincoat and placing his sidearm in his shoulder holster for the first time since he came to Glencoe.

'It's about ten miles north of Fort William. About twenty-six miles from here, heading along the A82, sir.'

'Dixon, contact Inverness and brief them on what's happening. Ask them to get the duty sheriff to grant a warrant.'

'Yes, sir. I'm on it now.'

'The rest of you put your vests on. This guy may be armed. We can't take chances … George, you come with me.'

It was a cold night with an icy wind coming off the loch that bit into exposed skin, but no one cared about the cold. The squad of detectives and uniformed officers piled into their marked and unmarked police vehicles, allowing Dorsey's car to pull out first to lead the task force. Using the GPS coordinates and Google Maps, Mitchell pinpointed the house deep in an area of woodland well off the main road. The obvious fear was that the suspect would see them coming and disappear into the woods or turn it into a hostage situation. They'd have to take this guy by surprise by dumping the cars on the A82 and making their way to the house on foot. The main objective was to rescue Erin Keenan alive.

They passed at speed through the Highland village of Spean Bridge, which was dead at this time of year. The only tourists around were obsessive Munro baggers, who seemed to love being miserable and wet just to say they had climbed some mountain that no one else had ever heard of or cared about. Dorsey stopped at a lay-by. The rest of the police vehicles pulled up on the grass verge behind. 'George, can you ask DI Crawford and DS Grant to follow us and tell the rest to remain here until we need them? I don't want any unarmed officers anywhere near that house until we apprehend the suspect and secure the area.'

When they reached the turn-off that led to Sloan's house, Dorsey stopped the car and they got out. He went to the back and opened the boot, taking out two bulletproof vests and handing one to Mitchell.

Crawford and Grant approached, chewing gum and looking like they had psyched themselves up for a walk-on part in *Gunfight at the OK Corral*. Dorsey knew what he was about to tell them was not going to go down well, but he was more interested in having his back covered than making them like him. 'If Sloan was going into Fort William, it's unlikely he's at his house. We're going to take a walk up there and check it out. You two stay here in case ...'

'What!' interrupted Grant. 'Why would we do that? This is an Inverness case! You can't just shut us out when there's a bit of fucking action!'

'DS Grant, if you don't shut up, you can go back to Inverness right now and stay up there. I don't have time to debate matters with you. Do what you're told or fuck off right now.'

'Bill,' Grant pleaded, turning to Crawford for support.

'John, just shut up ... What's it you want us to do, Frank?'

'I want you two to stay here to cover our backs. If he's not at the house and turns up, let him drive up to the house. You can come in behind him and arrest the bastard when he reaches the house. I'm more interested in finding Erin Keenan.'

'Okay, we'll have your back. I only hope she's still alive. Right, John, get in the car,' ordered Crawford, opening the passenger door for Grant, who had the look of a man who had just been betrayed by one of his own for an outsider.

Dorsey and Mitchell headed towards the house. The darkness engulfed them the further they walked from the main road until the moon slowly emerged from behind the clouds. The road was no more than a muddy path, wide enough for one car only. The adrenaline was pumping through their bodies, increasing the nearer they got to the house.

A biting wind was now howling through the trees and around the house. There was no car parked outside and no sign of life. Dorsey went to one of the front windows and shone his torch into the darkness. The beam picked out a couch and coffee table with beer bottles lying around the floor. The living room looked a mess.

'Frank, we're still waiting for the warrant.'

Dorsey checked the front door handle. It was locked. 'George, see if there's an easier way to get in around the back,' ordered Dorsey.

A few kicks had the front door off one of its hinges, and the lock was now lying on the hall floor. But it still wouldn't open. Dorsey put his shoulder hard against the door, but he couldn't get it to budge more than a few inches. He shone the torch around the doorframe to see what was keeping it from opening. The door was now jammed between the frame and a floorboard in the hall that was slightly proud of the others. He tried to force it again, but it was jammed tight. He took a few steps back and gave the door another kick. The frame came away with the door and the whole thing collapsed into the hall. When he recovered from the effort, he saw someone coming through the hall towards him. He immediately drew his sidearm.

'Frank, you've made a bit of a mess here. The back door was open.'

'Fuck, George. You scared the life out of me!' he said, putting his gun back into his shoulder holster. 'I could've put a bullet in you. Why didn't you at least turn on the lights?'

'They're not working. He must live off the grid. There's probably a generator in here somewhere. I hope this is the right house.'

'Don't say that. Help me move this fucking thing.'

'Look!'

Dorsey turned to see the headlights of two cars coming slowly up the farm road. He was eventually able to make out the Volvo bumping over the rough track. He turned to Mitchell. 'He's trapped now; that old car has no chance of heading off-road in this place. Phone the backup and tell them to get up here. I want this fucking house taken apart.'

Sloan pulled up at the front of the house as the car behind drew up beside it. The two Inverness detectives got out of their car with their guns pointing towards the Volvo. 'Police! Get your fucking hands up!' Crawford shouted as he moved cautiously to the driver's door. Grant covered the passenger's side.

Crawford carefully opened the driver's door and pulled Sloan by the scruff of his coat onto the ground. He fell roughly and howled in pain. The stunned suspect was turned on his back and cuffed. 'The dog is in the back,' Grant shouted, putting away his gun and opening the back door. 'It's definitely the one that went missing!'

The other police vehicles were now making their way along the road to the house, beams of light bouncing across the dark sky. Dorsey ordered the rest of his team to join in the search of the property. The lack of a warrant didn't seem to bother him, as they made their way through the house. Sloan and the dog were taken to Glencoe Police Station.

Each room was systematically searched as the hope of finding Erin Keenan quickly faded. The fact that she had not already called out could only mean she was not there or she was already dead. It didn't look good.

The detectives turned the place upside down. The threadbare carpets were lifted and wood panelling ripped from the walls, but there was no cellar or secret chamber found. It was obvious from the number of empty bottles and cans scattered around the house that Sloan lived from one beer to another. The man did not seem to have any time for modernity. Apart from an old radio, there was no television, no computer, and even his cooker looked like it was originally made to burn peat but was now attached to a gas bottle. There was nothing of evidential value to show that anyone had ever been imprisoned, let alone murdered there.

The only outbuilding was used to store firewood, a heavy-duty shredder and half a dozen crates of beer. As his team of detectives continued to search the surrounding area, Dorsey went to his car and got his cigarettes. He was desperate for a drink, but the temptation of helping himself to one from Sloan's hoard of beer quickly passed. With the wind still blowing from all directions, Dorsey gave up trying to get a cigarette lit and put it back in his packet. He could only wait for his squad to finish their task and secure the house and surrounding area for the forensic team to arrive.

DI Crawford approached, carrying two shotguns. 'Frank, she's not in there and there's nothing to indicate she ever was. This is all we found of interest. If he's got a licence for them, then fine. The place is secure. I guess the only thing to do is to get SOCOs in to see what they can find. If he's our man then he must keep his victims somewhere else. There's nothing in there.'

'Okay, thanks, Bill,' said Dorsey. 'George, phone Kilbride at Inverness and tell him what he needs to know. Then phone Dixon and see if she has got the warrant and find out what time it was granted. This might be another screwup.'

Dorsey ordered the crime scene to be cordoned off. He then ordered the task force back to the station, leaving one detective and two uniformed officers behind to wait for the forensic team to arrive. He had an interview to do.

The atmosphere in the incident room was one of uncertainty; there was no obvious feeling that they had cracked the case, not yet at any rate. While the suspect was in the detention room and his lawyer was contacted, Dorsey planned the best approach to tackle the interview.

The tag on the dog confirmed it was Hannah Bain's cockapoo and a quick check by Mitchell confirmed Sloan didn't hold a firearms licence. That was enough to charge and hold him under the Firearms Act, giving them the right to oblige Sloan to provide a DNA swab. It would also give the forensic team more time to check his house and surrounding land.

The best scenario would be to crack Sloan during the interview and for him to break down and confess to everything, although that was unlikely. They had no idea of his mental condition and he could be desperate to get it all off his chest.

Those detectives who had stayed on after their shift had finished and left for home. Dorsey retreated to his office to concentrate on the salient points he intended to put to Sloan during the interview.

There was a knock at the door, and PC Dixon put her head around the door. 'I think the dog needs the toilet; shall I take him for a walk?'

Dorsey had almost forgotten about the dog and its welfare. At least Dixon was always there to keep an eye on things. 'Yes, but don't lose him,' he said with a smile. 'When you get back, leave the dog with someone else and go home. You've been on duty now for fourteen hours. I'm starting to think you need the overtime.'

'Can I just take him home with me until the morning? He's never going to settle down in here.'

'Okay, can you phone Hannah Bain and let her know we got him back?'

'I've already done it. Her number is on the dog tag. She'll come tomorrow to pick him up.'

'Just make sure we have a few pictures taken of him and the dog tag. She must've asked if we found her friend.'

'She did. All I could tell her was that she's still missing.'

Once she had left with the dog, Dorsey went back to checking his interview questions, wondering if he'd get any answers to them, fully aware that he could be facing the standard 'no comment' response that all lawyers advise their clients to make during police interviews.

The solicitor arrived, an elderly man whose wispy grey hair was all over the place. He looked like he had just got out of his bed and was blown there by the wind. Dorsey left Mitchell to give him a run-through in relation to the charges arising out of the unlicensed firearms, theft of the dog, attempting to pervert the course of justice, and the reasonable suspicion that he was responsible for the abduction, wrongful imprisonment, and murders of Lena Kaminski and Evinka Janik, and the abduction and wrongful imprisonment of Erin Keenan. The lawyer didn't look in the least fazed by the sheer magnitude of these charges and allegations and simply asked to see his client.

The two detectives had more experience than most at police interviews. Mitchell prepared the tape recorder while Dorsey ran through his notes until the custody officer arrived with Sloan.

After exchanging a few words and explaining the procedure, the recording button was pressed to begin the interview. Dorsey asked everyone present to introduce themselves for the benefit of the tape and then went over the preliminary matters including explaining the suspect's right to remain silent. It was only when he read over the list of allegations that Dorsey noticed a change in Sloan's demeanour. He stared at Dorsey with utter contempt, smirking with a derisory grin, showing a mouth of discoloured teeth and gaps that were hard to look at. Dorsey moved slightly back in his chair to avoid getting another whiff of Sloan's disgusting breath.

Sloan then gave his name, age, and address without hesitation before sitting back and folding his arms. Dorsey decided to start with the shotguns and move on to the murders and abductions once he had Sloan under pressure and answering questions freely.

'At 9.20 p.m. tonight, you were arrested outside your home address at Crowe Farm Road, Spean Bridge. Do you own or rent another house?'

Both Dorsey and Mitchell knew the response to this basic, but important question would tell them what type of interview this would be. Sloan just stared hard at Dorsey, breathing heavily, anger barely contained, as though he was ready to explode into a tirade of abuse. But then in a quiet voice he replied, 'No comment.'

'I assume that your response to all my questions will be the same?'

'It depends on what questions you ask,' said Sloan, causing the solicitor to raise his eyebrows.

Dorsey knew from experience that some suspects, despite the legal advice given to them to make no comment, couldn't help themselves. The tactic was always the same: tease them into answering questions they felt comfortable with. So, he changed tack and decided to ask about the least serious matter Sloan was facing. 'Let's start with the dog that was found in the back of your car. Who does the dog belong to?'

'It doesn't belong to anyone. It's an animal and belongs to no one.'

'You had it in your car.'

'Only because I was looking after it until it was well again.'

'What was wrong with it?' asked Dorsey, trying to remain as calm as possible. As long as the suspect was talking, his job was to keep him talking. The big questions would come later.

'I found it a couple of months ago. The poor thing was caught in a snare in Craggy Woods, near Kinlochleven. It was in agony. I cut the snare off and took the dog home to look after it until it got better. Are you telling me that's a crime?'

'There was a tag on the dog's collar that had the name of the owner and a contact number. Why did you not phone and tell her you had the dog?'

'Because the dog had a better chance of recovering with me. If the owner had taken it to a vet in that state, then it would have been put down for certain. That's why I didn't phone. Get a vet to look at the dog's left leg now, just above the paw. It was cut through to the bone. I used manuka honey, which is not cheap, to gradually get the skin to close over and heal. Now you wouldn't know to look at that leg there was anything wrong with it. All I was doing was going home when one of your fucking thugs put a gun to my head and pulled me out of my car and gave me this bruise on the side of my face. So, fuck you. Charge me if you like, I'd do the same again.'

'You must have known that the dog was being sought as part of a murder enquiry?'

'No, how'd I know that? The dog never said he'd murdered anybody.'

'Do you think this is funny?'

'No, I don't, but this is a fucking frame-up … Murder, abduction, what the fuck!'

'If you knowingly failed to report that you had the dog we were looking for, then you could be charged with attempting to pervert the course of justice.'

'I didn't fucking know! I don't have a television and I don't read newspapers. So prove I knew anything. I knew nothing about this until my lawyer told me ten minutes ago.'

'We found a radio in your house?'

'If you can get that to work then you can keep it.'

'Okay, as you know we recovered two shotguns from your house, which we've checked and you don't have a licence to own these guns. What's your …'

'Chief Inspector,' interrupted the lawyer, 'before you ask any more questions, I'd like a moment to speak to my client.'

Dorsey looked hard at the lawyer, but he didn't want to get into a discussion with him while the tape was still running. 'For the purposes of the tape, this is Chief Inspector Frank Dorsey suspending the interview with Angus Sloan at 23:16 hours.'

'George, can you take Mr Sloan back to the detention room while I have a word with Mr Irvine?'

Once Mitchell left with Sloan, Dorsey waited for a few moments before speaking. 'Is there a problem? You had enough time to speak to your client before the interview.'

The solicitor took out a handkerchief and wiped his glasses before simply requesting to see the search warrant.

'We didn't need a warrant. We were acting in an emergency to save a life,' explained Dorsey, who knew he was on thin ice when trying to argue the nuances of the law with someone who looked like he had drafted the Declaration of Arbroath.

'Whose life did you save? There was no one found in the house.'

'But we didn't know that at the time.'

'Let me get this right. Your colleague advised me before the interview that you searched my client's house because you suspected that he was a serial killer on account that he had someone's dog that had run off from its owner a couple of months ago. My client then tells me he never saw a warrant, which you have just confirmed you never had. You raided his house clearly based on a hunch that he had abducted and imprisoned another young woman there. You found no evidence in the house other than two shotguns which you say he doesn't have a licence for. Is that it?'

Dorsey had underestimated the old lawyer, who he thought looked dishevelled and half asleep when he arrived at the station. Appearances can be deceptive; he was a smart man. 'That's an argument you'll no doubt have with the procurator fiscal in court. We're here to conduct an interview, not to debate the legality or otherwise of a search that recovered two unlicensed shotguns.'

'He's given you an explanation for the dog. The search of his house was clearly illegal, and as such, the two shotguns are inadmissible as evidence. The reality is that you found nothing to connect him to the murders and abductions. If you are going to charge my client with anything I suggest you do so, otherwise release him. He will, on my advice, be answering no more of your questions. So, if you allow me a further consultation with him, we can get this over with and we can all get home.'

'With all due respect, he's not out of the woods yet. We'll resume the interview in fifteen minutes once you've had a chance to speak to him.'

After discussing the situation with Mitchell, they agreed to go through with the interview, even though it had already gone pear-shaped. If he followed his lawyer's advice and went back to making a no comment interview, they would still charge Sloan with the possession of the two shotguns and require him to provide a DNA swab. That would buy more time, at least to let the forensic lab check the DNA and anything else they had recovered at the house.

Chapter 27

Sunday: 12th of November 2023

It was past midday before Dorsey woke from a deep sleep that left him shattered and feeling lethargic. His whole body was exhausted, and he wasn't even sure if there was any point in getting ready and going into the office. He wanted a cigarette but forced himself to get up and have a shower. It took a while for the water to revive him. He gradually turned off the hot tap, letting the cold water batter his body from its stupor.

He shaved; the three days' growth was making him look unkempt. He needed a haircut, but that would have to wait. Feeling much better, he put on the dressing gown provided by the hotel and made himself a strong coffee. The cigarette had now become a need more than a want. Pulling the curtain back from the window, the watery grey light looked cold and damp. It was miserable. The balcony was soaking wet and the chairs and table were drenched from what must've been a biblical downpour during the night. He wasn't going to be put off, and took a towel from the bathroom and wiped the wet chairs.

There was little he could do about the chilly breeze that was coming up from the loch, but the shower had made him more able to endure it, at least until he had his coffee and smoke. He watched a couple of seals that had come to the near shore as a small fishing boat buffeted them in its wake.

It was after two before he decided it was time to check in with the station to see what the latest situation was with Sloan, who had been kept in overnight after providing a DNA swab. He was wondering why no one, not even Mitchell, had contacted him. He called the station. It was Dixon who answered.

'It's DCI Dorsey. What's happening?'

'Sir, I was about to phone you. We just got the DNA results back … They're negative.'

'Shit, I had my doubts, but it's still a bummer.'

'Forensics found nothing either. The place hasn't been cleaned in years, and the only fingerprints they found were Sloan's. His car also came back negative. There was no forensic evidence relating to any of the young women found.'

'Okay, get Sloan to sign a disclaimer for the two shotguns and release him. The search won't stand up in court, and his explanation for the dog is believable, even though it was probably caught in his own snare … I'll be in later.'

With no leads, no suspects, and the investigation back in a cul-de-sac, the only thing they had to show for all their work was the recovery of the dog. He got dressed and drove into Glencoe.

By the time he got to the station, Sloan had already been released. There was only a skeleton squad on duty to allow the other detectives to have a break from the relentless workload. Sundays were always quieter anyway; the number of crank phone calls was also at a minimum on the Sabbath for some reason.

Dixon made him a cup of coffee. He must have looked like he needed it. She then handed him copies of the DNA findings and the provisional CIS report. 'I thought we had him, sir.'

'So did I.'

As he scanned through the forensic reports that clearly exculpated Sloan, there was a knock at the door. The duty sergeant entered. 'Sir, Hannah Bain is here to collect her dog.'

'Tell her I want to speak to her.'

Dorsey didn't recognise the young woman who came into his office. She bore no resemblance to the confident-looking person in the picture taken at Glen Etive. The jet-black shoulder-length hair was back to its natural mousy brown, swept back and tied in a ponytail. She wore very little makeup and no longer looked like she had bats for pets. He smiled and indicated to her to take a seat. She nervously shook her head, tightly holding on to the dog's lead as if afraid she'd lose him again.

'Thank you for finding Skye,' she said, her voice trembling and tears welling up in her eyes.

'I didn't find him. Someone saw him in a car and phoned in. We just went and got him back. He seems to be none the worse for his ordeal.'

'But you didn't find Erin?'

'No, we hoped they'd be together.'

'Is she dead?'

'I don't know. We are still trying to find her and there's still a chance she may be alive. I'd be lying if I said I knew for certain what's happened to her.'

'It's all my fault,' she wept, the tears now running freely down her cheeks.

'It's not your fault. How can it be your fault?'

'She didn't want to go. She only went with us because I begged her to go.'

Dorsey thought there was more to what she was saying, but he didn't want to ask her any direct questions as she looked like she was ready to unburden herself with whatever guilt she was carrying. He took a tissue from the box on his desk and handed it to her. Her hands were shaking.

'Why don't you sit down, and I'll get us both a cup of coffee and I'll get one of the officers to take Skye for a short walk.'

'I'd really like a cigarette, but I know you're not allowed

to smoke in here.'

'Well, who's going to stop us?'

He went into the main incident room and asked one of the uniformed officers to bring two coffees. When he returned, Hannah was still visibly upset, but she had dried her cheeks and looked a bit more composed. He was never great at small talk, but knew there was something important she wanted to tell him.

The coffee arrived, and Hannah reluctantly let Dixon take Skye for a walk.

She smiled for the first time when Dorsey closed the door over, taking an ashtray from a drawer in his desk and a packet of cigarettes from his jacket pocket. He offered her one.

'I won't get into trouble for this?'

'No, but I might.'

After a couple of draws and a timid sip of coffee, she began to unburden herself. 'The reason Erin didn't want to go was because she wanted to break up with Duncan.'

'We know that.'

'Yeah, but the trip was already booked and paid for, and I talked her into not telling him so we could all go away for the weekend. It was selfish of me.' She began sobbing again. 'Duncan was such a shit to her. She was frightened of him and I feel guilty for making her go on the trip. I thought she would be okay because we were there.'

'Did Duncan assault her?'

'No … I don't know. He might have. He's now going out with someone else as though Erin never existed. I shouldn't have talked her into going. It's all my fault. I can't bear to think she's dead and lying up here in a bog somewhere … All my friends think she's been murdered.'

'Don't blame yourself. Whoever abducted her is to blame, and maybe Duncan Webster for making her run off that night.'

'Will you find her?'

'I'll do everything I can to find her. Why have you changed the way you dress and look?'

'Because of the abuse I was getting online. People were accusing me of murdering Erin. It's fucking nuts … Sorry.'

'That's okay, *fuck* is one of the most underrated words in the English language.'

She smiled again, taking a long, nervous draw of the cigarette.

'Why would anyone accuse you of murdering Erin?'

'Because there are morons out there who think that being a goth somehow makes you evil or believe in the devil. I just liked the music and the way it made me feel when I dressed up. It gave me confidence.'

'There are a lot of ignorant people in this world, and the best place to find them is on social media.'

'After what happened, people who know nothing about me were posting all sorts of horrible things online. Some were suggesting that the three of us murdered her and disposed of the body, and that's why we didn't report her missing until the next day. It's amazing how many comments and likes that got.'

'If you are prepared to allow us access to your social media, then we can track down these people and ...'

'No, I'd rather forget about it. I've deleted all my social media apps.'

'Okay, so long as you are not online they'll soon give up. Are you still seeing Jack Hardy?'

'No, we split up a couple of weeks ago.'

'I'm sorry to hear that.'

'He didn't want me to tell you. He thinks we'll go to prison,' she said and began crying again.

Dorsey suddenly felt a rush of adrenaline but waited until she wiped her tears before asking her another question. 'Did something happen the night Erin went missing that Jack is afraid you'll tell us about?'

'Yes,' she said through sighs and sniffles.

'Do you want to tell me now?'

'We were taking drugs that night, some hash and eccies.'

'Ecstasy?'

'Yes.'

'Did Erin take anything?'

'Yes. She smoked a joint and took one ecstasy pill. We all took one each.'

'Where did the drugs come from?'

'I don't want to say.'

'That's okay. That doesn't matter.'

Dorsey knew what she was telling him would be inadmissible in court, but he wasn't interested in getting convictions for a couple of joints and a few ecstasy pills. He wanted to find out what actually happened that night. 'Is there anything else you want to tell me that may help us find her?'

'After she ran off, we searched for her everywhere, but it was dark and we eventually gave up. Duncan then decided to drive down to the main road to see if he could find her.'

'Just Duncan?'

'Yes, he was gone for more than an hour, maybe even two hours, but he couldn't find her anywhere. Am I going to go to prison?'

'Hannah, what you have just told me is not admissible in court, but I need you to give a formal statement after you speak to a solicitor. He will no doubt advise you not to answer any questions, which is your right to do. I don't need that done right now, and you can go home and arrange to see a lawyer. You will be contacted when we require you to be interviewed.'

'We never thought she'd be abducted by a serial killer. Oh my God.'

'We don't know that … Now, how did you get here?'

'My dad drove me. He's waiting outside.'

'You take Skye and go home. We have your number and we'll call you and arrange for you to give a statement.'

'Will I have to come back up here?'

'No, it will be done in Glasgow.'

Shortly after she left, Dorsey sent an email to London Road CID ordering them to arrange the interview with Hannah Bain under caution. He provided the details of what she had already told him and the original reports of the case. Once they had her statement, Jack Hardy and Duncan Webster were to be brought in and re-interviewed under caution on suspicion of possession of drugs and attempting to pervert the course of justice. He wasn't hopeful that this would lead anywhere; once the lawyers were involved, the advice was always the same.

That evening when the phones had stopped ringing and the station had gone quiet, Dorsey and Mitchell headed for the pub. The backshift would now have the task of sifting through the remaining alleged sightings of Erin Keenan, most being anonymous calls and probably from the same time-wasters that had phoned in before. The culprits knew how to withhold their numbers and to hang up before the calls could be traced. The other regular callers were those making bizarre allegations against their neighbours. All had to be logged and followed up, even where there was only a semblance of credibility to the accusations.

The chef at the hotel had little culinary imagination. It was either a mild chicken curry and boiled rice or steak pie with chips and peas most nights. Dorsey almost stunned Mitchell when he ordered the chicken curry.

'I think you've done the right thing,' said Mitchell.

'What, chancing the curry?'

'No! Dropping the shotgun charges against Sloan. Still, I thought we'd have heard from his lawyer again about the state we left his client's house in.'

'I sorted that. Joiners are going out tomorrow to repair any damage, Sloan's been advised.'

'Where do we go from here? We've no other leads whatsoever.'

'I think we need to have another look at Duncan Webster and Jack Hardy … Anyway, let's not think about that until tomorrow, I've got a splitting headache.'

'There's the food now, anyway,' said Mitchell, who wasn't one for taking chances, as the plate of steak pie, mashed potatoes, and peas was put in front of him.

'I may have made a mistake. The steak pie is looking good.'

'Always stick to what you know,' said Mitchell, before placing a large forkful of hot food in his mouth.

A few days later, Dorsey got a call from the CID in Glasgow. 'Boss, I've interviewed Bain, Hardy, and Webster. They all gave no comment interviews.'

'I take it you put it to Hardy and Webster that we have evidence from Hannah Bain that they were all taking drugs that night, and that Webster was driving his camper while under the influence of both drugs and alcohol.'

'Of course, I also threatened to charge them all with attempting to pervert the course of justice by lying in their original statements. They all looked as guilty as sin but still refused to comment. I had no option but to release them. That's what happens when there are lawyers involved.'

'Okay, what Hannah Bain told me is inadmissible. If she was not prepared to say it on tape with a lawyer present, then it's as good as useless. Thanks for trying.'

'Okay, Boss, if you need me to do anything else just let me know.'

Chapter 28

Monday: 13th of November 2023

The rain was pouring down and the bogs around Glencoe looked saturated. The rivers ran fast as the mountain gullies emptied into them relentlessly. The roads were quiet for a Monday morning. He drove up to the checkpoint.

Please Son, slow down. Don't give them any reason to stop you.

'Don't worry, Mother. I know what I'm doing.' He changed down the gears and looked in the mirror, brushing the fringe of his hair away from his eyes.

He knew that the police cars no longer blocked the road leading to the roundabout at Ballachulish. They now simply parked on the grass verge and waved most of the cars through the checkpoint with only a cursory look into the front of the driver's window. He held his NHS card up to the window and smiled as he passed the glum, rain-drenched police officers.

He drove towards the Ballachulish Bridge as the daylight began to lift the darkness from the surrounding hills. He couldn't get Daisy out of his mind. The more he thought of her, the more aroused he became … It was unbearable.

He had to pull over into a lay-by and began looking at pictures he had saved on his phone. He unzipped his trousers and began masturbating. Eyes closed and face contorted, he tried desperately to keep the memory of Daisy undressing in his mind. He quickly relieved himself, letting out a pitiful whimper. He sat for a moment, breathing heavily. He could hear her screaming. His mind had blanked out what happened that day. All he could remember was watching the police frogmen recovering her body from the loch. He began banging the steering wheel with his fists in his frustration and shouting, 'Daisy … Daisy … Daisy!' He quickly came to his senses when he noticed a marked police car in the rear-view mirror slowing down before pulling in behind him.

He took a deep breath, reaching for the NHS card. He put the lanyard back around his neck, trying desperately to think of a plausible reason why he was sitting in a lay-by in the middle of nowhere at that time in the morning. His heart was racing. The police car just sat behind him. He was tempted to drive off when the driver's door suddenly opened and a uniformed officer got out.

He rolled down the window as the officer approached his car. 'Is everything alright?'

'That's what I'm supposed to ask you. Is there a problem with the car?'

'No, it's fine, Officer. I just pulled over to look for my locker key. I thought I might have left it at home this morning.'

'And did you?'

'No, it was in my jacket pocket,' he said, showing the officer the key.

'Do you have any identification on you? Your licence?' asked the officer.

'No, but I have my work pass.'

The rain was dripping from the peak of the officer's hat as he studied the picture and the information on the NHS pass before handing it back.

'Are you heading to work now?'

'Yes. In Fort William. I work in the hospital, in the geriatric ward.'

The officer made a cursory look into the rear of the car. 'Can you open your boot for me?'

'Why? There's nothing in the boot.'

'I'd still like to have a look for myself.'

'Do you have a search warrant?'

'No, but do you want me to get one?'

'No … I just don't know why you have to look in the boot, that's all. I'm going to be late for my shift.'

'Are you going to open it or not?'

'Yes.'

'Just give me the key, and I'll open it. No point in you getting soaked as well.'

He handed the officer the car keys and began to panic. He could not remember what was in the boot. Beads of sweat began to trickle down the side of his face. He was hyperventilating and took one of his pills to calm himself down.

He listened as the officer struggled with the key in the lock. The car jerked slightly when the boot was finally opened. He could see the officer standing staring into the boot for a moment before bending down. The noise of things being moved about worried him. He still couldn't remember if there was anything still in it.

He let out the breath he wasn't aware he was holding when the boot door was banged closed.

Son, smile at the nice officer, don't let him think you have anything to hide.

He rolled down the driver's window as the officer approached.

'This is a good old car you've got. You can't beat the Germans for quality. It must be, what, fifteen years old at least?' he guessed, handing back the keys.

'Yes, it still runs well.'

'Okay, you can go. The road ahead is waterlogged in some places, so drive carefully.'

'Thank you, Officer. I will.'

He slowly manoeuvred the car back onto the edge of the road. The police officer suddenly shouted at him to stop.

He watched him approach, stopping at the rear of the car. *What the fuck is he doing now?* He listened to the boot being opened again, and then a heavy-handed bang made him jump.

'That's it now. I didn't close it properly. I think you need to have that lock looked at.' The officer then turned back to his own car.

Being careful not to drive off too quickly, he continued onto the road. As he changed up the gears, the police car remained stationary in his rear-view mirror. It finally went out of view when he took a sharp bend. A twisted smile of relief spread slowly across his face.

You're such a clever boy. They'll never catch you.

'I know, Mother … but I need to find a Daisy.'

Chapter 29

Saturday: 2ⁿᵈ of December 2023

The beginning of winter was bitterly cold and Glencoe was beginning to look desolate. The hordes of tourists had long gone and many of the pubs and hotels had closed for the rest of the year.

With the investigation dragging on week after week without any new leads, most of the detectives were becoming despondent. They needed a breakthrough, and they needed it soon. Dorsey took the train back to Glasgow to see his son, leaving Crawford in charge while he was gone.

He spent the day with Daniel and managed to tempt him away from his gaming console with tickets to see an IMAX 3D movie at the Science Centre. Out of the four options, Daniel predictably picked *Top Gun: Maverick*. Dorsey prepared himself for two hours of high-fiving, loud Americans laden with testosterone, banging on about how great they were. Lost in a world of nonsense for a couple of hours, he was surprised that he actually enjoyed it.

Daniel was now wanting to become a pilot when he left school, another change of career. He was planning to be a doctor only a couple of weeks before; at least he hadn't decided to become a terrorist yet. They got a taxi back to Newlands just as the heavens opened up.

After dropping Daniel back home, he said his goodbyes and left. With Liz at a work's night out, he decided to simply head back to the city centre and get the train back to Glencoe.

It stopped raining. He walked to Strathbungo for some fresh air and to have a look at all the old haunts he used to drink in when he was younger. Most of the pubs had changed, others had gone. When he reached the Allison Arms, he decided to go in and have a pint. He still had plenty of time to catch the train and be back before the shift change and the debrief. The pub hadn't changed in years. The bar was quiet, and he got served straight away. He had hardly sat down with his pint when he got a call from Knox.

'Frank, I've spent the last fifteen minutes trying to figure out the best way to tell you this, but there isn't a better way other than to tell you what Cullen has told me. You're off the case.'

'I'm off the case? What the fuck does that mean?'

'As of today, you're no longer in charge of the Glencoe investigation. I'm sorry, Frank. I did tell him he was making a mistake, but he's been under pressure from the negative media. He also had a meeting yesterday with the Lord Advocate and the lawyer for the Keenan family, who were suggesting maybe it was time to get someone new to look at the case with fresh eyes.'

'Hope you told him where to go!'

'Maybe not the way you might have put it, but I told him if anyone could catch this killer it was you. He said he was meeting the chief constable this evening to tell him his decision. But, as it stands, from today you're no longer in charge of that investigation.'

'Well, just tell that weasel Cullen it was him that insisted I take over the case. This is not happening. Fuck it!'

'Calm down, Frank, it's out of my hands.'

'The Lord Advocate is a political appointee of the SNP government; they can't be allowed to decide on operational matters in an investigation. If you let them take me off this case because some fucking lawyer in a wig tells them to, then I'll be handing in my notice!'

'Frank, don't do anything hasty. You've nearly six weeks of holidays due to you. Take them now and go on a cruise

213

with Liz. Let someone else deal with this nightmare of a case.'

'Are you serious, a fucking cruise?'

'Well, take her to … Frank … Frank?'

Dorsey left the bar, his pint untouched, and walked to the taxi rank, ignoring the repeated calls from Knox. He eventually hailed down a taxi. 'Queen Street Station, mate.'

The journey to Tyndrum was a form of torment that he had never experienced before, torn between feelings of anger, resentment, and failure. Although he didn't understand why, he knew he had to get back. He stopped himself from phoning Mitchell and sent a text instead. *George, I am on my way back, can you ask the day shift to stay behind?* The phone immediately buzzed. He switched it off, not wanting to explain everything over the phone, even to Mitchell.

The drive to Glencoe from Tyndrum helped to calm his thoughts. Maybe it was for the best. He had never given up trying to find the missing student, but he had to accept what everybody else at the station had believed for weeks, even months: she was dead and lying in a bog.

He parked outside the police station, feeling that most of the detectives would be delighted when they heard that he was finally gone. Like a worn-out football manager fighting relegation only to run out of games, it was time to go.

By the time he got back to Glencoe village it was nearly eight o'clock, and the day shift would be getting ready to head home. He knew he had to face them, and he was as well to do it when the full squad was there to see his humiliation.

Mitchell was standing at the front entrance, his face grim. 'Frank, I'm sorry … I've asked the day shift to stay back until you got here. Everyone is in the muster. They all know. Mackie phoned about an hour ago and spoke to Crawford.'

'Well, George, let's get this over with.'

Never in all the years he had been a police officer had he ever walked into a muster room of detectives that was in total silence. He made his way to the other end of the room and stood with his back to the incident boards that held all the pieces of a cryptic puzzle he had failed to solve. He looked around at the solemn faces that he had come to know as good, hard-working detectives.

'This will be the last time I will speak to you as the senior officer in this case. I am aware that you have already heard that I have been taken off the investigation and a new senior officer will be appointed.' He coughed; he was more nervous than he had ever been in his career.

'I want to thank every one of you for your tireless efforts to solve this case, and to find Erin Keenan and bring the killer of Lena Kaminski and Evinka Janik to justice. If there have been any shortcomings in how this investigation has been handled, those failures are my sole responsibility. I am confident that you will continue to work to the best of your abilities to bring this matter to a successful conclusion. In that you have my full confidence. As of tomorrow, I intend to hand in my resignation. I don't have anything else to say.'

'Frank, before you head off, you should know that if you are taken off the case we will all be resigning first thing tomorrow,' said Crawford, looking back at his fellow detectives, who were all, to the disbelief of Dorsey, nodding in agreement.

'No! You have to stay here. Find Erin Keenan and whoever killed those two young women!'

'Sir,' interrupted one of the detectives, 'when you first turned up at the Lairigmor ruins to take over this case, we all thought you were a conceited arrogant bastard, and you probably still are.'

'Don't hold back.'

'It had to be said, sir. But that night, when you held up a picture of Erin Keenan and said to us that if she was your sister or daughter, you'd all still be out looking for her, it made me think about my own daughter, and every day I get up to go to work, that's what I think about. If she was missing, I'd never stop looking for her.'

'Most of you have families to think about, mortgages to pay.'

'We know, sir,' said another detective standing beside Crawford. 'But we've also got to do the right thing, and you can't order us not to. It's not your call. We've never worked on a case where we've been driven so hard day after day, but we all know that you're here in the morning before we even start and still here sometimes after midnight.'

'George, fucking help me here.'

'They're right, you are an arrogant bastard at times, but if you let them take you off this case, then you're letting down the families and everyone in this room. You're the only person in this room who thinks Erin Keenan is still alive, and because *you* think it, we're all prepared to put our own doubts aside and try to find her. So don't let them take you off the case without putting up a fight. If you do, you're not the Frank Dorsey I know.'

'Boss, I have already spoken to CS Mackie and told her our position,' said Crawford. 'We don't want another SIO.'

'Fuck,' was all Dorsey could think to say.

'Sir,' shouted Dixon from the open door at the other end of the room. 'That's the chief constable on the phone.'

The phone call from Chief Constable Rankin was awkward, and it was clear that the mutiny had been placed at his door when CS Fiona Mackie passed the buck on to Cullen, who lost his nerve when he heard the number of detectives who were prepared to resign.

'Frank, I have overruled Cullen. You're still on the case. He should have spoken to me before he made that decision.'

'Still on it, or in charge of it?'

'In charge, of course. I know you were given a poisoned chalice when you took this case. It's one thing to have to find a missing person, but that has become time-precious since

216

the discovery of the two bodies. You haven't even been on this investigation for four months and have discovered two victims that nobody was looking for.'

'Actually, the first body was found before I was involved in the case.'

'Okay, that may be so. But as I explained to Cullen, we cannot be dictated to by lawyers and politicians who have no idea about the amount of work involved in this type of investigation. I'm not taking you off this case, now or in the foreseeable future. You have my full confidence.'

'Thank you, sir. That means a lot to me, but I've had enough. I think you *should* get someone else to take over the case. Like your deputy said, a pair of fresh eyes. Maybe he should take it on?'

'Okay, you don't have to be facetious, Frank, but I understand your position. Why don't you take a few days off and think about it? I can send CS Mackie down, maybe it's time she got her wellies out.'

'I've made my mind up, sir, but I'll stay here until you can find a permanent replacement.'

'Okay, Frank, I guess there's no point ordering you to do what you don't want to do. But I hope your threat to resign was just to call Cullen's bluff?'

'No, it wasn't.'

'Well, let's get this done without making it a rod for the media to thrash us with. You stay in post until I appoint your replacement.'

'Okay.'

'Frank, when I heard that there were a dozen detectives, virtually all of whom hadn't worked with you before, threatening to resign en masse, I knew we had the best man to solve this case. You can't buy that kind of loyalty. I hope by the time I get someone to take over you'll have changed your mind.'

'Thanks, sir.'

Dorsey just sat for ten minutes, staring at the wall opposite. He had a sense of relief now he would soon no longer be burdened with the case.

Chapter 30

Sunday: 3ʳᵈ of December 2023

The next morning, Mitchell handed his boss a copy of the newspaper with the story of his alleged sacking. They say good news travels fast but bad news travels faster. Now his sacking was in the public domain, the fact it was overturned would mean nothing to those who thrive on the downfall of others. *Schadenfreude* was a human condition that even the most virtuous were guilty of from time to time. Dorsey just looked briefly at the headline: *The Bodies in the Bog Case: Chief Inspector Frank Dorsey sacked.*

'Police Scotland seem to have more leaks than Scottish Water,' said Mitchell.

'I take it you're not going anywhere, Frank?' asked Crawford, who was bringing in a trolley load of files with all the statements taken over the last few weeks by uniformed officers that still had to be looked at for possible leads.

'Bill, I appreciate what you and the others did yesterday. The chief constable has overruled Cullen and asked me to remain in charge of the case, but I think maybe it's time for a new SIO to take over. I told him that I would wait until he found someone else before handing over the case. That means it's my decision. Now you and the rest of the squad have no reason to resign. If you can let them know the situation, I'd be grateful,' said Dorsey, taking a folder of statements from the trolley to peruse.

After an hour of reading statements of no consequence to the investigation, his phone buzzed – it was Liz. He hesitated for a moment before answering. 'Hi, Liz. How are you?'

'Frank, I heard they've taken you off the case.'

'Where did you hear that?'

'A colleague told me. She saw it online. Is it true?'

'It is and it isn't.'

'What kind of answer is that? Are you off it or not?'

'I was taken off the case by Cullen yesterday, although he didn't have the guts to tell me himself. He got Knox to do it.'

'So, you *are* off the case!'

'Cullen was later overruled by the chief constable, but by that time my whole team knew about it. You can't be undermined to that extent and still retain the respect you need to lead hardened detectives in a complex triple murder enquiry.'

'Triple murder? Did you find another body?'

'No, but apparently I'm the only person here who believes Erin Keenan may still be alive. Even George thinks she's dead, but no one told me how deluded I've become until yesterday. That's why I told the chief constable that it was time for someone else to lead the investigation. I've had enough.'

'Until you find her dead or have some other evidence that confirms she's dead, then she *is* still alive! I've never thought of you as someone who cared what other people thought. If you think there's a chance that she is alive then you must keep looking for her … Frank?'

'Yeah, I'm still here. They've still to appoint a new SIO. I said I'd stay on until they find one.'

'Frank, please phone your boss and tell him you've changed your mind. You'll never live with yourself if you give up. If everybody else thinks she's dead, then the investigation will just go cold. If there's even the slightest chance she's alive, you'll find her. I know you will!'

Dorsey didn't know what to say. He wasn't expecting this reaction. If anything, he'd have thought she would be pleased he was off the case.

'Are you still there?' asked Liz.

'Yeah, I don't know what to say to you. I have already made my decision.'

'Right! Now you're just being fucking stubborn. Your pride's been hurt. Get over it and do your fucking job! If you stay on, I'll speak to my boss and try to get time off to come up.'

'I've never heard you swear before, it suits you.'

'Fuck, Frank, will you phone him or not?'

'Okay, so long as you agree to come up.'

'I'll be there even if I have to threaten to resign myself. Now phone him!'

'It's Sunday, I'll do it tomorrow.'

'Do it now. You must have his personal mobile number.'

'Okay.'

'Text me when you've done it. I need to go. I've got a bath running. Look after yourself. Helen told me that you were looking worn out yesterday.'

'Helen! I didn't know you were in contact with my ex-wife?'

'I told you that I know the lawyer she's been seeing. He gave her my number a few weeks ago when she couldn't get a hold of you. Something about your son being in trouble at school for punching another boy. She phoned again last night to say she was worried about you.'

'Okay, it just seems a bit weird that you two are on talking terms and you're a friend of that fucking arse of a lawyer she shacked up with.'

'Frank, I didn't phone her. She phoned me. The fact I know Richard Hamilton is neither here nor there. I know hundreds of lawyers. I need to go. Remember to text me.'

There was now more pressure on him not to resign. He had never heard Liz being so forceful, but then he had never seen her cross-examining witnesses. Then he thought about what Mitchell had said in the muster room: '*If you let them take you off this case, then you're letting down the families and everyone in this room. You're the only person in this room who thinks Erin is still alive ...'*

He rarely had reason to speak to the chief constable, probably half a dozen times in his career. Now he had the discomfort of speaking to him twice in two days. Rankin could not have been any more supportive and ended with a promise to put the gutter press in their place by issuing a statement that the recent news reports of Dorsey's removal from the investigation were without substance.

After feeling that a weight had been lifted from his shoulders, he took on the burden once more with new energy and belief. Liz's rant, strewn with swear words, was exactly what he needed to knock him back into shape. Now he had to inform the whole squad and civilian staff of his change of heart. This was going to be even more embarrassing than when he had to tell them he had been sacked.

Chapter 31

Monday: 4th of December 2023

They had been on the hillside for over three hours when the accident happened. Ryan lay on the wet heather where he had come to rest after slipping on a moss covered stone, before tumbling over rocks and through a tangled web of brambles. His hands and face were covered in small cuts and scratches. He tried to sit up. 'I think it's broken,' he groaned, feeling his left ankle. 'I don't think I'll be able to walk on it.'

'Oh my God!' shouted Lucy, the wind blowing in her face as she gradually made her way down to him.

'See if you can phone for help.' He managed to sit up, his face grimacing with pain as Lucy tried her mobile.

'I can't get a signal,' she sighed, putting the mobile phone back in her pocket. 'Can you try your phone?'

'The battery is dead,' sighed Ryan as he looked down the hillside towards Tyndrum in the distance. 'I'll never get back down like this. Lucy, you'll have to try to make it to the road. I can't walk on this and it's going to get dark soon.'

'No, Ryan, I can't leave you here.'

'You'll have to. You might get a signal on your phone when you get down to the road.'

'Okay,' she agreed reluctantly. 'I think it's going to rain.'

'We can't do anything about that, just go! I'll be alright.'

Lucy began her descent over the rocks and onto softer ground, but the hill was steep and slippery. She turned back, becoming more anxious when she could no longer see Ryan. She used her hiking poles to keep her from slipping as the wind tried its best to knock her off her feet.

She stopped to catch her breath and looked at the few cars and lorries travelling along the A82. The road seemed so near, but was still a long way down and surrounded by a forest of trees. She carried on, afraid it would get dark before she made it to the road.

She eventually reached a large outcrop of rock and was not sure how to get on to the next level. Moving along to a more manageable drop, she slid down on her backside, scraping her hands on the coarse rock. She wiped the blood on her jacket when she got to the bottom. She got up and struggled on through the waterlogged bog, her boots sinking in the mire and draining her strength. All she could hear was the sound of the wind as it swept over the hillside, her hands now numb with the cold. Her breathing was heavy and she began to perspire, the layers of clothing under her puffer jacket trapping her body heat. She forced her way through a thicket of gorse bushes and onto a stony path. Ahead, a dense forest lay between her and the main road. She decided to try her phone, but it wasn't in her pocket. She began to panic, realising it must have fallen out when she slipped over the rocky outcrop. It was too late to go back for it.

The ground was now easier to walk on and she followed the path through the high columns of trees that blocked out most of the fading daylight. She hurried along the path, breathless. All she could hear was the trees creaking and the wind whistling through them. Her heart was racing and beads of sweat were forming on her brow. She walked faster, her boots crunching the twigs and pine leaves underfoot.

Then the path suddenly disappeared under a tree that had fallen over and become overgrown with brambles. There was no path on the other side, only more brambles sticking out in every direction, making it impossible for her to go any further. She had to turn back and find another way.

The wind was now swirling above the canopy and one gnarled tree groaned and looked like it was about to crash to the ground. She forced her way through a gap in the trees, long, bony twigs grabbing at her clothes and hair. The steepness of the ground propelled her forward. She reached out, grabbing low hanging branches to slow herself down but lost her footing, falling into the side of a tree trunk and cracking her head. She got to her feet and continued, determined to get help for Ryan. The moon emerged from the clouds, casting long shadows. The last of the daylight had gone. She hurried on down the hillside in spite of the burning pain in her legs.

Eventually the light from isolated houses appeared on the other side of the glen. The sky was now dark and a scattering of stars had emerged between the clouds. It took another ten minutes before her efforts were rewarded. The trees began thinning out and she could see the road.

She jumped over a ditch to the grass verge at the side of the road. She sat down, utterly exhausted. She had made it.

It began raining, the wind blowing tiny shards of icy rain into her frozen face. There were no cars coming from either direction. She began walking towards Tyndrum. She wanted to run to get help for Ryan, but the strength was already sapped from her legs.

She walked on until the headlights of a car appeared in the distance, heading towards her. The car slowed down, eventually stopping on the opposite side of the road. A door opened. She turned to see a man standing outside the driver's side, the rain and wind lashing against him. He shouted, 'Do you need a lift? You can't walk in this.'

She stood and stared in his direction, unable to see his face. She thought about Ryan lying in pain, depending on her.

'Hurry up if you're coming,' the man shouted. 'This is only going to get worse.'

She walked over to him. 'I need help, my boyfriend is up there somewhere. He thinks his ankle is broken,' she said, pointing back up the hillside, which was lost in the darkness. 'Can't you just phone for help?'

'I don't have my phone. I left it at work. I was just heading back to get it. Jump in, we'll need to go and get help. He'll not last long up there in this weather.'

She walked to the passenger door and got in. The man's hair and face were soaking wet. He put the car into gear and made a U-turn. He drove in the direction of Tyndrum, which was at least three miles back the way he came.

'What's your name?' he asked, handing her a bottle of orange juice.

'Lucy,' she answered.

'You remind me of someone … Her name was Daisy.'

Chapter 32

On the platform in the school hall, Dorsey sat at a trestle table alongside the local councillor. He was a big man with curly red hair who had insisted another meeting was necessary to deal with the concerns of the local community. Dorsey had suggested to CS Mackie that she should attend, but she declined. He wasn't disappointed or surprised, and asked Mitchell to take her place instead. Despite the weather, the hall was packed. Tea and biscuits had been laid out, and those attending huddled in groups around the more vocal individuals in the parish. A damp smell prevailed as the old radiators coughed and creaked to heat the place.

The local press was present in the form of Kitty Murdoch, a reporter from the *Oban Times*, who was one of the first to take a seat, a MacBook on her lap and rainwater dripping from her coat. She had covered the case from the beginning and was still writing regular articles about it, even when the rest of the mainstream media had moved on. There was only so much you could write about a case that had had no leads for months.

Dorsey liked the young reporter; she was not aggressive or annoying like some he had dealt with over the years. After the death of Alex Munro, he had emailed her information about the Military Cross that Munro was unfairly denied. Kitty wrote a touching obituary and started an online petition to have the medal awarded posthumously. It was now being supported by the local community and dozens of veteran soldiers who had served with Munro in Afghanistan. The constituency MP had even asked questions in the House of Commons, which resulted in a promise from the PM to investigate the matter. Dorsey was now expecting a call from Colonel Chambers, accusing him of breaking his word as a gentleman.

The councillor banged the table with his fist to get the attention of the hall. 'Can you take your seats?' he shouted, the tone in his voice carrying the gravitas of someone accustomed to public speaking. Soon the rows of chairs began to fill. 'If there's no seats left, just stand at the back of the hall.'

The councillor then introduced the two detectives. Dorsey spoke first and proceeded to give an update in relation to the investigation, acknowledging that despite the best endeavours of the police, the killer remained at large. He acknowledged that the passage of time meant the police now believed Erin Keenan had met the same fate as the two bodies recovered in Lairigmor. He confirmed the investigation was now officially a triple murder enquiry and that the search for the body of the missing student would resume if an area was identified for the police to concentrate their limited resources on.

'If this goes on, it's going to devastate this area. My bookings for next year are way down, half what they should be. Who'd want to come here on holiday if there's a bloody lunatic running around murdering people?' complained the owner of a hotel in North Ballachulish.

'I can't do anything about that,' replied Dorsey, who hadn't thought about the impact the murders were having on tourism.

'Well, Chief Inspector, you could try to catch the killer,' shouted a man at the back of the hall, who got an immediate chorus of support.

'We launched the largest manhunt in the history of this part of the country ...'

'But you haven't a clue who you're looking for,' shouted another disgruntled local. 'You even arrested poor Alex

Munro, God rest his soul, and he was the man who actually found one of the bodies!'

'Alex Munro was never arrested. We were grateful for his help and obviously shocked when we heard of his death.'

'You arrested Angus Sloan,' shouted another man, getting to his feet and pointing accusingly.

'We've had to question many people in this investigation. I am not here to discuss who we questioned or why. All those questioned have been eliminated from the enquiry.'

Mitchell stood up, knocking his chair over. 'If more of you lot came forward and provided a mouth swab then we wouldn't have wasted our time interviewing so many people, whom we could've easily eliminated with a simple DNA test! Alex Munro was asked twice to provide a DNA swab but refused to do so. That's why we had to question him.'

There were angry shouts and curses from the disgruntled locals in the hall. Some were putting their coats on and leaving through the back door. Others remained, determined to get answers.

'Kitty Murdoch, *Oban Times*. Chief Inspector, do you think this monster is likely to kill again?'

'So long as he's at liberty, there is every likelihood he will not stop until he's caught.'

The answers given did not satisfy anyone still in the hall and questions dried up. The meeting came to a dismal end, with many more getting up and leaving, most not hiding their disgust at what they had to listen to.

'Well, that went well, Frank,' said Mitchell, getting to his feet and putting on his coat.

'You can't blame them, can you? Chief Inspector,' said the councillor, offering his hand. 'It's not that they aren't grateful for all the hard work you and your team are doing. They're just worried this thing might go on for years and destroy their community. Without tourism, many businesses in this area will simply close down altogether.'

'Thanks, Councillor, we're doing everything we can to catch this man. But I fully understand the feeling of the people you represent.'

'It probably feels like you're looking for a needle in a haystack when there might not even be a needle there to find. He could be living anywhere. Anyway, thanks for coming by,' said the councillor, putting his cap on. 'I'm off home now. Goodnight to both of you. It's a wild-looking night out there.'

Dorsey and Mitchell stood at the steps of the school hall and watched the last of the locals leaving the meeting. Mitchell's phone buzzed. He stepped back into the hall to take the call as Dorsey lit another cigarette and walked towards his car.

'Frank, hold on. That was the station. There's an incident involving a hillwalker who broke his ankle. A local sheep farmer found him and raised the alarm.'

'What's that got to do with us?'

'His girlfriend had gone for help a few hours earlier but must have got lost coming down the hillside. There's no record of her calling for help or attending the police station in Tyndrum, where they were staying. A mountain rescue team are searching for her.'

'Okay, let's go,' said Dorsey, getting into his car.

Chapter 33

It had now been snowing for two days and most of the minor roads were impassable further north. With its snow-covered rooftops, Kinlochleven had a magical feel to it. The mountains around the loch were shrouded in a mantle of powdery fresh snow, beautiful to look at, but treacherous to the unwary.

Dorsey woke after only a few hours' sleep and sat on the edge of his bed with his head in his hands. The name Lucy Potter had joined the other names that disturbed his sleep, night after night.

The missing hillwalker had not been found after a further day of searching the hillside. The head of the mountain rescue team had called off the search after her mobile phone was found and there had been no trace of her. It was immediately logged as an abduction.

The case was now drawing attention from all over the world as international TV crews began snapping up all the available hotel rooms and other accommodation in the area. How ironic, thought Dorsey, that this additional abduction had tipped the balance and the local business owners, who were complaining about the loss of tourism, were now doing well out of the notoriety of having a serial killer on the loose in the glens.

The gritters had been out early and the B863 to Glencoe was open as Dorsey and Mitchell headed into the station. Mitchell had one of the morning papers on his lap. He had already read the front page. It didn't hold back with its

231

criticism of the police investigation now that another young woman had been abducted, this time under their noses. Incompetence was clearly how the paper saw the handling of the case.

'What do we know about this missing hillwalker?'

'She's twenty-two and a primary school teacher from Edinburgh. She's also a lieutenant in the AR.'

'She's in the Army Reserves?'

'Yes. She was top of her survival course and very highly regarded as someone who can look after herself.'

'I take it her family have been informed?'

'Yes, her parents are staying in a hotel in Glencoe. Her father is ex-army and has organised a search party of locals and some ex-army volunteers from his old regiment. He's also offering twenty thousand pounds for information leading to his daughter being found.'

'That's not going to help. The phones will be inundated with oddballs … George, when we get into the station, can you contact Glasgow and ask the family liaisons officer to contact the Keenans?'

'That's already been done. They know about Potter.'

'Okay,' said Dorsey, keeping his eyes on the road. 'How the hell did he get past our roadblocks? We'll have to check every vehicle that was logged that night. Lucy Potter must have been abducted sometime between when she left her boyfriend and when the mountain rescue team arrived. That's only around three hours. I want the uniformed officers that were manning the checkpoints to submit their logbooks. I want to have a look at them.'

'That should already have been logged onto HOLMES.'

'That's if they've been doing their jobs properly. I'm beginning to think the suggestions online that a cop is the serial killer might be true.'

'You're not serious, Frank.'

'Nothing would surprise me in this fucking case.'

232

Chapter 34

In an overgrown field of weeds and bracken on the edge of an ancient woodland, a mature stag rubbed its antlers against the trunk of a tree. The stag stopped, dark eyes alert as it sniffed the air, before stretching down to eat the lichen and moss that fell to the ground around the exposed roots. Above, a barn owl was perched on the ruins of a chimney stack. It let out a long, harsh screech before flying off into the darkness.

The only sound was the drip, drip, drip of water. It was pitch black. She tried to think. Her mind was confused, but she knew something terrible had happened. Her eyes gradually adjusted to the darkness. *What the fuck!* She realised she was wearing a blue dress with nothing underneath. She called out, but her mouth was so dry, she barely made a sound. When she tried to sit up her head swooned. She felt a sickness rise in her stomach. Suddenly, she became aware of the strap on her ankle and the long chain it was attached to. A panic gripped her. She had to think. If only she could think … Had she lost her mind? Was this an asylum? Then she remembered the doctor. The injection, and slipping back into a deep sleep. *No, it wasn't a doctor.* Her mind began to clear. *Think! Think! How long have I been here?* All of a sudden, a lullaby started playing in her head. It was something she remembered from her childhood.

As the fog in her mind slowly lifted, the music stopped. She got out of the bed, dragging the chain towards where she now recalled there was a bathroom. The concrete floor was

233

cold on her bare feet. Shivering and confused, she slowly opened the door. *Think, think.*

She found the light switch. The bulb buzzed and flickered before it finally came on, a dim blue light that barely revealed the cold, dirty bathroom. Looking into the cracked mirror above the sink, she recoiled in terror at the reflection staring back at her. She hardly recognised herself. Her face was caked in makeup so thick and dry it resembled a Venetian mask from the Middle Ages.

Touching what was left of her hair, she removed a kirby grip and dropped it in the sink. She then wiped the red lipstick from her mouth with the back of her hand before washing most of the makeup off.

There was a constant drip from one of the taps. Staring at the bathtub, she recalled the water on her skin, his hands with their long, dirty fingernails. She began to gag, vomiting into the sink until her ribs began to hurt. After emptying the little that was in her stomach, she fell to the floor, shivering. The blue bulb above her head buzzed again like a giant blowfly.

As she lay there, other memories came back as though she was slowly being released from an evil spell. She remembered making her way down the hillside, deeper and deeper into the woods, until she eventually reached the road, where she got into a car. She couldn't remember the face, but the voice was soft and made her feel safe. She was on her way to get help for Ryan. He gave her a bottle of orange juice; it had a bitter taste. The last thing she could recall was the headlights of cars coming the other way, making her feel sleepy. Then nothing. *Think … Think!*

Using the side of the bathtub, she pulled herself back onto her feet. She remembered the intermittent flashing lights and being moved into various positions on the bed. She began thinking about what might have been happening to her while she was unconscious. The sudden fear that she had been raped made her feel sick again. She retched and heaved over the sink, but there was nothing to bring up.

She went back into the other room, the light from the bathroom revealing the starkness of the bare brick walls and the low, uneven ceiling criss-crossed with dark wooden beams. She looked for a way out, but the door was locked. There was no handle on the inside. It was impossible to open. She listened, but could hear nothing from the other side.

She moved slowly around the room, stumbling in the darkness. There was a small window, but it was boarded up on the outside. Apart from the wrought iron-framed bed and a small bedside cabinet, there was nothing to indicate it had ever been a bedroom. She lay back down on the bed and wrapped the duvet around herself. *Oh my God. Where am I?*

Chapter 35

The police station was now under siege from the world's media. Dorsey and Mitchell made their way through the scrum of reporters and photographers who were now virtually camped outside the police station. He ignored the raft of questions, some sounding more like accusations.

The front door was locked, and Dorsey had to bang on the glass panel to get in. 'For God's sake,' Mitchell said. 'How are we supposed to do our job with this circus following us around?'

Once in the station, Dorsey ordered the duty sergeant to get out from behind his counter. 'I want you and two constables to go out there and clear those reporters away from the building. Anyone who refuses to move, arrest them. They're obstructing this investigation.'

'Yes, sir, I'll get rid of them alright!'

The incident room was manic. Every one of the detectives was either taking calls or typing on their laptops. The incident board now had the picture of Lucy Potter on it. The lack of evidence in the four cases was baffling.

The four police officers who were on checkpoint duty the day Potter went missing were standing outside his office. He indicated to them to follow him in.

Dorsey took his jacket off and put it on the back of his chair before sitting down. The four officers stood to attention; the gravity of the situation etched on their faces. He opened a folder on his desk, reading the findings of the senior officer he had asked to investigate the logbooks. 'Your duty was to log every vehicle that passed through your checkpoints. Is that correct?'

'Yes, sir,' they responded almost in unison.

'From what I have here, that doesn't look like what you were doing.'

'No, sir,' said one of the officers, who seemed to be their agreed spokesman. 'Those were our original orders. Several weeks ago, we were ordered only to stop vehicles that we hadn't previously checked unless there was something we thought suspicious. We were following orders, sir.'

'Orders from whom?'

'Chief Superintendent Mackie, sir. I understand she had received several complaints from local businessmen and farmers about the constant backup of traffic on the A82. It was affecting their businesses. That's all I know, sir.'

'Okay, just go back to your duties.'

Dorsey sat for a while, wondering if there was any point in phoning Mackie to accuse her of undermining the investigation. He even thought of going over her head and phoning the chief constable, but decided neither call would make any difference to the fate of Lucy Potter.

There was a chap at his door. 'Sir, I've just had a call,' said PC Dixon, hardly able to contain the excitement in her voice. 'Someone has found a body on a farm, just a few miles from the Ballachulish Bridge along the A828, heading towards Appin.'

'Who found it?'

'Actually, it was an estate agent who was showing someone around the farmhouse that's been up for sale for nearly five years. I've got his details and the address of the property. I've asked him to wait there.'

'Is there any indication who it is?'

'He's sure it's female, but it's badly decomposed, and he didn't get too close.'

'Contact Inverness and let them know that we need

forensics down here immediately. Who else in here knows about this?'

'No one. I have just taken the call.'

'Well, keep it that way for now. I don't want this leaking to those reporters outside.'

'Can I help, sir?'

'Okay, I'll phone Inverness. I want you to set up a roadblock on the A828 just beyond the bridge and stop any journalist following me to the locus. Before you go, ask Mitchell to meet me at my car in ten minutes.'

Dorsey had just finished his call to Inverness when Mitchell got into the passenger seat. 'What's going on?'

'A body has been found on a farm not far from the bridge on the A828. I've just put the address into the satnav, but for some reason nothing's coming up.' He handed Mitchell the note with the address on it. 'Can you see if you can find it on Google?'

'Who found the body?'

'An estate agent, would you believe. He found it while showing a potential buyer around the property. He thinks it's female, but it looks like it's been there for a while. It's badly decomposed.'

'Do you think it's Erin Keenan?'

'I think I'll wait this time until I see it. If it is badly decomposed, it's not Lucy Potter. Have you managed to find that address yet?'

'Yes, take the road that goes under the bridge past the Ballachulish Hotel. It's only a few miles from there.'

'Okay, let's go.'

When they reached the hotel, they could see Dixon up ahead, standing beside her car. She acknowledged them as they passed with what was halfway between a salute and a wave. It made Dorsey smile, which was rare these days.

'That's Loch Linnhe on that side,' said Mitchell, who was watching their progress on his app.

'I think that must be the estate agent,' said Dorsey, slowing down and pulling over to the grass verge. 'He looks pretty shaken.'

'Well, unlike us, he doesn't expect to come across dead bodies doing his job.'

They both got out of the car and introduced themselves. The estate agent was a man in his mid-thirties, dressed like a country gentleman heading to a grouse shoot. He took off his glasses and wiped them as he explained the fright he'd gotten.

'Who owns this place?' asked Dorsey.

'This farm or junk yard, depending on whether you're trying to sell it or buy it. It's been on the market since the owner died over five years ago. I'm selling it for the solicitor who's been dealing with the estate. It's been run down for years and the house is a hard sell. This is only the second viewing it's had in all that time. I'll never get a buyer for it now.'

'Who owned it?' asked Mitchell, taking out his notebook.

'Robert Campbell. He lived here on his own and let the place go to rack and ruin.'

'We'll need keys to search the house,' said Dorsey.

'Here, you can take these. I guess I won't be needing them for a while.'

'Can you show us where you found the body?'

'Of course, just follow me.'

They followed him up a path that led to the farmhouse. He suddenly stopped and pointed. 'It's in that woodshed. I'd rather not go any closer.'

The woodshed was on the verge of collapse. The lower part of the body was underneath some rotten logs, and in spite of its condition, it was clearly the body of a young woman. She had the same jacket on that Erin Keenan had worn when she went missing. Dorsey knelt down to have a better look and lifted the right hand. He had no doubt of her identity when he saw the Claddagh ring still on the finger her mother put it on for her twenty-first birthday. For some reason he blessed himself, something he hadn't done since he was a child.

The drive to Inverness the next day was tough. Dorsey hardly said a word to Mitchell the whole way up. He knew nothing about the other two victims and only discovered things about them after their post-mortems offered up clues to their identity. This post-mortem was different. He had hoped against hope that he would find Erin Keenan alive and return her to her family. The sense of failure now overwhelmed him. He decided he would not view the body. He only needed Dr Jamali to give him her provisional findings.

The doctor met them in the reception area and took them to her office. 'We still require confirmation of her identification, but I have no doubt it's Erin Keenan. There's the ring, and what was left of the clothing. These correspond to what she was wearing when she went missing. I have passed them on to forensics to be examined further.'

'We'll need to confirm her identity before we inform the family that it's definitely her,' said Dorsey. 'How do we do that now, dental records?'

'Yes, I have requested them already. The body is too far gone for any formal identification by a family member. Unfortunately, the decomposition has been quite extensive, and it also looks like the flesh and some internal organs have been eaten by what I can only assume were rats from the size of the teeth marks.'

'That's not something the family need to know about,' said Dorsey, remembering what her sister, Orla, had said to him. *I miss her every day. Please find her.*

'No, it's not relevant to the cause of death and I intend to leave it out of my final report.'

'When do you think you'll be able to confirm her identity?'

'Sometime today. They may have already emailed her dental records. I haven't had time to check. I've already X-rayed the teeth, so it won't take me long to make a comparison.'

'Do you have any idea when she was killed?' Dorsey asked.

'It is clear the body has been there for months. It had become entangled with the surrounding vegetation and the body fluids have seeped into the soil, which support this. The compression of the earth under the body also confirms to me that it was there for some time. I'm waiting for the entomology results.'

'Entomology results?'

'Yes, I had an entomology specialist examine the ground in the woodshed and the body for insect infestation, which can help with the estimation of how long the body has been dead. She discovered that the remains had been colonised by the larvae of blowflies which feed on the flesh, probably when the weather was still relatively mild. She will provide her findings in the next couple of days, which I expect will reaffirm my belief she was put in the woodshed shortly after she was killed.'

'You don't think she was killed at the farm where she was found?' asked Dorsey as Mitchell continued to take the salient points down in his notebook.

'Unlikely. It looks like where she was found was a deposition site. She was killed somewhere else and dumped there, probably shortly after she was killed. Her injuries support this.'

'What *were* her injuries?'

'Don't be impatient, Frank. I was coming to that.'

'Sorry.'

'She suffered a fracture to the back of her skull. This is consistent with blunt force trauma, in other words, being hit or hitting something very hard. This was the probable cause of her death. There are also three broken ribs. One of the ribs pierced the skin. She would've been bleeding from that wound. There is also some sign of internal bleeding which would also have contributed to her death. It looks like she was struck by a vehicle, fell backwards and hit the back of her head on the road.'

'A road accident?' quizzed Dorsey, looking at Mitchell, who looked as perplexed as Dorsey felt.

'Well, it could've been deliberate, but that might be impossible to prove.'

'Is there any injury that would indicate she was punched?'

'No, I've checked for that, Chief Inspector. It seems that Webster might have been telling the truth. I have looked at the photographs of his hand you sent. I would have expected to find some injury if he punched her and suffered that extent of bruising. There are no fractures on any part of the facial area.'

'Maybe he punched her in the ribs,' suggested Mitchell, looking up from his notebook.

'No, she would've been in no condition to run off if he inflicted that type of injury on her. It was too severe to have been done by punching. It's rare for someone to inflict injury on that part of the body with their fists during a fit of anger. The injuries are consistent with a road traffic accident. It's likely whoever knocked her down decided to hide the body rather than admit to the accident.'

'Because they were drunk or under the influence of drugs,' suggested Dorsey.

'Webster,' said Mitchell. 'Who else is it going to be? He went missing for at least an hour, maybe as long as two hours, after she ran off. They all lied about that in their first statements. They all lied about taking drugs. He could have knocked her down by accident when he went to look for her. He probably panicked and decided to conceal what he did because he was driving under the influence. He had plenty

242

of time to get to the farm and dump the body. I think Knox might've been right all along.'

'Finding out who may have knocked her down is really up to you. All I can do is tell you how she died. I have taken hair and tissue samples for toxicology tests to see if she had any drugs in her system. It's highly unlikely the lab will find anything after all this time, as unlike the other two bodies, the internal organs have rotted away.'

'So this has no connection whatsoever to the other two victims, and might have just been an accident?' asked Dorsey.

'There is nothing whatsoever to link this body with the other two. I am pretty sure she was already dead before you took on the case. So, don't feel bad, Frank. You were never meant to find her alive,' said Dr Jamali, closing her file. 'The only consolation for the families is that she never suffered and was likely killed as soon as her head hit the road.'

'And she was not the victim of a perverted serial killer,' said Mitchell.

The drive back down was as solemn as the drive up. Dorsey was still trying to accept in his own mind that he could have done nothing to save her.

Just before they reached Glencoe, Dr Jamali phoned. She confirmed that the dental records proved beyond any doubt that the body was that of Erin Keenan. Dorsey thanked her and let out a deep sigh. He had lived with the picture taken at Glen Etive in his mind for months. It was now replaced with the morbid memory of the corpse in the woodshed.

'Frank, this is not our fault. She was dead before we took on the case. We were given a poisoned chalice by Knox.'

'I know, George. I know.'

'We still have Lucy Potter to find.'

'I know, and that's what we're going to do.'

Chapter 36

Sunday: 10th of December 2023

She gradually came out of her trance, moving between confused dreams of escapism and horrifying reality, sometimes not sure which was which. She could now feel a cold wind coming through the cracks in the window shutters. Her body was so cold it felt like she was going to have a heart attack. She pulled the duvet up to her neck and tried to stop shaking.

He had not been back for days. How long exactly, she couldn't work out. Since the last injection had put her back into a state of semi-paralysis, time had become ephemeral and impossible to gauge. She felt the side of her face where he had hit her when she tried to fight him off. It was still swollen and sore to the touch.

Slivers of light were now gradually seeping into the grim room as the sound of birdsong told her the dawn was breaking in a world she could not see, only remember. The fog continued to lift from her mind. Still wearing the blue dress, she tried to sit up. Drained of strength, she quickly slumped back down. A painful headache made the skin around her skull feel tight. She was so thirsty her tongue felt stuck to the roof of her mouth. She couldn't remember the last time she drank water. She forced herself to sit up again when she noticed a bag of food and bottles of water on the floor beside the bed. He was keeping her alive for some reason.

She struggled to open the plastic top on one of the water bottles, fingers aching. Channelling all her strength into the stubborn piece of plastic, it finally opened. She drank, gasping for air between long breathless gulps. The water revived her a little and she wiped her chin, determined to find a way out before he came back.

She forced her weak body out of the bed. Her stomach ached from hunger; she was losing weight. Determined to eat to keep her strength, she opened the bag of food he left, looking at the ring-pull tins of tuna and sardines, jars of pickles, a large bag of nuts and raisins, and oatmeal biscuits. Food that didn't need to be cooked. She ate what she could before lying back on the bed, exhausted.

Her eyes gradually adjusted to the gloom, and she focused on a large hook on one of the beams that ran the width of the ceiling. Her first thought was to try to remove it to cut off the leather strap around her ankle.

Determined, she stood at the end of the bed and steadied herself by gripping the hook in the wooden beam. It was tight and wouldn't budge. Ignoring the pain in her hands, she twisted it until it finally loosened. After several more twists, she managed to unscrew it. The effort made her lightheaded, forcing her to lie back down on the bed to recover. Taking deep breaths to clear her head, she recalled her first days of training as an army reservist, when she had to push herself through the pain barrier to finish the brutal course. *Never give up* was the regimental motto that she repeated in her head as she gathered her strength.

Fearing he might return at any moment, she quickly sat up and opened her hand to look at the hook. It was heavy, but useless for cutting through the leather strap. Her eyes shifted to the chain attached to a metal bolt in the exposed brick wall behind the bed. Desperately, she stabbed around the bolt with the pointed end of the hook, but the brick seemed impossible to break. Her regiment's motto became a mantra in her head. Her fingers ached, covered in blisters and red-brick dust, attacking the brick in a flurry of stabs until a crack appeared above the bolt. *Never give up. Never give up.*

She yanked at the chain. The bolt refused to budge, but the hole around it grew larger as fragments of the brick gave way.

She was still pulling at the chain when she heard the creak of floorboards. She lay back down and pulled the duvet around her. Her heart was pounding so hard she could hear the blood pumping in her ears. She pretended to be asleep as the sound of the padlocks being opened terrified her.

She could sense his presence at the foot of the bed. Then she heard him moving around the room, lifting things and muttering to himself. His voice changed back and forth, as if there was someone else in the room arguing with him.

He then sat on the edge of the bed, breathing heavily. He began to rub himself over his trousers. She froze as he pulled down the duvet. She could feel his eyes staring at her as he muttered, 'Daisy, I know you're awake.'

She suddenly sat up, unable to control her rage. 'I'm not fucking Daisy, you fucking freak!' She lashed out with the metal hook, drawing blood from his startled face as he jumped back, almost falling off the bed. 'You try to put a needle near me again and I'll fucking stick it in your ugly fucking face! You're nothing but a fucking freak!'

He wiped the blood from his face. 'You're *not* Daisy. She would never do that to me.'

'Because I'm Lucy! You fucking freak!'

'Stop it!' he pleaded, backing away from her, the voices in his head taunting him to do something. The bottom of his face began to spasm, his eyes now black with anger. He stood at the door as she screamed at him again.

'Let me go, you fucking weirdo!'

He turned and went out, slamming the metal door closed and frantically sliding the large snibs over before locking the padlocks. He sat on the floor outside the door, the voices in his head continuing to torment him. He began to cry, whimpering like a child. 'Mother, she hit me.'

Emboldened by his pathetic reaction, Lucy began pulling at the metal chain again. The rage that rushed through her body gave her the strength she needed. The bolt finally came free, flying across the room like a bullet and crashing against the metal door.

The noise of the bolt hitting the door startled him. The voices in his head became intense. *Kill her! Kill her!* He got up and went into the kitchen, pulling a drawer so hard it landed on the floor, scattering its contents. He picked up a large carving knife, the voices urging him on. He went back into the hall and unlocked the door.

She was standing beside the bed with the music box, her fist gripped around the pink ballerina. 'Come near me and I'll break it off and smash this fucking thing into bits.'

'Put it down, it's not yours. Put it down!' he demanded.

'I know, it's Daisy's … You fucking freak. I'll smash it. Get fucking out of here!'

He backed slowly out of the room with his eyes fixed on the music box. He quickly slammed the door closed. He began banging his head off the door. In his pique of anger, he was unaware that he had gripped the blade of the knife in his other hand so tightly it sliced open the skin. He suddenly realised what he had done and dropped the knife on the floor, staring at the raw gash as the blood dripped through his fingers.

Lucy moved towards the door and listened to him moaning as he struggled with the padlocks, arguing with himself like a spoiled child. She heard him go into the other room. There was a thud, the sound of something heavy falling onto the floor. She could feel the cold air on her feet as the front door opened and quickly closed again with a bang. The sound of a car driving away made her fall to the floor, exhausted. He was gone.

Chapter 37

Monday: 11th of December 2023

Duncan Webster's uncle protested as his beloved campervan was loaded onto a police recovery truck. He looked at the warrant again. He could not understand why this was happening. The two constables who had served the warrant refused to tell him any more than what was in the court order. The campervan was taken to the vehicle forensic unit to be examined.

After consultation with the Crown Office, it was agreed to offer Hannah Bain and Jack Hardy immunity from prosecution for any potential charges arising out of the possession of drugs and lying in their original statements. In exchange they agreed through their lawyers to provide full statements and be Crown witnesses in any proceedings that may be brought against Duncan Webster.

Once their statements were emailed to Dorsey, he ordered the arrest of Webster. He planned to interview him after the funeral of Erin Keenan, for which he drove down to Glasgow with Mitchell to attend. Knox met them outside Saint Andrew's Cathedral on Clyde Street, dressed in his full formal uniform. Dignitaries from across the political divide were in attendance.

When they went into the packed cathedral, Dorsey noticed Hannah Bain and Jack Hardy sitting in a pew at the back. Hannah smiled nervously at him, but quickly looked away. The organ began as they took their seats and an angelic voice began to sing *Ave Maria*. A heady smell of incense drifted out from the altar as the bishop began the Requiem Mass.

Desmond Keenan gave a moving eulogy for his daughter, which was hard to endure. Even Knox looked tearful. Before Erin's father left the pulpit, he thanked the police for finding their daughter. He expressed his family's gratitude to have her home and to be finally able to put her to rest. Prayers were also said for the two victims who were killed in much more sinister circumstances and for the safe return of Lucy Potter. The burial was to be private, away from the press who had gathered outside the cathedral. Dorsey left with Mitchell as soon as the service was over.

Duncan Webster was already in a detention cell when they arrived at London Road Police Station to interview him. His solicitor was on his way. Mitchell prepared the interview room, which had both video and audio recording equipment. It was all set by the time the solicitor arrived, who had a short consultation with his client before the interview began.

Both Dorsey and Mitchell were expecting the usual no comment interview when Webster was brought from his cell and seated beside his solicitor. Their job was to make him break down and admit to knocking down Erin and thereafter concealing her body to prevent detection. He would be told of the benefits of accepting his guilt, and if it was accidental, then now would be the time to explain what had actually happened. Dorsey then gave both the lawyer and his client the usual run-through as to how the interview would proceed, before nodding to Mitchell to switch on the tape.

The two detectives were surprised when Webster immediately began to freely answer each question Dorsey put to him. He admitted to lying in his original statement, as well as being under the influence of alcohol and taking an ecstasy pill before he drove the campervan down to the B863 to look for Erin. However, he emphatically denied punching her or being involved in any accident. 'I'd never do anything to harm her … Honest to God, I didn't. I loved her.'

'We have your uncle's campervan at our forensic unit. If

there's even the slightest chance it was involved in knocking down Erin, then they will find the evidence to prove it. If you admit it now and that it was an accident, then I'm sure your lawyer has advised you that causing death while driving under the influence is much better than facing a murder charge. If the prosecutor thinks you did it deliberately and that's why you concealed the body, then you *will* be charged with murder.'

'I didn't do anything to Erin.' He finally broke down and sobbed, looking forlornly at his lawyer for help. 'I only drove the camper to try to find Erin.'

There was a sharp knock on the interview room door and the duty sergeant put his head in. 'Sorry, sir, that was the DI at the vehicle forensic unit.'

'This is Chief Inspector Frank Dorsey. I am stopping the interview with Duncan Webster at 14:45 hours,' said Dorsey, nodding to Mitchell to switch off the recording equipment, before leaving the room to speak to the duty sergeant.

'Sorry for interrupting the interview, sir, but I was ordered to do so by the DI at the forensic unit. They found no incriminating evidence in the campervan and there was no damage or repair that would indicate it had ever been involved in an accident.'

'Okay, thanks.'

Dorsey decided to give Webster another chance to confess, but the responses were the same as before the interview was interrupted.

With no evidence to show that Webster was the one that knocked Erin down, Dorsey left Mitchell to formally charge him with what he had admitted. The interview was then concluded. Duncan Webster was released and told the matter would be reported to the procurator fiscal. Dorsey decided to let them figure out what to do with him.

After dropping Mitchell off at home, he headed back to his flat. Glasgow was overcast and the constant drizzle made it look miserable, but he had still missed it. There was something about the city that nowhere else he had ever been made him feel, but he was never quite sure what that was. It was just a feeling he got whenever he was away and came back to all the familiar streets and places that made him the man he had become. He was Glaswegian and proud of it. The rugged beauty of Glencoe was undeniable, but it did not have the same visceral impact on his senses that the tenements and pubs and the people of Glasgow did.

The flat was freezing. He turned on the heating. The radiators groaned and moaned as they slowly adjusted to the heat. He took off his black tie and changed out of his suit, hanging it up behind the bedroom door. It was overdue a trip to the drycleaners.

Hungry, he looked in the fridge, but the smell immediately repelled him. Grabbing a bin bag, he cleaned out the food that had gone off. The only thing that looked edible was a packet of unopened cheddar cheese. He hated drinking coffee without milk, and he needed a coffee. He would have to go to the shops.

He bought a litre of milk, a jar of coffee, and a packet of cigarettes and went back to the flat. He didn't see anything he wanted to cook and decided that he'd phone something in later.

When he returned, the flat was no longer cold. He turned down the boiler and put on the kettle before going into the living room. He switched on the record player that Liz had bought him for his birthday. He had only three vinyl records to choose from. He carefully removed Dylan's *Nashville Skyline* from the cover, placing it on the turntable and lifting the needle to his favourite track, 'Girl of the North Country'. With Dylan and Johnny Cash singing in the background, he went back into the kitchen and finished making the coffee.

He looked at his phone. There was a missed call from Liz and he pressed the redial button.

'Hi, Frank. How did it go today?'

'I take it you mean the funeral?'

'Yeah, it must have been hard to deal with that.'

'Not as hard as it was for the family.'

'Frank, are you okay? You sound a bit down.'

'I'm fine. Just listening to Dylan.'

'I take it that's the same Dylan record you play every time I'm at your flat.'

'Yeah, I need to buy a few new albums.'

'At least I know what to get you for Christmas … How did the interview go with Webster?'

'I don't think it's him.'

'Do you want me to come over?'

'I don't think I'll be much company. I'm shattered.'

'Okay, you need a rest. Have an early night. When this case is over, I'm booking us a holiday.'

'That sounds good. Just don't make it an Airbnb in Glencoe.'

'I still fancy Montenegro, but maybe it's a bit too cold this time of the year. We can decide nearer the time. Love you, Frank.'

'You, too.'

'You still can't say it, can you, Frank?'

Chapter 38

Tuesday: 12th of December 2023

The next morning, he could have easily slept until midday, if not for Mitchell's repeated buzzing of the intercom. He staggered to the hall and pressed the entry button, unlocking the front door. He went back to lie on the bed. The early night had drained the little energy he had left, which seemed to defeat the purpose.

'We don't have to go back up today,' said Mitchell, when he went into the bedroom and found Dorsey lying in a heap on top of the bedclothes. 'Crawford can hold the fort for a few more days. You need a rest.'

'No, we need to go back up. Can you make the coffee while I have a shower?'

Mitchell went into the kitchen to put the kettle on.

They got the train to Tyndrum and picked up Dorsey's car from the car park, heading back up the A82 to Glencoe. It was another grey day, but at least it was dry. They hardly looked at the stunning countryside surrounding them as they drove through Glen Etive.

'Frank, did you know that the bagpipes actually originated in the Middle East?' mused Mitchell.

'George, you are actually starting to sound like Michael Cain. Who cares where bagpipes came from?'

'Okay, I'll shut up.'

Dorsey began to feel guilty as he looked over and saw Mitchell quietly scrolling through Google on his phone. 'Okay, where in the Middle East?'

'I think that guy pissing at the side of that car looks

drunk,' said Mitchell, indicating towards a parked car in a lay-by near the turn off to the Glencoe Ski Resort.

'So long as he's not driving. That actually looks like … It *is*,' said Dorsey, slowing down to get a better look. 'It's the poacher we arrested. What's his name?'

'Angus Sloan,' said Mitchell, 'and he is pissed.'

'That's an old Ford Estate, not the Volvo he was driving when we arrested him. I think we better have a word with Mr Sloan before he kills someone,' said Dorsey, pulling in behind the Ford. 'George, can you do a PNC check on the car?'

They got out of the car and approached Angus Sloan, who didn't seem to notice them at first. 'Are you okay, Mr Sloan? Is this your car?'

'Who the fuck … It's my brother's,' said Sloan, zipping up his fly, as though he had just realised who was speaking to him.

'There's no one else in it,' said Mitchell, after checking through the passenger's side window.

'So, where's your brother?' asked Dorsey, now close enough to smell alcohol on Sloan's breath.

'He's dead,' said Sloan, turning to get back into the car.

'Hold on … Have you been drinking?'

'No. I've not been fucking drinking.'

'I think you have. You'll have to wait here until we get a breathalyser test done. George, did you get the PNC result back?'

'That's it through now. It's registered in the name of Robert Campbell. There's no MOT or insurance for this vehicle. That's the address …'

'Hold on, George … Mr Sloan, who is Robert Campbell?'

'I've just told you. He's my half-brother. Same mother, different father.'

'When did he die?'

'About five years ago. I don't normally drive this. My

car's off the road. What the fuck was I supposed to do?'

'Well, you were not supposed to be driving this for a start,' said Mitchell, now aware why Dorsey had cut him off.

'George, can you phone the station and ask them to send two uniformed officers with a roadside kit? Mr Sloan, can you give me your car keys and sit in the back of my car until we check if you're fit to drive?'

'This is a fucking joke. I've no' been drinking … I want my lawyer contacted.'

While they waited for the uniformed officers to arrive, Dorsey took a closer look at Sloan's car. 'We need to get this examined. Look,' said Dorsey, pointing to a hairline crack on the left-hand side headlight.

'Are you thinking what I think you're thinking?'

'It's too much of a coincidence. He had the dog, and the body was found on his dead brother's property.'

It was the longest six hours of Dorsey's life. He knew he had to be patient, but that was easier said than done. Even Mitchell found it hard to concentrate on anything else. With so many disappointments in the past, they agreed to keep what they suspected to themselves. Only DS Kilbride, who arranged for Sloan's car to be uplifted and taken to Inverness, was told.

Sloan was charged with numerous road traffic offences, including drink-driving after he failed the roadside and follow-up breathalyser test in the station. These charges were of little interest to Dorsey, but they gave him the time he needed to have Sloan's car forensically examined while he was under arrest and detained for his court appearance in the morning.

It was after six-thirty when he finally got the call from Inverness. He took a deep breath before answering. 'Jock?'

'Frank, I've just had the DNA results from the traces of blood found in a groove in the casing just under the left headlight … It's a perfect match.'

'It's definitely her DNA?' asked Dorsey, finally exhaling the breath he took before answering the call.

'Yes, and we also got a match from hairs and cloth fibres found in the boot. I think you've finally got your man for Erin Keenan.'

'So it was Sloan after all. Shit.'

'There's no doubt whatsoever. I'm preparing a report which I'll email to you within the hour so you can have it when you interview him.'

'Thanks, Jock.'

While he waited for the report to be emailed, Dorsey re-read Dr Jamali's post-mortem report of Erin Keenan. Everything in her report and the DNA evidence pointed to Sloan being the person who knocked her down and tried to conceal her body. He contacted Sloan's lawyer and advised him of the nature of the allegations. 'I intend to interview him this evening around eight. Can you be here in time, or do you want the duty lawyer informed?'

'No, don't bother with the duty lawyer. I'll be there. I would like to see a copy of the DNA report before I consult with Mr Sloan, if that's possible?'

'There will be a copy made available to you when you get here.'

Now that was done, Dorsey went out to the front of the office to have a smoke and to kill some time. The waiting was unbearable. It was cold, and so dark that the sky was strewn with stars that were impossible to quite take in. He could never get his head around what was up there.

Mitchell joined him a few minutes later. 'Orion,' he said, pointing to one of the brighter constellations and handing him a cup of coffee.

'I'm surprised you didn't start that with your usual *Did you know?* catchphrase.'

'Very droll, Frank … Did you know? Michael Cain never actually said that.'

'Every day's a school day with you … I take it the DNA report hasn't come through yet.'

'No, but this interview is going to be interesting.'

'The difference this time is we *have* the evidence.'

Chapter 39

The voices returned. *You must kill her. She's bad and will hurt you again.*

He touched the scar she had inflicted on the side of his face and swore she would pay, glancing down at the shotgun on his lap. A twisted smile spread across his gaunt face. As he turned to look back down the track, the bones in his neck cracked and he let out a breath of putrid air from his lungs and hissed.

His hand was crudely bandaged and throbbed with pain, making it difficult to change gear and get the car up the steep track that led to the house. He knew the wound was infected, but going to hospital was not an option. There would be too many questions.

The car hit a deep pothole with a sudden violent jerk, slamming his bandaged hand against the steering wheel. Screaming in pain, he watched the blood turn the gauze bright red. 'Fucking bitch!' he shouted, saliva dripping from his lips like a rabid dog. He took his pills, trying to calm himself as he finally reached the front of the house.

*

Lucy heard the car. Her heart thumping and legs shaking, she climbed onto the ledge, placing her feet between the tiny shards of glass still sticking out of the broken window frame. Terrified he would grab her from behind before she got out, she pulled the dress above her knees and jumped, unable to avoid the tangle of thorny branches below the window.

Suffocating her screams, the countless barbs pierced

258

her skin through the thin dress. She forced herself to get up, pulling the branches aside and forcing her way through the thicket of brambles. They tore and slashed her arms and legs, stabbing the soles of her bare feet. She gritted her teeth, absorbing the excruciating pain in silence. *Never give up. Never give up!*

She reached the woods. Her feet were bleeding badly and the pain made every step unbearable. Unable to endure it any longer, she lay down on the ground to try to remove the thorns. The dress was in tatters and wet with sweat. She was suddenly cold.

*

He could sense something was wrong when he opened the storm doors. There was a freshness that seemed unusual. He placed two cartridges in the barrel of the shotgun, jerked the breech closed, and slowly moved down the hallway.

At the far end, he yanked a heavy velvet curtain aside, revealing the metal door. There was a draught from the gap at the bottom. He could hear something banging. Fumbling with the keys, he eventually unlocked the padlocks. The door wouldn't open – there was something on the other side. He pushed hard, gradually forcing the door wide enough to see the bed that was pushed up against it. He squeezed through the gap into the room.

His face contorted as he stared at the chain lying in the corner with fresh blood on the leather strap that had been cut open. His heavy boots crunched on the shards of glass strewn across the floor as he went over and looked out of what was left of the window. The broken shutters were hanging from their hinges as the wind blew them against the outside wall. He banged his head with the barrel of the shotgun until blood ran down his face. Breathing rapidly, he screamed, firing one of the chambers into the grey sky ... *Fucking bitch!*

Lucy froze when she heard the bang echo through the woods like a clap of thunder, scattering a rookery of crows from the trees. Her breathing now erratic, she continued to pick the thorns from the soles of her feet. Nervously glancing back, she knew he would come after her. She listened, but apart from the wind rustling through the trees, she could now hear nothing. Desperate, she tore off the sleeves from her dress and tied them around her blood-smeared feet. She refused to give up. She had to keep going. She had to survive. She ran until she could run no more and eventually fell to her knees, gasping for air, her lungs on fire. Unable to go on any further she lay down, her body trembling with exhaustion.

The forest offered her some protection, but the gnarled trunks and branches of the trees also frightened her as they creaked and swayed in the wind. She shivered uncontrollably. The cold was so bitter that it penetrated her skin and chilled every bone in her body. What was left of the thin cotton dress gave little protection. All her survival training seemed useless. Even the Army Reserve wouldn't expect their recruits to survive barefoot and almost naked in such a hostile environment. *Get up, get up … Never give up!*

She forced herself to walk deeper into the woods. She had no idea where she was going, but she needed to get as far away from the house as possible. Her feet had become so numb she barely felt the pain anymore. She struggled through the undergrowth, desperate to find a way out before it got dark. *What was that?* She turned in every direction, the trees closing in on her. Startled, she could now hear the sound of dry twigs snapping underfoot, growing closer, moving quicker. She began to run again, twisted branches catching her hair like skeletal fingers. Suddenly, she tripped and fell to the ground, pain shooting through her ankle. She screamed as the crude wire snare tightened and cut deep into her skin.

She could hear heavy breathing coming towards her. Then the click of metal. She turned to see him standing over her, his face a twisted grin of triumph. She raised her hand to protect her face as he smashed the butt of the shotgun down on her head.

Chapter 40

Wednesday: 13ᵗʰ of December 2023

Lucy Potter's father and his friends continued to post her picture in every shop, hotel, pub, and restaurant for miles in every direction from where she went missing. The lamp-posts in Fort William, Oban, and every village throughout the Central Highlands were now plastered with her picture. Social media was once again gripped with the investigation and the amateur detectives, in spite of their previous failures, were back making up their wild theories and false accusations.

There was heavy snowfall during the night and the snowploughs were out early clearing the main roads. The rest of Glencoe was covered in deep snow that completely transformed the look of the landscape. Dorsey drove slowly behind a truck that was spreading grit along the B863 as he and Mitchell made their way to the station at Glencoe to start another day.

Dorsey slowed down and phoned Knox to arrange for the Keenan family to be informed of Sloan's arrest.

'Yes, it's all on tape. The DNA report did the trick. He's admitted knocking her and the dog down. When he realised she was dead, he panicked and put her body in the boot of his car and dumped it at his dead brother's property where it was found. He's now been charged with causing her death by dangerous driving and attempting to pervert the course of justice by concealing the body.'

'So, she was never abducted?'

'No, finding Lena Kaminski's body muddied the waters a

bit. Erin Keenan's body was found on the other side of Loch Linnhe. It was outside the search area.'

'Okay, I'll personally speak to the Keenans. This is good detective work, Frank. We might never have solved this if you had been taken off the case.'

'Thanks, Andrew. I'll leave it to you to tell Cullen. I've already emailed the file to the procurator fiscal's office in Inverness and informed Mackie of the arrest.'

'Okay, I'd better phone the Keenans now before it's leaked to the press.'

Dorsey shifted up a gear and put on the Bluetooth, which randomly selected Frank Sinatra singing 'That's Life' from his playlist.

'All this salt on the road is going to ruin the underside of your car,' said Mitchell, who wasn't much of a Sinatra fan. 'We really should be driving 4x4s up here.'

'This place is stunning,' said Dorsey, absentmindedly.

'I'd rather be back in Glasgow.'

It took twice as long as usual to get to the station. The weather had caused the press outside the station to dwindle down to a couple of local reporters, desperate for a scoop.

'You're wasting your time hanging about here in this weather,' Dorsey told them, before noticing that one of the reporters was Kitty Murdoch. She was having a cigarette and looked freezing cold. He decided if anyone deserved a scoop it was her. As soon as he got into the building, he phoned and gave her the details of Sloan's arrest. 'The family have just been advised, and there will be a press conference this evening in Inverness. At least you'll be the first to get it into print.'

Having broken one of his own cardinal rules, he went into the office to update the rest of the detectives and get back to the arduous task of finding Lucy Potter and catching the serial killer. Sloan's arrest and confession gave the detectives a much-needed boost. The gloom that had settled on the place after the discovery of Erin Keenan's body lifted.

Dorsey was about to make himself and Mitchell a coffee when his mobile buzzed. It was the forensic lab in Inverness.

'Frank, you asked me to do another familial DNA check,' said Jock Kilbride, with an unusual tension in his voice. 'I've just found someone related to our suspect. His name is Samuel Purdy. He was arrested six weeks ago for drug charges and was required to give a swab. There were segments of chromosomes in his sample indicating a family relationship. It looks like we have a match with the killer's DNA, probably a first cousin. I've got an address in Inverness for him. Do you want to have him brought in?'

'No, not yet. We're heading up. We'll decide what to do when we get there.'

Mitchell could tell from Dorsey's face that something was up. He had not seen a smile on his boss's face in weeks. This was more than a smile; it was a look of elation.

'Keep your coat on, George, we're going to Inverness. That was the lab. They've got a partial match of someone who's related to our guy. His name is Samuel Purdy. They think he may be a first cousin. They have an address for him.'

A sudden surge of energy passed through the station as the information was relayed to the detectives in the incident room. Computers were abandoned and half-eaten sandwiches and packets of crisps were dumped in waste bins as those named put their coats on and rushed to the car park.

When they reached the Ballachulish Bridge, Dixon switched on her patrol car's siren and activated the blue lights to clear the way ahead. A few locals stood and watched them pass and then went about their business. They had seen it all before.

More information was continually relayed to Dorsey as they travelled at speed on the gritted roads through village after village, past Fort William and on to Spean Bridge.

Suddenly, Dixon could see there was a problem ahead and slowed to a stop behind a long line of traffic.

She radioed to the detectives behind that she would check out the problem. Sirens and lights reactivated, she drove along the opposite side of the road, only slowing down when she saw the carnage up ahead.

There had been a three-car pile-up. Traffic police and two ambulances were already at the scene. The wreckage was scattered across the narrow road. The cars were clearly write-offs. One of the traffic officers approached her and confirmed there were three fatalities and two injured passengers still trapped in one of the mangled cars. The road would be closed for hours. There was no other route to Inverness that wouldn't require a major detour, adding hours to the journey. She reversed at speed back towards the tail end of the line of traffic and explained the situation to her boss.

Dorsey got out of the car and walked up to see the situation for himself. He phoned Inverness HQ before walking back down the line of traffic.

It took less than twenty minutes for a tiny speck to appear in the distance. The speck soon became a dot before finally transforming into a police helicopter, red lights flashing as it eventually came to land in a nearby field.

'How did you manage that?' asked Mitchell.

'It's not what you know in this life, it's *who* you know that matters.'

He instructed Dixon to tell the detectives in the other two cars to go back to Glencoe.

'What about your car, sir?' she asked.

'Here, take my keys and ask DS Grant to drive it back. When you get back to the station, find out everything you can about Samuel Purdy from social media. Call if you find anything of interest.'

As the convoy of police cars turned and headed back,

Mitchell followed Dorsey over a drystone wall into an adjacent field. They ploughed through the fine drifts of snow that came up to their knees to the waiting helicopter. They climbed into the small bay area with the help of one of the two-man crew and strapped themselves in. The helicopter engine fired back up and gracefully lifted its skids out of the deep snow.

Inverness looked like it had coped well with the two days of heavy snowfall. Virtually all the roads and pavements of the inner-city area were gritted and clear of snow. The outskirts were still covered in a veil of white.

The pilot was in constant radio contact with the police on the ground as he made a wide berth over the River Ness towards a five-storey block of flats where several police vehicles were already parked along the narrow road. The gritters had not reached this part of Inverness and it was still covered in snow and slush. The pilot signalled to Dorsey that he was planning to land on a nearby football pitch. A black van was already making its way across the pitch as the helicopter landed gently in the soft snow.

'That's DI Dylan Jackson of the armed response team. He'll take you to the address of the suspect,' said the pilot before flicking switches above his head and radioing back to his base.

'Thanks, Captain, but the guy's *not* a suspect,' said Dorsey, unsure why there was an armed response team waiting for him.

The pilot waved and went back to preparing his machine for lift-off. The rotor blades roared back into take-off mode as the two detectives jumped onto the ground.

Heads stooped, they walked towards the black Sherpa van, with the turbulence from the rotor blades blowing a blizzard of snow after them.

They were met by DI Jackson, the armed response team leader who was dressed in his full-body combat gear and looking more like a superhero from a Marvel comic than a police officer. 'How do you want to do this, Chief Inspector?'

'I didn't ask for an armed unit. The guy is only a potential witness.'

'Okay, sir. Jump in,' said Jackson, indicating with a nod of his head.

They got in the back of the van and squeezed in beside the adrenaline-pumped, gum-chewing armed officers of the Inverness response unit. The driver hardly waited for them to be seated before he drove off at speed. Dorsey began to think they knew something he didn't.

'Ace of Spades' by Motorhead was booming from the driver's cab. Dorsey assumed it was the kind of stuff they played before going into action. It all felt a bit surreal. He looked over at Mitchell, jammed between two of these RoboCops, his face deadpan as though he was just taking the bus into town to do some Christmas shopping. The music suddenly stopped and the police radio buzzed over the speakers. *'Suspect down and cuffed. I repeat, suspect down and cuffed.'*

'We'll be there in a minute,' Jackson shouted back, before 'Ace of Spades' came back on.

'Fuck,' was as much as Dorsey could think to mutter to Mitchell.

When they reached the block of flats, a young man was lying face down and cuffed on the pavement, with one of Jackson's men kneeling on his lower back. A stream of yellow urine was speeding through the snow around the man's groin area. He must have gotten the fright of his life when he was pounced on by one of Jackson's men, thought Dorsey, still taking in what was happening around him, as a crowd of onlookers enjoyed the drama.

'Can you get these people away from here?' he shouted to the other armed officers who were strutting around with their semi-automatic rifles across their chests as though they had just taken out Pablo Escobar.

'Get him up from there!' he ordered, showing his warrant card, and trying to control his temper. The officer glanced at it and got up. Dorsey lifted the man by the arm and chest onto his feet. 'Is your name Samuel Purdy?'

'No. Why is this happening? I haven't done anything.'

Dorsey looked at Mitchell, two pennies dropping at the same time. 'Where do you stay?' asked Dorsey, taking out the details he noted down from Kilbride.

'I live in Wick. It's my mother who lives here.'

'What flat number does your mother live in?'

'Flat 3/2, but that piece of paper you've got says block six, this is block nine.'

'Okay. George, get RoboCop to uncuff him and phone for a uniform unit to get here.'

'Can someone check on my mother?'

'Don't worry, we'll see she's alright.'

'These guys must be on steroids,' said Mitchell. 'Do you want me to go upstairs and stop Jackson's men doing any more damage?'

'Take this young man up to his mother and tell Jackson to stand down his men. This is not a fucking terrorist situation. I'm going to give Samuel Purdy a visit,' said Dorsey, crossing the street to an identical block of flats.

There were no lifts. The stairwell smelt like a public toilet and graffiti covered every wall. His picturesque notions of the capital of the Highlands were dented. He could've been in any rundown part of any big city. There were two flats on each floor, most with no names or numbers to identify them. He climbed to the third floor, and worked out the door on the left must be 3/2.

When he went to knock on the door he immediately noticed a pungent smell. He knelt and opened the letterbox and almost fell backwards. The stench made him gag. 'What the fuck?'

268

Regaining his composure, he kicked the door with the heel of his boot until the Yale lock gave way. He put on a pair of latex gloves. Holding his hand over his mouth, he walked slowly down a narrow, dark hallway towards a door where the putrid smell was emanating from. He opened the door and almost threw up, but managed to stop retching by holding his breath. 'What the …!'

Through broken slats in the closed Venetian blinds there was enough daylight to make out the bloated body of a male hanging from a hook in the ceiling, wearing nothing but black lingerie, with the black knickers pulled down to his knees. Scattered around the floor were disturbing pictures of dismembered female bodies. He picked one up and was positive it was of Lena Kaminski.

He could only look at it fleetingly as the sickly-sweet smell began to overwhelm him again. He had to get out before he threw up. He backed off down the hallway, still covering his mouth and nose. Unable to keep it down any longer, he got out the front door just in time to throw up on the landing.

He went back down to the front of the block of flats to get some air in his lungs. *Could Jock have made a mistake with the DNA match*? He gathered his thoughts. The pictures on the floor could only have been taken by whoever dismembered those bodies. If the body hanging from the ceiling *was* Samuel Purdy, then he *must* be the killer. Did he decide to end it all in that gruesome way to avoid being caught alive?

He phoned Jock Kilbride and explained what he had discovered.

'Frank, I'm a hundred percent certain the DNA I recovered from the database is Samuel Purdy, and that's his bail address. He's on bail for drugs charges. Possession of cocaine, I think. He has no other criminal record.'

'So, he's got no sexual offending history?'

'No, nothing he's been caught for. His DNA isn't the same as the profile we got from the crime scenes.'

'They must have been in it together.'

'Frank, I don't know, but the photographs you mentioned clearly link them. Look, I can be there in twenty minutes, don't cut him down.'

'Don't worry, I wasn't planning to. He's beyond any help. Looks like he's been here for weeks.'

Dorsey lit a cigarette. The adrenaline was pumping through his body and he couldn't get the 'Ace of Spades' out of his head. He crossed back over to where Mitchell was talking to DI Jackson.

'Chief Inspector, we were given the wrong address by CS Mackie,' said DI Jackson. 'We were told to wait for you, but to arrest the suspect if he tried to leave the building. I'm sorry, but my guys were only following orders.'

'Why was that guy knocked to the ground and cuffed when your guys couldn't have known which flat he came out of?'

'We were told there was only one flat still occupied in the block, and he came out the front door. What else were my guys to think? George tells me the guy you're looking for was only a possible witness. We got a message before we left which stated he was positively identified as the Glencoe killer.'

'Who sent you that message?'

'CS Mackie. She's obviously got the wrong information from the lab.'

'I think it's more likely she got the right information from the lab but didn't read it properly.'

'Maybe.'

'Well, thankfully your guys didn't shoot him. I hope you didn't frighten the life out of his mother.'

'She's fine, we just had a look around the flat. Her son is back up there with her having a cup of tea.'

Dorsey turned to Mitchell. 'Anyway, George, we've got bigger fish to fry. Phone Dr Jamali and see if she can get here as soon as possible. Here's the *correct* address. I found Samuel Purdy hanging from his ceiling. He's not smelling too great.'

Looking rather deflated, the armed response unit headed back to their base as a marked police car pulled up. The two uniformed officers were immediately instructed to cordon off the area, while Dorsey and Mitchell went to Purdy's flat. Dorsey had forgotten he had thrown up until Mitchell pointed out what he thought would likely be a piece of evidence outside the front door. 'Never mind that,' said Dorsey, taking a production bag from his jacket pocket and lifting his own vomit. He went down to the bins to get rid of it before the scenes of crime arrived. He noticed specks of blood in the vomit, but he had no time to worry about that. He threw the bag in the bin.

When he got back, Mitchell was outside the door retching. He was just able to keep his breakfast down or they would've probably had to order a skip. 'Fuck, Frank, I've never dealt with one as bad as that before. It's brutal.'

'God knows why they have to get into that getup to knock one out.'

'Yeah, some way to end your life, with a pair of women's knickers around your knees and a vibrator up your arse. Try explaining that to Saint Peter. I don't fancy Dr Jamali's job having to dig that out.'

Dorsey hadn't noticed the vibrator, but Mitchell did have a habit of looking in places most detectives wouldn't think to look for evidence.

Before the SOCOs arrived, Dorsey and Mitchell began door-to-door enquiries. At least, that was their intention. There was no answer from either flat on the ground or first floor. An old woman on the second floor, who was clearly hard of hearing, insisted she was the last person living in the block. The flats were due to be demolished and she was moving out at the end of the week. They carried on up the stairs, knocking on doors and looking through letterboxes. The building clearly had only two residents, one who could hardly hear anything and another, hanging from his ceiling, who could hear nothing at all.

They were heading downstairs when they met Jock and his team on their way up. He was carrying all sorts of equipment. 'I take it he's in there,' said Jock, wrinkling his nose. 'Is Dr Jamali here yet?'

'No, she's been notified and hopefully won't be long.'

'Here, you better put these on,' Jock said, handing Dorsey a forensic suit, shoe covers, and a mask. 'I think you should change those gloves as well; we don't want you contaminating the crime scene. Sorry, George,' he added. 'I've only the one spare Tyvek suit with me.'

'Don't apologise, Jock, I'm happy to wait out here. I've already seen what's in there.'

Dorsey handed Mitchell his jacket and changed into the forensic garb. He took a paper hanky from his pocket and made a couple of tissue nose plugs, packing his nasal cavities with them before putting the mask on and going back inside.

There was no electricity in the flat, so an LED light was set up using a portable generator. The full horror of the scene was now illuminated in a blue tinge that made the room feel like a mortuary lab. Jock began taking photographs of the paraphernalia around the body, the pictures scattered on the floor, the unopened packet of condoms, a bottle of wine, and a metal ashtray full of cannabis joints. He then lifted the pictures from the floor. They both looked at them. 'Six different corpses … all dismembered. These two are the ones found in Lairigmor. Are any of the others Lucy Potter?' asked Jock, in a matter-of-fact voice, as though he was comparing second-hand cars.

'No, I don't think so.'

'So, that's four other victims we know nothing about.'

'It looks like it.'

Jock continued to take more photographs, this time of the body from every conceivable angle. The vibrator poking out of the anus didn't even register a raised eyebrow. He had seen it all before. 'This kind of stuff is more common than most people would think,' he said, between flashes and clicks of the camera. 'It seems Mr Purdy was one sick, horny bastard.'

'And likely a serial killer, or if not, in cahoots with one.'

'He could be, but I'm not convinced. There's something not right about this.'

'I take it he slipped off the stool and choked?'

'Maybe, or he simply misjudged the pressure and passed out. Either way the result is the same, death by misadventure.'

'So, it looks accidental?'

'That's how it looks, but it's not my job to determine the cause of death. That grim task is for Dr Jamali. That's why she gets paid a lot more than me. It's odd that no one smelt him before now.'

'This block is empty apart from an old woman on the second floor. She didn't think anyone else was still living here.'

'Well, she was right on that score.'

'It's due for demolition.'

'There's no electricity, no carpets, no curtains, no light bulbs, no mod cons, only an old sofa and coffee table. It looks like a squat. Those old things were probably left behind by whoever lived here before him. I see there's a backpack over there. I bet he just keeps all his clothes in it ready for the off. It's definitely a squat.'

'Sorry, I'm a bit late,' said Dr Jamali, entering the room already suited and booted in her whites and face mask. She stared at the bloated body for a moment. 'He's been hanging there for a while from the stench of him.' She then noticed the vibrator. 'What some of you men will do for a wank!'

The doctor's unexpected crudeness caused a smile to be shared between the two men, which, even with their masks on, she could see in their eyes. She liked to shock every now and then; it made her day more interesting, but she wasn't expecting the retort from Jock. 'The last time I tried that, all I got out of it was haemorrhoids.'

'I can get you a cream for that.'

'Enough of the banter,' said Dorsey. 'The smell in here is making me want to throw up.' He almost said 'again' but managed to stop himself just in time. Being sick, even outside a crime scene, was for rookies, not a chief inspector with over twenty years under his belt.

'Do we have a name?' asked Dr Jamali.

'Samuel Purdy,' said Dorsey. 'Although we still need him to be positively identified.'

'Okay, Samuel, this is not the best way for your mother to find you.' She started taking her own photographs of the body; everything else in the room was the SOCOs' concern.

Once satisfied she had taken enough in situ snaps, she began to give the body a rudimentary examination, dictating her findings on a small digital recorder. She pulled over the coffee table and stood on it to have a closer look at the ligature and to examine the knot at the back of the neck. She continued almost whispering into her recorder what she thought might explain why Mr Purdy expired in such an undignified way.

Dorsey heard her refer to 'autoerotic asphyxiation' more than once. It sounded less distasteful when *she* said it, as though it was a common way for young men to accidentally kill themselves.

When she had dictated what she needed, she turned to him. 'You're not telling me this is our serial killer?'

'I'm still trying to figure out what the hell he is. Jock managed to get a familial match with the killer's DNA, which would make him a blood relative. Have a look at these,' he said, handing her the macabre pictures recovered from the floor around the body.

'Lena Kaminski and Evinka Janik. Who are the others?'

'We don't know, but I'm pretty sure that none of them are Lucy Potter.'

'So, he's killed at least four more.'

'I don't think anybody's listening to me,' said Jock, who was going through the backpack of clothes. 'He's *not* the killer, at least not the one we're looking for.'

'If he's not, he's involved in some way,' responded Dorsey.

'Could he have got these pictures off the dark web?' asked the doctor.

'Possibly,' said Dorsey. 'We need time to process all this. I'm going down for a smoke. Let me know when you're finished in here and we'll get this body down and over to the morgue.'

Chapter 41

Dorsey decided to stay overnight in Inverness to attend the PM in the morning. It was a place he knew very little about. It was quite small and more like a large town than a city. Mitchell booked the Grange Hotel on Waterside Street. They went for a few pints in a pub facing the river. Dorsey couldn't get the smell of Samuel Purdy's decaying flesh out of his nostrils and wondered if it had permeated into his clothes.

'That's another four young women murdered and they were not even flagged up during this whole investigation. It's bizarre,' said Mitchell, staring at his beer as though he was waiting for permission to start drinking it. 'This is now up there with the Yorkshire Ripper case and look how long it took them to solve that … We could end up finishing our careers up here.'

'The only hope we have now is if relatives of Purdy come forward when we release details of his death. Obviously, I'm not expecting the psycho cousin to come forward, but nothing would surprise me in this case. Someone must know him.'

'Do you really think there are two of them involved?'

'Unless Jock is wrong about the DNA, then there must be two of them. The photographs show he was either the killer or his accomplice. We've now got to start another full-scale search for the other victims in those photographs, but where do we start?'

That evening, they had dinner in the hotel and then went through to the bar for a few pints to unwind. It was a day of drama and both were exhausted. It was snowing again and it reminded Dorsey that he still had to buy Daniel's Christmas present. He had given up trying to surprise him. Nothing seemed to please him and he was now old enough to know what he wanted. He phoned him while George was at the bar. 'Daniel, how's things?'

'Everything is okay, Dad. Have you found the killer yet?'

Dorsey was surprised. It wasn't like Daniel to show any interest in his job, and it was a question even he wasn't sure of the answer.

'No, not yet, Son.'

'Why is it taking you so long?'

'There's over five million people in Scotland. If you can tell me which one it is then you can have my job when you leave school.'

'I don't want *your* job. I want to be a lawyer, like Richard.'

Maybe he deserved that response, but he was still not expecting it.

'Are you coming back for Christmas?' Daniel asked.

'Of course, that's why I phoned,' Dorsey replied, pushing his jealousy to the back of his mind where it usually festered. 'Do you have any idea what you want this year? You mentioned a smartwatch before, are you still wanting one?'

'No, Richard is getting me that.'

'Okay. That's fine. Is there anything else I could get you?'

'Dad, I need a new bike.'

'What's wrong with the one you've got?'

'It's a bit naff. Richard took me to a cross-country tournament in the Campsies last week. All the other bikes there were proper mountain bikes. I really want a Falcon ZX200, but you can buy me a cheaper one if that's too expensive.'

Dorsey felt like telling him to get Richard to buy it, but he noted down the name and the specialist website to order it from. 'I might struggle to get it before Christmas.'

'There's plenty of time. That's mum shouting on me. I need to go down for my dinner. I'd better go.'

'Okay.'

Before he could say anything else, Daniel ended the call.

'Is everything alright?' asked Mitchell.

'Yeah, do you know anything about mountain bikes?'

'Only that they're not cheap.'

Chapter 42

Leaving Mitchell to have a lie-in, the following morning Dorsey took a taxi to the morgue. He was early and had to wait for almost an hour before Dr Jamali arrived. He spent his time looking at mountain bikes on his mobile. He took a deep breath when he saw the price of the one Daniel wanted. It was nearly one thousand pounds. That wasn't going to happen. Even five hundred pounds was more than he wanted to pay for something he knew would end up in the garage with Daniel's other bike that rarely saw the light of day. Then his hatred for Richard Hamilton resurfaced, putting an end to his scrolling and looking at bikes that all looked the same to him. If it had to be the Falcon ZX200, then that's what he was getting.

'Morning, Frank. You're here early. Did you get a coffee?' asked Dr Jamali, shaking a flurry of snow from her umbrella.

'No, I had something at the hotel this morning before I left.'

'Give me ten minutes to get ready.'

The morgue had that clinical blue light and smell about it that Dorsey found hard to endure. He stood aside as two lab assistants wheeled the body into the room and transferred it onto the dissection table. Dr Jamali was already dressed in her autopsy garb and sorting out the frightening array of surgical equipment. The apparent cause of death often wasn't the actual cause, necessitating a brutal and invasive examination to reach a final determination.

Before the examination began, an assistant took dozens of photos of the corpse, which had to be turned on its back and on its sides for a complete digital record that could be used later in a court or fatal accident inquiry. The ligature, underwear, and the protruding vibrator had been removed at the locus and were already being examined in the forensic lab back at police headquarters.

The doctor took hair samples from various parts of the body and scrapings from under the fingernails, placing them in sterile containers to be sent to the toxicology department along with the samples of blood she was now carefully extracting.

She turned to the main task: the dissection of the body. With the clinical precision of someone immune to normal thinking, she made an incision, opening the skin from the left clavicle to the sternum before repeating the same procedure on the other side of the body. She then ran the scalpel all the way to the pubis, slicing the torso open in the standard Y-shape. The body released a pungent odour of decay that made Dorsey adjust his mask around his nose.

The Y-incision gave access to all the vital organs protected by the ribcage. Dorsey winced at the sound of the ribs cracking as they were forced apart. The doctor then used the scalpel to cut the veins and arteries that connected the heart to other parts of the body. It was removed and placed on a steel worktop next to a large stainless-steel sink. One of the lab assistants put the heart into a clear plastic bag before laying it on a digital scale. He noted the weight and placed it in a refrigerated container for the doctor to examine later. The same process continued in relation to the lungs, liver, pancreas and other internal parts that Dorsey didn't recognise.

'They all look healthy enough, no sign of any disease,' said Dr Jamali, as much to herself as to Dorsey who was standing so far back, he might as well have stayed in the waiting room. She then removed the stomach and emptied an unrecognisable brownish mush into a plastic container and set it aside.

'This doesn't look right, Frank. I think you should come closer to look at this,' she said, running her forefinger along the ligature marks. 'If he died of asphyxiation, I would have expected the ligature to have caused much more damage to the skin. The neck muscles are not showing the bruising that I would also expect to find in a strangulation with such a relatively thin cord.'

She then used her scalpel to open the neck area, pulling back the skin to expose the neck muscles around the larynx and oesophagus. 'There is no damage to the mastoid or hyoid muscles and no bone fractures of the cervical vertebra.'

'What do you think that might mean?'

'I'll obviously have to complete my full examination and see what the toxicology tests find out.'

'But what do you think now?'

'Provisionally, so don't hold me to this, the ligature marks don't appear to have occurred perimortem. I'd expect to see other injuries if he lost his footing or passed out. The sudden weight on the neck would have caused more damage to the muscles and neck bones. I think he was already dead when the ligature was put around his neck.'

'Okay, that would mean he was murdered.'

'Yes. The crime scene and body were staged to look like an autoerotic asphyxiation took place.'

The doctor peeled back the foreskin of the penis and attempted to take a swab. 'There is no sign of semen. I would've expected some residual traces if he was masturbating prior to losing consciousness. In the flat, Jock used luminol light on the floorboards around the body, the underwear, and on the photographs. He found no traces of semen that would indicate the deceased ejaculated prior to passing out.' She signalled to her lab assistant. The morgue was plunged into darkness until the doctor turned on a handheld luminol light, which she hovered over the groin area. She then moved on to the hands before asking for the lights to be switched back on. 'Nothing that would be consistent with sexual arousal any time prior to his death. This supports my theory that this was all staged. It seems you're dealing with more murders in one investigation than most detectives up here deal with during their whole careers.'

'But if he didn't die of asphyxiation, how was he killed?'

'I think the toxicology tests may give us the answer to that question.'

Dorsey had no option but to extend his stay in Inverness. He went back to the hotel to find George having lunch. He joined him but wasn't hungry, so he ordered a cup of coffee. He explained Dr Jamali's suggestion that Samuel Purdy was murdered and her reasons for taking that view. Dorsey skipped the details of the PM examination; he was still trying to get the images of the dissection out of his head. George's choice of liver and mashed potatoes for his lunch was not helping.

'What kind of human being are we dealing with here? Psychopath doesn't seem to do him justice anymore,' said George, taking a slice of the liver and covering it with onion gravy.

'The only thing I can think of is sadist. I'm going out for a cigarette,' said Dorsey, who couldn't look at George dissecting the liver any longer.

After George had finished his lunch, they took a taxi to the divisional headquarters to speak to Jock Kilbride and see if he had a similar view to Dr Jamali.

They were directed to the forensic labs by a young PC who looked like he should still be at school. They had to use their warrant cards to get by the security officer at the labs, who was insistent on seeing their identification.

Jock appeared in a white coat with a brown folder under

his arm. 'I got a call from Dr Jamali after you left the morgue this morning,' he said, skipping the pleasantries. 'She told me about her provisional findings, which I'm in total agreement with. It was definitely a staged homicide.'

'Okay, so Purdy *was* murdered.'

'Yes. The lack of semen at the crime scene is the first thing. Then there's the fact that Dr Jamali also found no sign of prior sexual arousal. This strongly suggests this was all staged. Even more important is the lack of injuries to the neck that she would expect to find. That is consistent with what I've found. Have a look at these,' he said, producing several photographs from the brown folder which showed the blue nylon ligature. 'The knot in the cord isn't right and isn't tight enough to have choked him. If he slipped or lost consciousness then the sudden weight of his body, and any struggle, would've meant the ligature would've tightened around the neck way more than it had. This knot was tightened by hand. Since there are no other obvious injuries to the body, he must have been poisoned and then put into the position we found him in.'

There was no more room for doubt in Dorsey's mind. The Glencoe killer also murdered Samuel Purdy, who was related to him by blood, at least through a familial DNA match. The question was why?

'Frank, I found his phone under a mattress in the bedroom at the flat. My IT guy managed to bypass the pin number. There are dozens of contact details but there's one that may interest you.' Jock switched on the black Samsung phone and opened the contact page, scrolling down to *Mum,* and a phone number. 'It's an Inverness landline number. I haven't phoned it. I thought that was something you'd want to do yourself. You can use my office.'

'Thanks, this may finally be the lead we've been looking for, but I can't tell her over the phone that her son's been murdered.'

'I think our IT expert will be able to find the address for you from the landline number. Give me a few minutes.'

A short time later, Dorsey and Mitchell were sitting in the back of a marked police car as it travelled to the address that was linked to the phone number. They had no idea what to expect when they got there. The journey was double-edged; on one hand, they had to tell a mother that her son had been murdered, a grim duty at any time, but on the other hand, she may have the information that long months of the investigation had failed to uncover – the identity of the killer.

The police patrol car pulled up outside a row of semi-detached houses in a quiet suburban street, which surprised both detectives as they had been expecting something a bit grimmer. 'It's that one over there, sir,' said the driver. 'Number sixty-five.'

The detectives got out of the car and made their way to the front door along a garden path that had been cleared of snow and slush. Dorsey took a deep breath, then exhaled as he pressed the doorbell and turned to look at Mitchell. 'I'm not looking forward to this.' He pressed the doorbell again.

The door opened and a middle-aged man answered, a newspaper folded in his hand. He looked annoyed, as if they had interrupted him before he'd finished his crossword.

'What's up?' he asked.

'I'm DCI Dorsey and this is DS Mitchell. Are you the father of Samuel Purdy?'

'No, thankfully not. I'm his stepfather.'

'Is his mother home?'

'Margaret,' he shouted, turning his head back into the house. 'It's the police looking for Sam. They want to speak to you.'

'Can we come in?' asked Dorsey.

They followed the stepfather into the living room. It was warm and bright, unlike the place where they found Samuel. Margaret came into the room from the kitchen, immediately switching the television off. 'What's wrong?' she asked, the concern for her son obvious in her voice and her worried eyes. 'Has he been arrested?'

'No, Mrs Purdy.'

'It's Mrs Symonds,' said her husband, 'and it has been for fifteen years.'

From experience, Dorsey knew the only way to tell a mother that her son was dead was to come right out and say it. Beating around the bush was a tactic that did nothing but add confusion and upset.

They stood and watched as if the pain that his words had caused her had stabbed her in the heart. The newspaper and the unfinished crossword were lying on the floor as the husband tried to comfort his distraught wife. 'What happened to him?' asked the stepfather, now showing real concern on his bewildered face.

'We believe he was murdered.'

'Oh my God, no, not my boy … There must be some mistake.'

'Murdered!' repeated the stepfather, pulling his distraught wife closer to him. 'How was he murdered?'

'We believe he may have been poisoned,' replied Dorsey, the image of the body hanging from the ceiling in black lingerie and the vibrator sticking from the anus flashing into his mind. 'We are still waiting for the pathologist to confirm this, but that's her provisional opinion.'

'I knew he was back. I just knew it,' she said, as if in a trance. 'Sam was scared of him.'

'Why was Sam scared? Who's back?'

'My nephew, Zachary Hicks. He's evil. He murdered my poor Daisy. Now he's murdered my boy.'

She began sobbing, her upper body shaking with the shock. They waited for a few minutes until she looked back up at them, hoping for answers. Dorsey took the opportunity to press ahead. 'Mrs Symonds, we're so sorry for your loss.

We *must* find your nephew. Do you know where he is?'

'How should we know?' replied her husband. 'We've had no reason to be in contact with that monster after what happened to Daisy.'

'Can you tell us what happened to your daughter?'

'I'll tell them,' Mr Symonds said, patting his wife's clasped hands. 'About fifteen years ago, Margaret was going through a messy divorce. The kids, Daisy and Sam, were sent off to stay with her sister. Give me a minute.'

He got up and went into another room, returning a few minutes later with some old newspapers. 'The police said it was an accident,' he explained, handing them to Dorsey, who read a short article in the *Oban Times*.

Police are treating the drowning of Daisy Purdy, a fifteen-year-old schoolgirl, as suspicious after her body was recovered from the River Esragan. They are appealing for information from anyone who was in the area between the hours of 8 p.m. and 6 a.m. on Wednesday the 22nd of July 2008.

'Hicks was the last person to see her alive and he told the police a pack of lies,' said Mr Symonds, who sat back down beside his wife, who was now staring into another world.

'What was Daisy wearing when she drowned?'

'She was wearing a blue dress. My sister made it for her,' whispered Daisy's mother, almost to herself.

Dorsey looked at Mitchell as another piece of the jigsaw dropped in place. He turned back to her husband. 'Was he charged with anything?'

'No, Hicks told the police it was an accident. That she slipped and fell into the river. He said he tried to save her, but she went under and he couldn't reach her. All lies.'

'He pushed her in. I know he did,' said the distraught mother, her voice now clear and angry.

'Why do you think he'd do that?' pressed Dorsey.

'Sam told me after she drowned that they were both scared of him. He used to bully Sam and constantly follow Daisy about, staring at her and saying things he shouldn't have been saying to anyone, never mind his cousin. Disgusting things. Sam even caught Zachary going into her room and looking through her underwear. The disgusting animal. My son confronted him and got a punch on the face, and the pig threatened to kill him if he told anyone. Sam was only a boy, fourteen at the time.'

'Did Daisy know he did this?'

'No, Sam was too frightened to tell her, but she hated Zachary and was always telling him to keep away from her. My sister was too busy drinking gin every day to know what was going on.'

'Did the police know all this at the time?'

'It was all in her diary. They took that, but said it didn't mean he was responsible for her death.' Then Margaret broke down again, sobbing into her hands and muttering curses to herself. Dorsey waited for the wave of emotion to break, not wanting to press her too hard.

After a few minutes she wiped her face with a tissue and found her composure again. 'He was at the funeral and I could see a twisted smirk on his face, staring at me at the graveside, enjoying our pain. He's evil. He was always a strange child. I think it was in his blood. His father wasn't much better. He used to beat my sister whenever he got drunk, and he was drunk a lot back then. He was killed in an accident at his work when Zachary was about six. Betty got a large insurance payout … That's when she bought the old farmhouse and turned it into a holiday home. She spoiled Zachary. He got what he wanted. She was useless, or maybe she was frightened of him, like she was of his father.'

'What age was Zachary Hicks when Daisy drowned?'

'He was sixteen and training to be a chef at the Portland Hotel in Perth at the time.'

'Did the police take a statement from Samuel?'

'Yes, he gave a statement and told them everything, but they said it wasn't enough to charge his cousin because there were no injuries on Daisy's body to show he attacked or forced her into the river. That Detective Mackie, she was hopeless.'

'Was that Detective Fiona Mackie?'

'Yes, she was the one that decided it was an accident. I saw her on the TV a few weeks ago. She's obviously a big shot now. She even sounds different ... posh.'

'Margaret, where does your sister live now?' asked Dorsey.

'Betty's dead, she died about six years ago. We never spoke after what happened. She took her son's side. They must have let the bastard out.'

'Out of where?' asked Dorsey, trying to tease out everything he could without her breaking down again.

'About eight years ago he was accused of assaulting a teenage girl in Perth. They didn't even charge him. He was sectioned and sent to a psychiatric hospital, and the last we heard he was transferred to Carstairs. We thought he'd never get out, but about a month ago, just after Sam's name and address appeared in the local newspaper for a drugs charge, he told us that his social media accounts were being hacked and he was getting threatening and abusive messages all the time from a fake account. He freaked out when one message ended, *Did Daisy know her brother was a disgusting homosexual?* He told the police, but I don't think they took it seriously. It was on a gay dating site.'

'How long has your son been living in the flat at Rowan Street?'

The stepfather answered. 'He only came back to Inverness about six months ago. He'd been living in London for years and hardly phoned his mother twice in all the time he was away. He turned up here a few months ago, looking

288

for money. We gave him what we could. When we heard he was arrested about six weeks ago for drugs, he phoned looking for more money to go back to London. I told him we didn't have any. That was the last we heard from him.'

'Margaret, we need to find out where your nephew is now. Where did your sister live?'

'She lived in Perth, but spent most summers in her holiday home in Argyll. It was an old farmhouse with a small bit of land in the middle of nowhere. That's where I sent the kids for a holiday the year Daisy drowned.'

'Who owns these properties now?'

'I don't know what happened to them after Betty died. I didn't even know she was dead until months later. I assume she left both properties to her son. I might still have the address for them if you give me a minute.'

Chapter 43

Dorsey tried to find out everything he could about Zachary Hicks before he left. The Symonds had no photographs of him, which was understandable, and the description Margaret gave of her nephew when he was sixteen was not much use for a man now in his early thirties. It was already starting to get dark, and he phoned ahead to get a task force ready for the journey back down the A82. He then phoned the CID in Perth, instructing them to find out who was now living at the address the Symonds gave him. If it was Zachary Hicks then they were to obtain warrants, arrest him, and search the house. Dorsey was confident that the house in Argyll was a much more likely place for Hicks to have carried out his crimes and not raise suspicion.

When they reached the police HQ, DI Jackson and his men were already in operational mode, another heavy metal song blasting from his Sherpa van. This time it was 'Paranoid' by Black Sabbath. Dorsey opted to have a patrol car drive him and Mitchell back down the A82 toward the address of the holiday home, which was now located on the GPS on the driver's dashboard computer. He phoned the PF's office and gave them details to obtain a warrant. 'I need this within the next two hours. If the sheriff's got a problem with granting it, give him my phone number.'

The A82 was now completely cleared of snow, the bulk of it pushed onto the verges by snowploughs, but it was still treacherous. The driver was obviously accustomed to the twists and turns in the road and barely took his foot off the accelerator, turning into corners at a speed that left Dorsey and Mitchell struggling to stay upright in the back. Even DI

Jackson's driver was having difficulty keeping up, flashing his headlights repeatedly. 'Officer, we're not in a race,' said Dorsey, who was starting to feel nauseous. 'Can you slow down so we get there in one piece?'

'Sir, he's the best driver in the division,' said the constable in the passenger seat, who was clearly also a bit of a speed freak.

'Ayrton Senna was once the best driver in the world,' said Mitchell. 'Look what happened to him. Slow down now!'

'Sorry, sir.'

The countryside was now in darkness as they passed through Spean Bridge and then Fort William. The tension was unbearable as cars pulled aside to let them pass. Dorsey phoned the station at Glencoe and spoke to Crawford. 'Bill, we have our suspect's possible location. His name is Zachary Hicks. Can you set up roadblocks on the B845 at Barcaldine and Inveresragan on the other side? We don't have a description of him, but he's in his early thirties. Detain any males in that age group, unless they can satisfy you of their identity. Don't accept a driving license. He may be using a fake. Take your sidearm and throw half a dozen stab-proof vests into your boot. We might need them. We're still waiting for a warrant. We'll be there in around an hour.'

'Okay, we're on our way.'

A helicopter suddenly appeared overhead, the chopping sound of the rotor blades getting closer. 'Constable, can you get in touch with the pilot of that helicopter?'

'Yes, sir,' replied the driver, pressing buttons on his control panel radio. 'Captain, I have DCI Dorsey here. He needs to speak to you.'

The radio crackled back over the noise of the rotor blades clipping in the background. 'Copy. Go ahead, Chief Inspector.'

'Sir, you're on speaker direct to the cockpit.'

'Captain, can you hear me?'

'Yes, Chief Inspector … Go ahead.'

'Stay away from the target until we are ready to move in,' shouted Dorsey over the racket. 'I don't want to spook this suspect. He may still have Miss Potter and use her as a hostage.'

'Copy, Chief Inspector. We'll land at the helipad in Glencoe and wait for further instructions … Just to warn you, there's a blizzard heading in. We may not be able to take off again.'

'Okay. We'll see what it's like when we get there.'

'Good luck, sir. Roger and out.'

They reached the Ballachulish Bridge and crossed to the south side of Loch Leven, turning onto the coastal road along Loch Linnhe, which was so thinly gritted that some parts of the surface reflected large areas of ice in the headlights. They slowed down, the back wheels slipping on the ice. The driver had to go down the gears and drive into a skid on one corner that nearly took them over the edge and down the hillside into the loch. Even the constable in the passenger seat was gripping the dashboard and swearing under his breath. The rally driver that had left Inverness was now driving like his granny and was as worried as the rest in the car about losing control on a surface that no one could rely on.

DI Jackson and his two Sherpas were now so far behind that their headlights had disappeared into the overwhelming darkness. They could now see the blue lights of the roadblock in the far distance. It began to snow.

Dorsey's phone buzzed. He could barely look at the screen, his mind distracted with the fear of going over the edge and ending up in the loch. The text was from the CID in Perth.

The house on Thistle Street was sold to the present owners by the trustees handling the estate of Elizabeth Hicks. We checked with the local solicitors who dealt with the sale. The conveyance of the property was completed five years ago on

292

behalf of a trust set up in the name of Zachary Hicks by his mother.

A blizzard was taking hold and visibility was almost zero. The snow was falling so heavily that the roadblock suddenly disappeared. The landscape had been devoured by snow and darkness. They could be anywhere. The patrol car was now moving so slowly it was in danger of stalling.

The wind suddenly changed direction and the blue flashing lights reappeared up ahead. The driver pulled up just in time, narrowly avoiding skidding into the marked police car that was blocking the road.

Crawford approached the patrol car, his head and shoulders covered in frozen snow. Dorsey rolled down the back window as a sudden gust blew large snowflakes into the backseat. 'No one's passed here since we arrived twenty minutes ago. It's the same on the other side. If he's in there, he's still there,' shouted Crawford over the howling wind.

'Okay, can you tell Constable Dixon to move the car off the road? DI Jackson is not far behind us. They might not see the car in time to stop.' Dorsey then tapped the shoulder of the constable in the passenger seat. 'You remain here with PC Dixon. Bill, you come with us.'

Crawford got into the vacated passenger seat, bringing more snow in with him. He had two stab vests on his lap for Dorsey and Mitchell.

They carried on along the treacherous road for another three miles before the driver slowed down to a stop. 'Sir, the house is half a mile up this road on the right,' he said, looking at the GPS monitor. 'Do you want to drive up to it now or wait for DI Jackson?'

'Keep driving,' ordered Dorsey, taking out his sidearm from his shoulder holster. The driver turned up a road that only he could see was there. They drove through snow that had not been touched since it had fallen. The only guide was the hawthorn hedges on either side of the track. The headlights reflected nothing but the falling flakes of snow. They hadn't gone far when the backend of the police car suddenly slipped sideways, causing one of the back wheels to sink into a deep rut at the side of the hedge.

The driver changed gears and tried to free the car. The wheels began spinning in situ. 'Sir, I can't get any traction. I think the back wheel is in a ditch.'

'Okay, you wait here for DI Jackson. Bill, you come with us. George, can you phone the PF and see if they've got that warrant granted yet?' said Dorsey, putting on his protective vest and handing the other one to Mitchell.

Chapter 44

The wind was now so strong they had trouble walking. Their torches were only able to light up a few feet ahead, the beams becoming dispersed in the overwhelming blizzard. The snow that lay ahead of them was deep and untouched. There was no sign of footprints. They reached a garden fence. Its gate was bolted over and locked with a padlock. Dorsey noticed a pole attached to the fence and he wiped the snow off the plaque at the top; it was a *For Sale* sign that looked so old it could have been put up during the Great Depression. They climbed over the gate and continued up to the two-storey house that looked like it was made of snow and ice.

He turned to check on Mitchell and Crawford, who were breathing heavily, their breath coming out like white clouds of diffused crystals. 'George, can you check again and see if we've got that warrant?'

Mitchell took off his gloves and looked at the messages on his phone. 'It's with the sheriff. They were waiting to get it emailed back from the clerk's office once he signs it.'

'Well, that's good enough for me … We'll check this out first,' said Dorsey, his torch scanning over what looked like an old barn. The gate was closed over with just a metal pin and was barely attached to its hinges. His heart beating fast, he opened it slowly. He shone his torch onto a large table that seemed to be moving. He recoiled when the light reflected off the frenzied eyes of dozens of rats covered in blood and gorging themselves in a feeding frenzy. 'Fuck,' he shouted when he saw pieces of meat hanging from what looked like butcher hooks. It took him a few seconds to make out what looked like a skinned rabbit. The other carcasses were so rotten it was impossible to even guess what they were. He backed out, not sure what to make of it.

'Look,' said Crawford, wiping snow away with his arm to reveal the number plate of a car parked on the other side of the barn. 'He must still be here.'

'Let's get this bastard!' said Dorsey.

They moved up to the front of the house. The storm doors were locked as though it had been shut up and abandoned. Dorsey shone the torch on each of the windows. The shutters were all closed over and padlocked.

'Look!' shouted Crawford above the howls of wind, pointing to the bobbing headlights coming up towards the house in the distance. 'It must be Jackson and his men.'

It took a couple of kicks from Mitchell to break the bracket off the rotten wooden door frame. Dorsey forced one of the storm doors open with his shoulder. The inside door was unlocked.

They cautiously moved into the hall, their flashlights revealing a staircase to the left and a number of closed doors along the right-hand side. Mitchell found the light switch and clicked down the brass button, but nothing happened.

Dorsey's fingers were numb with the cold, making his gun feel heavy. He was worried he might not be able to pull the trigger. He moved along the hall, nodding to Mitchell to take the first room as Crawford carefully made his way up the stairs.

He opened the second door. The room was in total darkness. He searched for the light switch. The bulb flickered before coming on, barely lighting the room. He took in the bizarre sight of what looked like a Victorian sitting room frozen in time. There was a birdcage in the far corner that looked like the original occupant was still in it. There was another stuffed animal on a small table beside the fireplace. He wasn't sure if he was looking at a stoat or a pine marten, but whatever it was it didn't look happy. An old Singer sewing machine was lying on its side on the floor with rolls of fabric strewn about it. The paraphernalia of dressmaking was everywhere. A piece of identical blue material that the two bodies had been wrapped in was pinned to a mannequin. A strange sensation ran through his body. He tightened his grip on the gun, fearing Hicks could rush at him from the shadows. He eventually backed out of the room, satisfied it was clear.

Mitchell was already back in the hall, moving slowly forward, the beam of their torches darting from side to side. 'Frank!' he shouted, before pulling away a heavy velvet curtain, revealing a metal door and an array of padlocks lying on the floor. He stood aside as Dorsey pushed the door open.

The wind was blowing snow in through the broken window, covering much of the floor and the bed that was lying in an odd position in the middle of the room. There was nothing much else other than a small bedside cabinet and a few tins of food scattered on the floor. 'This must be where he kept them,' said Dorsey, his torch coming to rest on a long metal chain lying next to the bed. 'It looks like she might have escaped.'

'I don't fancy her chances if she did get out. She'd be lucky to last a few hours in this weather,' said Mitchell, as they looked around the grubby bathroom.

A shot rang out.

'Crawford!' shouted Mitchell.

They both raced up the stairs, stopping at the top steps when they saw Crawford lying sprawled on the landing. Dorsey pushed forward. Mitchell was close behind. The floorboards creaked beneath their feet as they slowly approached the far bedroom.

Dorsey shone his torch down at Crawford. He looked dead. Then, out of nowhere, a tinkling melody began to play. Dorsey glanced at Mitchell, who looked blankly back at him.

Crawford groaned. He was still alive.

Dorsey's finger tightened on the trigger, causing a painful cramp in his hand. He stepped over Crawford. There, standing in the bedroom was Hicks, wearing a blue dress and blonde wig, his gaunt face covered in bright makeup. He was holding a large butcher's knife, his black eyes staring with the madness of his deranged mind, his head moving from side to side in time with the tinkling notes of the music box on a bedside cabinet behind him. The music stopped.

'*It* tried to steal it.'

'Drop the knife!' yelled Dorsey, pointing the gun at the grotesque face grinning back at him.

Hicks sneered. 'It tried to steal Daisy's music box. Daisy loved her little ballerina.'

'What the fuck are you talking about? Drop the fucking knife. Now!'

Hicks let out a high-pitched scream and lunged forward with the knife raised above his head. Dorsey struck Hicks's head with his gun and followed up with a full-force punch to the face. The outdated Laura Ashley wallpaper was splattered with blood from Hicks's burst nose. The knife fell from his hand, the point so sharp it stuck upright in the floorboard. Hicks whimpered and crumpled, collapsing in a heap on top of Crawford, who let out a painful groan.

Mitchell quickly dragged Hicks off Crawford onto the landing area, before kneeling on his back and cuffing him. 'Frank, are you okay?' he shouted, looking up at Dorsey, who stood slumped against the open bedroom door with Hicks's blood splattered on his face.

'Yeah, I'm fine, see how Bill is,' Dorsey replied, both his hands now throbbing in pain.

'Bill, can you hear me?' shouted Mitchell, checking Crawford's chest under his slashed Hi-Vis jacket. Hicks's knife hadn't penetrated the dense inner core of the stab vest. It had saved his life.

Crawford opened his eyes. 'Fuck, what happened? Did I get the bastard? Oh, my fucking head,' he groaned, touching the area that hit the balustrade when he fell backwards onto the landing after Hicks had attacked him with the knife.

Mitchell helped Crawford sit up against the door frame, his face ghostly white and looking dazed.

'We've got him at last,' said Dorsey, looking down at the prostrate body of Hicks, who was lying face down and whispering to himself like a disconsolate child.

'Mother ... Help me.'

Downstairs, DI Jackson and his men began piling into the house with their semi-automatic rifles and testosterone fully loaded. The floorboards bounced under their boots as they went from room to room.

'The suspect's down!' shouted Dorsey to DI Jackson, who was now making his way slowly up the stairs, the laser dot of his semi-automatic rifle darting from side to side.

With the help of Mitchell, Dorsey turned Hicks onto his side. 'Where is Lucy Potter, the young woman you abducted?'

Hicks just grinned, the blood from his nose running into his mouth.

'Answer the fucking question!' shouted DI Jackson, kicking Hicks hard in the ribs.

Hicks let out a scream.

'Enough of that!' ordered Dorsey, looking sternly at Jackson. 'Get him up.'

Once Hicks was on his feet, Dorsey asked him again. 'Zachary, where is the young woman you abducted?'

'Which one?' smirked Hicks, his teeth red with lipstick and his own blood.

'The one you abducted ten days ago.'

'That's for me to know and for you to find out.'

'Right, fuck this,' said Dorsey, tempted to let Jackson

loose on him. 'Zachary Aaron Hicks, I am arresting you for the murders of Lena Kaminski, Evinka Janik, and the abduction of Lucy Potter. You do not have to say anything, but anything you do say …'

Once he had finished reading Hicks his rights, Dorsey ordered Jackson to take him to Inverness. Hicks was too big a catch for a small police station like Glencoe to deal with. They would interview him in the morning.

'George, can you call in an ambulance? DI Crawford might have a concussion.'

'I don't need a fucking ambulance,' shouted Crawford, wiping sweat from his face. 'It's a fucking drink I need.'

'Get an ambulance here,' insisted Dorsey. 'He hit his head!'

Once Hicks had been taken downstairs, Mitchell pointed to a bullet hole in the wall. Crawford had missed Hicks by a country mile. 'Bill, when was the last time you were at the practice range?'

'We have a practice range?' laughed Crawford. 'Here, help me down these fucking stairs.'

'Quiet, what was that?' shouted Dorsey, moving along the hall to a door in an alcove that had a padlock on the outside. He stepped back and kicked the door open. The latch flew off with a loud clatter. He took out his torch and shone it into the darkness.

There, sitting on a mattress on the floor with her mouth gagged and hands tethered in front of her with cable ties, was Lucy Potter. Her face was bloodied and bruised. Dorsey slowly moved towards her. 'Lucy, it's the police. Don't be frightened. You're safe now.'

After removing the gag and untying her hands, he held her tightly. 'You're safe now, Lucy. That bastard can't hurt you anymore.' She began sobbing and shivering violently. He turned to Mitchell, who was standing at the door with Crawford. 'George, have you phoned that ambulance?'

'It's on its way.'

Chapter 45

Dorsey carried Lucy down to the front of the house. She was exhausted and barely conscious. He lay her on the stretcher, her body shivering violently as the paramedics wrapped her in a thermal blanket and put her on a drip before lifting her in the ambulance. Dorsey ordered the reluctant Crawford to get in with her.

'Frank, I'm fine, it was just a bang on the head.'

'Let the doctors decide if you are okay or not,' said Dorsey, not willing to take a risk after what had happened to Munro.

Now a multiple crime scene, holding all the clues to the hideous perversions of Zachary Hicks, the two-storey farmhouse was lit up from every possible angle. The police helicopter struggled against the wind as it hovered above, its searchlights scanning the ground. Soon, the gathering storm threatened to bring it down and it quickly retreated back to Glencoe.

The SOCOs radioed in from Fort William; it was as far as they could go. The snowdrifts were blocking the roads further south. They were planning to return to Inverness and try again in the morning.

A decision was made to cordon off and secure the house and to evacuate the area until the morning. Uniformed officers had the task of guarding the house and the barn overnight.

Dorsey and Mitchell were driven back to their hotel by PC Dixon. They were exhausted.

The Stag's Head was already preparing for Christmas, and a large tree was in the foyer. The stuffed wildlife had garlands of tinsel on them to make them look more festive.

Neither detective was hungry. They went into the bar where Dorsey ordered two large whiskies. It was only then that he realised there was blood splatter on his jacket. He took it off and turned it inside out. It would have to be lodged as a production in the morning; he knew Crawford's use of his firearm would be independently investigated – a process that always infuriated him. They could even suspend Crawford until that was done.

'Cheers, we finally got the bastard,' said Mitchell.

'What matters is that we saved Lucy Potter.'

'We've stopped him from killing any more innocent victims.'

Dorsey didn't respond. His mind was numb. They sat in silence, lost in their own thoughts, too tired to talk. They finished their drinks. Dorsey ordered a bottle of Glenfiddich, and they went up to their rooms.

He poured himself a glass of the expensive malt whisky and went out onto the balcony. It had stopped snowing. He wiped the snow off one of the chairs and lit a cigarette. He sat in the cold, looking into the darkness. The snow-covered mountains were only a faint outline. He drank the whisky neat. The heat felt like an anaesthetic rushing through his body. He looked at his phone. There were messages from Knox, Cullen, and the chief constable. He scrolled through without reading them. On the verge of tears, he phoned his son.

'Dad?'

'Daniel, never forget I love you …'

'God, Dad, what's wrong?'

'Nothing's wrong, but I miss you.'

'Dad, you sound weird. Are you alright?'

'I'm okay. We found the girl.'

'I knew you would. So why do you sound so sad? Will I get Mum?'

'No. I phoned to speak to you.'

'Okay, but I don't like it when you're unhappy.'

'I'm just tired, Son. I'll come and see you as soon as I get back.'

'Did you catch the serial killer?'

'Yes.'

'Good … Did you kill him?'

'No, he's in custody … I've managed to get the mountain bike you wanted. It should arrive before Christmas. I'm not looking forward to trying to wrap that up.'

'Dad, I don't care about the bike.'

'Now you tell me. Any idea how much that cost me?'

'I didn't mean it like that. I'm just glad this case is over. Mum thinks you're making yourself unwell.'

'I'm okay. I'll speak to you soon. Goodnight, Son.'

'Goodnight, Dad … I love you.'

He took the bottle of whisky and poured what was left of it over the balcony. It was a crutch he didn't need. Daniel had finally spoken to him like his son again. That was all he needed. Maybe he had finally forgiven him. He began to feel unwell and went into the bathroom and vomited in the sink. There was more blood this time and he knew he couldn't put it off any longer. He would have to see a doctor. What he read online wasn't good. He didn't want to die young like his father. He washed his face and looked at himself in the mirror. He now looked older than he remembered his father had before he died.

Chapter 46

Friday: 15th of December 2023

The phone buzzed again. He tried to find it in the folds of the bedclothes, but he gave up and lay back on the pillow. The empty bottle of whisky was lying on the floor where he left it. He remembered sitting on the balcony speaking to Daniel, and the strange stillness of the loch.

He found the phone. Apart from the text messages, there were now dozens of missed calls. He looked at the numbers; Mackie and Knox had phoned twice, and there was even a missed call from the chief constable. He phoned Mitchell.

'George, are you up yet?'

'Yes, I'm downstairs, I'm having breakfast. Will I order you something?'

'No, I'm not hungry.'

'Frank, you need to come down, it's all over the news.'

'I need a shower. I'll be down shortly. Just order me a coffee.'

He showered and shaved; his eyes looked like he had drunk the bottle of whisky. He made a coffee and went out to the balcony. The sky was blue, a blue that looked infinite and breathtakingly beautiful. The icy winds had gone back to where they came from and the loch was calm, even benign. The mountains were covered in a blanket of brilliant white, the winter sun melting the fringes as the gullies ran fast with meltwater, cascading down to the loch.

Dorsey and Mitchell arrived at the station in the patrol car that was sent to pick them up. The press were there waiting. They pushed past the torrent of questions and flashing cameras. This was the one part of the job that Dorsey hated, facing the same bastards who were happy to see him crucified, who were now rushing to help him down from the cross and put him up for sainthood. The questions were all about Hicks. It was the killer they wanted to know about, not the victims.

The incident room was equally disconcerting. The whole team of detectives and uniformed officers stood along one side of the room and cheered and clapped as he walked in with Mitchell. He raised his hand to calm them down, forcing a smile. 'This was a team effort, so don't do yourself a disservice by giving me all this shit. I want to say one thing – you never gave up and you supported me when others were happy to throw me under a bus. For that, you have my eternal gratitude. Now, let's get back to work.'

Dorsey and Mitchell returned to the locus.

Jock Kilbride, in his ill-fitting white overalls, approached the two detectives as they drove up to the front of the house. 'Frank, you'll have to come and see this,' he said, leading them into the house and to an anteroom in one of the ground floor bedrooms that looked like a women's clothes shop. There was a rack of clothes covered with a clear polythene sheet, which had clearly belonged to the victims. Their shoes and underwear were in cardboard boxes and stacked in a corner. The fingerprint specialists were now taking lifts from anything the killer or his victims may have touched.

'I've been able to work out that the clothes and shoes make up seven separate outfits, including the clothes that Lucy Potter was wearing when she was abducted. That would correspond with the number of pictures of dismembered bodies found at Samuel Purdy's flat. There's also some jewellery belonging to the victims, mainly rings and chains.'

Dorsey lifted a gold chain and crucifix from the box of jewellery. 'I think this belonged to Lena Kaminski.'

'I found these,' said Jock, handing Dorsey a Swedish

passport and a driving licence in the name of Greta Lind. 'There's also this.' He handed over a Bank of Scotland credit card in the name of Tracey Henderson. 'I have found nothing to identify the other two.'

'Sir, I found this in a room upstairs,' said one of Jock's team, producing an Ordnance Survey map of Glencoe and Glen Etive. He unfolded the map and spread it out on the floor. There were six X marks made with a black Sharpie, two of which were in Lairigmor.

'I think Hicks clearly has a problem with letting go of incriminating evidence. First the clothes and personal belongings, now this,' said Mitchell.

'The four other marks are in the Rannoch Moor area. What do we know about that place?' asked Dorsey.

'Well, if you thought Lairigmor was remote and desolate, this is on another scale,' said Jock. 'But, if these markings are correct, then we shouldn't have much trouble locating the bodies.'

The scenes of crime officers carried on meticulously working their way through each room, collecting and bagging evidence. Their first task that morning, of photographing everything in situ, had already been completed.

Dorsey contacted Cullen to get the resources he needed to initiate a search of Rannoch Moor.

'My God, so you think there's four more bodies there?'

'Yes, sir, we may already have found evidence in the house to identify two of them.'

'Okay, I'll get CS Mackie to put together a task force to start a search of Rannoch Moor. Can you send her the map coordinates you recovered? And Frank, you did a great job finding this monster and that poor girl ...'

'Lucy Potter, sir. Her name's Lucy Potter and she's a young woman, not a girl.'

'Yes, of course. I spoke to her father today. She's expected to make a full recovery.'

'I'm not so sure she ever will. Physically perhaps, but not mentally. How can she?'

.

Chapter 47

Monday: 18th of December 2023

The muster room was packed – even the admin staff from the church hall had been asked to attend. Dorsey asked his senior officers, DI Crawford, DS Grant, and DS Mitchell, to stand with him as he addressed the room. Before he could begin to speak, those in the muster broke into applause. He raised his hands to bring it to an end.

'On the 6th of September this year, I was unexpectedly asked to become the SIO in the ongoing search for Erin Keenan, whom we all now know turned out to be the victim of a road traffic accident. Angus Sloan's decision to conceal this crime, probably because he was drunk when he knocked her down, resulted in the discovery of these other more heinous crimes perpetrated by Zachary Hicks.

'I can confirm that the bodies of the four other victims have now been recovered from Rannoch Moor. Once formally identified, their families will be informed. The evidence gathered from the house in Argyll and Samuel Purdy's flat is overwhelming. Hicks is a psychopathic serial killer, who would have gone on to kill more victims if we hadn't stopped him. As most of you are aware, Hicks has been transferred to Carstairs State Hospital as the Crown's psychiatrists have confirmed he is mentally insane and unfit to plead. There will be a court hearing in due course to determine whether he will ever be fit to stand trial.'

'Sir,' interrupted one of the detectives. 'Could he get off on an insanity plea?'

'He could, but that will not change the outcome. The court

will still impose a hospital order on him that will effectively mean that instead of prison, he will spend the rest of his life in Carstairs. Remember, in spite of his mental state, Zachary Hicks is still the person responsible for the murder of seven innocent human beings. We believe the six young women he abducted and murdered were all complete strangers, picked at random. We also believe he may have been responsible for the murder of Samuel Purdy's sister, Daisy, nearly sixteen years ago. That case will be reinvestigated by the cold case unit based in Glasgow. Thankfully, Lucy Potter was saved from a similar fate and I understand she is recovering well from her ordeal.'

'What happens now, sir?' asked PC Dixon.

'You'll all be returning to your normal duties and divisions. I'll be shortly heading back to Glasgow with DS Mitchell. It has been an honour to lead you all in this extremely difficult investigation. Thank you all for your hard work and dedication. You all should be proud of yourselves.' He turned to Crawford and shook his hand. 'Thanks for all your help, Bill.'

'It was a pleasure to have worked with you and George on this,' said Crawford, now shaking Mitchell's hand.

'Bill, I have some things I need to do before we head back to Glasgow,' said Dorsey. 'Can you take my place at the press conference this evening?'

'Of course. What will I tell Cullen?'

'Just tell him I've got better things to do.'

Dorsey had spent the rest of the day writing letters to the families of the victims as PC Dixon sorted out the belongings that were to be returned. He placed Lena Kaminski's gold crucifix and chain in an envelope addressed to her parents. He wasn't sure if it would give them any comfort to have it back. He had a strange feeling of emptiness once he had finished the last letter. Now all the victims' belongings had been boxed and taken to the post office, he and Mitchell said their goodbyes and left. Dorsey was pretty sure they would have no reason to ever return to the station.

After a fleeting downpour, Glencoe was basking in what was rare winter sunshine and a rainbow stretched from one side of Loch Leven to the other. They drove through the village to the graveyard. Mitchell waited in the car. Dorsey had one last farewell to make. He walked towards the only grave that had flowers on it. The headstone seemed fitting; a small Celtic cross made of grey granite. He didn't really know Alex Munro, but his death still affected him. He noticed something in the middle of a wreath. It was Munro's military medal. He bent down to look at it.

'There's not been many here since he was buried,' said Eileen Munro, as she walked along the gravel path towards him with Major at her side.

Dorsey turned towards her, feeling slightly awkward until she smiled. 'Kitty Murdoch told me what you sent her to help get his medal.'

'It was only right … Without Alex, we'd never have found those two bodies in Lairigmor and discovered that there were four more on Rannoch Moor. Hicks would have probably gone on killing. Your brother was a good man.'

'I know, and Alex respected you. I'm glad you came to say goodbye to him. He would have liked that.'

Chapter 48

That evening, what was to be the last press conference in the investigation was chaired by Cullen, flanked by Mackie and Crawford in Inverness. The press cameras clicked and strobe lights flashed as the world media jostled for the best pictures. CS Mackie began to read a prepared statement detailing the history of the case. Once she was finished, she asked for a minute's silence to remember the victims and their families. The room fell still.

Once the minute's silence was over, Cullen spoke briefly.

'This has been one of the most difficult murder investigations that we as a police force have ever had to deal with in our history. It is certainly the most disturbing that I have ever been involved in. I, first of all, wish to thank our police officers of all ranks for their dedication and work ethic in this horrendous and disturbing case. As a result of their tireless endeavours, Lucy Potter was found alive and the serial killer who had stalked the central Highland region undetected for years was finally brought to justice for his heinous crimes. As this matter is still under investigation and the bodies of those young women recently discovered in Rannoch Moor have still to be formally identified, we are unable to comment further.'

'Kitty Murdoch, *Oban Times*. This is a question for CS Mackie: did you fail to do your job properly when you led the investigation into the suspicious death of Daisy Purdy in 2008? Is it not the case that the family provided incriminating statements against Hicks as the person responsible for Daisy Purdy's murder?'

'I resent your question, Miss Murdoch. There was no

evidence that Daisy Purdy was murdered. The case was fully investigated. I think you should check your facts before you make defamatory accusations.'

'I have checked my facts and have spoken to a retired detective who has told me that *you* decided the death was accidental, even though the evidence found in Daisy's diary pointed to Hicks having an unhealthy interest in her and she and her brother were afraid of him. This detective felt that your decision to treat the death as accidental was taken with undue haste because you were distracted by a promotion you had applied for at the time.'

Cullen banged his fist on the table. 'We're not here to answer scurrilous accusations. We are here to answer questions about the successful conclusion of this investigation. Hindsight is a wonderful thing, Miss Murdoch. I would be careful what you say next!'

'Is there any reason why the SIO, Chief Inspector Frank Dorsey, is not here? It was his case after all,' asked a reporter from BBC Scotland.

'I've no idea why he is not here … I think that answers your question,' said Cullen, his face still flushed with anger. 'This press conference is over.'

Ignoring all further questions, Cullen abruptly closed his file and stood up before making his way out of the noisy press conference. The veins on his neck were pumping with rage as he marched through the hotel with Mackie rushing to keep up. When he reached the hotel foyer he turned to her. 'I want to see all the paperwork regarding the investigation into the drowning of Daisy Purdy. I hope for your sake that you didn't fuck up.'

'Yes, sir,' replied Mackie, dropping her file on the floor.

'For God's sake, Mackie!' shouted Cullen as she went down on her knees to pick up the scattered documents. Cullen then turned to Crawford, who had sauntered up to them with his hands in his pockets. 'Why the fuck was Frank

Dorsey not here?'

'I spoke to him this morning. He said he had more important things to do than suck up to the media.'

Cullen let out a deep sigh. 'Maybe he's got a point … This press conference was a fucking disaster.'

Before the press conference was even over, Dorsey was already back in his flat in Glasgow. On the kitchen table he found a note under a packet of cigarettes that was on top of an old-looking copy of Pink Floyd's album, *The Wall*.

I know I shouldn't have, but I've tidied up the flat and made your bed. I've also booked that holiday in Montenegro, my treat. I bought this Pink Floyd album in a charity shop today to add to your collection. Although, I'm not sure if four vinyl albums can be called a collection. Frank, I am so proud of you. Love, Liz xxx

He removed the record from the sleeve. It looked in pretty good nick for an album that was older than he was. He carefully put it on the turntable, respecting the care the previous owner must have taken of it. He eventually fell asleep on top of the newly made bed, after listening to and feeling 'Comfortably Numb'.

Acknowledgments

In writing this novel I am grateful for the support and encouragement I have received from family and friends who have read early drafts and given valuable constructive criticism, in particular my partner, Lesley Walker.

My gratitude extends to everyone at Ringwood Publishing, in particular my editor, Shona McKenzie, and support worker, Kerry McGahan.

About the Author

Charles P. Sharkey has worked for over 30 years as a criminal lawyer in Glasgow.

Picking Daisies is his fifth novel with Ringwood Publishing. His successful debut novel, *Dark Loch,* was followed by *The Volunteer, Memoirs of Franz Schreiber*, then *Clutching at Straws*, of which *Picking Daisies* is the sequel.

Somewhat of a renaissance man, he has also had concurrent careers as a landscape gardener and as a singer-songwriter, with a number of his songs being recorded by other artists. His first studio album *Strange Hotel* has been well received, with more to follow.

Other Titles by this Author

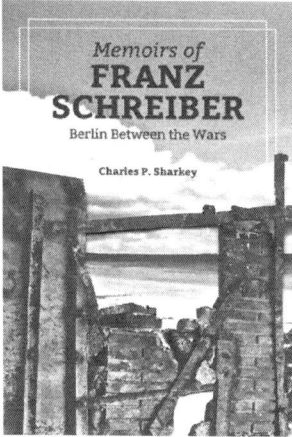

Memoirs of Franz Schreiber

Charles P. Sharkey

Memoirs of Franz Schreiber gives a unique perspective on the trials and turmoil of life in Germany during the First World War and the lead-up to the Second World War. When Franz and his mother get the news that his beloved father would not be returning to their home in Berlin from battle-fields of the First World War, their lives changed in unimaginable ways. Following Franz as he grows into a man, the effects of war are endless, and the story of his life is littered with love, tragedy and danger.

ISBN: 978-1-901514-64-3
£9.99

The Volunteer

Charles P Sharkey

The Volunteer is a powerful and thought-provoking examination of the Troubles that plagued Northern Ireland for almost three decades. It follows the struggles of two Belfast families from opposite sides of the sectarian divide.

This revealing novel will lead the reader to a greater understanding of the events that led from the Civil Rights marches in the late Sixties, through the years of unbridled violence that followed, until the Good Friday Agreement of the late Nineties.

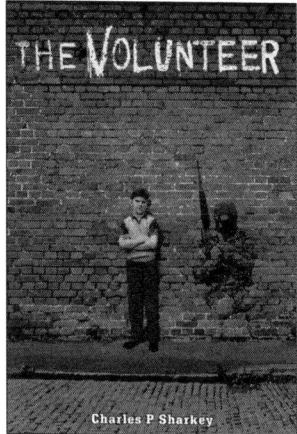

ISBN: 978-1-901514-36-0
£9.99

Dark Loch

Charles P Sharkey

Dark Loch is an epic tale of the effects of the First World War on the lives of the residents of a small Scottish rural community.

The crofters live a harsh existence in harmony with the land and the changing seasons, unaware of the devastating war that is soon to engulf the continent of Europe.

The book vividly and dramatically explores the impact of that war on all the main characters and how their lives are drastically altered forever

ISBN: 978-1-901514-14-8
£9.99

Clutching at Straws

Charles P Sharkey

Set on the gritty streets of Glasgow in the depths of winter, Inspector Frank Dorsey and his partner DC George Mitchell are called to investigate a dead body they believe to be linked to the Moffats, one of the most notorious crime families in Glasgow. However, as they begin to delve further into the case, it becomes apparent that they have a complex web of connected mysteries and murders to make sense of. Furthermore, it appears some of the victims had been sent a cryptic anonymous text message days before their death that warns of divine punishment for the criminals of the city.

ISBN: 978-1-901514-72-8
£9.99

How does the message relate to the murders, and how are the Moffats involved? Will Inspector Dorsey be able to crack it before more bodies turn up, or will he be left clutching at straws?

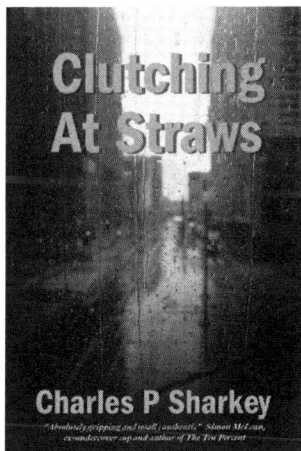